CHASE THE WILD PIGEONS

CHASE THE WILD PIGEONS

John J. Gschwend Jr.

Chase The Wild Pigeons

http://civilwarnovel.com

ISBN: 978-1-105-18247-1

Printed in the United States of America

Dedicated to my family and the ones who persist and never give up

Note

The American Civil War was one of the most defining events in our country's past. It changed the course of history so that we have become the greatest and freest nation on earth.

Slavery was also a large stain on our history. Many today can't understand how such a merciless institution could have existed in this country. But it not only existed, it helped develop our country into what it is today.

African-Americans in bondage scraped out a life in the worst of conditions. They created a culture from the hardest of hardships. This is a history we must never forget, and we must know the true history of it. I could not imagine the life of waking up each morning knowing I belonged to another man, no matter how I was treated.

In this story I use dialect and words that are offensive to people today of all races. However, in 1863 this was everyday life, no matter if it was offensive or not. I researched extensively slave narratives, diaries, and letters. I desired to put the reader right there in that slice of time. Please know this was my only intention.

History is concrete; it only happened the way it happened. However, the record left behind may not always be the absolute truth. This novel was born from my research and my love of history. I sincerely hope my characters and my story live in the truth.

Best wishes,

John J. Gschwend Jr.

They Are No More

American Chestnut

It has been estimated the American Chestnut tree once numbered over 3 billion. It was an important tree in the eastern forests of North America. It could reach over 150 feet tall and 10 feet in diameter, and it was prized for its tasty nuts and the rot-resistant wood. Twenty-five percent of all trees in the Appalachian Mountains were American Chestnut trees. In the early 1900s, a blight swept through the forests of the East, and now there are few large chestnut trees left there, mostly shoots and saplings that struggle before the blight finally extinguishes them. The great chestnut forest exists no more.

Carolina Parakeet

The Carolina Parakeet lived in the forests of Eastern United States. The beautiful bird was mostly green with a yellow head and orange cheeks. The noisy emerald flocks sometimes raided agricultural fruits and grains. This, along with man's destruction of its native forests, may have been its undoing. It was considered extinct by the 1930s. These beautiful birds could once be seen in vast, colorful flocks, but now they are no more.

Passenger Pigeon

In the 1800s there are estimated to have been over 4 billion passenger pigeons—some say 5 billion. By these estimates, forty percent of all the birds at that time in North America were passenger pigeons, perhaps the most numerous bird to ever exist on earth. They were hunted relentlessly, and their habitat was destroyed for man's use. There are locations all over Eastern America named for these birds: *Pigeon Forge, Pigeon Roost, Little Pigeon River.* People of that time would have never believed the bird would someday be absent from the sky. Many today don't know they even existed. The last birds died in the early 1900s. Martha was the last passenger pigeon in captivity to die. She passed away at the Cincinnati Zoo in 1914. They once blackened the sky like dark clouds—now they are no more.

Chapter 1

Darkness crawled across the overgrown graveyard. The headstones were bent and canted from neglect and shoved aside by determined bushes and saplings. A smoky fog had rolled in off the Mississippi River, floating through the cemetery like many ghosts.

Joe snuggled in behind a big headstone, knowing the Yankee sergeant would be coming soon; he had learned the soldier's routine well. Joe looked over his shoulder; his partner was hidden behind a square, green-furred headstone. That's right, Curtis; stay alert. We can't afford to be caught, have to complete our mission for the cause.

Joe didn't know why these Yankees had held up here in Helena instead of going on down to Vicksburg where the fighting was. It didn't matter; they were here, and he was going to do his duty.

He settled in for the wait, had to have patience. He placed his face against the stone, cold and damp. He felt the inscription with his fingers. Curious, he backed off enough to read it. There barely was enough light, but he made out:

Allen Buford
Born 1802   Died 1851
May the angels guard him for eternity.

Joe felt a shiver, thought about looking for the angels.

"Psst!"

Joe started, then whirled. Curtis was pointing. Joe turned. The big Yankee was coming down the path. In the late gloom, his uniform appeared more black than blue. It was him, Sergeant Davis of Iowa.

Joe buried behind the headstone like a lizard under a shingle. Everything was automatic now. They had planned it well. They had practiced the escape. He was ready. He felt an electric screw in his chest and drumming in his ears, but he was ready.

The Yankee drifted down the dark, foggy path like a demon. He was a huge man, the biggest Yankee at Helena. He stopped at the exact place Joe had planned, slowly scanned the area, his Springfield rifle covering the area in a smooth circle, the bayonet on the end like a medieval spear.

Joe tried to melt into the back of the headstone. He knew Curtis was doing the same.

The Yankee finally seemed satisfied he was alone. He dropped a handful of leaves by a stump. There was a convenient chunk of firewood standing about eight inches beside it. The big man leaned his gun against a headstone, then unbuttoned his pants, and they fell to his ankles. He lowered his shining butt down on the stump and firewood—a homemade privy. Soon the music began—he was sputtering and spewing like a clogged flute.

Joe grinned. He had heard the soldiers call it the "Arkansas Quickstep." They had all sorts of afflictions and diseases, living in cramped quarters and not being used to the southern climate.

Curtis giggled behind him.

Sergeant Davis snapped his head in that direction. "Who's there?"

Joe turned toward Curtis, but his partner was hidden well. He's going to get us shot, Joe thought. He was usually scared of his own shadow—now he's laughing.

Davis turned back, must have assumed it was the wind. The sputtering began again.

Joe got to his knees. He was going to do this right. This mission would go off perfectly. He squeezed the weapon in his hands.

Davis grunted and his rear popped like a cork shot out of a bottle.

Curtis snickered.

Davis yelled, "Who the hell is over there? Answer me, damn it!" He reached for his musket.

Joe knew it was time. He leaped to his feet, jerked the rope in his hands. The rope snapped tight, catapulted leaves and sticks from the ground, then snatched the chunk of firewood from under Sergeant Davis's right cheek. Davis's arms fanned the air for purchase, but found none. His left cheek let go of the stump, and he landed butt-first into his own stink.

Curtis screamed laughter.

Joe struck out for the escape route. "Come on, Curtis!"

Davis tried to stand, slipped, and fell back into his mess. "Who the hell is over there?"

Joe stopped.

"No, Joe, keep going," Curtis said. "We've been lucky so far, let's don't push it."

Joe grinned. He turned toward the darkness that hid Davis and whistled "Dixie."

Davis replied instantly: "Joseph Taylor! You little runt!"

Joe cut out for home with Davis's yells fading behind him.

***

It was black dark when Joe ran up to the house. He snatched the backdoor open and flew in, his union kepi pulled down tight on his head, and his blonde hair dark with sweat. The kitchen, as always, smelled of sweet wood smoke. A brown hand grabbed his shoulder as he slammed the door. Joe turned to see Aunt Katie Bea glaring at him. She meant business. She always meant business.

"What you doing running in the street like that?" She let his shoulder go and crossed her arms—her business position. "I done told you over and over to stop running after dark. One of them Yankees gonna shoot you yet. You know they jumpy."

"Pshaw, I ain't worried about them Yankees."

"You be worried when I tells your uncle." She jerked the kepi off his head and shoved it into his chest. "A twelve-year-old boy ain't got no business running in the street after dark." She went to the stove and stirred in a steaming pot.

"Now Aunt Katie Bea, you know you ain't going to tell Uncle Wilbur on me." However, he knew well that she was subject to tell. He peeped into the pot. "Mmm, what ya cooking?"

"We is having stew." She smiled—she could change expressions in a twinkling. "That nice Yankee colonel is in the parlor with your uncle right now. He gonna take supper with us this evening."

Joe looked down the hall, then turned back to Katie Bea. She was short, only five feet. Joe was almost as tall as she was. Her hair was straighter and her skin was lighter than most Negroes Joe knew. He believed she was mostly white, probably a quadroon, but they were all the same to him.

Peter came through the backdoor with a load of firewood. He was Katie's sixteen-year-old son. Even though he was a big boy, Joe believed he could take him if it ever came down to it. Joe could take most anyone.

"Peter, that's enough firewood," Katie Bea said. "Lawd, it too hot in here now. The kitchen should be outside the house like it supposed to be." She mopped her brow with her apron. "You, go put the cow up after you stack that wood." She straightened her apron and went into the hall leading to the parlor.

"Boy, I heard what you did," Peter said as he stacked the firewood by the stove.

Joe grabbed a spoon and stole some stew. "What ya talking about?"

"You know what I'm talking about. Someone put a chicken snake in that private's knapsack down at the river."

"Weren't me."

"You and your friend Curtis."

"I didn't even see Curtis yesterday."

Peter stood and smiled. "Who said anything about yesterday?"

Joe hated him when he outsmarted him like that—wise ass darky.

Katie Bea came back into the kitchen. "Boy, get outta that stew." She shooed him away. "You two get ready for supper."

"I need to tend the cow first," Peter said and smiled at Joe before he went out the door.

Joe stuck his tongue out, and Katie Bea popped him with a rag.

"Boy, show some manners. I ain't raising you to be no heathen. Now go tell the gentlemen supper will be set in just a few minutes. Get outta here and worry them a spell."

Joe crept down the hall, stopping short of the parlor. The door was open and he could see the men, but the hall was dark and they couldn't see him. Joe had often played as if the hall were his cave.

He stopped to listen. He had learned that the only way for a twelve-year-old to learn anything was to spy, but it was important not to get caught. He had learned that the hard way—had he ever.

Colonel Frank Russell sat with his legs crossed at the end of the sofa, and Dr. Wilbur Taylor sat across from him in his favorite chair. Dr. Taylor smoked on his pipe as he usually did while in the parlor. That pipe smelled sweet. Joe would smoke one when he got the chance. He would try it now, but he knew Dr. Taylor was wise to that because he never left it where Joe could sneak it.

Joe glanced back down the long hall—it was safe. Katie Bea couldn't see him, so he settled in to listen.

"For the life of me, I can't begin to understand why you would leave Pennsylvania for this God-forsaken place," Colonel Russell said.

"I didn't anticipate there would be a war, that's for sure," Dr. Taylor said, poking in his pipe. "I just wanted a change, and this fast-growing, frontier town fit the bill, and it's on the river so I'm still close to civilization."

"There are plenty of small towns up North," Colonel Russell said, dragging a large cigar from his shirt pocket. Dr. Taylor lit it for him.

"I can't put a reason that I chose the South. It is all America—was America."

"It is still all one America. We will make sure of that."

"I do pray it all turns out for the best. You see, Colonel, I have a brother that took a bride from Mississippi and moved there and another brother that moved to Virginia, Joseph's father. I guess that is strange to you."

"Very strange indeed, Doctor. The first chance I get I'm going back North."

"I like Southerners—they are a charming people, chivalrous and kind."

The colonel exhaled and talked through the smoke: "Charming, chivalrous and kind? Are we talking about the same race that we've been fighting? Hell, slavery alone nullifies all that."

"Most have nothing to do with slavery."

"They sure are suffering a terrible war to keep the merciless institution."

"You are more aware than I that there is more to this war than the institution of slavery."

Colonel Russell waved a dismissal. "I know, Doctor. I sure didn't come here to start a war with you. I know you are a transplanted Yankee and are good to the Negroes. Hell, you treat your slaves like family."

Dr. Taylor stood. "Sir, Katie Bea and Peter are not slaves!"

Russell slowly rose. "Dr. Taylor, please, I do apologize. I've offended you, and here you have so graciously invited me to dine with you. Please let us sit." He sat back down.

Dr. Taylor smiled weakly and eased into his chair.

"I just thought since they lived in the house with you and the boy that they were your servants." He blew smoke. "You and Katie Bea are not—"

Dr. Taylor shot up from the chair again. "Colonel, you overstep you bounds, Sir!"

Joe had never seen his uncle so riled. Maybe a fight was brewing. If Uncle Wilbur had trouble, Joe would hit the colonel low—that was always his best strategy.

Colonel Russell stood. "Doctor, you are absolutely correct, and I do apologize again." He bowed his head, and smiled. "And I'm damned if you don't sound like a Southerner."

Joe saw his uncle relax as the men sat.

"Well, Colonel, I reckon I see how you could have made the mistake. You are a guest in my home, and I should apologize to you also."

Colonel Russell nodded and puffed on the stinking cigar.

"Katie Bea's husband was a good friend, and when he died, I took them in," Dr. Taylor said.

"He must have been a very dear friend for you to feel that indebted."

"I could never repay the debt that I owed him, but Katie Bea and Peter are family to me now—not a debt to be repaid."

This was getting too boring for Joe, so he pulled the kepi down tight and marched into the parlor. He saluted. "Hi, Colonel."

"Joseph, pull that cap off in the house," Dr. Taylor said.

Joe slid it off.

The cigar smoke was heavy and not at all as pleasant as the pipe smoke.

"What have you been up to, you little Rebel-Yankee?" Colonel

Russell said, smiling.

Before he could answer, Dr. Taylor cut in. "If he and his troop keep getting into mischief, I will take a belt to the captain while the private watches."

The colonel laughed, asked, "You and your troop wouldn't know anything about a snake in Private Funk's knapsack, would you?"

Joe realized with all the choking cigar smoke and the interrogations that this was not a good place to be.

"Aunt Katie Bea said supper would be ready in a few minutes." With that statement, he slipped back toward the kitchen.

He was at the washbasin in the kitchen when someone knocked on the door. Katie Bea went to answer, but before she made it to the door, it became a pounding. She opened the door. It was jerked from her hand.

It was Sergeant Davis. "Where is that damn boy?"

Joe slipped unnoticed into the dark hall.

"Don't you be a-coming in this house talking to me in that fashion," Katie Bea said.

"You listen to me, darky. That little devil has messed with me for the last time, and an ass-whooping is what he will get."

Dr. Taylor charged past Joe and into the kitchen. "Sergeant, what is the meaning of this intrusion?"

"I mean to give that boy a licking. You folks don't seem to be able to handle him."

"You get out of my home this instant!"

At that moment Peter came through the door. "What is that smell?"

"What does it smell like, boy? It's shit."

There were a couple more soldiers outside; they laughed.

Davis grabbed Peter by the shirt, snatched him inside, and slammed the door.

Joe was formulating a plan when Colonel Russell moved past him in the hall.

"Davis!" Colonel Russell barked when he entered the kitchen.

"Sir!" Davis shot to attention.

"What are you doing?"

"Colonel, it's the boy again. He has gone too—"

"I will not have my men barging into civilian homes and

threatening the inhabitants. I am a guest of Dr. Taylor and you—"
He sniffed. "What is that smell?"

Joe giggled in the hall.

Davis headed for the hall. "You little—"

"Sergeant!" Colonel Russell yelled. "I will have you locked up."

Davis stopped. "But Colonel—"

"That boy has been here all evening," Russell said.

Davis stared at his colonel for a long minute. Slowly he said, "Very well, Colonel."

"Now, I suggest you leave this house," Colonel Russell said.

Davis continued to stare for a time; then he slowly turned to leave.

"And Sergeant," Colonel Russell said, "get cleaned up."

***

Davis slammed the door. The soldiers waiting outside burst into laughter. He shot a look at them, and they fell silent like crickets. Slowly he felt anger fester. Joe was at the parlor window whistling "Dixie."

***

"Then what happened last night, Joe?" Curtis asked as he threw a six-foot spear over his skinny shoulder.

"The soldiers heard me whistling 'Dixie,' and they took to laughing. Then Uncle Wilbur snuck up behind me and grabbed me by the collar."

"Did he whoop ya?" Curtis, with his snaggled-toothed grin, looked down at Joe.

"He had a conniption fit, with Colonel Russell there and all."

"But did he whoop ya?"

Joe threw his own pointed stick over his shoulder. "Sakes alive, Curtis, he whooped me across the butt with his shoe. Now, shut up before I give you a sockdologer across your lip."

"I knowed it. I knowed it." Curtis kicked his bare foot into the air. "You get walloped more than any one person in the whole big world."

The boys trudged down the muddy streets. There were few citizens on the streets, mainly soldiers and contraband Negroes. The local white folks stayed indoors as much as possible. Joe believed them to be cowards.

Joe saw the mud ball coming and weaved. It smacked Curtis.

Curtis grabbed his arm, but he said nothing.

Joe scooped up a glob, quickly made a ball and sailed it back toward the attacker, catching the Yankee private in the back as he tried to escape.

"Damn it, Joe," the private said, "I'll flank you next time."

"You had better bring your whole company." Joe, looking at Curtis holding his arm and pouting, said to the private, "Casualty for casualty."

The private laughed and went into a house he and some others had homesteaded.

Joe had heard Helena was once a busy and growing town—that was before he had arrived. Now it was rundown and ragged. It was still busy though. In fact, more people were in town than ever before: Yankees. The soldiers had been rough on the town since they had arrived a year ago. Only a few stores remained now, and one was Dr. Wilbur Taylor's mercantile.

Dr. Taylor had figured since he was a Northerner, the occupying army would be lenient toward him. They were. In fact, he was doing more business than ever now that the small river town's population had increased with the blue army. Because Helena was on the Mississippi and an occupied town, the store sold items that many parts of the South had a difficult time getting: coffee, candles, sewing needles, flour, and Joe's favorite, hard candy.

Many of the town's people had little money to buy things from the store, so they traded eggs, milk, vegetables, and the like—if the Yankees didn't steal it first. Joe saw a lot of trading across the picket line, especially cotton. He knew his uncle was making big money from trading cotton. Joe believed the Yankees were interested in getting white gold above all else.

Joe and Curtis propped their sticks by the open door and went inside the store. Joe liked the smell of the place with its coffee, tonics, lamp oil and a blend of a hundred other smells.

As the boys walked in, Dr. Taylor retrieved a bottle from a high shelf and gave it to an old woman. "Mrs. Cooper, just give James a couple teaspoons of this as the pain bothers him."

"Dr. Roy said a while back it would not be fitting to give him too much laudanum," she said.

He placed a tender hand on her back. "Mrs. Cooper, at this stage of his illness it will give him some comfort, and it can't do anymore harm. Dr. Roy will agree."

When the woman left the store, the two boys were waiting at the long counter.

"What are you two about?" Dr. Taylor said, as he placed two sticks of candy on the counter.

They snatched them up and went to work on them.

"We're a-going fish sticking," Curtis said, chomping the candy.

"What?" Dr. Taylor said.

"We made some spears, and Curtis knows this hole where we can stick some catfish and gars," Joe said.

"Yeah, my pa used to fetch me there all the time before the war," Curtis said.

Dr. Taylor shot a mean look at Joe. "Joseph, I forbid you going through the pickets. It has become very dangerous of late. You know that."

"The hole is inside the lines, Uncle Wilbur." If Joe had known this was going to happen, he would have never stopped in.

"Where?"

"Just a little south," Curtis said.

"The Negro camp is south, and you boys will not go there. There is enough disease and dying with these Union soldiers without you catching something from those poor, overcrowded Negroes."

A tall black man came through the backdoor with a sack across each shoulder. Joe had never seen him before. He was broad across the chest and dark as night—Joe had never seen a Negro so dark. He must have just come from the darkest jungles of Africa.

"Lucius, set those sacks along the wall there," Dr. Taylor said.

"Yessuh."

Lucius handled the sacks as if they were full of feathers. Joe had moved similar sacks around before, and he knew they were heavy. Lucius stacked them neatly and went back through the backdoor and into the storage room.

When Lucius disappeared into the back, Joe resumed. "We won't go to the Negro camp, will we, Curtis?"

Lucius came back into the store with another load, and Curtis, wide-eyed, watched his every move.

Joe elbowed Curtis. "Will we?"

Curtis didn't answer, but gawked at Lucius as if he had seen a bear.

Joe elbowed him. "We won't go there, will we, Curtis?"

Curtis turned to them, "Oh. No, sir, we won't."

"All right then, boys, but you make your presence known to the soldiers at all times. Don't try to sneak by any of them."

The boys agreed and fled the store before Dr. Taylor could change his mind. On their way out, they bumped into Peter coming in.

"Hey, slow down," Peter said. "The Yankees are already here, no need to run now."

The boys grabbed up their spears. "Going fishing. See you at supper," Joe said. With that, they trotted down the muddy street.

***

"Peter, I trust you procured everything we needed from the boat," Dr. Taylor said.

"Yes, sir." Peter handed a ledger to Dr. Taylor.

"Where is Theo?" Dr. Taylor asked, studying the ledger.

"He's coming. He doesn't feel well." He was drunk again, but Peter didn't want to say it.

Theo waddled through the door. His large belly stretched his trousers, and his face was almost as red as his hair.

"Are you not well?" Dr. Taylor asked.

"I think I'm coming down with something, and that's a fact." He flopped down in a chair at the end of the counter, drew a blue handkerchief from his vest pocket, and mopped his face.

"You just sit there for a time, and I will look you over in a few minutes," Dr. Taylor said.

Peter didn't know how a man could let himself go as this fat man had. Peter prayed for the man often, but it was going to take a heap more praying he believed.

Dr. Taylor squeezed Peter's shoulder. "How did it go, my boy?"

"Well, we retained what we needed," Peter said, looking down at his shoes.

"Your first time handling the buying and that is all you have to say?"

"He ain't handled a thing," Theo said. His pumpkin head hung low on his chest as if it were too heavy for him to lift.

"What do you mean by that?" Dr. Taylor asked.

Peter felt the shame come over him like a hot wind.

Theo raised his big head. "I mean they didn't take him for serious, and that's for sure." His belly jiggled as he stood and put a hand on the counter. "They laughed at the boy. They wanted to know why a nigger was a-doing a white man's business."

Peter stared at the floor, felt like sinking right through it.

Dr. Taylor looked at Peter. "Is this true?"

"Damn right it's true," Theo said, slurring his words and getting too loud. "Tell him boy. Tell him how they laughed on you. Tell him how they said, 'Look at the monkey reading the writing.' Go on, tell him."

"That is enough!" Dr. Taylor said. "You will mind your tongue, or you will find another job."

"He's right, Dr. Taylor." Peter forced himself to look up. "They laughed at me. They wouldn't deal with me."

Dr. Taylor patted Peter on the back. "There will be another day, and I will go with you. We will make it right."

Peter felt the corners of his eyes burn. He went to a shelf and straightened bottles. He didn't want Dr. Taylor to see if a tear betrayed him.

Dr. Taylor told Theo to go home.

"We still have the rest of the day left, and I need to earn more money," Theo said, hopelessly pulling up on his pants.

"You are of no service to me in this condition. Go home."

"That ain't no way to be doing a sick man."

"Do you want me to examine you and see just what your illness consists of? I should think not."

Theo huffed and staggered out the door.

Dr. Taylor turned to Peter. "Son, you go on home and help your mother."

"But I can help out here if you need me."

"No, boy, it has been a stressful day. Go on home. Go through the back and tell Lucius he is finished for the day. I will be home a little later."

On the way home, Peter felt his confidence slowly return. Dr. Taylor had said he would make things right. He was the best of men and Peter loved him for it. When Peter talked to the Lord tonight, he would give thanks for him.

Chapter 2

Smoke hung over the Negro camp like a gray ceiling. The camp—more like a garbage dump—sprawled down the river, yet still inside the levee and the safety of the Yankee lines: flimsy stick shacks and makeshift tents, made from anything the refugees could find. A pigsty couldn't have been muddier or nastier. This type freedom had to be worse than the slavery from which they had escaped, Joe believed, but that was their business.

"Dr. Taylor said don't go into the Negro camp," Curtis said.

"We ain't going all the way around the camp when the pond is just yonder." Joe pointed to a small cypress brake. "We'll just be going in a small part of the camp. Those darkies ain't going to hurt you."

Curtis shadowed Joe, scanning every little thing like a scared hound. The refugees started noticing the odd couple with their spears over their shoulders: one blonde, shorter, with a Yankee kepi; the other, tall and skinny, brown hair, and no shoes.

"What is that smell?" Curtis whispered, wrinkling his nose.

"Smells like a privy," Joe said. He wondered how they could live in such filth. Why did they follow the Yankee army here to live like this?

Joe stopped by an old woman beside a ragged tent stirring a board in a simmering black pot and shooing flies. Curtis ran into his back.

"Nation, Curtis," Joe said, "what's the bother with you?"

Curtis said nothing, continued to glare all around as if he expected a wolf to attack at any minute.

Joe peeked into the pot. It was a thin liquid, but smelled good. "What you cooking, Aunt?"

"Juss a soup," she said, taking her eyes away from the pot just long enough to take his measure.

"Ain't much in it, is it?" Joe asked, still examining the pot.

A black man came from the tent and another walked up from behind the boys. Curtis eyed both men and moved closer to Joe. Joe never took his attention from the pot.

The woman glared at Joe. "We ain't got much to put in it, now is we?"

He inspected the woman, noticed how skinny she was. Her dress was faded, thin, and ragged. He saw more feet than shoes, felt sorry for her, poor ignorant darky.

"I tell you what. We are going fishing with these here spears," Joe said. "Why don't I fetch you a big catfish to go in that there pot?"

The man from behind moved up to Joe. "Where is you gonna get that catfish?"

Joe sized him up—he was ragged, too, and overdue for a good scrubbing. He was black, but had a white film over his skin like scales.

Joe pointed to the cypress brake. "Curtis's Pa use to take him and catch them right over there."

The two men laughed.

The man from the tent said, "Boy, does you know us niggers is done caught every fish out of these holes around this here camp? We done got every rabbit, every squirrel, every coon, possum, snake, turtle, bird, you name it. We is also fishing that old river, too, for all we can get."

Joe looked at Curtis; he was trembling, afraid of the wind. He turned back to the men and smiled. "Well, I don't know about all that there. I reckon we can fetch you a fish or two."

The woman dropped her board into the pot and pointed back toward Helena. "You boys best get on out of this camp before something happen to you."

"Now Mae, let them boys be," said the man from the tent.

"They's going to catch us a ole catfish."

Other men migrated up and gathered around the boys, boxing them in.

Curtis tugged at Joe's sleeve. "Let's go."

Joe ignored him and leaned on his stick. "You colored folk don't know how to fish is all. Now, me and Curtis here, well that is another matter altogether."

The crowd laughed.

A voice from the crowd asked, "You think you can catch enough for all us niggers?"

The crowd roared with laughter. It was becoming a carnival.

The man from the tent was not laughing now and grabbed Joe by the arm. "You look here, boy. We is starving to death. We is dying in this here filth, and we don't need no cracker coming here funning us."

The man's breath was rotten and his teeth—what were left—were black around the edges.

Joe looked him in the eyes. "Why don't you go back to your master then?"

The man raised his hand back to swing, but it was stopped in midair by another hand.

The crowd fell silent as Lucius let the man's hand go. The man rubbed his wrist, but said nothing.

"You boys best get on back to town," Lucius said. "I heard Dr. Taylor tell you to stay away from this here contraband camp."

Curtis was sobbing, but Joe felt his own face burning. "I aim to go fishing."

Lucius looked down at him, and with his bullfrog voice said, "Go ahead, but beings I work for your uncle, I'm bound to tell him you was in the Negro camp."

"I ain't scared of these darkies." Joe tried to walk passed Lucius.

Lucius stopped him with an iron grip to the shoulder. He pulled him away from the others. Curtis hurried behind them.

"Boy, Peter say you is from Virginia. I don't know what they is like there, but you is in Arkansas now, and niggers here is desperate."

Joe jerked loose when Lucius relaxed his grip. "Niggers are niggers!"

"Boy, you is hard-headed. It all the same to me; these people can put you in that pot for all I give a damn; I'm just worried for my work."

Curtis whimpered, "Come on, Joe." He tugged at him.

"What it going to be boy?" Lucius said. "You want me to tell Dr. Taylor?"

Joe looked up at him. He would tell—damn darkie. "Come on, Curtis."

Joe threw the spear over his shoulder. He parted the crowd as he marched back toward town with Curtis in his wake.

***

It was almost dark when Peter heard Joe coming down the street. Peter was in the little barn sharpening hoes for tomorrows gardening, but it was no mistaking that it was Joe. He was the only person around with a harmonica, and on top of that, he was playing *Shenandoah*. He knew other songs and played them well, but *Shenandoah* was his favorite.

He had been playing the instrument the first time Peter had seen him. Peter could still remember clearly last year when the boat pulled up to the wharf. Joe was sitting on a trunk playing. Soldiers and men with carpetbags were standing around listening, not wanting to get off the boat until he finished the song.

Joe had traveled alone from just above Memphis. Rebel marksmen firing at the riverboat had accidentally killed his mother and little sister. Joe's mother had taken them to the pilothouse to get a good view and see how the boat was driven. They were not there a minute when bullets shattered the window, leaving Joe's mother and sister dead, and him alone. Dr. Taylor had come unstrung when he had received the horrible news.

Joe, his mother, and sister were on the boat because his father had decided it would be safer for his family to stay with his wife's family in Texas and wait the war out. Dr. Taylor was to help them get to Texas once they got off the boat at Helena. With Joe's mother gone, Dr. Taylor kept him at Helena.

Peter listened now, as the playing grew closer. He loved to hear Joe play.

Peter put down the hoe and file and hid by the barn door. He saw Joe tucking the harmonica into his shirt pocket. As he reached the kitchen door, Peter leaped out. "Boo!"

Joe jumped and turned. He laughed. "That was a good one,

27

Peter. You gave me a start, I tell you."

Katie Bea opened the door. "You two get in here and stop that deviltry."

Dr. Taylor was sitting at the table when the two boys went in. Peter instantly knew something was wrong—Dr. Taylor was staring at the lamp and not watching them as they walked in. Peter always noticed those things, but Joe never did. He didn't now as he raced past Peter to get to the washbasin first.

Peter blessed the food—he always did. He felt it an honor, and he knew the Bible better than most.

Joe grabbed a roll at amen and crammed it into his mouth. Peter smiled, but tried not to laugh, because he could tell Dr. Taylor was not up to that.

Dr. Taylor looked up from his plate. "Joseph, what did you do today?"

Peter knew Dr. Taylor already knew the answer. He always knew when he asked that way, and Joe had usually been up to no good.

"I've been with Curtis all day," Joe said, shoveling a spoonful of potatoes into his mouth.

"I told you not to go to the contraband camp," Dr. Taylor said.

Peter saw Joe suddenly stop chewing. Joe was caught like a rabbit in a trap.

"Lucius is lying. I never went to the Negro camp."

"I haven't seen Lucius," Dr. Taylor said.

Peter choked on his milk. Joe fell for that every time. Joe knew how to get into trouble easier than anyone, but he had no clue how to get out.

"Dr. Roy saw you there," Dr. Taylor said. "Other than a few of the missionaries, white people are as plentiful as hen's teeth in those shanty camps."

Joe didn't say anything, but he chewed more slowly.

"Boy, a few of the lucky ones in those camps are being shipped north. I'm afraid the vast remainders are subject to deprivation and all manner of disease. God knows we are subject to catch something here, with all these soldiers coming down with this or that, without you going out there, too. Above that, I forbade you to go there."

"Yes, sir," Joe said. "I'm sorry, Uncle Wilbur. I won't listen to Curtis again."

Peter wanted to laugh aloud. Joe had never followed Curtis—never. Joe was the leader.

"I never saw Dr. Roy," Joe said. He poked a spoonful of peas into his mouth.

"He was a good distance from you, and to be honest, he said he just saw two white boys. I added two and two."

"Speaking of Dr. Roy, why don't you doctor here like you did in Pennsylvania?"

Peter wished Joe would not ask such questions. Peter knew the answer.

"We'll talk on that another time," Dr. Taylor said. He pushed his chair away from the table and placed his napkin by his plate. He took his hat from the hat rack. "I've got to go to the store for a spell."

"Ain't the supper fitting?" Katie Bea asked.

"It was first rate, but I forgot I told the new man that he could stay in the back of the store. I need to stroll down there and check in on him."

Joe was gulping his milk and almost strangled. "Uncle Wilbur, wait. I would like to go with Curtis tomorrow to see his Granny at LaGrange."

"LaGrange!" Katie Bea said. "Lawd sakes, that is five miles or more."

"After pulling your shines today, you expect me to let you go?" Dr. Taylor said.

"If I don't go, Curtis will have to go alone."

Dr. Taylor thought on it for a minute. "All right, just wait until the sun is good and high. I know Mrs. Wilmar will watch out for you. And Joseph, the cavalry is skirting the town. Don't hide if you see them. Make sure they see you in the open. I don't want them mistaking you for a bushwhacker. Understand?"

"Yes sir."

Peter saw Dr. Taylor smile as he walked out the door. Joe sure could come it over him.

"Aunt Katie Bea, why don't Uncle Wilbur doctor much anymore?" Joe crammed another roll in his mouth.

"He just don't."

"But why?"

"Hush up, boy. You ask too many fool questions. Finish your

supper."

Peter thought about it; maybe when they were alone he would tell Joe about Pennsylvania.

Peter stared at his plate, remembered it too clearly. It seemed the whole town had the fever. Peter sure had it, and he never would forget; he was weak as a kitten. Dr. Taylor worked around the clock, helped everyone, and everyone recovered, except for one: Mrs. Hattie Taylor, his wife.

Dr. Taylor had blamed himself. No one could talk sense to him. He quit his practice and most days he sat in his study, day in and day out. But one day he came home from a short trip and told Peter and his mother to pack; they were bound for Arkansas.

Katie Bea didn't want to leave Pennsylvania and go back down south. She had her freedom now and was afraid to go to Arkansas. However, she finally relented; Dr. Taylor and Mrs. Taylor were all the family she and Peter had. With Mrs. Taylor gone, she figured she had better take care of Dr. Taylor.

That had been over five years ago. It seemed as if it were yesterday.

"Peter," Katie Bea said. "Peter."

"Uh—Oh!" Peter felt embarrassed for daydreaming.

"You can study that plate all you want to, but you might get more out of it if you eats something on it," Katie Bea said.

Joe laughed and sprayed potatoes on the table.

Peter laughed back as Katie Bea hit Joe with a towel.

***

The sun was peeking over the river when Joe and Curtis exchanged dirt clods with the pickets. Joe escaped without a wound, but Curtis caught one in the back; however, the boys faired better than the Iowans, who were still cussing and laughing when the boys went down the hill and out of sight.

Away from the hills of Helena and Crowley's Ridge lay farmland. Many of the fields were unplowed and littered with weeds, but here and there was a plot of corn or a patch of cotton, coming up green in the warm weather. The boys saw a few Negroes chopping, and they waved as the boys passed. Joe wondered why a few loyal servants stayed with their master when the Yankees were practically here at the door.

Large houses were in ruins. Some were missing sides or fronts where the lumber had been stripped. Broken furniture littered the yards, and ragged, abandoned clothes hung from the bushes. But the things that stood out the most were the many chimneys where the houses hand been burned to the ground. They stood silent and lonely like giant tombstones.

In contrast, some houses remained whole and were even occupied. Gardens grew nearby. They saw dogs and cats in the dooryards, but few farm animals—chickens and pigs were prized by the soldiers, blue and gray.

As the boys passed by a small house close to the road, an old man sitting on the porch called for the boys to come over. Dust squirted between Curtis's toes as they stepped from the road and up to the ragged gate. The old man was digging in a corncob with a knife. Joe reckoned he was making a new pipe.

"You boys a coming from Helena way?" he asked, still digging in the cob.

Joe leaped upon the porch to get a better look at the cob. Curtis stayed in the yard.

"Yes, sir," Joe said.

The man shot brown spit over the porch rail.

"We're going to LaGrange to see Curtis's Granny, Mrs. Wilmar."

"Mrs. Wilmar? Bertha Wilmar?"

"Yes, sir, that's right."

The man looked down at Curtis. "Well, I'll be damned, right here and right now. You's little Curtis Wilmar."

Curtis climbed onto the porch. "Yes, sir."

"Boy, you has growed a heap since I last seed you." The man turned to the door and called, "Bess. Bess, come look who's here." No one came. The old man scratched his head. "Reckon she's out by the barn picking them damn blackberries again. She's going to get chiggers, I swear."

Curtis hesitated, but asked the man's name.

"Confounded boy. I'm Frank Crawford. I knowed your folks all my life. I's been away a time, but the war has brung me back."

Curtis smiled big, moved closer. "Yes, sir, I remember you. You use to help Pappy with his hay."

"That's a fact—that's a fact. Me and your Pappy growed up together in Kentucky." He hit Curtis on the arm. "Now tell me why you two boys is a coming down this here road. It's the long way to LaGrange."

"My uncle said the other road was too dangerous," Joe said.

"Why, I spect your uncle is probably right on that head. Who's your folks?"

"I'm from Virginia. My father is fighting for General Lee."

"Do tell. You got people in Helena?"

"I'm staying with my uncle. He lives there now, but he was from Pennsylvania."

Frank frowned. He spit again and stared at Joe. "He a Yankee?"

Joe stared back at the man. "No, sir, he's a doctor."

"Something happen to Dr. Roy?"

"No, sir. My uncle don't doctor anymore, except when Dr. Roy needs help. He runs a store."

"Don't doctor no more? I ain't never heard such truck."

"That's a fact," Curtis said.

"Ba!" Frank said. "That's just like a Yankee."

Joe realized right then he didn't like this old frog.

"Tell me Curtis, what is them Yankees up to in Helena?"

"They just drill and march around. A lot of them are dying of consumption and the like. They're burying them all over the place."

Frank smiled. "Now ain't that first chop."

"We better get going," Joe said. He wanted to get away from this man before he said what a boy shouldn't.

"Wait right there. I'll be right back." Frank set the cob down and went into the house. He reappeared shortly holding a small sack. He handed it to Curtis. "Take this here to your Pappy. He probably ain't crossed the picket line to get none."

Joe could smell the coffee.

"You boys see anybody, ya'll chunk it into the weeds. Don't tell nobody where you got it."

"Did you get that coffee from the Yankees you don't care for?" Joe said.

Frank spit again, this time he hit the porch rail. "Maybe I killed one of them Yankees and took it."

Joe stepped off the porch and headed to the road. "I doubt it."

***

Joe and Curtis traveled farther from Helena and saw fewer fields and houses. Crowley's Ridge rose high to the east. It resembled a small, long mountain, running north and south. Joe knew better. It was actually a maze of steep hills and deep gullies. A few roads cut through it, but other than that, it was almost impossible to travel through. He and Curtis had tromped all through it, eating beechnuts and muscadines, and playing war. However, that was before the Yankees had become jumpy. Now it was too dangerous—they would shoot you for a bushwhacker.

About four miles from LaGrange Joe heard a rumbling coming from the direction of Helena. He turned to see a large cloud of dust rising.

"Come on, Curtis, let's hide behind the trees," Joe said, leaping off the road.

Curtis stood. "No, we told the folks we would stay to the road."

"Nation, Curtis, we'll smother in the dust. In case you haven't noticed, this road is dusty, not like the muddy streets in town."

Curtis wouldn't budge. Joe kicked the hickory he was standing behind and trudged back to the road. He wouldn't leave his friend standing there alone. He pushed Curtis's shoulder, almost knocking him over. "Chicken."

The rumbling grew and the big cloud drew near. As the troopers neared, Joe saw the horses were only in a slow trot, but still the dust rose like smoke.

When the Yankee troopers came along side, Joe heard one call his name, and one passing by reached over and knocked Joe's kepi from his head. Soon it was too dusty to recognize anybody, and Joe and Curtis raised their shirts over their faces. Confound Curtis, Joe thought. If he wasn't so all-fired scared, we would be in the woods and out of this dust.

It only took a few minutes for the troopers to pass, but it seemed forever to Joe. He didn't know how many there were—at least a hundred or two. It seemed like a whole army when you were standing next to them eating their dust.

Joe beat at the dust on his clothes and gave Curtis another push.

They had walked for another mile or two when they came upon a large tree; some of its large limbs hung over the road. When they got closer, Joe saw the berries in the road; it was a huge mulberry tree. Bunches of birds were swaying the limbs like a breeze.

Yellow, red, and green parakeets were squawking and fluttering about the tree, along with an assortment of other birds. Joe tossed a stick at the birds. Some flew out, but circled and came right back. The parakeets walked on the limbs and hung upside-down. Joe laughed at them—they seemed awkward compared to the other flitty birds.

"I'm going to get me some of them mulberries, too," Joe said. He shimmied up the leaning trunk.

Curtis set the bag of coffee down and climbed up, too.

Their fingers and faces soon turned purple from the fruit. They laughed and threw berries at each other. They threw berries at the parakeets, which had worked their way to the other side of the tree. The birds seemed to have gotten used to the boys and continued gorging on the berries.

Joe had grown hot walking on the road; now in the tree it seemed much cooler. He believed he could play up there all day. There wasn't a worry in the world—no Dr. Roy to tell on him, no Katie Bea to make him clean up, and no Uncle Wilbur to give him a whipping.

Suddenly a bird messed right on Joe's nose. Curtis laughed so hard, he almost lost his grip on the limb. Joe smeared it off with a leaf. Then he stood on a large limb with his back to Curtis and unbuttoned his pants.

"What are you doing?" Curtis asked.

Joe didn't answer, just started giggling. Soon he was peeing down on the road.

"Hey! Don't get Pappy's coffee wet."

"I ain't going to get the old coffee wet. I can aim like a rifle."

Curtis chucked berries at Joe while he was peeing.

Joe tried to write his name in the dust on the road, but he kept giggling and pee went everywhere. Finally, he finished. "Don't you have to go, Curtis?"

"Yeah, but I can't go from no tree," Curtis said. "I might fall and break my neck."

"Pshaw," Joe said. "I ain't scared of falling. I can climb like a squirrel. Watch this." He tucked his kepi into his pants, wrapped his legs around the big limb, and rolled under the limb. He swung upside-down. "Look, I'm a parakeet. Yahoo—yippy—"

"Joe, listen! Listen! Be quiet!"

Still hanging upside-down, Joe fell silent. He heard popping sounds coming from the direction of LaGrange.

"What is it?" Curtis asked.

"Gun shots." Joe climbed back up onto the limb.

Joe listened as the firing intensified. He saw the dust rising in the distance. It grew closer, and he heard the rumbling of hooves.

"Let's get down and hide," Curtis said.

Now he wants to hide. "No, they will go right under us. All we have to do is be still."

"What do you reckon it is?" Curtis asked.

"We'll soon find out. Here they come."

Soon the lathered horses were thundering under the tree with the blue troopers whipping them hell-bent-for-leather. Joe saw some of the saddles were empty, and some horses had red paint on their backs. A strange feeling came over him. There should be Yankees on those saddles. Where were they?

Dust floated up into the tree and Joe gagged. He smelled the horses as they pounded under him. The dust soon blocked his view, but not before he saw the look on the men's faces: absolute fright. They looked as if they had seen a horrible monster. He could think of nothing else that could scare someone so.

He heard more popping coming from down the road, and through the dust, he could barely see the gray troopers coming. Then he heard a yell and a thump under the tree. The dust moved away enough for him to see that one of the Yankees had been shot from his horse.

The young trooper rolled over on his back, and at that instant, he looked straight at Joe. Looking into those eyes, Joe felt the terror. The man seemed to stare forever—pleading for help, but it was only a brief second, and Joe saw the man realize there was no help in that tree. The man scrambled to his feet, holding his left arm. As he stood, Joe saw another trooper had come back for him. As the horseman bent, Joe heard a shot and saw a red spot magically appear in the middle of the man's chest, and he toppled from the horse. The trooper on the ground grabbed for the reins.

A Rebel reined his own horse next to the Yankee. Joe looked back down the road and saw this man had outdistanced the rest. The man pointed his revolver at the Yankee.

"I'm your prisoner," the Yankee said.

"Good, very good indeed. We treat our prisoner like y'all treat y'all's," the Rebel said, then shot the man in the face.

The Rebel climbed down from the horse and looked back toward the approaching gray troopers.

Joe heard his own blood swooshing and pounding in his ears. He prayed the cold-blooded killer couldn't hear it. He tried not to breathe, but he was panting like a dog.

The man went through the Yankee's pockets. He pulled a ring from the dead man's finger, then noticed the sack of coffee, picked it up, and smiled.

Joe saw a stream of water trickling down and splashing near the man. Then it moved up onto the man's hat. Joe followed the stream up. Curtis was sprawled on a big limb with one of his legs hanging, and pee was dripping from his big toe. Joe looked at Curtis's face. Curtis looked back at him. He was crying and shaking. Joe looked back down at the man. Please don't let him notice.

But the man did notice. He looked around, then looked up and saw the boys. He pulled his revolver. "Shit!" He stepped away from the pee, pulling his hat off and shaking it.

Curtis cried, "Don't shoot—don't shoot!"

"Shut up, and you boys come down out of that damn tree."

As the boys climbed down, other troopers galloped by chasing the Yankees. Curtis hit the ground first, and the man shoved him to the ground. Curtis whimpered. One pants leg had a wet streak down it.

"You pissed on me, boy!"

When Joe's feet touched the ground, the Rebel jerked the Union kepi from Joe's pants. "What do we have here?"

Joe looked at Curtis and felt sorry for his friend. He turned on the man. "What does it look like?" Joe tried to take the kepi from him. The soldier backhanded him, knocking him to the ground.

Curtis cried louder. The Rebel raised his hand to slap Curtis, "Quit that blabbering, mind ya, or I'll give you what he just got."

Joe scrambled to his feet. "Give me my hat!"

The Rebel pointed the revolver at Joe. In his face, it looked like a stovepipe. "I'll give you a hole in the head," the man said.

Two horsemen pulled up to the man. One was a captain. Other men galloped on.

"Put that weapon down, you fool," the captain said. He dismounted from his horse.

"The youngun there had this," the man said shaking Joe's kepi.

"Get on that damn animal and head back to LaGrange," the captain ordered.

The man grabbed his horse.

"Give me my hat," Joe said.

"Joe, let him have it," Curtis said, whimpering and wiping his nose.

"Hell, no. I want it back." Joe stood straight with his fist tight at his sides.

The man looked at the captain and threw it back at Joe. He mounted the horse and raced back down the road.

"Boys, what are y'all doing here?" the captain asked.

Curtis sniffled, "We—we—"

"Keep quiet, Curtis. We don't have to tell them nothing."

The captain studied Joe for a minute, then turned to the other soldier. "Corporal, tell the lieutenant not to get too close to Helena. Bring them on back. The colonel is sure to be at LaGrange wanting to know the particulars." The corporal leaped on his animal and galloped hard toward Helena.

"Why won't you boys talk to me? I'm from Arkansas, too." He pointed to the dead Yankees. "There is the enemy, not me."

"He was—he was trying to surrender," Curtis whimpered.

"Yeah, and your man shot him in the face," Joe said.

The captain pulled his hat off and raked his fingers through his dusty hair. Joe saw the top of his left ear was gone, probably shot away in a previous battle.

"That's bad for sure," the captain said. He put his hat back on and looked straight into Joe's eyes. "But boys, they do the same to our men. They captured ten of our boys a while back, and not one made it to Helena. They drowned them. This is war, and war is just plain mean. We all do bad things, and that man Franklin that shot these boys here is the worst. He saw three of his brothers shot to death with a cannon, and now he aims to kill all the Yankees single-handed." He turned to Curtis. "Where are you from, boy?"

"Helena."

"Don't talk to him, Curtis."

"Mind you, I'll talk if I want to. Your pa is fighting for General Lee, and you won't talk to our own army."

"How many soldiers they got in Helena, son?"

"A whole bunch," Curtis said.

"More than three thousand, maybe four or five," Joe said, placing his kepi back on. "You aim to attack Helena?"

"No. Just wondering what they had over there. The number of cannon and things like that."

"Captain, they have a fort and some mighty big guns. They will give you a cocked hat if you climb those hills to get to the town, and that's a fact."

The captain smiled at Joe, then looked toward the direction of Helena. His men were coming back.

"Have they been digging?" the captain asked.

The boys looked at each other, puzzled.

"Have they been digging?" The captain asked again. "Trenches, breastworks?"

"They've been digging graves for their men that have died of sickness," Joe said.

Slowly he looked down at the dead Yankee with the bullet hole in his head. He really saw the man's face for the first time—at least with his own mind clear and not the worry of being found in the tree. Suddenly he felt sick and found it hard to keep from crying.

The captain mounted his horse. "Son, I would advise you to not wear that hat in this country."

Joe reached up absently to pull it off, but stopped before his hand made it to the kepi. He slowly lowered his hand and kept his gaze on the dead Yankee.

"Captain." Joe couldn't stop his voice from quivering. "War is horrible, ain't it?"

The captain followed Joe's gaze to the dead man. "Yeah, son, as horrible as it gets."

"I watched that man get shot. I looked straight into his eyes when he was on the ground and didn't even noti..." Joe wiped his eyes. "Captain, that man's name is Lieutenant Nathan Randall from Iowa." Joe looked up at the captain, pulled the kepi tight on his head and squaring his shoulders. "He's the man that gave me this kepi about a month ago. I believe I'll wear it."

The captain nodded, looked at Joe for a long minute, wheeled the horse around, and joined his men heading back toward LaGrange.

As the Rebel troopers rumbled by, Joe looked back down at the dead man one last time. Now he realized war was not just a stray bullet shot into a pilothouse from some unknown shooter or the pain of having to leave your father behind in Virginia. War did something to you inside when you witnessed it up close—something indescribable and horrible.

"Joe, let's go home," Curtis said.

Joe took one final look at dead Nathan Randall. How did he not recognize Nathan when the man was looking up at him in the tree? Did he know me? Joe wondered. It is the last Nathan will see of war. Joe hoped it was the last he would see of it, too.

They started back toward Helena. Joe pulled his harmonica from his pocket and tried to play *Home Sweet Home*. A week earlier, he had played the song much prettier for Lieutenant Randall as a trade for the kepi.

Chapter 3

"Bless it!" Peter dropped the hammer and shoved his thumb into his mouth; he should have been paying more attention to fixing the gate, instead of watching the Yankees. He couldn't help it; something was going on around town. The Yankees were busier than before, a lot more drill and urgency about everything. They even worked in yesterday's rain. They were digging in the surrounding hills west of town and fussing over the cannons up there—even right behind the house. There was more excitement now than last month when the bushwhackers ambushed the Iowa cavalry, killing so many of those troopers.

Peter placed another board on the gate and nailed it in place without hitting his thumb again. As he finished with the last nail, he heard swearing and laughing coming from the other side of the house. When he went around there, it was as he had suspected. Joe was the one laughing. He was always the one in the middle of it. Heck, he witnessed the shooting of those troopers. He was drawn to trouble like flies to honey—maybe he drew the trouble instead of the other way around.

A wagon had stalled in the road with the tongue lying in the muddy street. Two soldiers, Sergeant Davis and a private, were trying to back two stubborn mules back to the wagon.

"Back up there, you hardheaded mules," Joe said, "and you four-legged ones need to back up, too." He slapped his leg and laughed.

"Damn you, boy," Sergeant Davis said. "If you're the one that fixed this wagon, I'm going to fix you." He slid and tripped in the mud. The private fell over him. The mules spooked and trotted down the street.

"This is why y'all are up here and not at Vicksburg. General Grant wants to win." Joe went to his knees, laughing.

A short piece down the street, Lucius halted the mules. He wrapped his huge hands around their noses. "Whoa, mules." They tried to throw their heads, but Lucius held them. He forced them back to the wagon. "Back, mules, back."

"Look there," Davis said to the private. "Now there's a man that knows how to handle animals."

Peter stood next to Joe as Lucius helped the soldiers hook the team back to the wagon. "Did you see that?" Peter said, pointing to the mules.

"What?" Joe asked.

"The way Lucius forced those animals back."

"Oh, yeah, he's a strong one."

Peter looked down at Joe; he was watching the men and giggling. Joe thought nothing of Lucius's strength—not really. If Lucius were to pick up one of the mules, Joe would probably believe he could pick up the other one himself. Peter shook his head. Now that Peter thought about it, Joe was probably the one that sabotaged the wagon.

The soldiers boarded the wagon, and Davis flipped Lucius a coin.

"Obliged, Massuh," Lucius said, showing teeth.

"Hey, boy," Davis said, looking at Joe. "Let him take care whoever tries to come it over on Sergeant John Davis. That's a fact."

"Pshaw." Joe waved the warning away. "I wasn't born in the woods to be scared by no owl."

Lucius approached the boys as the wagon creaked down the street. Peter was almost six feet tall, and Lucius towered over him. Peter instinctively stepped back, remembering how Lucius handled the mules.

"Is Dr. Taylor home?" Lucius asked.

He was looking at Peter, but Joe answered. "Yeah, he told me to tell you to go around to the parlor door. He's expecting you."

Lucius started for the house, but Joe grabbed his shirtsleeve.

"How did you make those mules back up like that?"

Lucius reached down, grabbed Joe under the arms, and picked him up to his eye level as if he were a feather.

Peter's heart raced. He couldn't let this big man hurt Joe.

"Them there mules," Lucius said, "they's scared of me."

Lucius glared at Joe. He was dark, and his eyes were coal black, surrounded by whitish yellow. Peter thought of a cat.

Joe smiled. "Yeah, mules are funny like that I reckon. Back home, I saw one act plumb crazy when a little mouse ran through the feed trough."

A smile slowly grew on Lucius's face until his teeth showed so white that they were in perfect contrast with the rest of him. He hawed a deep baritone laugh.

Peter breathed easier as Lucius put Joe down and went for the parlor door.

***

Katie Bea let Lucius in. "You can wait here in the parlor, Lucius. Dr. Taylor be with you in a spell."

"Obliged."

When Katie Bea left the room, Lucius looked the parlor over. He had never been allowed in a fine home before. A big rug covered most of the floor, fancy curtains on the windows, and pretty furniture, probably soft; he was sure he would never find out. The room smelled like a cedar tree, not like rotting hay or musky blankets, as he was used to. There was a huge fireplace; he had never seen such a sight. Above it hang a big painting covered in glass, and in it, he could see the reflection of Dr. Taylor in an adjoining room. He was getting money from a metal box on his desk. Lucius could see something gold by the box, maybe a watch. Dr. Taylor placed the gold object back in the box and closed the lid before Lucius could tell what it was. Then Dr. Taylor sat at the desk and started writing in a book.

Lucius found the writing not worth watching, so he looked around the room more. This time he noticed the subject of the picture: a white woman.

The last thing he needed was to be caught looking, so he scanned the hall and adjoining doorways to make sure no one was watching.

The woman had pale skin, almost a real white—not darker white like most white people. Her hair was brown and tied high on her head, and she was smiling, but it wasn't a real smile; it was a picture smile. She wore a gold necklace.

Lucius moved closer. The necklace seemed familiar, but how could it? He had never been that close to a white woman—never. He had never been that close to a picture either. There was something about the necklace. It had two gold birds with red glass eyes. They were in a gold circle with small white glass stones. The birds were either kissing or feeding each other.

"What are you gawking at?" Katie Bea had appeared at the hall door holding a plate.

"I's not gawking."

Katie Bea lowered her voice. "Dr. Taylor catch you looking at Mrs. Taylor in that fashion, he'll have you skint."

So, it was Dr. Taylor's dead wife.

"Here, take this plate and keep your attention on this here food. You sit there on that hard chair." She pointed to a rocking chair by the window. "Don't you spill none on the floor."

"Thank you. You is a kind woman."

She started for the hall, stopped, looked back, and then shut the hall door as she left.

Lucius tried not to look, but there was something about that necklace. It would come to him. He always remembered—sometimes he had to study on it, but he always remembered. Black folks had to remember. Yes, they had to remember if they wanted to hand down history.

Lucius was sopping the last of the bean juice when Dr. Taylor came from the study. Lucius shot to his feet. He had the feeling of being caught doing something wrong.

"I see Katie Bea prepared you something to eat."

"Yessuh. She a fine woman."

"Let me take that plate." Dr. Taylor set the plate on the mantle. "Lucius, I wanted to see you, not only to pay you your wages, but I may need you to do more."

"Yessuh, anything you say."

Dr. Taylor counted out the coins and dropped them in Lucius's calloused hands. They felt nice. They were cold and shiny, and they clinked as he placed them there one by one.

Dr. Taylor looked up at Lucius. "You ever made this much money before?"

"I's never made no money before. I's never even had no money before."

Lucius studied Dr. Taylor's gentle face. If there were such a thing as a good white man, maybe he was one.

"I need you to help me out," Dr. Taylor said. "I need you to keep an eye on Theo. I suspect he is drinking whiskey and even taking laudanum while at work."

"Yessuh, Mas—Dr. Taylor. If you will forgive a darky, why don't you hire somebody else beside Massuh Theo, another white man?"

"There is no one else in town that can do the work that Theo does. The qualified people left when the Yankees came. Well, there are some, but they think my buying cotton from the Yankees is a horrible deed. Oh, I know there is a lot of corruption going on—I'm no fool, but if it can help some of these farmers hang on until this horrible war is over by me purchasing cotton, so much the better."

Lucius nodded at the doctor's every word, but he was thinking differently: you can fill your fat pockets with money from the thieving Yankees, and it is fine by me if you want to fool yourself.

"Will you help me out, Lucius?"

"What you need me to do?"

Dr. Taylor smiled and opened the door. "Just do the job you were hired for, helping around the store, and when I'm not there, keep an eye on Theo. That's all you have to do. There will be a little extra money in it for you."

"But why trust ole Lucius?"

"When Peter's not there to look after Theo, you're all I have. I'm hoping I can trust you. You wouldn't betray me would you, Lucius?"

"Oh, no suh. I's always been a good and trusty nigger. You can count on Lucius to do the good thing. Yessuh."

He felt the doctor pat his back just before he shut the door.

Keep an eye on the fat white man. He could do that. He could keep an eye on many things.

Lucius walked down the street back toward the store. He passed a black woman with her son in tow. He knew she was looking for work, too. The contrabands came from the filthy camps every day and begged the Yankees for something to do to keep from starving, just as he had, but he was lucky to meet Dr. Taylor. A few men cut wood for the steamboats or joined the new black regiments. Lucius wouldn't. He wanted his freedom now, and the army didn't seem like freedom to him. The women looked for work as cooks, washerwomen, or seamstresses, but many went hungry anyway. Too bad for them.

Lucius turned as he passed the woman and child. Suddenly he remembered—he knew he would. He didn't believe in God—no, he had seen too much hell on earth, but some power must have led him to Dr. Taylor's home. Something led him to that necklace. Oh yes, he remembered it real good now.

***

Joe ran his hand along the cannon. It was hot on top, but cool on bottom, even in the late June scorcher.

From this high ridge west of town, he could see all of Helena: below the Catholic Church, Uncle Wilbur's house left of that, Fort Curtis with its large guns, far left, and the Mississippi River on the other side of town—he could see steamboats on it. They appeared small from atop the hill. One had guns sticking from it like a floating pincushion. The town had a blue tint with all of the Union soldiers about it. They spilled out of the town and along the river. The biggest Negro camp lay south. Three more hilltops had cannons on them, too, and the troops had dug large ditches far in front of the cannons. The big guns were trained on the roads leading into town. He saw trees had been cut and now blocked the roads. The troops had been working up on the ridges for weeks, and they were still digging and bracing.

"What do you think of all of this work, Joe?" Captain Varner asked. He placed his hand on the cannon beside Joe's hand.

Joe looked around again. "Sure are a lot of guns."

Joe liked Captain Bob Varner. He had red hair and always smiled, but he couldn't understand how Captain Varner and the rest of the Missourians could be Yankees. It didn't make sense. He knew there were Missouri regiments in the Confederate army. How could it be both ways?

"Yeah," Captain Varner said. "I just hope it is enough to stop the Rebels." He patted the gun.

"Do you really believe they will attack Helena?"

"I don't know." He looked down at Joe. "I hope not. God, I hope not." He pulled his cap off and swatted at a wasp trying to enter the cannon muzzle.

"Do you hate the Confederates?" Joe asked, and took a swat at the wasp, but missed, too.

"No, I don't hate them." He put his cap back on. "I don't hate anyone."

"Then why did you join the Yankee army?"

Captain Varner stared down the road to the west. "I don't remember anymore." He thought for a long minute. "I guess to preserve the Union. I don't know." He looked at Joe. "That must sound strange to a young boy like you—me not remembering why I joined up to fight."

Joe looked at him, but didn't know if it was strange or not, so he didn't answer.

"I have a brother in the Confederate army," Captain Varner said. "For all I know, he could come right up that there road and attack this very battery some day soon."

"I hope that doesn't happen," Joe said. He really meant it. He didn't want Captain Varner's brother killed, and from what Joe could see, if an enemy came up that road, he didn't have a chance. "Maybe this war will be over soon, and you will see your brother again."

"Now that is a capital thought, Joseph." He rubbed Joe's head. "And I hope you see your father real soon."

"Captain Varner, can you keep a secret?"

"Depend upon it."

"I want to go home. I want to find my pa."

"Maybe this war will be over soon and you will be able to."

"Oh no, Captain, I aim to strike out soon." Joe set the kepi straight on his head.

Captain Varner took hold of Joe's arm. "Boy, don't take this war so lightly. Virginia is hot with fighting. I'm sure your father would want you to stick right here."

Joe looked at the soldiers all around them. He eyed the big guns, then looked down at Fort Curtis.

"Joe, I know what you're thinking, but there may not even be a battle here." Captain Varner made a sweep with his arm. "This may all be for nothing. Most of my men believe there is not a large

Confederate army within two hundred miles, just a little cavalry keeping us bottled up scared."

"I want to see my pa, Captain. He's all I've got left in the world, and I don't even know if he's alive. He was fighting with General Jackson, and now I hear Jackson is dead. I want to go home to the Shenandoah."

To the west, Joe saw cavalry coming down the Little Rock Road, the only road not blocked by the felled trees. The blue uniforms were coming toward Helena fast.

Captain Varner yelled at a man standing in the long ditch. "Corporal, run over to that road and see what they have found." The corporal saluted then bounded down the hill.

A sergeant working on one of the ditches came up to the captain. "These here rifle pits are more than ready, sir."

Captain Varner watched the rear of the cavalry as it went below the hills and into the streets. "They are back soon, Sergeant."

"That they are, sir." The skinny sergeant drew a dirty handkerchief from his shirt pocket, pulled his round glasses off, spit on them, and smeared the mud around on the lenses until they were fairly clean. Then he turned toward some soldiers that had followed him. "You men get back to work."

Joe didn't see how the men could do any more to the trenches.

Captain Varner turned to the sergeant. "What is your opinion?"

"Sir, it could mean about anything. If the captain would like, I will fetch up one of them horse boys and find out."

"No. There is no need for that. I'm just being impatient. Corporal Stewart will be back directly."

Joe saw the captain was acting strange. He didn't seem scared, but nervous. He looked the way Joe felt when his Aunt Alice would come on the cars to visit. Joe would watch every passenger leave the car, hoping none was his aunt, hoping she had missed the train.

Shortly, Corporal Stewart raced back up the hill. He almost bowled Joe over when he slid to a stop in front of the captain. Joe probably would have hit the ground if Captain Varner had not caught him.

The corporal was panting. "Sorry, boy." He bent, placing his hands on his knees.

They all waited.

He straightened, and took a deep breath. He began to speak,

stopped abruptly, and looked down at Joe, then back up to the captain.

"Go ahead, corporal; if the Confederates are upon us, it's not going to matter now who knows," Captain Varner said.

The corporal nodded briskly. "Sir, a trooper said they couldn't get as far as Lick Creek. He said there is a large body of cavalry out there, bigger than anything they've seen, yet. They skedaddled on back here."

"Very good, corporal. That will be all."

"They're coming, Captain," the sergeant said. They're screening for the infantry.

"Yes, Sergeant, I believe you can hang your hat on it."

Joe didn't know what it all meant, but he knew Lick Creek was only about five or six miles west of town.

Captain Varner squeezed Joe's shoulder. "Joe, I think it is best you don't come back up here for a spell."

"And boy, if the Rebels do attack, stay in that house," the sergeant said.

As Joe headed down the hill, he thought about what the sergeant had said: "If the Rebels do attack." This was all madness. He liked these Yankees. They were like everyone else once you got to know them. However, most of the men who had lived in Helena before the Yankees arrived were now Rebels. The men in the Shenandoah Valley were mostly Rebels—his pa was a Rebel. Rebel, Yankee, Union, and Confederate—names, just a bunch of names. He looked back up the hill at the many blue uniforms. All of those men had names. The men in gray would have names, too. He looked at the cannons atop the hill; the hill was named Graveyard Hill. Graveyard Hill—that reminded him—tombstones also had names.

***

Peter's muscles were still aching when he stepped through the parlor door. Dr. Taylor was a good man, but he believed in hard work. Mending the gate wasn't enough; he also had Peter clean all of the shelves in the store today. Katie Bea was darning socks when he dragged through the door.

"Dr. Taylor had me working like a slave today," Peter said as he piled on the sofa. When he faced his mother, her bottom lip was quivering.

"Oh, child, don't say such." She put her hands close to her face as if in prayer.

I'm sorry, Mam." He hated more than anything to see her upset.

"Oh, Peter, Dr. Taylor is so good to us." She wiped her eyes with her apron.

"I know he is, Mam." Peter really didn't know what he had done to upset her so.

She went back to her sewing. She stopped crying and became firm. "Peter, long as Dr. Taylor alive, you be free."

"Yes, Ma'am."

"I don't know what we could done if he had not took us in when your poppa died." She smiled. "He liked your poppa so much. They's good friends in Pennsylvania."

Peter loved to see her smile. She was a pretty woman, and when she smiled, she glowed with prettiness. When she told stories of his poppa, she always smiled. If Poppa could have lived, maybe she would smile more often.

He had heard the stories many times. Peter's father, as a teenager, had been a runaway, and Dr. Taylor's family, while on a trip to Virginia, had found him sick, hiding in a ditch. They had smuggled him back to Pennsylvania. Years later, Dr. Taylor had been bitten by a snake, and Peter's poppa had carried him across his shoulder five miles to help. There were more stories, and Peter loved to hear them.

"Peter, we is going north, the first chance we gets."

He looked at her, but he didn't understand. What did she mean they were going north? Dr. Taylor had not said anything about it. Peter had heard there might be a Rebel army on the other side of Crowley's Ridge. It would be dangerous.

"Do you hear me, boy?"

"Who's going?"

She put the sewing back down and took his hands in hers. "You and me is going."

"Us!"

"Oh, Peter, I was a fool to come down here, to bring you down here."

But how could they go? He didn't understand.

"You is growed up to be a handsome, strong, young man." She smiled. "You look so much like your poppa." Her smile disappeared. "If something happen to Dr. Taylor, we be slaves down here."

"But we have our free papers and—"

"Them papers don't mean a thing. They ain't worth a Confederate dollar. I's got money, and I's going to talk to Dr. Taylor. He will help us get back to Pennsylvania."

"Mam, we can't go now. There is a Rebel army out—"

"We can go!" She stood. "We is going. I's been a slave. I's lucky to be freed when my missus died when I's just barely a woman. I don't aim to be a slave again. If that Rebel army take Helena, where you think we go then?"

He took her hands and tugged until she sat back down.

"Mam, let's do what Dr. Taylor thinks best. He is a very smart man. He loves us. He would not tell us wrong."

Tears welled in her eyes. "Peter, if something happen to me, promise me you will go north to Pennsylvania."

"Nothing is going to happen to you." He squeezed her hands.

"Promise me that, boy, you hear." Tears made small streams down her pretty face.

"I promise," he whispered. "I will go to Pennsylvania. I promise."

***

It was late morning when Lucius and Theo began taking inventory in the small storeroom behind the store.

Lucius watched the fat, red-faced man climb the ladder. He was dripping sweat, and it wasn't even warm, yet.

"I don't know why he don't get that damn nigger boy to do this," Theo said. "Hell, he done gone and learned him to read and write like white folks."

"Dr. Taylor say we is to do it," Lucius said.

Theo wheeled on the ladder. "Shut your mouth, boy!" Theo thumped his forefinger on his own chest. "I'm the boss on this here job. Do you understand that, boy?"

"Yessuh, Massuh." Lucius grinned. "Lucius know his place."

"Just because you are a big nigger, don't matter none to me. You understand?"

"Yessuh, I understand."

"Good." Theo turned and climbed to the top of the ladder. He pulled a rag from his hip pocket, wiped dust from a crate on the top shelf, and wrote something in his ledger. He mumbled as he scribbled, "Inventory July 3, 1863. Well, tomorrow is the Fourth of July, probably won't be no fireworks around this dull place."

Lucius looked at the man, such a fat, lazy, worthless, white cracker that grunted with every move. He pursed his lips like a fish when he wrote in the book. Lucius wondered what the man would look like with a cotton sack dragging behind his ass.

Theo started down the ladder. "Get me a dipper of water, and you best not spit in it."

"Oh, no, Massuh, I ain't thought about such shines." As Lucius went out the door, he thought he would rather put poison in the sorry man's water.

Theo made sure he was gone and rolled a barrel from the corner of the storeroom. He removed an old cloth, uncovering some bottles, grabbed one of them, pulled the cork, and turned it up.

From a crack in the wall, Lucius watched. He smiled at the worthless jackass and turned to the well.

Lucius cranked the windlass. Sweet well water, he thought—not the filthy ditch mud like they were drinking in the nigger camp. He ladled a dipper full. It was clear and fresh. White folks always had it sweet. Blacks had the scraps, like dogs. At least Dr. Taylor was allowing him to stay in the back room of the store; he could get some of the benefits like a white man. That Dr. Taylor was a strange one.

As Lucius enjoyed the water, he noticed the change in the hills around Helena. He had not really left the store much in a couple of weeks, especially since he slept there, too, so he really hadn't paid much attention to the goings on around town. Now he noticed the soldiers. They were thick as flies on the hills west of town. Something was about.

What would he do if the Rebels took the town back? Swim the river again, that's what. Try to make it to Memphis; there were freed slaves there, too.

"Boy, you going to fetch me that water or not?" Theo yelled from the storeroom.

Lucius rushed the water to him. Theo, waiting outside the door, snatched the dipper, spilling some on Lucius's feet.

"Massuh Theo, what is them soldiers doing up in them hills?" Lucius said, pointing toward Graveyard Hill.

Theo chugged from the dipper, dribbling water down his shirt;

he turned toward the hills. "They look like they are getting ready to fight." He shoved the dipper back at Lucius. "I reckon they believe our boys are going to take Helena back. And with the way them Yankees have siphoned men to Vicksburg, our boys might just skip right in."

Lucius stared at the soldiers. He felt the muscles working in his face.

Theo smiled. "Yeah, you niggers will all be dead. Well, maybe not. They might just herd you over them hills like a bunch of cows." He snickered.

Lucius endured the fat cracker's laugh, but some day—some day soon, the bottom rail will be on top.

Chapter 4

The new barn is going to be capital, Joe thought. The new colt will love it better for sure.

"Hand me that hammer, Joe," his pa said, smiling down from the ladder. He always smiled when he worked. He was the best pa in the Valley, and he was good to Joe and his sister, Sarah. Joe would be like him some day.

The Valley was so green this year. Wildflowers painted the hillsides, and the sky was as blue as Sarah's eyes. It was perfect weather for romping, and that was just what Joe planned to do when the barn was finished.

Joe heard his mother singing from somewhere in the house—birds could not sing prettier. She was probably combing Sarah's silky hair; she always sang when she did that. Joe loved it, but he wouldn't tell anyone.

His pa drove the nail with the hammer: bang, bang—bang—bang—bang, bang—

Joe bolted upright in the bed. It took only seconds to realize he wasn't in Virginia—he was in Helena Arkansas, and the banging was coming from the hills behind the house. He threw the mosquito bar open and ran to the window. It was dark, but he could tell the shots were coming from the west side of Graveyard Hill.

Joe heard the long drum roll. Soon Yankees were swarming like bees around a hive. Men were running below his window so close he could have dropped a rock on their heads if he had a mind to.

There had been a lot of activity in the early morning for about a week now, but this was much more—now there was shooting. The Confederates had really come!

He grabbed his clothes from the chair and scrambled to get them on. He tried to get both legs in one pant leg, fell to the floor, jumped up, staggered over to the bed, and finally lined everything out. If he didn't hurry, he was going to miss it. He crammed his kepi on and headed down the stairs toward the kitchen. He reached the door, and Dr. Taylor caught him.

"Joseph, go to the parlor. Now!"

It was dark in the kitchen, but he didn't have to see his uncle to know the expression on his face, nothing to do but follow his order for now.

In the parlor, Katie Bea and Peter were sitting quietly on the sofa. They were like lost puppies. Joe eased down in the rocking chair. He desperately wanted to go outside, but Dr. Taylor stood watch at the window.

A small lamp, turned low, barely illuminated the room. Joe looked at the clock. It was 3:30, a long time before sunup, and the time dragged as the shooting grew closer.

After a spell—seemed like forever, Joe couldn't stand waiting in the chair, felt like a tied coon. He slipped over to the other window while Dr. Taylor was preoccupied with the happenings outside his own window. It was dawning and a heavy fog blanketed everything. Joe could barely see the hill behind the house. Small flashes illuminated the fog atop the hill, like an approaching storm—eerie. First, he would see the ghostly flashes like small specks of lightning and a short time later, he would hear the reports.

Suddenly the room quaked; the whole house shuddered as the cannons erupted atop the hills. Katie Bea screamed, and Joe felt his heart jump in his chest.

"Joe, get away from that window!" Dr. Taylor said. "Peter, help me."

They dragged the sofa to the fireplace. Katie Bea placed a quilt on the hearth and frantically beckoned the boys to her. Dr. Taylor pulled two big chairs next to the sofa, making a huge barricade, surrounding them and the fireplace. He climbed across the sofa and drew everyone near. He said nothing, but as he looked into Katie Bea's eyes, Joe saw the worry.

"What do it mean?" Katie Bea asked. She was trembling.

"The Confederate army is trying to push into the town," Dr. Taylor said. "The batteries up there are firing on them."

"Sweet Jesus!" Katie Bea said. She grabbed Joe's hand and squeezed so tight that it hurt. "Do you think the Rebels will take the town, Doctor?"

Dr. Taylor took her other hand. "The Federals were ready for this. That is why they have been up at 2:30 every morning, lately. They have four batteries up on the hilltops. I believe they can easily hold the town."

Joe believed it, too. He had seen those guns in the hills, and he had seen the big guns in the fort. He also knew that gunboats were always coming and going on the river. In fact, the Tyler was there yesterday and probably there this morning. It had some great-big guns. But, if the Yankees had big guns, surely the Rebels did, too. Then Joe remembered the trees the Federals had felled across the roads leading into town. The Rebels would have a hard time getting their guns across those obstacles.

He couldn't stand the sitting—too much was happening. The shooting grew hotter, like popping corn in a kettle. He stood to see over the sofa. He could barely see through the window. As the dawn grew, the sky flashed like a thunderstorm.

Dr. Taylor jerked Joe's arm. "Get down, boy! Do you want to get killed?"

Another boom thundered, jarring plaster from the ceiling, then another, and another. The windows rattled, pictures fell to the floor, and the whole house seemed to shiver. Joe had never heard thunder as frightening as the big guns. Surely, the house would crumble any minute.

Someone pounded at the door. "Dr. Taylor!"

Dr. Taylor hesitated, crawled across the furniture, looked back, opened the door to find a Yankee private there.

"Sir, Colonel Russell requests that you come with me."

"What about my family?" Dr. Taylor pointed toward the barricade.

"He ordered me to bring only you."

Cannons thundered again, jarring more plaster from the ceiling.

Both men instinctively ducked.

"Private, you can tell the colonel my family is my first responsibility."

"Doctor, two of our surgeons are in the hospital with malaria. The colonel has ordered me to bring you at the point of the bayonet if I have to." He looked at the barricade. "Sir, your family will be as safe there as anywhere else with you there or not."

Joe stood to crawl across the sofa, but Peter pulled him back down. How dare that private threaten his uncle?

Dr. Taylor grabbed his bag off the table and turned to the barricade. "I will be back soon. You just stay right there. Peter, take care of them while I am gone."

After the door closed, Joe turned to Peter and Katie Bea.

Katie Bea had her face in her hands, sobbing. Peter's eyes were closed tight, and though he was silent, his lips were moving rapidly forming just the right words for God to hear.

Joe agreed it was a good idea to pray. He wondered if the soldiers were praying. Then he remembered Captain Varner. He wondered if he was facing his Rebel brother up on Graveyard Hill. It occurred to Joe: were brothers praying for each other at the same time they were fighting each other?

***

Lucius stared out the backdoor. He didn't frighten easily, but the hell going on in the hills scared the hell out of him. He had once seen fireworks, but nothing compared with this. The very earth shook as the cannons from the fort pounded.

A heavy fog floated about three feet above the ground; everything below the level of the fog was clear, everything above was lost in a ghostly cloud, only the explosive flashes cut through it. After a while, the stinking smoke from the guns mingled with the fog, creating a horrible stew.

Lucius went back into the room, had to think. If the Rebels took the town, the Negroes would be rounded up like cattle, just as Theo had said.

The cannons fired again, jarring items from the shelves in the store.

He went into the dark store. It was dawning, but the fog and smoke denied the light. He lit the lamp on the counter and picked it up. It slowly glowed bright. Shadows played like ghosts as he looked about the store.

Suddenly a loud noise rang out beside his head—his breath caught in his throat. He swung the lamp around. The light fell on the wall clock as it chimed four times. He took a deep breath, and went back to looking around the store.

He knew what he was looking for, but he didn't know where they were kept. He had seen Theo sell one. He searched all of the shelves; then he remembered. He moved around behind the counter and placed the lamp on it. He slid a wooden box from under the counter. Knives of all types were in the box, and their blades reflected the yellow lamplight. He found the one he wanted, a long Bowie Knife, about a foot long with a leather sheath. He tested the blade—it was sharp. He raised his trouser leg and crammed the knife into his boot.

He went back to the back room, gathered his few belongings, and wrapped them in a blanket. He blew the lamp out and cracked the backdoor just enough to see the battle going on behind the town. If the gray backs took the town, he knew what he would have to do.

***

How long would this go on, Peter wondered. Surely everyone was dead by now. It was after 8:00 and the shooting continued in all directions it seemed.

The Taylor house was situated between the fort and the hills. When the big guns from the fort joined the fight, Peter felt as if the cannon balls would come right through the parlor.

"I can't stand this," Joe said, and scrambled across the barricade. He fell on his face, then got to his knees and crawled to the window.

"Joseph!" Katie Bea screamed.

Jesus, the boy is crazy, Peter thought.

Peter climbed the sofa and chairs and ran to where Joe was staring out the window.

He grabbed Joe's arm. "Have you lost your—" He saw where Joe was looking. The fog was shifting; some places it was heavy, and others it was disappearing like cooling steam. Through the broken cloud of fog and smoke, he saw gray soldiers at the top of Graveyard Hill. In the center of the soldiers, he saw a nightmare—the Confederate's flags. "Oh God, no."

The house rocked again as the cannons from the fort fired, but he could not move. Suddenly dirt erupted around some of the Confederate soldiers and they disappeared in an instant, as if the hand of God had plucked them from earth. More of the tiny men vanished as the cannons on the other hills shot at the Rebels. Peter found himself fixed, could not look away. It wasn't real—it couldn't be. It just couldn't. God would not let anything be so horrible—except for hell.

All at once, a screaming streak came from the river and ran over the city like a trail of brimstone. It screamed like fury, then exploded among the Confederates. A great gap opened up in the men: brown and gray and red. It appeared to Peter as if the lower region, itself, had opened up to swallow the men. Still he could not look away. He could not believe. He could not move. No man would allow such things to happen. No man would do this to another man.

The screaming shell from the river came again, but this time it missed its mark and landed farther down the hill, closer to the house, exploding earth into chunks of brown spray.

"The Tyler," Joe whispered.

Peter looked down at Joe instinctively, but he didn't see him. His mind still saw the shells exploding among the men on the hill.

"Those big explosions are shells from the Gunboat Tyler," Joe whispered again.

Peter looked out the window again. Soon the shell came across the town once more, screaming, whistling, screaming, and exploding.

Screaming—screaming! Suddenly Peter felt a jolt in his brain. His head cleared, as if awakened from the worst of dreams, but it was no dream. Screaming—he realized his mother was screaming his name.

Peter grabbed Joe and slung him under his arm. He raced back to the barricade and shoved Joe across. Katie Bea grabbed them both, hugged them in a frantic embrace.

The screaming and exploding continued, again and again. It grew closer. It sounded to Peter as if it were crawling down the hill and toward the house like a serpent. He knew the Rebels were coming. The explosion told it as much as a town crier could.

The house jarred violently. Windows shattered, mortar sprinkled from the fireplace and small boards fell with a rattle.

"Lord God, help us!" Katie Bea prayed.

The picture of Mrs. Taylor fell and smashed across Peter's head. He felt no pain.

Men were all around the house. Peter heard them swearing as they shot at the Rebels, heard the leads from the Rebel's muskets thudding into the house.

With the windows shattered, the sulfur smell of the spent gunpowder drifted into the house like a plague.

Peter watched Joe coolly take his kepi off and shake the dust and glass from it. Joe started to rise again. Peter snatched him down. "Don't you get up again! You hear me!"

Joe ignored him, formed a queer look on his face. Peter wondered and then followed his gaze. A small hole had appeared in the sofa. It was ever so tiny.

Peter's heart pounded fast, faster than God meant for a heart to ever pound. He slowly turned. He didn't want to look—he was afraid to see.

A small trickle of blood oozed from a perfectly round hole in his mother's neck. Her eyes looked far away. She folded into his arms. The battle outside didn't matter anymore. It could have been on another planet—or in hell where it belonged.

***

Joe almost pulled the door from its hinges. Smoke met him like a brick wall, and he had to stop when he staggered from the porch. The air smelled like rotten eggs.

The big guns in the fort fired again. Joe covered his ears, but it was too late, and he suddenly heard humming in his head. A shingle slid from the house and hit his shoulder. Splinters flew around him as the mini balls struck the corner of the house like angry bees.

The cloud of smoke drifted and Joe saw Yankees, like phantoms, all around the house, shooting back toward the Confederates. They were yelling and cussing. One was lying in the garden—his eyes were open, but Joe knew they saw no more.

Joe stepped away from the porch, saw Confederates coming toward the house—he thought of lava flowing from a volcano as they moved down the hill. Through the clouds of smoke, he saw the small puffs coming from their muzzles.

He had to find Uncle Wilbur—never mind the Yankees or the

Confederates. He reached to see if his kepi was in place—it was. He didn't want to run through the town if it wasn't—he didn't want to look like a Confederate. He darted across the yard toward town. Immediately, he felt something tug at his shirt. He found a small hole in his sleeve. He ran faster.

He ran through Yankees and out to the street. Red pain hit his face. He found himself on the ground, dazed for a second, then saw a bayonet stuck in the ground by his head. He followed it up to a wild-eyed Yankee. The man's face changed as he recognized Joe.

"Damn you, Joe, I nearly killed you!" The soldier jerked the bayonet from the earth and sprinted toward the house.

Joe didn't recognize the man. His face was black and smutty. Joe had seen the soldiers practice shooting, so he knew the black was from the man tearing open the paper powder cartridges with his teeth, and as black as the man was, he had shot a lot.

Joe hurt, and he wanted to lie there, but there was no time—he had to find Uncle Wilbur.

He hurried to his feet, charged between two houses, and now he could see the fort. Fire and smoke belched from the big guns. He threw his hands to his ears. It was all hell—nothing shorter. He ran east. He would have to go around the fort.

As he barreled down the street, he looked back. The Confederates were still swarming off Graveyard Hill and down toward the house. Great holes were erupting in their ranks. The Gunboat Tyler was lobbing the screaming shells with devastating results.

When he moved around to the east side of the fort, above the yelling and confusion, someone called his name. It was Sergeant Davis, a bandage around his head and a bag across his shoulder.

"Dear God, boy! What are you doing? Did you come to see the elephant?"

Joe didn't know what in the world he was talking about.

"Find you a hole to climb in, or you're going to get killed, boy!"

"I'm looking for Uncle Wilbur."

"Lord, Joe, couldn't you wait until after the damn fight?"

"Katie Bea's been shot!" Joe screamed above the battle.

Davis shook his head slowly and grabbed Joe's shoulder. "Look, boy, I can't help you now. I've got to get back with these rounds." He pointed toward some men. "Follow those wounded men.

They'll take you to the doctor, I'm sure." He patted Joe's arm and trotted south, followed by two more men with bags.

Joe followed the wounded men into a house. He didn't remember who owned the home, but he knew the Yankees had been using it for some kind of headquarters.

The smell hit him first. It smelled like hog guts. Men were lying all over the floor; most were groaning, some were crying. One was even screaming and holding what was left of an arm. As Joe gawked at the screaming man's arm, he tripped over a man on the floor. Joe looked down and saw a piece of pink gut hanging from the man's belly. Joe looked away. It was like seeing something private that he shouldn't see.

Joe wandered into the next room. He found a surgeon attending a man lying on a table. Joe looked closer to see the table was really a door lying across two big chairs. The patient was swearing as the surgeon dug in his leg with some kind of fancy knife.

"Joseph, what in God's name are you doing here?"

Joe turned. A table was next to the wall, and Dr. Taylor was wrapping a bandage around a man's head.

"Uncle Wilbur—Uncle Wilbur, Aunt Katie Bea's been shot!"

"Boy, I told you to stay there at the house."

Joe realized he hadn't been understood. He grabbed Dr. Taylor's arm. "Katie Bea has been shot."

"Is she all right?"

Suddenly Joe could not see clearly—his eyes were filling with tears. He wiped at them with his sleeve. "I don't think so."

The room shook from a volley of blasts from the fort.

The surgeon told Dr. Taylor to go see about her. An assistant took the bandage from Dr. Taylor.

Outside hell was still brewing. No one could have told a story as horrible as this. If Joe had not known better, he would have sworn it was Hell from the Bible.

Colonel Russell stopped Joe and Dr. Taylor before they got to the house. His eyes were wild like a frightened horse. "Where in the hell do think you're going?"

"I'm going home. Katie Bea is injured," Dr. Taylor said.

"Damn it, Doctor, there are men dying all around us. This army will need you. The fighting is right behind your house. Hell, they may take your house any minute. You stay your ass right here!" He hit the ground with his sword tip.

"I'm goin—"

"Doctor, I don't have time for this shit." Colonel Russell stopped a running soldier. "Private, you don't let this doctor go toward the fight. You keep him right here. He's no good to this army dead."

The private saluted, and Colonel Russell went toward the fort.

Dr. Taylor reluctantly relented.

Joe wanted to go. He knew the private wouldn't shoot them. "Uncle Wilbur, we have to see about Katie Bea."

The private raised his rifle.

Dr. Taylor grabbed Joe's shoulder. He spotted some wounded soldiers leaning against a shed and went to help them. "Joe, help me here."

Joe stared at the private. He would remember the man. What sort of a man would stand in the way of a doctor?

"Joe, help me!" Doctor Taylor said.

The battle raged, and more men came to the back of the shed to be tended. They found the doctor like flies find a dead dog. Dr. Taylor sent the more serious ones to the house with the surgeon. Joe assisted as best he could, but his mind was on the house just two blocks away and Katie Bea.

Some Yankees brought up a few captured Rebels to be treated. They wouldn't talk much, but when they did, they seemed angrier with their commander, General Holmes, than with the Yankees.

One grumbled, "We have been betrayed by that old man. Only a handful of defenders in Helena—pshaw!"

After about an hour, the battle sounds petered away. Slowly the cannons fell silent, and the smoke drifted toward Mississippi. The Yankees cheered. Joe looked around the shed to Graveyard Hill. The American flag had replaced the Confederate one.

Joe stared up at the hill and felt the whole of his inside sink. Men in gray uniforms were strewn down the hill like a gray and red blanket. Blue soldiers walked among the dead Confederates. Joe's eyes began to blur and the soldiers looked like blue Negroes in a gray cotton field.

"Come on, boy," Dr. Taylor said.

Joe believed all of the Confederates were dead, but then cannons sang out north of town, but there wasn't much to it.

"Joe." Dr. Taylor shook Joe's arm. "Let's go while the soldiers are rejoicing and while that private has his attention elsewhere."

They made their way toward the house. Yankees were everywhere, some cheering, some crying, and some escorting gray prisoners toward the river. All of the soldiers were smutty and black and wild.

When they finally made it to the house, Joe's thought of war disappeared. Katie Bea—what about Katie Bea? What about Peter? Were they still alive?

He ran to the door; it was open. Most of the plaster had fallen from the ceiling, and the parlor was covered in white dust. No windowpanes were left—they were shattered on the floor. He stared at the barricade. It sat alone in front of the fireplace like a tomb—no movement, no sound, except the cheering men outside.

Dr. Taylor came through the door and dropped his bag. They pulled the chairs and sofa away from the fireplace. They found Peter holding Katie Bea's head in his lap, smoothing her hair. Joe saw blood from Katie Bea's wound had run down Peter's arm and had pooled on the hearth.

"There, Mam, Dr. Taylor is here. He has finally come, and everything will be fine now," Peter said.

Tears started down Dr. Taylor's face as he knelt. "Peter, Peter."

Peter slowly looked at Dr. Taylor.

"She's gone, Son."

Peter, bewildered, looked down at his mother.

"Mam." Peter sobbed. "Tell him you're not dead. He can fix you."

Dr. Taylor took hold of Peter's bloody hand. "I'm sorry—so very sorry."

"But Dr. Taylor, you can save her. I know you can. You're a doctor. You can save her."

Dr. Taylor began to cry. "I can't save her—I can't, Peter. I can't save her any more than I could my own Hattie."

Peter cried, "No, Dr. Taylor! No! She's not dead. She's just tired. She's exhausted. It has been a horrible day and she needs rest. She has just fainted. She will be—"

Dr. Taylor threw his arms around Peter and wept.

Joe ran to the porch, had to get out. A thin cloud of smoke, just a wisp, floated on the air. A few shots came from the distant north—only a little popping, and the rotten egg smell was not as strong now. More prisoners were being prodded down the street.

Joe stepped off the porch and went out onto the street. He looked back at the house. It was battered good, but it could be repaired.

He looked back up to Graveyard Hill. It appeared so much different from yesterday. He never would have believed the Confederates would have ever taken Graveyard Hill with its great-big guns. What makes men charge cannons?

Poor Peter. What will it be like now with Katie Bea gone?

He hoped Dr. Taylor would be all right. He was mighty unstrung.

So this is what Pa is facing in Virginia.

Joe started toward town. Maybe Theo would have the store open. That hard candy would be good now, maybe clear his throat of smoke.

Joe turned his back on the house. He turned his back on Graveyard Hill. He turned his back on the war. There would be time to think about it later—but not now. He would wait a spell until the smoke cleared and the blood had been washed away—maybe then it wouldn't be as real.

Chapter 5

Lucius stood inside the doorway of the store cleaning the shelves. The morning sunlight flowed through the open door; dust floated in the sunbeam like a wisp of smoke.

Theo dropped a five-pound sack of salt on the counter and smiled at the pretty, young lady there to buy it.

"Well, now, Mrs. Simmons, I reckon we are better off for it that them Yankees whipped the Johnny's. The long and short of it is: if the Yanks hadn't won the battle last week, you might not be a-getting this here salt." He pulled a ledger from under the counter. "We are right fortunate to get merchandise from them Yankee riverboats, I tell you." He grinned and laid his fat paw on her hand.

Mrs. Simmons grabbed the salt from the counter. "I could have gotten by without the salt if it would have helped us in our revolution." Her dress brushed against Lucius as she marched from the store.

When she cleared the door, Theo mocked her, "I could have gotten by without the salt."

Lucius stared at the fat, sweaty man. What side did Theo fall on, Yank or Secesh? Neither side would want such a worthless beast. If the gray boys had won the battle, he would have talked that up to be the best thing.

"What are you staring at boy?" Theo asked. He spat in a can.

"Nothing, Massuh." Lucius turned back to his dusting. Theo was pushing him to his limit with that big mouth. It would be so easy to bring him down a peg.

An old woman entered the store. She wore fine clothes, but not as fine as they once had been, and she carried herself so high and mighty. Lucius had never seen her before, but he knew her all the same. He had seen her kind; she was the missus of a plantation, no doubt on that. As she walked by Lucius, she looked at him as if he were a smelly horse. Where were her slaves now? He would have felt top feather just to slap her—so high and mighty. She turned back as she approached the counter and gave him another sour look.

Lucius spotted a necklace on her. It had a big thing on it. He couldn't remember what it was called, sounded like roach or was it poach?

Although the necklace wasn't the same, it reminded him of the picture of Dr. Taylor's wife and the necklace she wore in it, the two gold birds with the red eyes. His mother had told him of the birds when he was a boy. The birds had come from the other country—gold birds with eyes of fire—African birds.

He had loved those stories. They took him away from hard times, away from bondage to free Africa. Free to run like a deer, free to hunt like the mighty lion. A man was a man over there, not a piece of property.

"Lucius. Lucius!" Theo called.

Lucius heard Theo, remembered where he was, and started dusting again.

Theo shook his head. "I need you to deliver a sack of flour for Mrs. Hodges."

Lucius put the duster on the shelf and went to the far wall where the flour was stacked. He tossed the fifty-pound sack over his shoulder like a rag.

"Will there be anything else, Mrs. Hodges?" Theo asked.

"No, thank you, Theo. That will be all."

Theo scribbled something in the book.

Lucius followed the old woman through the door. Theo called for Lucius to close the door on his way out.

As Lucius passed the window, he saw Theo dash to the storeroom. Lucius grinned at Theo's disgusting weakness. The weakness was a key, and Lucius would someday have that key in his pocket.

***

Peter scrubbed the kitchen floor for the second time that morning. They had cleaned and repaired the house after the battle, but it didn't seem to be enough. Mam would want it clean, so he labored at it. It must be spotless; it must be the way she would have cleaned it.

Dr. Taylor came into the kitchen. Peter felt him looking at him, but he didn't look up or stop scrubbing.

Dr. Taylor sat at the table. "Peter, come sit with me."

Peter reluctantly dropped the sponge into the bucket, dried his hands on an apron, and sat across from Dr. Taylor. He didn't want to be there; he wanted to finish the floor.

Dr. Taylor smiled softly. "I miss her too."

Peter believed him, but she wasn't his mother. No one felt the tearing pain in the heart as he did. No one cried all night as he did and tried to hide it so no one would know. It was his mother, not anyone else. She was the only family he had in the world.

Dr. Taylor lit his pipe, pulled back from the table, and crossed his legs. He drew at the pipe, stared out the kitchen window.

"When your father died," Dr. Taylor said, still looking toward the window, "God gave me the wisdom to take you and Katie Bea in. When Mrs. Taylor died, you two filled a void—an indescribable hollow." He turned to Peter. "Peter, you are my family now and I love you as a son."

Peter felt the corners of his eyes burn. He always believed Dr. Taylor thought a great deal for him, but now he had it from his mouth. A warmth fell over him as complete as sunshine.

"I've thought on it, and we are going back to Pennsylvania. I came to Helena running from something that I can never outrun."

God can help you, Peter thought, but he didn't say it. He was still struggling with his own sorrow.

"I will sell the store. I'm sick of trading cotton. Some of the officers are even trading escaped slaves back to their masters for the cotton. I want no more of this." He reached for Peter's hand. "We will go home, and I will resume my practice, and we will build from there."

Peter felt the first bit of hope since the day of the battle. It could never be as it was when Mam was alive, but it could be good again.

He remembered friends there he had not thought of in years. He remembered the way it was then. It would not be that way now, but it could still be good. It would be better than Helena.

"I need your help more than ever to keep up with that boy." He squeezed Peter's shoulder.

Peter smiled.

"I have to return him safely to his father. I pray he is alive." Dr. Taylor squeezed Peter's hand. "Will you promise to help me take care of him, Peter?"

"Yes, sir." Peter would do anything for him.

Dr. Taylor winked, then pulled a golden object from his vest pocket. Peter knew it well.

"This is for you, Peter." He placed the object in Peter's hand. "I had this made for my Hattie years ago. She loved them so. It was such a treat for her when they came in the spring, so many, so beautiful. She loved a painting of the birds by Audubon, so I had this made from that likeness."

Peter looked at the present and felt a rush in his heart. He had always admired the precious piece of jewelry, with its uniqueness. He knew it was dear to Dr. Taylor. He also knew what it meant to receive such a gift. Dr. Taylor could have given it to Joe, but he hadn't; he gave it to him. Peter knew what love meant, and he held it in his hand.

Dr. Taylor moved around and placed a tender hand on Peter's shoulder. "It is worth a good deal of money, but to me, it is worth more than treasure."

Peter understood. This was the treasure of the heart.

"Hattie said it represented an abundance of love. I reckon I can't think of anything more abundant than those birds."

"No, sir, I'm not sure God made anything more abundant." Peter looked up. And God never made a better man than Dr. Taylor.

"It is now yours, and do with it as you see fit. I hope you never have to part with it, but you do what your heart calls, as I have. We never know what the future holds."

Peter pulled the object to his heart. This was pure love—nothing else, for you cannot sell love—you can only give it away.

***

Joe dug another minie ball from a tree and placed it in the sack with the others. Curtis dug at another tree. They had a big collection now. However, the collection of weapons was the biggest prize. They had found two muskets, four knives and a hatchet. The boys had hid them in a hollow gum just outside of town, except the hatchet—it stayed in Joe's belt.

The Confederates had made their headquarters at the Polk Farm west of Helena during the battle, and the boys had found the goodies between town and there. Joe had shown some of the Yankees the leads, but he kept the weapons a secret. He didn't know what he and Curtis would ever do with them, but they were there if they wanted them.

This day Joe and Curtis were behind the Nunnery, below Graveyard Hill. They had found a lot of lead. Joe knew they would—he had seen the battle rage there.

"Joe, look!" Curtis said, pointing at a fat stump.

Joe saw a big hole in the stump. There was a cannonball in there for sure.

Curtis knelt down beside the stump and started digging with his knife.

Joe grabbed him by the sleeve. "Get up from there, and let me cut it out with my tomahawk."

He and Curtis called the hatchet a tomahawk. Joe had even learned to throw it and actually hit what he was chucking at— most of the time.

Joe hacked away with the hatchet. He hit the big lead projectile, making a twanging sound. This would be a great trophy.

Suddenly someone grabbed the back of his shirt and snatched him away from the stump.

"What in the hell do you think you are doing, boy?" a private shouted.

Curtis broke and ran toward the Nunnery like a long-legged swamp rabbit.

"Don't you know this is one of those shells from that gunboat? It didn't explode, and here you are hacking away at it like an idiot. It will blow you up in a twinkling." The private crossed his arms, looked at Joseph, and shook his head. Then he looked down at the shell again. "Step aside, boy." He bent down to get a closer look.

Joe stuck the tomahawk back in his belt. He looked at his shirt. The private had ripped it when he jerked him from the stump. He looked down at the soldier, now digging splinters away from the shell and mumbling something about the boy being stupid. Joe recognized the man, the private that had pointed the gun at Uncle Wilbur and wouldn't let them go to Katie Bea the day of the battle.

Joe felt his face grow warm and a faint humming grew in his ears. Joe looked around, saw no one—Curtis was nowhere to be seen. Joe looked back down at the private's ass and smiled. Joe raised his shoe back to the sky and let it fly.

The private's head hit the stump. He screamed.

Joe laughed. The man must have thought the shell had exploded.

"Damn you, boy!"

Joe cut out.

The soldier was on his heels.

Joe flew around the corner of a fence. Curtis was hiding behind it. Curtis screamed and broke into a run. He almost bumped into the private as he ran back the way they had come.

Joe knew the man was right on his tail, but he laughed at Curtis—he was such a flicker. Joe cut to the right and headed for a small woodshed, which had its top blown out during the battle. He could hear the man panting behind him. Joe ran around the shed and dove like a rabbit through a hole in an upright-staked fence.

The soldier smacked the fence headfirst. "Shit!"

Joe looked back, but the soldier wasn't chasing him. He eased back to the fence and peeped through a crack. The soldier was sitting on his butt, holding his head, blood running down his face. Joe poked his lips to the crack and whistled "Dixie." When he looked back through the fence, the man was cussing and staggering toward it.

Joe laughed and cut out running. He looked back, but the soldier had not tried to climb the fence. Joe laughed. There was no way that soldier could—

He tripped, tried to grab hold, but there was nothing but air. He tumbled, felt vines tug and rip as he fell. His back smacked the ground. He looked up. He had fallen into a deep gully, breath knocked from him.

He couldn't breathe. His lungs begged for precious air. No air! He couldn't push or pull a breath. No air! No air! He rolled over, crawled in the bottom of gully like a snake—no, a worm. It was past forever now. No air! Would he die right there in that gully? No one would know where he was. His chest hurt, and only a silly wheeze escaped his throat. The air wouldn't move—either direction. Panic screamed at him. Suddenly something gave, and he felt his breath stutter and jerk, then finally—finally, a burst of sweet—sweet relief. He sat and drew in the good air; breath was never so good.

Slow he regained himself, saw the gully was like a thousand others on Crowley's Ridge, about ten feet deep or so. He and Curtis had played in many like this one.

All at once, a rotting smell came over him completely, like a soaking rain. Sweet air hell, now he gagged and choked. He turned and looked straight into the face of a corpse.

He crawfished, turned, and tried to climb out of the gully. He scrambled, grabbed a root, tumbled back down. He clawed at the dirt. He tried to scream, but gagged instead. He turned and ran up the gully to where it was shallower and wallowed from the pit. He ran toward home.

He stopped, but didn't know why he would do such a foolish thing. He saw the corpse in his mind—a Confederate soldier. He knew he should go to the house, but he couldn't. He had to see.

He placed his kepi over his mouth, and with the other hand, he raked the creeper vines from the top of the gully. The body was sitting in the ditch, as he must have died. Flies busied themselves, and worms squirmed and wiggled. Joe turned away and gagged, turned back. He was drawn like the flies. The man was a captain. His sword lay across his lap, and he still held a navy colt in his right hand.

Joe's pa was also a captain and had such a revolver. Joe knew this was not his pa, but he suddenly felt worried for him. Surely this was someone's pa. He was dead and rotting in a gully at Helena, and no one in the whole world knew it, except Joe.

He no longer felt sick. The flies and worms didn't bother him so much now. He felt sorry for this man's family, wherever they were, and thought it was good they didn't know his fate. But more than anything, Joe wanted his own pa. It was settled in Joe's mind right then and there, right in front of a rotting, forgotten soldier in a stinking ditch, in a hell-hole called Helena Arkansas. Joe was going home. He was going to the Shenandoah Valley to find his pa. He prayed he wasn't a dead captain in some forgotten ditch like this poor man.

***

The next morning Joe had some clothes laid out on his bed. He examined each piece before cramming them into a carpetbag. He would have to travel light, so he needed only a few garments.

He reached under the bed and retrieved a doll and a mirror. They were cherished possessions of his sister and mother. He had always kept them close by. He looked at his reflection in the mirror, but in his mind it was his family he saw.

Things would never be the same. Why hadn't he been nicer to Sarah? Why did he pull her hair and make her cry? She was such a pretty sister, such a lovely girl. If only he could do it over again, he would be good. But he couldn't do it again because she would not be in the Valley when he got there. His mother would not be there either—no homemade pies, no more kisses when he didn't feel well.

Joe wiped at his nose. He stuffed the mirror and doll in the bag. He had to keep his head clear, had to find his pa. He had to find his way back to the Shenandoah Valley.

He stuck in matches he had swiped from the kitchen. He put in some hardtack he had gotten from one of the soldiers, but he knew he would have to be starving to eat that brick.

He thought of something else, went to the door—no one around. He crawled under the bed and drew out the heavy revolver. He dropped it. It sounded like an anvil hitting the floor. He scooped it up, crammed it into the bag, and threw the bag under the bed.

Soon there were steps and the door flew open.

"What are you doing in here?" Peter asked. He studied the room just like Katie Bea used to do.

"You ain't got no business busting into my room."

"Dr. Taylor wants me to keep an eye on you, and keep an eye on you I will."

"Why?" Joe immediately wished he hadn't asked the ridiculous question. He wanted Peter to leave. He didn't have time to mess around.

Peter looked Joe in the eyes. "What are you up to?"

Joe sat on the bed. Peter was sharp. He was the sharpest colored person he had ever known—too smart. Joe had heard it said that a

72

smart darky was more trouble than a loose mule in the corn patch.

"You ain't got no business in here, so skedaddle."

Peter leaned on the door facing. "You are still in the house an hour after sunup—you're up to no good."

"Pshaw!" Joe clasped his fingers behind his head and fell on the pillow. "Go find a dead skunk to meddle."

Peter smiled. Joe had not seen that since before the battle. He didn't understand it, but it felt good to see Peter smile.

Peter left the room, and soon Joe heard him outside calling to the cow.

Joe pulled the bag from under the bed again. He hefted the heavy colt and aimed it about the room. His pa had taught him to shoot, and he held the gun next to his face as he remembered those days. He smelled the spent powder, like rotten eggs—like the cannon smoke. Only one round had been shot. Had that captain killed someone with that shot?

He thought of his pa. Had he killed anyone? Of course he had by now. Surely, he had been in battles like the one in Helena. However, there was a difference; Helena stayed put—it didn't go looking for another fight, but the soldiers did. The battle had to come to Helena, but the soldiers followed the war—they caused the battles. His pa had probably been in many battles. He may have killed many men. More than likely, he had been shot at time and time again.

Joe heard talking outside his window. He looked down to see Uncle Wilbur talking to Peter, then Peter went into the barn and Uncle Wilbur came into the house. It was early morning, too early for him to be home from the store. Joe put the revolver in the bag and shoved it under the bed. Why was he home? Joe went down stairs.

Joe found him in the parlor.

Uncle Wilbur was looking at the picture of his wife propped on the mantel. He heard Joe and turned. "Come here, boy."

Oh, no, what was he in trouble for now? It couldn't be too bad; Uncle Wilbur was smiling. Joe sat on the sofa beside him.

"Yes, sir?"

"I hear you are about town kicking soldiers in the hind side these days. Could this be true?"

Joe smiled and shrugged his shoulders. He didn't know, yet, if he was in trouble. You had to wait and see about these things. You have to take care and not give yourself away.

"Well, I told this informant there was no possible way this could be my Joseph no, sir, not my Joseph Taylor."

He was funning. He had not joked in a long time. Joe was beginning to worry—maybe Uncle Wilbur was losing his mind. It had been a hard two weeks since the battle. Things had changed so much—Katie Bea was gone.

"It doesn't matter now," Uncle Wilbur said. "Those soldiers won't be bothered by you much longer. We are going to Pennsylvania."

Is the war over? Another thought struck Joe—if they go toward Pennsylvania, they may go through the Shenandoah Valley; at any rate, they would be going that direction. It would be good to have company on the trip.

"I believe it will be safer up there for you two boys," Uncle Wilbur said. He patted Joe's leg. "I'm from Pennsylvania, but you know that. That's where all the Taylor's are from, including your father."

"Pa's from Virginia."

"No, Joe, your pa is my baby brother, and we grew up in Pennsylvania—the three of us: me, Josh—your father, and the oldest, Zeke."

"Uncle Zeke lives in Mississippi."

"That's right, but we were born and grew up in Pennsylvania."

Joe scratched his head.

"All right, Joe, it's like this: Zeke married when he was a young man to a girl from Mississippi."

"How did he meet a girl from Mississippi?"

"She was visiting relatives."

"Oh." Of course, everyone visits. Sometimes they stay all summer.

"Your pa moved to Virginia when he married your ma to farm land that our family owned. He loved it so much he stayed."

Joe was putting the pieces together. It was beginning to make sense. Families were like creeper vines—they sprawled out in all directions, but joined to one vine.

Then it occurred to Joe, if he had family scattered north and south, surely the soldiers fighting did, too. He remembered Captain

Varner from Missouri fighting for the North, and his brother fighting for the South. This war was like a cruel game—you simply chose sides and killed each other, and for what? What could be that important?

Uncle Wilbur rose from the sofa. "Joe, I need to get some work finished in my office."

Joe started for the door, hesitated, turned. "Uncle Wilbur, since all of the fighting is in the South, it will be safe in Pennsylvania, won't it?"

Dr. Taylor stood for a long minute and was silent. Joe thought it strange. The whole world was strange, it seemed.

"Son, they had a big, horrible battle up there. In fact, Lee lost and was withdrawing from Pennsylvania the same day Vicksburg fell—the same day of the battle here in Helena. They fought for three days and thousands of men died. To put that in perspective, I believe less than two hundred died here."

Three days! Thousands! Joe found that almost impossible to believe. The battle at Helena only lasted one day, that seemed forever, and he saw the dead men sprawled out on the side of Graveyard Hill like so many felled cornstalks. They were many—too many, but they weren't thousands.

"In fact, the battle here in Helena hardly made the papers," Dr. Taylor said. "Grant's victory at Vicksburg on the Fourth of July and Lee's defeat up there were bigger news."

Joe remembered the dead captain in the gully. He had died in the battle here at Helena. Joe's pa was probably in the big battle up there; after all, he was in General Lee's army. Simple math said Joe's pa's chances of dying were much greater than the captain in the gully, yet that captain was food for the worms. Joe felt a shudder in his chest.

"Do you think Pa was in that battle?"

Dr. Taylor appeared reluctant to answer, but he did. "Yes."

"Was it fought in a town like Helena?"

"It was fought around a town that I have been to many times: Gettysburg."

***

From down the street, Lucius watched the white-headed boy leave the house. The door opened again and that high-feather nigger, Peter, chased after him. They exchanged a few words, which

Lucius couldn't hear from that distance; then they walked together down the street. He let them get out of sight before he went to the door. The streets were empty except for a few soldiers about a block over. He knocked on the door.

He had made the delivery quickly, so time was good. Take care of business here and be back at the store on time.

Dr. Taylor opened the door. "Lucius—is there a problem? Did you make the delivery to Mrs. Baker?"

"Yessuh, I made the delivery just fine. I just needs to talk to you, suh. It about Theo."

Dr. Taylor opened the door wider. "Come in."

Lucius stepped into the parlor. The painting of Mrs. Taylor stood out above all else. It wasn't hanging, but was propped on the mantle, and the glass was missing, but the subject still stood out like the moon over the open Mississippi.

"What is this about?" Dr. Taylor sat in the soft chair and motioned for Lucius to sit.

"No, suh, I'll stand." Lucius looked at the floor.

"Dr. Taylor, I saw Theo drinking whiskey or something like it at the store."

Dr. Taylor nodded.

"He keep it in the storeroom, so's you won't see."

"I suspected it was so." Dr. Taylor stood. Shaking his head, he walked to the mantle and placed his hand on it. He looked absently at the painting.

Lucius peeked out the window—no one was on the street.

Dr. Taylor turned around. "Lucius, you have done well. Come here; I said you would be rewarded, and I am a man of my word."

Lucius followed Dr. Taylor into the study. He stood at the door while Dr. Taylor wrote something in the book.

"I knew I could trust you," Dr. Taylor said as he pulled the key from his pocket and opened the metal box.

Like the strike of a copperhead, Lucius grabbed Dr. Taylor around the neck from behind. Lucius's muscle hardened as he squeezed. The doctor wheezed and gasped and clawed at the air.

Lucius smiled, said, "Doctor, you's been good to me, but it just no good." He wrapped his huge hand over the doctor's mouth, and slowly the doctor sagged in his arms. After a short time, Lucius let go and the doctor crumpled to the floor.

He stepped over the body and didn't look down.

He grabbed the metal box and rifled through it. It wasn't there! He jerked open the desk drawers, but he couldn't find it. He knew it was there the last time he was at the house—he had seen it.

He kicked the doctor's body. "Where is it, Doctor? You ain't going to keep it from me. It mine, and I aim on getting it!" He kicked the body again and pulled at his own hair.

He had to think. Where is it? It could be anywhere in this big house. Maybe it was at the store. Maybe— A smile slowly grew on his face. Of course. The smile grew larger. The boy! Who else would know, but the boy?

Lucius grabbed a handful of coins from the box and closed it back. He stepped over the body, turned, and kicked it again.

He opened the door slowly. Good, no one on the street. He slipped out of the house. Must walk slowly. Can't draw suspicion. As he rounded the corner, he felt at ease. No one had seen him go in or come out of the house.

He thought of the little Taylor boy. He didn't like the cocksure boy anyway. He grinned. Now, we will see what makes the white-headed boy scared.

Chapter 6

It was already after ten in the morning when Joe knocked on Peter's door. It had been a week since the funeral, and Peter was spending too much time in his room.

"Peter?" Joe put his ear to the door. "Don't you want some breakfast?"

Nothing.

Joe went back down to the kitchen. The women of Helena had been fussing over him, and now there were all kinds of food on the table. He cut a big hunk of bread and smeared it with muscadine preserves, then poured fresh milk from a bucket into a cup.

Milking had always been Peter's job, but since he was holed up in his room, Joe had tried his hand at it. He only had a little milk in the bucket; the cow had seen fit to kick it over twice.

Joe munched on the bread, thought again of his plan. He had been thinking about it for days—that is, when the ladies would give him rest. Four different women had already insisted he stay with them.

Then there was Theo trying to take over the store. But why did Joe care—he knew he was leaving soon. Besides, it was hard to think while the smell was so good coming from all of the food on the table. Joe smeared butter on a biscuit.

It just didn't seem right that Uncle Wilbur would die from a heart attack. He seemed too healthy, but Dr. Roy had said it was his heart. It still hurt to think on it. He had to push it from his mind, or he would think of Ma and Sarah, too.

Butter dripped down Joe's shirt, and he smeared at it with his arm.

Poor Peter, he was closer to Uncle Wilbur than anyone else. He was like a darky son. That was funny: "darky" and "sun."

He will be right as rain by and by. Peter was a big boy, and he should be able to take care of himself. Joe had to leave, that was just the short of it. Peter would have to fend for himself. Joe had to find his pa. After all, he didn't own Peter. He was a free man.

Joe poured more milk from the bucket and sloshed it onto the table. It ran down the tablecloth and onto the floor.

"Look at you," Peter said.

He had walked into the kitchen unnoticed. He grabbed a towel from the hanger and wiped at the spill.

"About time you came out of that hole," Joe said. "Want something to eat? Mrs. Kelly's biscuits are first rate."

"I don't want anything from those people." Peter attacked the spill with the towel.

"It's real good." Joe had smeared preserves around his mouth.

Peter looked up. He was crying. Joe felt his heart get heavy.

"Haven't you seen how those people have treated me since Dr. Taylor died?"

Peter went to the washbasin with the milky towel. Peter wiped his eyes, then sloshed the towel in the water. Joe thought on it, but he didn't know what Peter was talking about.

"You're just too young to understand," Peter said as he hung the towel on the peg.

Joe took offense, but said nothing this time.

"They fussed over you and hugged you, and offered you this and that, but they said nothing of the kind to me," Peter said, wiping his nose. "But they did find it in their hearts to tell me, 'Darkies ain't supposed to be in the parlor with white folks.' Mrs. Furley was even nice enough to fix me a plate of cornbread and beans and told me to go to my room to eat it. And I overheard them say how wrong it was that I was living in the house like I was white. None of them cared that I loved Dr. Taylor as a son loves a father."

Peter went to the window and stared toward the street.

Joe nibbled at his biscuit and watched Peter. Poor Peter, he doesn't know what he is missing. This biscuit is good.

Peter turned from the window. "Sooner or later someone will come for you, and I will have to go to the Contraband camp."

Joe swallowed the last piece of biscuit. He thought about the Negro camp. He wasn't worried about someone coming after him, because he was leaving for Virginia soon, but he hadn't given Peter enough thought.

"No one is coming after me," Joe said.

"Yes they will."

"They ain't done it. I'm going home."

"What?" Peter sat at the table.

"I already had it planned, and would have been gone, too, but for Uncle Wilbur dying." Joe finished the milk with two gulps.

"Have you forgotten the war? Virginia is where most of the fighting is."

"I ain't scared. I'm leaving real soon, and I've got it all planned out. The way I got it figured, I will go to Uncle Zeke's in Mississippi first, then strike out from there. And now that I think on it, you're going with me."

"I don't think so. This is ridiculous. I'm going to have to tell..."

Joe smiled. There was no one to tell, and he saw the realization come over Peter like light from a freshly lit lamp. He would go, and it wasn't just because he was afraid of the contraband camp. Joe knew Peter, and Peter wouldn't let him strike out alone. Peter was a good darky that way.

***

That night Peter lay awake in his bed. Mosquitoes buzzed outside the net, and an owl softly hooted somewhere in the hills behind the house. Maybe it was a spirit of one of the dead soldiers. Oh, but that was ridiculous, and not in harmony with Christianity, and he knew he should stop having those wicked thoughts. A soldier laughed somewhere in the night and a dog barked, then yelped; someone must have kicked it to shut it up.

Peter climbed from the bed and knelt on the floor, clasped his hands together. "Oh, Father in heaven, show me the way. I am lost—I know not what to do. Please guide Joseph and me as you did Moses. Give me a bright guiding star as you did the Wise Men. Oh, Holy Father, give me the strength and the ability to make this journey. Help me to look after Joseph. Help me to protect him from the evils of the world. Give me the guidance to choose right from wrong, good from wicked, and love instead of hate. Thank you, God. I humbly ask this in the name of Jesus. Amen."

Peter slipped back into bed. He tossed and turned; his mind was heavy. He ran plans through his brain, but none bore fruit. There appeared to be no safe way out. There was no one to confide in; it was his responsibility alone. It was a great weight, like a heavy sack of cotton dragged down an endless row. He closed his eyes, but leaving Helena kept swimming in his head.

He heard a sound downstairs. Mice maybe? No, that didn't feel right. It was a shuffling sound.

Peter eased his door open. There was a dim light downstairs. Maybe it was Joe. He opened Joe's door; he was sound asleep in his bed, just where he should be.

What was it? He could wake Joe, and they could climb through Joe's window—Joe did it many times; he had a rope that he didn't know anyone suspected, especially Peter.

That was ridiculous. Joe probably left the lamp on in the parlor before he went to bed.

Peter crept down the stairs. He stepped on a creaky board, froze, listened, only heard the clock. Slowly, he descended the rest of the stairs. The parlor door was ajar, and the light was definitely coming from there.

There was a strange smell in the house. He sniffed; it was familiar: dirty clothes, no—a horse blanket or the like. He couldn't place it, but he had smelled it before.

The light coming from the parlor moved. Peter jerked back from the doorway. He took a few deep breaths, then peered around the opened doorway. The light was coming from a candle sitting on Dr. Taylor's desk in the study.

Peter slipped behind the sofa and moved closer to the study. He peeked over the sofa back. He saw movement above the fireplace. It was reflection in the new glass on Mrs. Taylor's portrait.

He could make out a man in the reflection. He appeared to be searching for something. It was a black man. It was Lucius!

Lucius looked over the shelves, then looked under the desk. He pulled a knife from his boot and pried open the desk drawer. He fumbled through its contents, then pulled out Dr. Taylor's lockbox. "There it is, maybe the boy put it back," he whispered loudly. He pried it open with his knife.

What could he be looking for? Why had he come in the middle of the night, and how did he know about the box? This was not good—not good at all.

Peter knew it was time to get out of the house. If this man was brave enough to come in the night and sneak into the house, no telling what he was capable of. First, he had to get Joe. They could go out through the window.

Peter crawled behind the sofa. He knocked something over. It was Joe's spear. Peter froze.

He listened for footsteps, but could hear nothing for the blood rushing through his ears and his own heavy breathing. Sweat dropped down on his hands as he squatted closer to the floor.

He strained to hear. The clock on the wall sounded like a hammer pounding with each tick. That's all he heard—no owls, no dogs.

"Oh Lord, please give me the strength. Please show me what to do. It's not just for me, but for Joseph, too. Please let that man leave our home. Please don't let him harm the boy. Oh sweet Jesus, please. Amen."

Peter inched up from the back of the sofa after a long wait. The candle flickered. The outside door was open. Lucius had fled. He must have been scared when he heard the spear fall. Peter scrambled to shut the door, then locked it. He was probably more frightened than I was, Peter thought.

Peter would make sure the rest of the house was locked. Tomorrow he would try to figure out why Lucius was in the house. He and Joe would visit the colonel in the morning. But what did it matter? They would be leaving soon, anyway.

He went into the study to blow out the candle. He should just let it burn. What did he have to lose if the house burned to the ground? Someone else would get the house soon—soldiers probably. If they didn't live in it, they would tear it down for the—

Something slammed into him. His neck felt like fire, as it was being twisted. He felt something sharp under his chin.

"Don't you squeal or I'll cut you like a pig," Lucius hissed. He tightened his grip and pressed the knife to Peter's chin.

Peter knew the knife was there, but he was too afraid to feel the pain. He was strong, but this man was iron. Lucius's stinking breath was heavy like rotten meat, and now Peter knew where the horse blanket smell had come from.

"Boy, you is going to tell me what I needs to know," Lucius said. "I know you is a smart nigger. I's going to let this here knife down a bit, but don't you figure I can't strike fast."

Lucius lowered the knife and moved around to the front of Peter, the knife only inches from Peter's face.

Peter's fear grew to anger when he saw Lucius's face.

Dr. Taylor had done so much for this man, and here he was now.

"Look at you," Lucius said, snarling. "Got that fine gown on, just like you's a white man."

"What do you want?" Peter asked.

Lucius grabbed the gown and cut it from Peter's body so fast that at first Peter didn't realize what had happened. Lucius looked at it with disgust, then threw it to the floor and stepped on it.

"Now, boy, you stand there black just like me," Lucius said, sticking the knife back under Peter's chin. "I ask the questions. You understand?"

Peter felt his eyes burning, but he was determined not to cry. He would not be shamed in front of this beast.

"Do you understand me, boy, or is I got to cut something else?"

"I understand," Peter said slowly.

"Good. Good," Lucius said, smiling. "Do you see that white woman over the fireplace?"

"I see her."

Lucius grabbed Peter around the back of his neck with his big hand and pushed him toward the picture. "You see those birds hanging down off her neck?"

"I see the necklace."

"Where is it?"

What would this runaway slave want with a necklace? He must be crazy.

Lucius put the knife to Peter's neck. "Where is it?"

"I don't know."

Lucius wheeled Peter around. "Listen to me, boy. Tell me where it is and I'll be gone. Don't—I kill the white boy."

Peter looked straight at Lucius's face. The flickering candlelight danced in his eyes. Peter had not noticed before, one eye was brown, but the other eye was almost gray. They looked like snake eyes or maybe cat eyes. He was like some wild animal ready to pounce.

"I told you, I don't know where the necklace is."

Lucius slammed his giant fist into Peter's face. Peter was on the floor dazed before he realized what had happened. Lucius jerked Peter from the floor, twisted Peter's arm behind his back. Peter groaned and spit blood. Blood spilled from his nose and mouth like red gravy.

He couldn't think. Bright lights flashed and pulsed in his brain. The world was spinning. The floor was falling.

"Come on!" Lucius said. "When I get my hands on the boy, we'll see what you know." He pushed Peter toward the stairs.

The world came and went as Lucius twisted Peter's arm and shoved him forward.

The pain in his face brought him to reality in a hot wave. It hammered. He had to do something or Joe might get worse. His mind was trying to form plans, but things were gray. His brain wouldn't perform.

All at once, the grip on his arm went loose, and he heard something crash to the floor. He turned. The room was still spinning. Slowly—seemed forever, but it was only seconds; his brain cleared, and he saw Joe standing over Lucius holding a large revolver. He was holding it like a hammer, with the barrel in his hand.

Lucius stirred, and Joe hit him again. Lucius lay still. Joe brought the butt of the revolver down on Lucius's head a third time. It sounded a like a hammer striking wet wood. Joe reared back to hit him again.

Peter grabbed Joe's arm. His senses were coming around.

"Let go Peter. I'll deliver him to hell right here and right now."

Holding firm to Joe's arm, Peter looked at Joe—no fear in Joe's face, only determination. Peter had always known since the first time he saw the boy that he was brave, but he never suspected this level. He took the revolver from Joe.

"You're bleeding," Joe said. He turned and kicked Lucius. "You rotten, stinking thief."

"Stop, Joe. He's done." Peter looked at the gun. "Where did you get this?"

"I found it on a dead soldier." Joe tugged on the gun, and Peter let it go. "I'm leaving now while it's dark."

At first, Peter didn't understand; then it registered. "Why now?"

"After this, do you think the people in this town will let me stay here in this house alone with just you? No. They will ship me off somewhere, and who knows what they'll do with you."

Joe was thinking clearly. Peter had not thought of this. However, Joe wasn't the one with a busted face. Joe was right. What would happen to them after this?

Joe grabbed up the candle and went up to his room. Peter followed. Joe pulled his bag from under the bed.

"You're already packed," Peter said.

"You need to hurry up and pack, too," Joe said, digging something else from under his bed. "We are going to need some money. We will get it from the store."

"You mean steal it?"

"That was Uncle Wilbur's store and his money. Now it is ours and rightfully so."

Peter went to his room and lit the lamp. He poured water into the basin and dabbed at the blood on his face. It stung, but the real pain was the pain of the unknown.

If they stayed, it would be as Joe said. If they left, what would it be? How would they make it? How would they get to the North with war raging all over the South? It would be hard enough for Joe, but a Negro traveling the roads would invite every trouble possible.

Peter looked at his reflection in the mirror. His face was beginning to swell, but it was not going to be too bad. Not too bad? He argued with himself. How was he going to get Joe out of here? Oh God, how? He wept. The tears brought a flood of pain, memories of Mam and Dr. Taylor, and Helena before the war. It would be easier to just sit down in the floor and wait. He could wait for what happened next. It was too hard to think on. It would be impossible for them to undertake this journey.

He spotted his Bible by the basin. He picked it up and pulled it to his heart. It was a comfort—it was always a comfort.

Joe came into the room. "We need to go, Peter."

Peter squeezed the Bible. He nodded.

"You need help packing your stuff?"

Peter shook his head, not looking back at Joe. "Just give me a few more minutes."

Joe left.

"Dear God, watch over us, and give us a guiding star." Peter began loading his carpetbag.

***

The store was dark and quiet when Joe unlocked the door. He lit the lamp on the counter. He searched under the counter where Uncle Wilbur had always kept the change money. It wasn't there.

"Someone might see us," Peter said.

Joe wasn't worried about being seen. He was eager to find the money.

"That damn Theo has the money," Joe said, hitting his fist on the counter.

"Don't you swear in that fashion. I don't care what kind of fix we're in."

Joe looked at Peter and felt embarrassed for cussing.

"Let's get some food and get out of here," Peter said. He appeared anxious as he looked out the big, front window.

Joe searched around the store with his lamp held in front. "Here." Joe threw Peter a sack of coffee beans.

Peter caught it. "We don't drink coffee."

Joe collected some candy from the counter. "Think, Peter. They don't have coffee outside of Helena." Joe smiled. "Better than gold."

Peter smiled back and dropped it in his bag. He plucked a handful of candles from a shelf and put them into the bag, too. "We need more matches. They are on the shelf by the door."

Joe went toward the door that opened to the back room. He found the matches and put them in his bag. He noticed a dark shape in the door. He raised the lamp. It was Theo. Joe stepped back.

"What are you doing here?" Theo said.

Joe quickly gained control. "I own this store now."

Theo stepped out into the lamp glow. He held a small pistol in his hand, and it was pointed at Joe. Not good.

"Now what do you know about running a business?" Theo said. He pointed the small revolver at Peter. "I know that boy don't know nothing."

Joe would love to cram that gun down Theo's big fat throat.

"You can have the store. Just let us have a few things, and we'll be gone," Joe said.

Theo staggered toward Joe with the gun waving. "Well now, I can't let you take things out of my store. How would I realize a profit?"

Joe smelled whiskey, saw the bottle in Theo's other hand.

"Theo, put the gun down," Peter said.

Theo swung the gun back toward Peter. "Don't you tell me what to do you high and might—"

Joe threw the lamp at Theo. It hit him in the face, and shattered on the floor. Theo dropped the bottle, sloshing whiskey down his pants. The flames jumped to the spilt lamp oil, then whooshed to the whiskey.

Theo screamed and beat at the flames on his leg.

Peter yelled, "Let's go!"

A small sack fell from Theo shirt. Joe scooped it up. He knew the bag—Uncle Wilbur's money sack.

They ran out the front door.

A voice in front yelled for them to stop.

Joe barely made out a soldier pointing a musket at them. A glow was growing in the store as the flames caught.

Peter stood closer to the store, and the fire illuminated his face.

"Tom," the soldier yelled to someone behind him, "darkies have set the Taylor store afire."

A gunshot blasted from within the store.

Instantly, Joe knew it was Theo shooting at them. This was not a good place to be.

Peter grabbed Joe by the arm and pulled him toward him.

The soldier shot and white smoke filled the air. Then he yelled, "The nigger's got a white boy!"

"Come on!" Joe said, and the two boys ran behind the store.

Joe heard more soldiers. It was definitely not good.

Peter stopped Joe. "Where are we going? We can't go home. Soldiers are all over town."

"Come on!" Joe said, breathing hard. "We'll escape through the camp."

"What camp?"

"The nigger camp. Now come on."

They ducked through alleys and ran through gaps in fences. This was almost fun, Joe thought. It was too easy. He knew all of the nooks and crannies. He looked back and Peter was on his heels. It didn't look like fun to him.

***

The contraband camp was a small city. It was dark, but fires sprinkled here and there giving it an eerie illumination, and shadows danced on the makeshift tents of rags. A dog howled to the south, and frogs and crickets harmonized the night.

However, it was the coughing Peter noticed the most. One cough could not be separated from the others. They ran together like words in a song from some ghostly chorus, some low and muffled, some high, wheezing tapering to a losing breath.

The air was foul, like the low end of a barnyard: chicken mess, cow pee, blended with the smell of rotting hay. The whole town of Helena had an outhouse smell with all of the soldiers crowded there, but not like this. Peter never knew the smell of death before, but that smell was here. He now knew why Dr. Taylor did not want them ever to come here.

"This is a horrible place," Peter whispered as they entered the edge of the camp. "These poor people."

He turned to Joe. Joe was looking back toward town. Peter immediately saw the fire. It was glowing about a quarter of mile away.

"It's the store," Joe said.

Small lights were popping on all over town and in the hills, too. Peter knew they were lamps and torches, but from here, they looked like lightning bugs.

"Joe did you hear what that soldier said? He thought I was nabbing you after setting the store afire."

"Yeah, I heard him. That was Bill Franklin yelling at Tom Ryan."

"They think I burned the store," Peter said.

Joe said nothing, only watched the glow of the burning store and the lights lighting up all over town.

Peter reflected. It would be easy for anyone to think I had gone insane: Mam was killed; Dr. Taylor was dead. What if Lucius was dead? They will find his body. They will conclude that I had killed him. Joe was missing and the soldiers saw him with me. Since the store was on fire, Theo may be dead, too.

"They couldn't tell it was you," Joe said, still looking toward town. "When Bill yelled at Tom, he didn't call your name. He said, 'Niggers,' not Peter, and he knows you."

Peter remembered. Joe was right. But that could be worse. Someone innocent could get the blame.

"What y'all doing here?" a voice came from behind them.

They both turned at the same time. Peter saw a black man with nothing but rags on. Peter was trying to think of an answer when the man spoke again.

Staring down at Joe, the man said, "Well, if ain't the little massah what going to catch us a fish."

A skeleton of a woman came from one of the tents.

"Mae, look what done come back," the man said. "Reckon he got them fish for us?" He laughed. He stirred in a fire and got a small blaze going.

Other people were looking out of their tents and shanties, and a few men came up.

A one-eyed man pointed toward town. "Look, they's coming."

Peter saw a trail of lights coming from town. They were moving quickly toward the camp.

Joe looked at Peter, then turned toward the gathering crowd of Negroes. He pointed at Peter. "They are after my boy, Peter. We need y'all to help us."

"We ain't helping nobody," the one-eyed man said. "Y'all is bringing trouble on us."

The crowd had grown large, and they were agreeing with the one-eyed man.

Peter saw what Joe was trying to do. They wouldn't help a white boy, but maybe they would help him.

"Please help us," Peter said. "They will take me from my young massah, and he is so good to me."

Some laughed and mumbled, "Poor nigger."

The crowd was more interested in the trouble coming from town. They walked past the boys and watched the lights coming, discussing what to say and how to avoid the coming trouble.

Mae motioned the boys to her tent. Peter pushed Joe that way. He didn't know what she wanted, but their options were slim.

She disappeared into the tent. Peter heard talking from inside, but he couldn't make out the words. Joe had his ear to the rags, trying to listen when Mae came out with a skinny boy. He appeared to be around seven or eight.

"Follow Bo; he will fetch you outta here," Mae said.

"Thank you," Peter said.

Before the words left his mouth, Bo had darted from the camp and through the weeds, with Joe on his tail. Peter hesitated for a second, but realized if he didn't act swiftly, he would lose the boys.

The younger boys were bobbing through the weeds and darting around stumps like rabbits. Peter had a difficult time keeping up, but Joe's blonde hair was like a beacon. They were heading east. That meant toward the river.

Peter knew they couldn't swim the river—it was a mile wide here. Mud gushed around his shoes as they ran through the bog, then they went up and over the levee. Now that the time was at hand, he didn't want to cross it at all. Confederates held the other side. He had his free papers, but he still didn't want to go over there. They could go up through Missouri, not east into Mississippi. Joe was the reason—he always found trouble.

Peter almost tripped over Bo, squatted down by some weeds.

The Mississippi River spread out before him like an ocean. The water glimmered with the moonlight. The river was so vast that Peter couldn't see the other side.

Joe was excited. "Look, a boat."

Bo pulled weeds and sticks from what resembled a boat or canoe. From the dim light, it appeared old and rotted. It was about ten feet long and four feet wide.

"God above, Joseph, we can't cross the river in that rotten thing—we'll drown for sure!"

"We have to. What else are we going to do?"

"We will just tell the soldiers what really happened. They will believe you."

Joe asked Bo where the boat had come from as he helped pull the brush from it.

"Two niggers tried crossing over from Mississippi in it," Bo said.

"Did they make it?" Joe asked, as the two boys dragged it to the water's edge.

"Naw, the Rebs shot 'em, but the boat washed up on this here side, and we fetched it."

Peter figured that's what will happen to them if they get in that boat, only it would be the Yankees doing the shooting.

Joe shoved the boat into the water. There wasn't much current close to the bank.

"Are you coming?" Joe asked, as he picked up a long board from the bottom of the boat.

"Joe, you can tell them what happened, and things will be set right," Peter said.

Joe started paddling with the long board. "You tell them."

Peter threw his bag over his shoulder and jumped into the water. He grabbed the boat.

"Joseph, you are not going to leave me in this fix!" Peter snatched the board from him. "Now, you get out of this boat and tell the soldiers what happened."

Peter saw Joe suddenly look past him. Peter turned and saw Bo was gone. Then he saw the lights shining above the levee toward the camp. He heard loud voices, then popping.

"Shit, they're shooting the niggers!" Joe yelled. "Get in the boat—get in the damn boat!"

Peter had to think—what should he do? He sure didn't want to cross the river, but they were shooting. What was going on up there at the camp? Were they really shooting innocent people? The Yankees wouldn't shoot unarmed men, would they? Would they shoot before Joe could tell them what really happened? Mam said go north. He had promised her. The Rebels were east. He was free, but he was black.

The lights were coming from the camp.

"Damn it, Peter, get in the damn boat!" Joe screamed.

The row of lightning bugs was coming.

Peter turned and flung the board into the boat. He pushed the boat hard and jumped in. Joe grabbed the paddle and stroked hard at the water. Peter pulled the board from Joe's hands. He made a quick calculation, raised his knee, and drove the board down across it. The board made a loud crack. He handed Joe half, and they took stations on each side of the boat and went to work. They quickly hit the current.

Peter looked at the bank again. Someone was standing in the water, a big man. Something glimmered in his hand. That's all the moonlight would reveal.

A sudden current wheeled them around, and Peter turned to

help Joe straighten the boat. They tried hard to go straight, but it was no use; the current pushed them downriver.

Splinters flew from Peter's paddle, followed by the report of a gun. He turned and saw the lights on the bank. There were many men now. The big man in the water was gone. They didn't shoot again. Peter reckoned they were afraid they would hit Joe.

Fright shot up Peter's spine, and he stroked harder and harder. The dark trees on the east bank slowly came into view, but they were still a long way off.

Joe was on his knees in the front of the boat pulling hard with his paddle. His blonde hair glowed in the moonlight. As slow minutes passed the lights on the west bank slowly blinked out as the men left.

"They can't get to us now," Joe said. "We are halfway across."

Suddenly, the boat shuddered. Peter heard scratching coming from the bottom of the boat. It wheeled around hard, and the paddles hit bottom. The current drove against the boat like a train. Something wasn't right; they appeared to have picked up speed. Peter marked a tall tree on the east side of the river. The current was screaming by, but they weren't moving.

"We've hit a sandbar right smack in the middle of the river," Joe said. "We have to be careful, or we will get swamped."

The mighty current was pounding the boat. Either bank appeared miles away.

"Let's try to hold the bow into the current, and I will push us off," Peter said.

As he stepped from the boat, it jerked free from the sand. He lost his grip. The current swept his feet from under him. He rolled and tumbled in the rushing water, tried to stand, but the water slammed him back down. He lost sight of the boat. The depth of the water went from inches to feet to inches. Water filled his mouth. He gagged and choked. His pants went to his knees. He grabbed at them, but tumbled harder. He thought he heard yelling, but the river roared like a monster.

Think, Peter, think, or you will surely drown. You can't stand because the current is too strong. Just float—just float like a log, and when you come to deeper water, swim. He let his legs float free, and he skidded along the sand. That's it—that's it. He could see nothing but water as he spun and bobbed—no boat.

His head struck something hard. The pain was instant, and he saw lights in his head. His body wheeled around and lodged against something. He felt something pulling at his shirt. He heard a voice, or was it just the rattling from the knock on the head. Hands pulled on his arm.

"Peter!" Joe yelled. "Peter, grab hold."

Peter realized it was Joe and the boat. He tried to stand, but the water was suddenly deep. His pants were only on one leg now.

"Work your way around and climb over the back, so we don't tip over."

Peter made his way to the back, and with the little strength he had left, heaved himself back into the boat. He spit and coughed muddy water as he lay on his back.

He lay there with his chest heaving, could have drowned, but The Almighty saw fit to save him. What a fix. What a fix indeed. Here he lay in the bottom of a boat, in the middle of the Mississippi River. It would only get worse from here.

Clouds had covered the sky now. The moon still glowed behind them enough to give a ghostly light.

Wait. There was one star shining through. It stood out in perfect contrast. It hung over the eastern bank like a beacon. Is that my guiding light? It was the only one in the whole sky. It was in the east. It had to mean something. All right then, Peter thought, all right.

Joe started laughing. When Peter rose, he saw Joe pointing. Peter had lost his pants. They both could have died, and came close to it, but Joe was laughing.

After he was about out of breath, Joe stopped laughing and pointed to something the boat was lodged against. "This here snag's got us."

Peter examined the snag. It appeared to be a tree, half buried in the sand with four or five large limbs reaching from the water. It must have lodged there in low water, and over time was covered with sand. No matter, with God's help, it had saved them.

They pushed free, and the current slung them from it. They were back in deeper water. They both paddled hard, and the eastern bank crept closer and closer as the Mississippi pulled them south.

Peter wiped sweat from his brow and thought about the man standing in the water with the glimmering object in his hand. He was a black man—a big black man. Peter had no doubt who he was.

Peter saw Joe's shoulders moving up and down as he paddled. He was laughing again. Peter looked at his pants wadded up in the bottom of the boat.

Chapter 7

The dawn crawled in slow as a turtle. The birds awoke first, like a noisy choir, but they sounded better than the annoying mosquitoes Joe had fought all night. The birds were in perfect harmony with the river, or at least that's what Peter had said when he first awoke. They were just birds singing, and just the river rushing to Joe, but Peter always said such foolishness.

They had camped on a sandbar behind willows and driftwood. It was no fun to Joe because they had no fire; Peter was afraid the Yankees would discover them. Joe reckoned he was right.

Soon, up river, Helena came alive. Riverboats built steam and, smoke rose in the air like clouds.

The two boys moved up the riverbank. After struggling around drifts and briars, they came to an old road. Joe reckoned a ferry probably landed there before the war. He was sure Peter knew the road, but he didn't ask him about it; he was acting queer: pouting, and other times, praying, or mumbling to himself.

Peter stopped at the road and stared across the river. He began to cry for no reason. Joe didn't know what to say.

Joe looked across at Helena. It was like a painting. The red glow of the dawning sun brushed the river and spilled over on the town, which sat at the base of Crowley's Ridge like a bird in a nest. Smoke floated up lazily from two riverboats at the wharf, and tiny men, like ants, crawled around the wharf and on the boats. From here,

Helena was beautiful.

Joe thought of Curtis, still over there. He remembered Uncle Wilbur and Aunt Katie Bea; they would never leave Helena. It might have been a nice place if not for the war and too many Yankees piled in it. He did have fun there sometimes, in spite of the Yankees. Uncle Wilbur had said the place was lovely before the war, and Curtis had harped on it. However, there was a war, and the place was now overcrowded with Yankees.

Joe looked at Peter again—poor Peter. If it weren't for over a half mile of muddy, racing water, Joe believed Peter would go back.

He noticed the stick over Peter's shoulder and the wet clothes tied to it. He had to turn away when he started giggling, remembering Peter in the boat without his pants.

Joe started down the road, and Peter soon followed. Peter could lead later, when he was finished pouting. When they turned from the river, the woods engulfed them like a vast tunnel, and the mosquitoes found them again. It was darker than by the open river, even as the sun rose. Giant oaks stretched to the sky, bigger than any oaks Joe had ever seen.

The morning grew, and the sunlight fought its way through the canopy. Often they would see the white tail of a deer bounding or hear the whistling snort. Other unidentified animals made their noises, too.

Peter walked closer to Joe as they moved deeper into the woods and away from the river. He scanned the woods like a soldier and kept looking back.

"What are you looking for?" Joe asked. "There are no Yankees over here."

"I'm not worried about Yankees."

"Then what are you scared of?"

"There are creatures in these woods."

"Creatures?" Joe giggled.

"Yes, creatures."

"There ain't nothing in these woods but deer and coons and the like." Joe laughed at the thought.

"That's fine, Mr. Audubon, but you didn't hear what I heard last night."

Joe hadn't heard anything last night, except mosquitoes.

"That's right," Peter said. "You were sound asleep, sleeping like a baby."

Peter was a step ahead of Joe, now. Joe saw he was surer of himself, knew something Joe didn't. He had heard the noise and Joe hadn't.

"What noise?"

Peter, still walking, turned and said, "Well, it was around midnight I reckon when I first heard it." He turned back and continued walking.

Joe waited for more, but Peter was silent and kept on walking. "Nation, Peter, you heard what?"

Peter said over his shoulder, "A scream."

A panther, Joe thought. Smiling, he said, "You really heard a wildcat?"

"Indeed I did." Peter didn't look back.

"Was you scared?"

"Yes, I was very afraid."

"What did you do?"

Peter turned as he walked. "Well, since we couldn't build a fire because we didn't want to be found by the Yankees, I took a—"

A rustle came from a downed treetop in front of the boys.

"Putt-putt-putt." A black animal streaked in front of Peter.

Peter yelled and dropped his stick and carpetbag.

The wild turkey darted up the road, running side to side trying to decide the best exit, gave up, and took to the air. A few wing beats and it disappeared through the woods.

Joe fell to the ground and grabbed his chest as he rolled on the road.

Peter, breathing hard, finally realized what had happened as he watched the turkey take flight; then he saw Joe lying in the road behind him. "Joe—Joe, are you all right?"

Joe turned over and faced Peter. His face was beet red, couldn't get his breath. After a time it finally came. The laughter came out in a wheeze at first and then a belly laugh.

Peter laughed, too, as he helped Joe to his feet.

Joe finally exhausted the laughing and dusted himself off.

Peter gathered his stuff from the road and turned back toward Joe. "We had better get out of these woods before the mosquitoes eat us alive."

Joe picked up his bag. "Yeah, and we don't want the 'creatures' to get us. 'Putt—putt.'"

They both laughed.

***

Late morning they came to a clearing. It turned out to be a long, narrow lake, surrounded by cypress trees. The water appeared black, but upon closer inspection, it was indeed clear; Joe could plainly see the garfish swimming just under the surface of the water. He liked gar as fish went. They had long snouts with a bunch of teeth. They were the best fish to chuck a spear at.

Peter said he remembered a bridge across the narrow lake when he was last here. No bridge now.

"Look, Peter," Joe said, pointing to a fishing pole lying on the opposite bank with the line still in the water. "Somebody's was just here fishing. There is a fish on the line; I see it jerking."

Joe saw some sort of bird flutter up through the trees, and like a rabbit, a little Negro boy shot out from behind one of the large cypress trees and beat it up the road. He appeared to be around nine or ten, and running seemed to be his calling. That's queer, Joe thought. "What's on the other side of the lake?"

"It was about four years ago when we came over here, and there was a bunch of slaves cutting trees up the road a piece. A few miles farther there is a place called Walnut Lake, I believe."

Joe looked across the lake and spotted a boat hidden under some brush. He stripped, except for his kepi and stepped into the cool water. It felt good in the late August heat. He slapped a mosquito on his butt, and Peter laughed. He swam over to the boat and pulled the brush from it. It was a poor job of concealment.

As he paddled across, the boat began filling with water; Joe slid his foot over the hole. He barely made it to the other side before it sank.

He put his clothes back on before the mosquitoes drained him. He hacked a stick with his tomahawk to plug the hole. "That should fix that wagon."

They paddled to the other side and placed the brush back over the boat. Peter wouldn't have it any other way—that's how they had found it.

They climbed the bank from the lake. Joe stopped. "What's that, a church?"

"I didn't hear anything," Peter said.

Joe shrugged his shoulders. Maybe he had water in his ears from the swim, but it sounded like a bell.

They walked about a half mile and came to a vast field. Corn, oats, sorghum, and cotton lay in neat rows. New girdled trees still dotted the fields like scatter telegraph poles.

There were a good many buildings up the road. When they were closer, Joe saw a large house, as large as any in Helena. He also saw cabins, barns, and a gin house. Split rail fences lined the roads and surrounded the house. The whole place appeared like magic in the middle of the wilderness. Everything was neat and orderly, nothing like anything he had seen in Yankee-occupied Arkansas. Wagons were by the barn, but Joe saw no mules or oxen. Now that he thought on it, he saw no animals at all: no horses, chickens, fowl, cows, pigs—nothing. He saw no people either.

"Must be deserted," Joe said as they walked the road toward the house.

"No, they are hiding," Peter said.

"From who?"

"From us."

"Pshaw, why would they hide from us?"

"That boy back there at the lake must have been a sentinel," Peter said. He looked around as if he were looking for a bear to jump out at them.

Peter was making sense. Joe hadn't thought about that.

"You have that blue cap on," Peter said. "That little boy must have thought you were a Yankee."

"Well, that little piccaninny. I ain't no damn Yankee."

They walked toward the steps of the big house. It was a beautiful red, brick, two-story house. A huge veranda ran the length of it. There were two big chimneys, one on each side of the house. A white picket fence picked up where the split rail fence stopped—the gate was open.

Suddenly Negroes appeared everywhere. They came from behind wagons, from around the house and barn. Joe believed if he looked up, they would be dropping from the sky. Two had guns, and they were trained on Joe and Peter. The others had pitchforks, sickles, and other things that might poke or gore a nasty hole.

One of the men with a rifle had white hair. He said, "That plenty far nuff, Yankee."

"He ain't even nothing but a boy," another said.

"I ain't no Yankee," Joe said.

"Fetch that ax off your belt and drop it on the ground," white head said.

"I ain't dropping nothing." Joe put his hand on the tomahawk.

Both guns were brought to shoulders and readied.

"Don't shoot!" Peter said. He stepped between the guns and Joe. "He's just a boy. We came from Helena. We are just passing through on our way to New Albany."

"I don't need no darky standing my fight," Joe said.

"Shut up, Joseph!" Peter didn't take his eyes from the men with the guns.

"What sort of nigger is you?" the old man asked.

A wise-ass nigger tending my affairs, Joe thought.

"Y'all put the guns away, Cluck," said a voice from the veranda.

Joe saw the prettiest woman he had ever seen. She had the longest, golden hair, and her skin was like cream. She wore a blue, velvety hoop-dress—it was perfect on her.

"Yessum, Missus," said the old man.

Joe looked at the old man. Cluck. Joe knew darkies had some queer names, but that one beat the band.

"Missus, Carl, I believes is done gone and made a mistake," Cluck said. He done seed that Yankee cap and believed they's Yankees. Most likely he's asleep again, and they done got too close and scared him fo he seed who they was."

"I's sorry, Missus," Carl said from under a wagon.

"Get outta there, boy, and gets you a bird and gets back to your post," Cluck said.

Carl squirted from under the wagon and skedaddled toward the back of the house. He tripped and fell in the dirt, scrambled to his feet and high-tailed it back toward a barn.

"Don't you be sleeping, you hear!" Cluck called after him.

Joe pulled his cap off and stepped in front of Peter. "Hi, Ma'am. My name is Joe Taylor, and this here is Peter."

"Hello, Joe. I'm Mrs. Hampton Donner."

"Nice to meet you, Mrs. Donner." It was nice to meet her indeed.

"Did I hear your servant say you had come from Helena?"

"Oh, Peter ain't my servant. He's a free nigger. He belongs to nobody."

All of the Negroes studied Peter as if he were a new prize bull.

"We do not say that word here," she said. "We say darky or Negro.

Joe noticed Cluck stick his chest out when she said this. Joe shrugged his shoulders. What ever the pretty woman liked was tops with him—nigger, Negro, whatever. "Well, anyway, we did come from Helena," Joe said, and I reckon we ain't never going back."

"I see," Mrs. Donner said. "Do come in to my home, Joe. I would like to hear more about Helena."

That was fine with Joe. He was hungry, and he knew this handsome lady would surely feed him.

"Come on Peter," Joe said as he started up the steps.

"Oh no," she said. "Darkies mustn't come through the front door. That simply will not do." She turned to Cluck. "Cluck, do see to Peter."

"Yessum, Missus." Cluck turned to Peter. "Come on, Peter; let's see is Bessie still got some of them biscuits left over at the kitchen." He turned to the rest of the servants. "The rest of you nig—darkies get back to work and bring them animals in from the woods."

***

Cluck took Peter around the big house to a small brick building with a large chimney. From there, Peter saw a smokehouse, and two teenaged Negro boys putting meat in it.

"If y'all is getting that meat back in the smokehouse that soon, y'all ain't hid it far enough from the house," Cluck yelled. "If they's really Yankees, they'd done fetched it all."

Peter saw that Cluck was some kind of boss. The boys lowered their heads as they put the meat away.

"Foolish young niggers," Cluck muttered.

When they went into the brick building, Peter discovered it was a large kitchen—the whole building. The fireplace was enormous with an arsenal of pots and pans hanging all over it. There was a long table with benches on both sides and a couple of smaller tables. Skillets, tongs, saws, forks, many sizes of spoons, a paddle, and many other implements for cooking were everywhere; they hung on pegs, sat on shelves, and even hung from the rafters. The floor was made of long flat bricks.

A big Negro woman was busy at the pots when they walked in.

She had a blue rag around her head and a towel over her shoulder. Her big rear seemed to be charging in all directions as she moved around the fireplace. Peter felt guilty for his bad thoughts, but her rear reminded him of the two tomcats Joe had tied in a sack.

"Bessie, is you got any of them biscuits left from this morning?" Cluck asked. He sat on a bench at the long table and told Peter to sit on the other side.

Bessie turned from her pots and studied Peter for a long spell. He was embarrassed at her staring.

"I don't feed no coloreds from this here kitchen til dinner or supper, lessen they's house servants, or else Missus say so." She eyed Peter with suspicion.

"Oh, no, this here ain't your average colored slave. This here bees a free man. The little white marster with him say so," Cluck said with pride, as if he had a stake in Peter. "Ain't that the truth, Peter?"

Peter hesitated for a second, "That is correct; I'm a free Negro."

"Did you hear that, Bessie?" Cluck slapped his leg. "A free Negro."

Bessie waddled over to Peter. "Is you really free?"

Peter squirmed on the bench. "I have my papers," he said as if he were talking to a paddy roller, but immediately felt foolish.

A giant grin blossomed across her face. "Ooh, Lawd, a free nigger." She sheepishly looked around as if someone else were in the room. "I means to say, 'a free darky.'"

She scooted Peter over on the bench and sat beside him. The bench creaked—Peter just knew it would break, but somehow it held the strain.

Her face reminded Peter of a bulldog, and he noticed she had a tooth missing in front, on the top.

"What it like?" she asked.

"Ma'am?"

She tapped Peter with her towel. "Listen at him call me Ma'am like I's white folk," she said to Cluck.

Cluck laughed and shook his head, then clucked his tongue.

So that's where he got his unusual name, Peter reasoned.

"Now you tell me what it like to be free," she said.

"I don't know any different," Peter said. "I was born free. I've always been free."

The smile fell from her face, and she looked down at a big wooden spoon she held. She studied it absently. "Always been free," she whispered.

Suddenly, Cluck slammed his hand flat on the table, frightening both Bessie and Peter. "Goodness sake, wife, get this here boy something to eat. Missus say fo to tend to him."

With a great effort, she rose from the bench and went to one of the small tables, covered with a cloth. She pulled the cloth off and retrieved a platter of biscuits. After sitting the plate in front of Peter, she went to a shelf and fetched a jug of molasses. She placed it on the table, gave him a weak smile, then went back to her pots.

Peter bowed his head and blessed the food with Cluck looking on. He gawked at Peter as if he had come from the moon.

As Peter poured molasses on his plate, the door swung open and a Negro girl strolled in. "Missus want something to eat fo the visiting young marster."

Cluck snatched the platter from in front of Peter. "Here girl, take this."

Holding the platter, she shyly looked at Peter, then at Bessie.

She looked to be about Peter's age, and pretty as a sunflower. She was a dark tan, but she appeared to have the features of a white person, slender nose, small lips, and straight hair.

"Go on, Lou," Bessie said softly. "Take that there food to the young marster."

She slipped from the room, but her eyes met Peter's, and he felt an unusual flutter inside—it was nice.

After she shut the door, Cluck said to Bessie, "Fetch Peter some more of them biscuits."

"That was the last."

"Is she white?" Peter asked absently, still looking at the door.

"Don't talk on that, boy," Cluck snapped. "Don't ever talk on that while you is here."

Peter started to ask why, but the firm look on Cluck's face changed his mind.

"I'll fix you up something else to eat," Bessie said. "I can rustle something up fo you can jump."

Cluck's face flipped to a smile in an instant. "Bess can sho do it." He clucked his tongue. "She the bestest cook in Mississippi."

**

A tall, black man in fancy clothes placed the platter at the end of a long mahogany table, bowed, and left the big dining room. Shortly he returned with a pitcher of milk and a glass. "Do Missus need anything else?" the man asked.

"No, John; that will do."

He bowed and left the room again.

"Sit down Joe, and enjoy a late breakfast," Mrs. Donner said. "I hope you don't mind my home. As you can tell, the war has impeded its completion."

Joe saw some of the house, indeed, wasn't finished, but said nothing. He plopped down in the chair and dragged a biscuit through the molasses. While pouring milk, he said through a full mouth, "This is a capital biscuit."

"Indeed, my Bessie is the finest cook around."

Joe polished off the first biscuit and attacked another. He soon had a milk ring around his mouth and crumbs down his shirt.

Mrs. Donner handed him a napkin.

"I venture to guess there was no shortage of flour in Helena," Mrs. Donner said.

"No Ma'am. With the Yankees there, we had everything."

"It has not always been so here," she said.

Joe immediately felt guilty. He knew the Confederacy was suffering because of the blockade. He set the second biscuit back on the platter.

She placed a tender hand on his. "Oh, no, Joe, I was not implying that we have a shortage of flour." She smiled sweetly. "Just the opposite. We have plenty, and salt, too."

Joe sopped the biscuit in the molasses. With a mouthful and molasses running down his face, he asked, "How do y'all get flour and salt?" Joe felt the molasses and smeared at it with a napkin.

"Let me just say we have ways, and Memphis is not so very far."

Joe saw something out the large window and hopped up to investigate. Slaves were coming from the woods with the animals: horses, mules, geese, pigs, and the like. Mrs. Donner stood beside Joe.

"What are they doing?" Joe asked.

"We had a spy at the lake."

"The little piccaninny!"

She looked disapprovingly at Joe.

"I mean the little darky...a...Carl."

"That is right. When he spotted you and Peter, he quickly gave the alarm. My people hastily hid the animals, food, and valuables."

Joe thought about it for a minute. He calculated the time it took to get there from the lake.

"Ma'am, Yankee cavalry would have went right through that lake. There would not have been time to hide anything."

"To be sure. We really didn't expect the Yankees to come from that direction, but we have our ways to be on guard."

"What about other roads? Do you have spies down them, too?"

"There is only the one road coming from the east, and we have ways to know in advance of an arriving party from that direction."

Ways? What did she have, a telegraph?

"Are there anymore white people on the plantation?"

"No, I'm the only one."

"No one? No overseer or nothing?"

"I don't require an overseer. I have Cluck."

Joe found it hard to believe she would let an old darky run the big plantation. He had always heard that Negroes would steal you blind, and then run off if not properly managed—or worse: kill you in your sleep.

"How many slaves do you have?"

"I have ninety-five servants."

"Where is Mr. Donner?"

"My, don't we ask a lot of questions? He was killed at Pittsburg Landing, along with two brothers."

"You mean to say no white folks will be coming home after the war?"

"My brother lives with me, but he is away at the present. He is a Partisan Ranger."

A bushwhacker, Joe thought.

Mrs. Donner took Joe by the hand. "Come, let us go out to the veranda."

Joe followed, his legs brushing her round hoop-skirt. She seemed to glide across the floor. She smelled like flowers, and her hair was as gold as ripe wheat. Her hand was softer than any hand he had ever touched before—small wrists, too. She made him feel tickly.

The double-layered veranda ran the length of the house with a pretty, white swing by the big front door. However, they sat on benches with fancy cushions.

From that spot, Joe had a grand view of the plantation. The fields stretched out far in every direction until they stopped at a line of woods. It was like a huge canyon or maybe a lake without water. The road, running east to west, cut the plantation in half. Little field roads crossed it here and there, like streets cross a pike. She owned all of this—just one woman.

A girl came upon the veranda and began slowly fanning Mrs. Donner with a big leaf. Joe saw she was an expert.

"How long have you lived here?" Joe asked.

"My husband began burning and clearing five years ago. As you saw, the house is still not finished. We are still breaking new ground every year."

How much more land could a woman need? He reckoned there were a thousand acres farmed now.

"Oh, it will be a grand plantation," she said. She smiled and held her hand across her breast. She appeared to be dreaming or thinking of something far away. "I shall require more servants, for I plan to plant more and more cotton."

"Can the Mississippi flood all of this?" Joe asked.

"My husband was an engineer, and he put the plantation on a rise. When the Yankees cut the levee on this side of the river down below, we only got a little water to the south."

Joe knew about the cut levee. It seemed Grant was going to try to get to Vicksburg by going through Moon Lake and eventually up the Yazoo. That way he wouldn't have to run the Mississippi River past the big guns at Vicksburg, but it didn't work. In the end, it didn't matter—he captured the town anyhow.

Another little girl came running from beside the house and stopped at the dooryard in front of the veranda. "Missus—Missus, some mo eggs done hatched and us got some mo babies!"

A grown Negro woman caught up to the little girl and grabbed her by the arm. "Child, I done told you, don't bother the missus." She curtseyed to Mrs. Donner. "Missus, I's sorry about May bothering you and the young marster, but she get so excited when them new babies comes. She juss plain don't know no better."

"Indeed, Ann, you must teach the young one to respect white people."

"Yessum, you sho right. Please forgive me."

Joe watched the hard frown melt away from Mrs. Donner.

"We shall let it pass this time. There is something to be said for a person taking so much pride in a new job."

"Thank you, Missus," Ann said. "Lawd, bless you."

Mrs. Donner stood. "Come Joe, let us go observe May's new babies."

As they descended the sprawling steps, Mrs. Donner took little May's hand. Joe noticed the contrast, one hand creamy-white and the other dark brown.

They rounded the big house and passed the kitchen house. Through the window, Joe saw Peter's back; he was sitting at a table eating.

Two young men walked by, and they bowed to Mrs. Donner as if she were royalty.

May tugged Mrs. Donner's hand and led her impatiently to a huge barn. There were two fine horses in big stalls. They appeared to be worth a lot of money because they were sleek and shiny—nothing like any horses Joe had ever seen.

May let go of Mrs. Donner's hand and ran inside to the back of the barn. "Come see, Missus!"

A big coop of some sort was attached to the back wall, about chest level, two feet tall, and around twelve feet long, divided into four sections—full of pigeons.

May stood on a crate in the far corner peering into the cage.

Ann opened the door, and a pigeon chopped at her three or four times with its wing. Ann gently nudged the angry hen from her nest, revealing two yellow, feather balls. They were ugly, with long beaks, too big for their heads.

"Oh, how precious," Mrs. Donner said, patting them with a finger.

"Yessum," May said, "and I's gonna train them real good." She looked up at Ann. "I means, me and Mammy is gonna train them."

Joe examined the coop. It had a one-foot square door cut in the wall of the barn. Little wooden pegs, spaced about an inch apart, hung from the top of the opening.

Joe pointed to it. "Is that a door or window?"

"Tell him about the door, Ann," Mrs. Donner said.

"Yessum. Them little sticks hanging swings in, but they don't swings back out. The pigeons can come in, but they can't get theyself back out."

"They're homing pigeons." Joe said.

"Yessuh, they is."

May screamed.

Joe whirled around. May was looking in a barrel next to the wall.

Mrs. Donner put her hand over her breasts and gasped.

Ann grabbed May's shoulder. "I done told you and told you not to scream when you see one of them rats in the feed barrel." She turned to Mrs. Donner. "I sho is sorry for the child scaring you."

Joe looked in the barrel. It contained corn, wheat, and some other grains. The barrel was almost empty, and the rat couldn't climb or jump out. He squealed and leaped, but he couldn't reach the top.

"I's sorry, Missus," Ann said. "Them ole rats always finds a way to get in the pigeon feed barrel."

"You must keep the lid secured, Ann," Mrs. Donner said.

Ann grabbed a stick from behind the barrel. Joe reasoned it was the "rat stick." She began whopping at the rat. The rat squealed and tried to leap to the top of the barrel.

"Oh, Ann, you shall get blood on the grain, and I can't bear that dreadful squealing," Mrs. Donner said.

"Let me get that ole rat," Joe said.

He took the stick. It was around three-feet long, a small fork on one end. Joe looked in the barrel, waited until the rat settled down, aimed the stick as he had done with his fishing spear, and stabbed the stick at the rat. The fork caught the vermin behind the head; the rat scratched and pawed, but he was pinned. Joe eased his hand in, grabbed the rat behind the head with one hand, and stretched the tail with the other. He brought the rat out, and it appeared even bigger when it cleared the barrel.

"Oh, my goodness," Mrs. Donner declared, putting both hands over her mouth.

"Ann, I need your help," Joe said, as he walked from the barn. Joe stretched the rat out on the ground, careful not to let go with either hand. "Take the tomahawk from my belt," he nodded toward the hatchet. "Now, just ease it in front of my fingers and put weight on it."

As the wedge slowly came down on the rat, it squealed. Ann

quickly applied more weigh and cut the rat's head off.

When Joe and Ann reentered the barn, Mrs. Donner and May were waiting. "How dreadful," Mrs. Donner said.

Joe looked closely at the pigeons. "Do they really come home?"

Mrs. Donner bent down eye-level with May. "Go tell Cluck that we shall let one pigeon go for the young master." May darted from the barn.

Ann pulled a big blue pigeon from the coop. The rat was soon forgotten. To Joe's surprise, the bird didn't resist. Six-inch ribbons were tied to nails on the barn wall: red, blue, black, and white. Ann tied a white one to the pigeon's leg and placed him in a covered straw basket.

Joe started to ask, "What is the rib—"

Cluck entered the barn followed by Peter. "Missus Donner, Ole Cluck don't think it bees a good idea to let the bird go." He took the basket from Ann.

"We have tied the white ribbon, Cluck," Mrs. Donner said.

"That don't make no never mind."

Joe had never heard a slave talk to his owner in such a manner.

Mrs. Donner slowly walked over to Cluck and held her hand out.

"Missus, you say you ain't gonna interfere with Ole Cluck."

"We have tied the white ribbon," she said evenly. "Now hand me the basket. The young master wishes to see the pigeon fly."

Cluck turned on his heels and headed for the door. "Oh, I takes it myself."

"Cluck," Mrs. Donner said softly.

Cluck turned and looked at Mrs. Donner for a long minute, then he turned to Joe. "If the young marster want to see the pigeon fly, Ole Cluck bees glad to oblige." With that, he disappeared from the barn and yelled to someone. "Put those mules to that wagon. We's going down the road a piece to let this here bird fly."

***

Joe and Peter watched the wagon disappear into the woods about a mile away.

Mrs. Donner sat on the porch in the swing, her hands in her lap. She sure was a handsome woman. If Joe was old enough, he would marry her for sure. However, he was only twelve, and she must be at least twenty-five. Joe stared at her. Her dress bellowed around her like a queen, and her smile melted him.

"Look, Joseph, here it comes!" Peter said, pointing to the sky.

Joe searched and there it was, coming like a bullet. It circled the house three times. Joe could plainly see the white ribbon fluttering under and behind the pigeon.

"Come on!" Joe said, as he ran for the barn. When they dashed inside, May was already standing at the coop on her crate. They ran to the coop and frightened the pigeons—they shuffled and scurried around inside the coop.

"Oh, the young marster ain't pose to scare the pigeons," May said.

Joe heard a fluttering outside, then the blue pigeon poked his head through the pegs, stood there for a minute, then pushed the pegs forward and dropped into the coop.

"Well, I'll be," Peter said.

Ann came into the barn and took the ribbon from the pigeon's leg. "Would the young marster like this here ribbon?"

"Thank you, Ann." Joe looked at the pigeon. "Ain't that something?" He crammed the ribbon in his pocket. "Ain't that something, Peter?"

Chapter 8

The rooster woke Peter before daylight. Soon after, a bell rang six or seven times—he remembered the bell in front of the big house. He sat up and brushed hay from his hair; he had elected to sleep in the barn, didn't want to intrude on the servants. Joe had better accommodations; he slept in the big house.

Peter heard voices, so he climbed down from the loft, had stood all of that comfort he could stand for one night. He went outside into an already warm morning, stretched. The eastern sky was beginning to glow pink as a distant owl hooted its farewell to the night, and chickens purred and clucked in the henhouse.

The slave quarters were already lit, and fires had been kindled, no doubt for breakfast. There were no lights in the big house, yet.

Trace chains jingled, and cowbells softly tinkled. The morning was alive, but soft as stockings on a wood floor.

A few feet away someone was gathering eggs. Evidently, they had been there for a time, and he hadn't noticed.

"Did you sleep in that ole barn?" asked a sweet voice.

Peter remembered the voice: Lou.

"I rested fine; thank you for asking."

She came closer, hugging the basket, her hair tied in a red cloth. He could barely see her pretty face in the soft dawning light, but he remembered it well.

"You sho do use fancy talk for a darky," she said.

"It's just the way I was raised."

"I hear you is free." She looked down at the basket, and then cut her eyes up to him.

"Yes, I am." He wanted to say something clever, couldn't think of anything.

"You come from Helena, too, I hear."

Peter nodded like a dumb animal. The right words eluded him.

"I hear they is a lot of darkies there what done run off from they marsters."

"I've been to the camps where they are gathered."

A pig squealed at the slave quarters. Peter turned to the sound, but it was still too dark to see; he turned back.

"You reckon them Yankees will ever come free us?"

Peter started to answer, but Cluck came out of nowhere before he found the first word. "Lou, you get them eggs over to Bessie and be quick! The white folk gonna be wanting they breakfast when they wakes up."

Lou scurried away with her head down without saying another word.

Cluck walked up close to Peter. "I know you is a free nigger and all that there, but you has to be careful what you says here."

"I didn't say anything out of the way."

"You don't say nothing about Helena and them Yankees. You don't say nothing about escaping. You don't say nothing about free niggers. Does you understand me?" He looked toward the big house. "Things is just like the missus want them to be, and if she happy, us niggers is right happy, too. I's seen times when it was bad; I don't want to see them no mo."

Peter wanted to say he meant no harm, but Cluck left before he could say anything. If there was a doubt about Cluck being in charge, it was gone now.

It grew lighter, and Peter watched more people spill out of the log cabins. Some loaded things into the wagons; others herded children to the biggest cabin—probably to be looked after by a woman too old to go to the fields. Soon all able hands would be working: hoeing, chopping, cutting timber, and all of the other hard work it took to keep a big plantation going.

What must it be like to be a slave? No freedoms. No freedom forever. Peter tried to think about it, but it was too big to understand. How could any free man know slavery? Peter was black, sure, but he belonged to no man. You could witness a slave toil and sweat; you could see him laugh and cry. You could observe the flesh of the being, but you could never see his soul—never know his heart. When slavery ends—and some day it will end, Peter prayed—the heart of the slave will be lost. Historians will never really know the soul of a person in bondage. Generations will pass, and with it, understanding will fade like paint in the sun. Peter thought on this. He looked at his hands—free hands. He was deprived sometimes, indeed, and he endured being black in a white man's world, but he was not in bondage. The Almighty had saved him from the wickedness of that horrible institution. "Thank you, Jesus."

"Put those mules to that wagon," Cluck called out in the distance. "You boys load up. It gonna be a long day."

Peter studied his hands again. He felt guilty being among these people. He had done nothing wrong. He owned no slaves, and he belittled no one, but he was a Negro, and he had not suffered slavery. He put his hands in his pockets. Maybe he could help somewhere until Joe awoke, show his worth to the rest of the blacks. He had helped in the kitchen all his life. He would go there.

***

Joe strolled out onto the veranda, his belly full of eggs and ham. That Mrs. Donner sure did have a good cook. The sun was already above the distant tree line, like a red ball. He saw a couple of wagons way across the field next to the woods, and he faintly heard the whacking of an ax. A cart, pulled by an ox, stirred up dust as it headed across the field. Chickens and ducks pecked around the dooryard, and a little piccaninny rushed in front of the steps chasing a goose with a stick. It looked like fun and made Joe want to chase after the goose.

This was, indeed, a fine plantation. It would be nice to live on such a place. Joe thought on it a minute—he changed his mind. The Shenandoah Valley beat it hands down. Besides, it took too many slaves to run this place, and everybody knows how much trouble they can be.

And speaking of trouble, where was Peter. They needed to make plans. Joe remembered seeing him in the kitchen house yesterday. Might as well look there first.

***

Peter was helping a big Negro woman knead dough when Joe entered the kitchen. The place smelled good, like a pan of bread. There was something bubbling in a kettle. Darkies always had something cooking in a pot.

"Smells mighty fine, Aunt," Joe said.

"Thank you, Young Marster." Bessie dipped in with a big wooden spoon. "Would Marster likes a taste?"

He was full, but what would one little taste hurt? It was beans, and as he suspected, it was capital. After he thanked the cook, he and Peter went outside.

"We're fixing to have to leave, I reckon," Joe said.

"Bessie there has already packed us some food," Peter said.

Joe had not thought about food. He was too full to think about it. He reckoned he wouldn't have thought about it until his belly started growling. Bringing Peter along was starting to pay off already.

"I reckon we need to get our bags, and I want to thank Mrs. Donner for her hospitality," Joe said.

Joe was going out the door when he heard shouting.

"Bird! Bird!"

Joe spotted a boy perched in some type of crow's nest atop the barn. He hadn't noticed it before. The boy scrambled down the ladder and ran around the barn. Ann and May ran to the front yard and looked to the sky where two pigeons circled.

"Red ribbon, Missus, red ribbon!" Ann shouted.

Joe and Peter hurried to the front yard and found Mrs. Donner standing on the veranda watching the circling pigeons.

The birds circled several times, then one lit on the barn while the other went to the coop. Soon the one on the barn followed the other to the coop.

"Double bell, Ann," Mrs. Donner said.

"Yessum." Ann went to the large bell by the veranda and pulled on the rope, making the bell ring twice. After a long pause, she rang it twice more, and repeated the process several times.

Cluck galloped up on a gray horse. "Ours, Missus?"

"Yes, Confederate," she said.

Some of the slaves ran in from the fields. Yet, others continued working.

"Hide the good horses!" Cluck yelled, as he walked toward the barn. "Take the bestest hams from the smokehouse. Take them good mules to the woods." Cluck was just going through the motions. Joe saw his orders were already being carried out automatically.

"They have a system," Peter said to Joe.

"That is correct, Peter," Mrs. Donner said, walking down from the veranda. "A red ribbon tied to a pigeon means our boys, a blue one, Yankees, and black, just strangers."

"White means no alarm," Joe said.

"Very good, Joe," she said. "You are very observant."

"But why are you hiding your property from our soldiers?" Joe asked.

"I only hide the fat."

"Ma'am?"

"If our boys see that we are doing well, they will take things. They will take meat from the smokehouse. They are always after horses and mules."

Some of the slaves were hauling items to the woods behind the house. There were even boys with big brooms sweeping the barnyard, hiding tracks. Eight milk cows were being led away—that left four. Mules and horses were taken from the barn and fields, but the sorry-looking ones were left along with the oxen. Joe saw the smarts in the plan.

Mrs. Donner addressed the boys, "Now you two don't let on about any of this."

This was too good. Joe wasn't going to say a word. What a plan. Not only was this lady pretty—she was smart.

In minutes, the plan was fully executed, with little evidence to tell the real story, just a slave grooming an old nag by the barn, four or five chickens, and a few ducks still pecked in the yard. The smokehouse door was shut tight. The little boy was chasing the goose with the stick again, and slaves were still working all around the plantation in wide-open view. The plan was perfect.

"Here they come, Missus," Cluck said. Then he led the horse to the barn.

Joe had heard the rumbling before, and he had seen the smoky dust cloud. No one had to tell him that they were coming.

"Maybe we should hide," Peter said.

"From Confederates?" Joe said. "I ain't hiding from nobody, and I sure ain't hiding from our own."

The front of the column stopped at the gate. The troops soon found the watering troughs. When the dust settled, Joe saw they were a ragged bunch. Some wore gray, some butternut, some even blue, but most were a mix. "Bushwhackers," Joe whispered.

It was hard to tell rank, but the first one to the gate was a captain. He was tall with long black hair and a droopy mustache. He stopped at the gate, took his gloves off, and handed them to a soldier behind him.

"Put these in my left saddlebag." He swaggered to the veranda. "How do, Ma'am." He pulled his hat off, revealing hair molded the shape of the hat.

"I am well, Colonel," Mrs. Donner said with a teasing smile.

The man looked back toward his troops, then back to Mrs. Donner. "I'm a captain—Captain Rowland."

"I've never seen you before, Captain. I know most of the officers from this area."

"We've come up from the south. Come to give General Chalmers a hand." He pulled at his mustache and studied Mrs. Donner. "Not much going on down in our neck of the woods, so we come here."

"I see. So what can I do for you, Captain?"

"I need to speak with the head of this here plantation."

"I am the owner—Mrs. Hampton Donner. I am a widow."

The captain looked back at his men again, then back to Mrs. Donner.

The soldiers tied their horses and began spreading out around the place. Some headed to the barn and others started for the slave quarters. One grabbed the goose and slung it under his arm. The bird raised a ruckus.

"Captain, please ask your men not to disturb my property."

"I'm afraid we will have to take some of your horses and mules," the captain said.

"Certainly that soldier can't ride the goose," she said, smiling.

The captain grinned and turned to the soldier. "Put the goose down, Phillips."

"But, Captain," the soldier said.

"Put the goose down, now!"

The goose hit the ground honking and running with his wings fanned, and the little boy with the stick in its wake. The soldiers laughed. Mrs. Donner laughed, too. Joe didn't.

"Now, Captain, please ask your men not to disturb my property until we have discussed the matter," she said, still smiling.

She was being too friendly to these bushwhackers. She should demand they leave, Joe thought.

"Ma'am, there ain't nothing to discuss," the captain said. "The top and bottom of it is this: we have to have those animals."

"Please, Captain, just step inside my home—we can talk...in private."

"Mrs. Donner, don't you bargain with that bushwhacker," Joe said. Joe had enough of this. The Confederates were supposed to protect the women of the South, not steal from them.

"Now Joe, you watch your tongue," Mrs. Donner said. "These fine soldiers are here to protect us." She smiled sweetly at the captain. "Please excuse the young boy. He is just passing through and doesn't know our ways. Now please step inside." She turned and went in before he could refuse.

The captain turned to his troops. "Sergeant, y'all just hold up here in the front yard while I discuss things with the lady."

A fat gray-haired man still on his horse said, "Sure Captain, discuss all you like." He laughed and the other soldiers laughed with him.

Joe shot up the steps. Peter tried to stop him, but he pulled free. He had to talk sense to Mrs. Donner.

The captain grabbed him by the shirt. "The little boy with the big mouth. What you doing with that Yankee cap on?"

"I would not let it concern you."

He slapped Joe, knocking his kepi off.

Peter ran for the steps, but two soldiers pulled their revolvers.

"Captain!" the sergeant yelled. "He's just a boy."

"Shut up, Sergeant!" The captain grabbed Joe by the collar and lifted him up until only the toes of his shoes touched the porch. "Boy, I'm going in here to see about this woman, and if you step through that door, I'll kill you." He shoved Joe off the veranda. He hit the ground hard. The captain shut the door behind him.

Peter helped Joe to his feet. Joe's top lip was bleeding. Peter picked Joe's kepi from the ground and placed it back on Joe's head.

The sergeant climbed down from his horse. "Are you all right, boy? You didn't fall on that ax, did you?"

Joe felt his bottom lip quiver as Peter dusted the dirt from his clothes.

"That damn arrogant captain, some day he will get what's coming to him," the sergeant said. He pulled a handkerchief from his pocket and dabbed at Joe's lip.

Joe pulled free from Peter and the sergeant. He wiped his lip on his shirtsleeve and smeared at his moist eyes with his fingertips. That captain would get his coming-ups sure enough and right now. Joe headed to the barn. Peter followed.

"Where are you going?" Peter asked.

Joe paid him no mind and went to the barn. He jerked the lid from the pigeon feed barrel, looked inside. Across the barn were four more barrels. He noticed the pigeon coop—all of the pigeons were gone. The blacks had hid everything, smart, very smart. Joe snatched a lid from another barrel—it was full of corn, another one half-full. The last barrel was a quarter full of some kind of beans. It also had what Joe was looking for: two fat rats.

Joe grabbed up the forked stick, jabbed at one of the rats. He missed; the rat shot up the stick and onto Joe's arm. He yelped and flung the rat. Joe looked at Peter. Peter grinned. Joe took better aim at the second rat. With a quick thrust, he caught the rat behind the head.

He marched to the front yard with the rat stretched out in front of him. The soldiers were puzzled, but said nothing. Joe took the rat to the captain's horse. Peter stopped beside the veranda. Joe tried to lift the flap of the left saddlebag with his teeth. Suddenly the flap flew up. Joe turned to see the sergeant. He smiled at Joe, but said nothing. Joe carefully dropped the rat inside, and the sergeant dropped the flap. The soldiers laughed, but not one tried to stop him.

Peter handed Joe his carpetbag. Joe looked back toward the big house. The door was still shut, and the house servants were all standing on the veranda. Mrs. Donner was not such a nice lady after all.

"I think we should leave before the captain comes out," Peter said.

Joe looked around at the slaves in the fields. He looked again at the house servants stationed on the veranda. Everyone was at their post. They were doing their duty, playing their part, including Mrs. Donner. It was a great deception—so was Mrs. Donner. Now that Joe thought on it, she wasn't so pretty after all. "Yeah, Peter, we best go." Joe knew they didn't have a part to play at the Donner Plantation.

***

They had walked for miles, and Peter's feet were sore. The country was different from the land around Helena and Western Mississippi, no giant oaks here, no grand plantations, just small farms, red earth, not black as it was closer to the Mississippi River. Peter liked the look of the area, and he reckoned Joe did, too, since he had been playing his harmonica for hours, happy as a lark.

"*Shenandoah* is a pretty song," Peter said.

Joe nodded.

"Do you know the words?"

"Naw, just learned the song when Mr. Von from the Valley gave me the Hohner. He was a sailor, and he learned to play it while on ship. He may have known the words, but he just taught me to play it."

Joe went ahead of Peter and started playing again. He had to be in the lead. If it made him happy, it was fine by Peter, better to keep an eye on him.

Peter looked back over his shoulder. The sun had set, and the western sky was just an orange smear. Peter had hoped they would make it to the town of Sardis before night, but he now saw that wasn't possible.

He spotted a small abandoned house off the road a ways, and he persuaded Joe to stay the night there. The house was old. It appeared to have been a log cabin that someone had made bigger by adding scrap lumber. Some of the windowpanes were cracked or missing, and the door hung by one hinge. There was a table in the front room with two chairs, and pans hung around the fireplace. The add-on lumber was a bedroom, and it had one old cotton-stuffed bed. Logs and kindling were stacked by the hearth, but a spider web spanned the fireplace. On the shelf was a jar of molasses, a little lard, molded bread, and a jar of popping corn. A basin and a cake of lye soap set on a rickety table in the corner. The place smelled like lamp oil. Peter had second thoughts about staying there. It might not be abandoned after all. The owner might only be away for a time.

Joe opened the backdoor. "Hey, look here." He held up something.

"What is it?" Peter asked.

"It's a pine knot torch. There is a jake back there. I reckon this is to light the way." He closed the door.

"Joe, I think we should move on. Whoever lives here may be back."

"Pshaw! They ain't coming back." Joe waved the notion away. He grabbed the popping corn from the shelf, pulled the lid off, and smelled the corn. "Smells good. Let's build a small fire and pop this corn."

"I really think we should move on." Peter said. "We may be trespassing."

Joe set the corn on the table and propped the front door up. "Nation Peter, there ain't nobody living here, besides we ain't going to hurt nothing."

Maybe Joe was right. It would be better than camping beside the road.

Joe stuffed old rags in the windows to keep the mosquitoes out, and Peter started the fire.

The stick holding the pot caught fire twice, but they were able to get the corn popped. The small house soon smelled delicious. They sat at the table eating straight from the pot. The glow from the small fire glowed and reflected a warm light over the small room. A rumble grew outside, and cracks around the doors and stuffed windows flashed, revealing a storm brewing. The wind was picking up, and the drafts down the chimney made the fire flame up, then die back down like a bellows. It was a safe feeling inside to Peter now that the weather had turned bad.

Peter looked at Joe chomping the corn. He smiled. "Joe, tell me a little bit about Virginia."

Joe's eyes lit up. "Well," he started, but his mouth was too full, and he had to hurry the rest of the corn down.

Peter laughed. Joe never had the patience to wait for anything.

They had found the well by the back porch with the aid of the torch, and a good thing, because Joe needed the water now. He took a quick drink, and choked, snorting water from his nose. Both boys laughed.

"I declare, Joseph, do you ever do anything slowly?"

Joe ignored the question and said, "Virginia is beautiful country, especially the Shenandoah Valley."

"Well then, tell me about the Shenandoah Valley."

Joe didn't hesitate. "The most beautiful farms you ever saw in your life. Clear streams and wildflowers and colored trees in the fall and there are beautiful mountains in all directions and caves—"

"Slow down," Peter said. It was pleasing to see the excitement in Joe after the hard times at Helena. "What do you like the best about the Shenandoah Valley?"

Joe pondered for a few minutes and said, "The mills, I like the mills the best."

"Mills?"

"Yeah, the mill always meant good times. It meant the corn was in after the hard summer work. We boys would play in the millstreams and that water was so cool. Boys from the area would choose up sides and have battles in the stream. I remember once I cut my foot on a sharp rock and Ma had a fit. She and Sarah fussed over me so. The blood just didn't want to stop, so somebody gave Ma a wad of moss from the stream to put on it. Sarah was trying to hold the moss on and I was laughing, because her hands were too small, and she got mad and told Ma to make me stop laughing, but I couldn't. She told Ma to make me stop bleeding if I couldn't stop laughing. Ma laughed, then Sarah laughed, and everybody looked at us like we were touched or something. We sure loved playing in that stream. I told Sarah when she got bigger...she...could..." Joe sniffed and rubbed his eyes.

Peter stood. "You know we have a long day ahead of us, so we had better turn in."

Joe wiped his nose on his sleeve. "I better go to the privy before I turn in." The wind howled and slammed the door open when Joe unlatched it. Peter shut it as Joe dashed for the outhouse.

Peter leaned against the door. Joe didn't reveal his feelings often, and it tugged at Peter's heart when he did. They had both lost so much because of this horrible war. No one should endure such hardship and heartbreak, certainly not a twelve-year-old boy. How much more could Joe take? Peter wondered how much more he, himself, could take. Joe was strong; indeed, stronger than any boy

Peter knew, but he was still only a child. They would have to stay strong—they would have to lean on each other if they were going to make it. But make it where? Virginia? Pennsylvania? That wasn't resolved yet, not to Peter's satisfaction. He would pray for an answer. Peter needed a heap of help finding answers now.

Joe came back in. "Ain't you glad we stayed here, now?" Joe asked, shucking clothes.

"It appears you were correct Joseph."

Joe grinned and jumped into the bed. He was soon on his backing humming *Shenandoah*.

Peter sat at the table watching the fire slowly die to coals, thinking how good it was that Joe could recover from bad feelings quickly. A trait he wished he had.

"Ain't you coming to bed?" Joe asked. "I'll let a darky sleep with me. This is a special circumstance."

Peter looked at the doorway to the little bedroom. Special circumstance. Peter smiled. Joe had never treated him as if he were inferior—he may have said some things, but his actions told another story. God knows, you always knew where you stood with Joseph Taylor. Well, unless you were the butt of one of his shines.

"I'll be there in a spell," Peter said. "I'm going to eat a little more of this corn." No reply. Joe always was able to go to sleep quickly, and he could sleep through anything, even this storm howling outside.

Peter stared at the front door. Behind it was still a long way to New Albany and the Taylor farm. Virginia was too far to even worry about. They may just stay put at Mr. Taylor's place until after the war.

After the war? How long would that be? It had already gone on forever—it felt that way.

Peter had been to the Taylor farm, so he could make it there, but he didn't know how to get to Virginia. He was only a child when they had left Pennsylvania—he had no idea how to go there. He would pray for an answer.

Peter stared at the door. Something was strange about it, but he couldn't put his finger on it. It was three wide boards held together by three narrow boards, which formed a "Z." But it wasn't the design of it. It was something else. Peter looked harder. There was something strange.

The door flew open. The wind blew the bowl of popcorn from the table, scattering white kernels over the dim room. Peter jumped from the chair. He caught his breath, just the wind. Nothing to be scared of, just the wind. He laughed at himself as he went to shut the door. He had seen a lot and had been through a lot, and now he was jumping at the wind.

He wrestled with the door. It had lodged against the wall, and the broken hinge had crossed and stuck. The wind and rain blew through the open door. Peter knocked the hinge free and turned to pull the door shut. He found a gun barrel just inches from his face.

A man stepped through the door. "All right, boy, you go ahead and shut that door," He had long black hair, which the rain had plastered to his big head, no hat. He had a bushy beard, greasy and nasty, a bedroll and saddlebags over his shoulder.

Peter slowly closed the door. His thoughts were on Joe. Please don't let him get hurt.

"Now then," the man said, "what's a nigger doing in this here house by his lonesome?"

Peter said nothing. He just stared at the barrel stuck in his face.

The man studied the room. His eyes settled on the dying fire. "Put some wood on that fire, boy."

Peter started for the fireplace.

"Wait a minute."

Peter stopped. He waited for the bullet to the back.

"What's in the other room?"

"Nothing." Peter knew the man would check. Maybe Joe had heard him and hid. But where?

"Nothing? Shit, I ain't gonna trust no lying ass nigger." The man eased toward the bedroom doorway. "Come outta there!"

Nothing happened.

The man looked into the room, then turned back toward Peter. Peter saw the man had a peg leg. "I reckon you are alone, ain't you?" He aimed the musket toward Peter again. "Move over there by that there door. I'll put the wood on the fire myself." He leaned the gun against the wall, dropped the load from his shoulder onto the floor, and threw a few pieces of wood on the low fire.

Peter took a step, and the man had the gun to his shoulder. "Boy, I'll blow that fuzzy head plumb off. Now sit your ass down in that corner."

Peter wondered if the man was a soldier, hard to tell Confederates. He was rough looking whatever he was. He was a filthy bruin, and the rain didn't seem to clean him up much, could smell his filth across the room, like dead fish.

Peter needed a plan, and he needed a plan fast, couldn't let the man harm Joe. He studied the gun. If the man would just move away from it a piece, maybe he could get to it. No, that was a bad idea. The man had already revealed how fast he could move.

The man pulled a piece of meat from his saddlebag. Peter didn't know what it was, but he sure wouldn't eat it, dirt and grass all over it. The man crammed the meat on the end of the pine knot torch and stuck it over the fire. It was disgusting.

"What the hell are you looking at, boy?"

"Nothing."

After a while, the man considered the meat done enough. He sat at the table, choked it down. He looked like a starving dog.

"Where did you run away from?" The man spit the words out along with bits of slobbery meat.

"I'm free."

"Free, my ass," the man said, throwing a piece of gristle into the fire. It hissed when it settled in the coals. "You won't be free tomorrow. I'll get a dollar for you somewhere, I'll be bound."

"I told you I'm free, and I have my papers."

The man threw the table over and grabbed Peter by the hair. He hurled Peter against the wall by the fireplace.

It happened so fast Peter didn't have time to react. Now his head hurt from hitting the wall, and his neck stung as if needles were sticking in it. Peter labored to his knees.

"Boy, from here on out, you speak only when I says you can," the man said, standing over him.

Peter had been called names many times by white trash, and he had learned to let it go, but he had never been handled before. The anger glowed in him like hot coals. "I said, I'm free." Peter tried to stand, but the room spun.

The man kicked him in the face. His head snapped back, and he fell over on his side. He was confused, lost understanding of what was happening, saw white lights, thought of Lucius and Helena.

The man brayed like a jackass.

Peter managed to get up on his hands and knees, couldn't

remember where he was, thought of Mam. She wanted him to go to Pennsylvania—was he there, yet? Where was he if not there? He saw his mother sitting on the floor beside him, reached for her.

The man stepped on his hand with the peg. Peter screamed.

"Go ahead, boy, scream. Ain't nobody going to hear you."

"Get off him!" Joe said.

The man wheeled around, almost fell.

Peter's hand raged with a fiery pain. He looked through a cloud, but he knew where he was now. The new pain was sobering. Joe had the big revolver leveled at the man.

"Who are you?" the man asked, staring at the long barrel.

Joe ignored the man, looked at Peter. "Are you all right?"

The man raised the musket. Joe fired. Blood sprayed on Peter. The man fell straight back like a felled tree, and the musket cart wheeled across the room. Joe cocked the hammer again.

The world was spinning slower as Peter gawked at the sprawled man. Was this real? Did this really happen? Things were beginning to focus again. The bullet had torn through the side of the nasty man's face, and his left ear was gone. The man's belly moved up and down slowly. Thank God, he was still alive.

Peter staggered to his feet, looked at Joe. "You can put that thing away. I don't believe he will be getting up soon."

"How are you, Peter?" Joe grabbed Peter's arm.

"I believe I'll make it, but—"

Joe grabbed his bag, shoved the revolver in it. "We need to get out of here."

Things were still fuzzy to Peter. "What?"

"He might have friends. We can use his horse if he has one."

Peter put his hand to his head—it pounded. "It's storming outside."

"It's perfect. Nobody will be on the road."

Joe was right. They could travel a long distance in the dark with the horse. Besides, Peter didn't want to stay in the house with the man.

Peter stood over the man, trying to get all of his own faculties back going. What made an evil person like this? The man moved. Peter jumped, then saw why the man had moved. Joe was pulling at the peg leg.

Joe jerked the leg off, inspected it, and threw it into the fire.

Giggling, Joe said, "He won't stand on nobody else's hand with that stick." Joe pulled the door open and went outside.

Peter looked down at the man again. Just a few months ago, everything was normal. How can all of this be happening? Mam and Dr. Taylor are dead. Lucius tried to kill us. Now Joe just shot a man as if it were a daily chore. Peter would pray harder than ever this night—he needed answers. Too much was happening, more than most people would ever see in a lifetime.

He heard a pop in the fireplace. The leg was blazing. Peter's hand throbbed where the man had stepped on it with that leg, and his face ached from the kick—he was still sore from Lucius's beating. He watched the leg smolder, and laughed. He could not control it—it spilled out like a cough. He went to the door. Joe was already on the horse. Peter turned back and looked at the burning leg. The world was still fuzzy, but he believed he could ride. He laughed again and turned for Joe and the horse.

Chapter 9

Joe was starving. It had been two days since Mrs. Donner's plantation, and now the food was gone. It had been a miserable two days, too. Joe and Peter had been wet, scared, lost, found, and lost again. They had steered clear of the main road and tried to avoid as many people as possible. They even passed through Oxford at night; Peter was scared someone would know they were on a stolen horse. It was ridiculous, but he would hear none of it. He would jump at his own shadow.

Finally, Peter knew where they were again. Joe hoped so—he wanted some food, and he wanted to sleep on a soft bed.

They arrived at the Tallahatchie River at Rocky Ford, Mississippi, and Peter said it would be just a reasonable walk to Mr. Taylor's farm from there. Joe wondered what a "reasonable walk" meant.

They crossed the river, rode a piece, then Peter wanted to abandon the horse.

"Are you mad?" Joe said. They dismounted the animal. "No one will know where this horse came from."

"I'll know," Peter said, pulling their things from the horse. "I have to live with myself for riding the stolen horse this far. I will ask God for forgiveness for the both of us."

"That man tried to kill you. It don't matter none we took his horse—spoils of war."

Peter slapped the horse's rump. It galloped back toward Rocky Ford, and Peter started up the road, said, "Thou shall not steal."

Joe threw up his hands, then picked his bag off the ground, and started after him.

Small farms scattered the area, and the locals took notice as the two boys passed, some even stared.

"I wish you would take that kepi off," Peter said. "I declare you are going to get us shot."

Joe ignored him, pulled his harmonica from his pocket, and started in with, *Home Sweet Home*.

The walk was longer than "reasonable," and Joe was relieved when they stopped at a fork. Peter chose the fork to the right, declared it the lane to the farm.

They headed down the lane, and Joe started thinking about his Uncle Zeke. He had never met him, never even received a letter after Uncle Wilbur died. Joe knew little about the man. How was this visit going to shape up?

"What's on your mind?" Peter asked.

"Ain't nothing."

"Oh, it's something. You have the harmonica to your lips, but you stopped playing five minutes ago."

"Why didn't Uncle Zeke come see about us when Uncle Wilbur died?" Joe finally asked, shaking spit from the harmonica.

"I reckon he doesn't know he is dead. I'd imagine he didn't even know you were in Arkansas; at least, Dr. Taylor didn't mention being able to get a letter to him. I know he had tried."

Joe felt a sudden heavy weight. How do you tell a man his brother is dead? He'd figure on that later.

"What's he like?" Joe asked.

Peter looked up the road, turned, looked back the direction they had come. "I believe this is the correct road, hope it is."

Oak trees grew so close to the narrow lane that their limbs intertwined overhead. It was cool and shady.

"Well?" Joe asked.

"Yes, this is the road."

"No. What's he like?"

Peter smiled and shook his head. "He is a very big man." Peter pondered. "Dr. Taylor wasn't a big man. Is your pa a big man?"

"Not too big."

"Oh. Well, Mr. Zeke is, and he doesn't talk much either. Above that, he didn't strike me as being too friendly."

Big and not too friendly, that is not a favorable combination, Joe thought. Maybe he and Peter could get a little food and shove right on down the road. He had hoped they could rest there a few days, but if things weren't too good, they could light a shuck.

Joe thought of something else. "Peter, I don't remember Uncle Zeke's wife's name?"

"Mrs. Lillie, and she is a very nice lady."

Maybe Aunt Lillie would fix them some food for the long road to Virginia. He never thought he would think it, but a good scrubbing with soap would be capital, too.

***

They had walked down the lane about ten minutes when they came to a large cotton field. Farther down the lane was the house. It was bigger than anything they had seen in a while, nothing like the Donner house, but still big. It almost seemed out of place in this country.

They moved closer, and Joe spotted the slave quarters. It was obvious Uncle Zeke was well off compared to the other farmers here about.

It struck Joe strange: Uncle Zeke was from Pennsylvania, and here he had slaves, and from the looks of the slave quarters, he had a passel. The more he thought about slavery and the war, the more ridiculous it became. The three Taylor brothers were from the North; one evidently now owns many slaves; one is fighting for a new country, which is bound and determined to protect slavery; and the last one, against slavery, died in an occupied town in the South. Joe had even heard that General Pemberton, the defender of Vicksburg, was from Pennsylvania.

And all of this fighting because of Negroes. Joe was beginning to think that was the problem. If there were no darkies, then there would be no war.

They walked toward the house, and a piccaninny ran to the house. A white woman came to the porch, couldn't be his aunt, too young. They walked by the smokehouse, and the smell floated out, inviting. Joe believed he could eat a whole ham. He hoped they would be happy to see him and give him something from that smokehouse.

Suddenly a Negro came around the smokehouse and stuck a shotgun in Peter's side. Before Joe could react, big arms were around him—he was lifted off his feet and something sharp was at his neck. Not again.

"All right, Yankee boy, what are you doing here prowling alone?" said a deep voice from the man holding him.

Joe couldn't see the man, but he could see Peter, and his eyes were big as plums. Then Joe saw a toothy grin grow on the old Negro as he lowered the gun.

"I declare, Marse," the old Negro said. "This here boy is Katie Bea's Peter. Look at how he has growed since us last seen him."

"Thank the Lord above, Seth," Peter said. "I was beginning to think I would be dead before you recognized me."

"I know I is a old man, but I ain't about forgetful like Marse. He didn't know you, and we's been watching y'all a coming for a spell."

Peter turned to the big man still holding Joe. "Mr. Taylor, this boy is Joseph, your nephew, Mr. Josh's son."

Joe felt the knife leave his neck, and he was lowered to his feet. When he turned around, he saw that Peter wasn't lying. Zeke Taylor was indeed a big man, at least six-five and weighed...a bunch. Joe reckoned the man was around fifty, but he looked like a bull.

Zeke put the knife in his belt and looked Joe over. He smiled bigger and bigger as he studied Joe. "Well, I'll be blamed. You sure do look like your mother, got that blonde hair and those blue eyes, and not too tall like the Taylor side."

"No sir, not too tall, but it don't hinder me none."

Zeke laughed, then said. "Why you got that Yankee cap on? It almost got you killed."

"I had some friends back at Helena that were Yankees, and one of them gave it to me."

Zeke looked at Peter, then back at Joe and slowly the smile faded. "What were you doing in Helena? Where are your folks?"

An older lady joined the younger one on the porch. Seth yelled over to her. "Missus, we got Marse Josh's boy here. We got Katie Bea's Peter, too. We sho is."

Joe couldn't believe how quickly the lady ran from the porch. One second he was talking to Uncle Zeke, the next his head was buried in her bosom. Joe was relieved when she finally released him. He was beginning to believe he was going to smother. She held

Joe's face in her hands, smiling and admiring him. She said, "Boy, I'm your Aunt Lillie."

He liked the looks of this woman, a sweet round face, a few gray streaks in her brown hair, but she didn't appear to be too old. Joe loved the attention. After all the hardships lately, this attention was pretty fine.

"Hello, Aunt Lillie; it is a pleasure to meet you."

She kissed him on the forehead. "Such a sweet boy." She turned to Zeke. "Come on, Ezekiel, dinner is on the table."

"That meat sure smells good in that smokehouse," Joe said.

"Oh, Honey, it tastes even better on the table."

Joe couldn't wait. He was starving.

"Seth, see that Floy feeds Peter," Zeke said.

Lillie said, "Oh, no! Peter is going to eat from my kitchen this day. He brought this boy to me, and he too shall have ham."

So they really were going to have ham, Joe grinned and nodded at Peter.

Zeke told Joe they would talk about Helena after dinner. Joe put Helena from his thoughts. Ham was the only thing on his mind now. Helena could wait. Nation, Virginia could wait on ham.

The younger woman's name was Fanny, Joe's cousin. She was pretty, and he saw the resemblance to Aunt Lillie.

The women fluttered around the table, setting dishes here and there. A black woman about Fanny's age was there, too, but she didn't help with the food. Instead, she tended to two babies in a crib in the corner. It was strange to Joe. Uncle Zeke had servants, but the white women were setting the table.

"Peter," Lillie said, "if my memory does not fail me, I remember you to be a good Christian."

"A pious Negro," Zeke grumbled.

"Zeke!" Lillie snapped.

"Lil, you know it is not fitting for Negroes to be at the table with white folks."

"This is my table, Mr. Taylor, so it is my say, not yours."

Joe looked at Peter. He had his eyes cast down at his plate. Poor Peter. Joe had not given it much thought about Negroes eating at the table with white folks. Peter and Aunt Katie Bea had always eaten at the table with him and Uncle Wilbur.

"Now, Peter," Lillie said. "Look up, Peter. That is a good boy.

Please bless this food for us."

Peter looked at Zeke. Zeke didn't appear angry, just a man of authority and wanted it known. He nodded, and Peter blessed the food.

After the meal, Zeke wasted no time asking about Helena. Joe found they didn't know about Uncle Wilbur's death. They had heard about the battle at Helena, but that was all. They also didn't know of Joe's mother and sister's death. The family huddled in the parlor as Joe told the stories. Lillie hugged and kissed him, while Zeke puffed on his pipe as Uncle Wilbur had. Zeke huffed, blew his nose a lot, and made frequent trips to look out the window as Joe gave details of the tragedies. Fanny sobbed loudly and said repeatedly, "You poor boy."

***

Joe only intended to stay on the farm a couple of days, but it turned into a couple of weeks. He would leave soon; he wanted to be in the Valley before it turned cold, but now he was enjoying getting to know his family.

The Taylor's had been fortunate. The farm was miles from the main road, and the Yankees had not been there. The war had been close—the Yankees had burned and vandalized New Albany just a few miles away, but so far, the Taylors had not experienced the horrors of war on the plantation. There had been hardships, though: shortage of supplies, such as coffee, salt, and the like, but not now. Now they traded cotton to the Yankees in Memphis and the suffering wasn't so great. In fact, the Rebels had hurt them more by taking some of the horses and mules.

Joe learned some of the neighbors were resentful of the Taylors. It seems they had been raided by the Yankees, whereas the Taylors had not. They believed it was because Zeke had been born a Yankee. Seth had told Joe it was all said behind Zeke's back—no man was brave enough to say it to his face.

Joe fell in love with Fanny. She was eighteen and a peach. She was Zeke and Lillie's only child. Fanny's husband, Robert, was away riding with General Chalmers. She was devoted to her eight-month-old son, Jack. Fanny was neither gruff like her father nor firm like her mother. She was soft spoken, charming, and smart—she reminded Joe of his mother.

The oddest character in the house was Fanny's seventeen-year-old Negro servant, Susan. They called her Zuey. Though she was a servant, she acted like family. She did no more around the house than the white folks. The only thing that set her apart was she took her meals in the kitchen and not at the big table with the rest of the family. She, too, had a son, James. He was about the same age as little Jack. When they were in the crib together, they could have passed for brothers. Joe didn't ask any question because Peter told him not to.

The plantation had fifty-five slaves on it, mostly field hands, working cotton and corn. There were more slaves on the place than any other farm for miles. The Taylors had no house servants other than Zuey, and Joe believed she wasn't a house servant anyhow. The cook on the place was Floy, Seth's wife, and she only cooked for the slaves.

Zeke was his own overseer, and he worked in the fields with the slaves. The Negroes had no doubt who was in charge when the big white man was around. Joe learned Seth was his second in command.

***

Peter found life at this Taylor home different from the last Taylor home. He was not treated cruelly by Zeke; in fact, he was treated well, but the warmth was not there, not like Dr. Taylor. Joe was given his own room, but Peter found his quarters to be little better than the slaves quarters—that was fine, but different to what he had always known. He had a room at the back of the house, which a hired hand once used. He did not eat with the family. He ate in the kitchen with Zuey. That turned out to be a good thing.

Peter found out what some thought of him when a teenaged slave named Stepto confronted him behind the corncrib.

"Well, now, ain't you a particular nigger," Stepto said, stepping in front of Peter.

Peter knew who Stepto was. He had learned many of the names. Stepto was smaller than Peter—most teenagers were smaller than Peter, but it was evident size didn't matter to Stepto. Peter saw trouble coming. "What do you mean, Stepto?"

Stepto looked Peter over. "Study them fancy clothes. You even got shoes. I spects you think you is good as white folk."

"I don't feel that way at all. You are just—"

"Don't you talk at me in that fashion. You ain't white, so don't be trying to come it over on me." He spit on Peter's shoes.

Peter took a slow, deep breath. "I don't want trouble." He tried to walk past, but Stepto grabbed his arm, more strength than Peter expected.

"We don't like niggers like you is. You and your massuh shirking around like lazy dogs."

Peter jerked his arm free. He could take the attack on himself, but Joe was another matter. He moved closer to Stepto. "You touch Joe, you even say an unkind thing, you will answer."

"That's right; answer to Marse, not you."

"Don't concern yourself with us too much. We will be leaving soon," Peter said as he turned to leave.

"You ain't leaving til Marse say so. Marse tell Seth you two is staying til this war is over, lessin' the other Marse Taylor come get the boy."

Of course, Peter thought, Mr. Taylor would not let Joe leave while the war was still raging. After all, Joe's father was probably dead—Peter would never say it to Joe.

Staying tight on the farm was, indeed, the smart thing to do. When the war was over—it probably wouldn't last too much longer—Peter could strike out for Pennsylvania, just as he had told Mam he would do.

Peter softened. "I'm sure Mr. Taylor knows best, and we shall do as he wishes."

"Well, now, I reckon you is a purty smart boy cause Marse ain't no man to cross. Why, he work harder than most niggers on the place, excepting me."

Peter smiled. "Stepto, I've never worked on a plantation, and since we are going to be here for a spell, you reckon you could take me under your wing, show me what to do."

Stepto looked suspicious.

"I've been watching you work," Peter said, "and I can tell you are the best field hand on the place. Joe and I both saw it right from the start."

He saw the minute the change came over Stepto: the strained muscles in his neck softened, and his swelled chest slowly dropped. Peter knew the last thing he needed was conflict with the blacks on the place.

"If you sho nuff wants to work, I reckon I can show you how,"

Stepto said, dragging his leathery toes in the dirt. "It won't be none easy for a soft nigger like you is."

"I do appreciate any help. Stepto, I knew you were first rate right from the start. I sure want to carry my weight around here."

Stepto looked down, then slowly looked back up. "Now, Peter, I was sho wrong on you. You is first chop. That's a fact."

Before another word, they heard a loud commotion. Joe was running and yelling and screaming and laughing with a large billy goat on his heels. He shot past Peter and Stepto. The goat skidded to a stop and looked at Peter, then Stepto, trying to make up his mind which one to charge. When Joe saw the goat had stopped, he picked up a stick and threw it at him. The goat charged after him. Joe laughed and took off. He tripped, and as soon as he was back on his feet, the goat butted him in the butt. Joe screamed, laughed, and cut out with the goat on his tail.

Stepto turned to Peter. "Young Massuh Joe is a might devilish."

Peter laughed. "Young Massuh Joe is a heap devilish."

Stepto watched Joe and the goat for a couple of minutes, turned to Peter. "Maybe you got more of a job than I studied on. Picking cotton gonna be easy. That's a fact."

Peter knew it was a fact.

***

Joe had roamed the farm freely. Zeke had really set no limits. In fact, he was busy working the fields during the day and paid Joe little mind and only spent time with him at the end of the long day, if then. Joe visited with the servants and even helped around the quarters, but he slipped away when it was time to go to the fields. He wanted no part of picking cotton.

The quarters had a pull on him, excitement there, especially in the evenings when the Negroes returned from the fields. Even though they worked late now that it was cotton-picking time, they still had enough energy for singing and visiting.

The slaves were all good to him except Floy. Floy was not nice to anyone, not even Zeke. It was odd; she was married to Seth, and Joe found him to be one of the kindest Negroes he had ever met. Floy had a big hickory stick, and she used it to run all the young ones from the cook cabin when they came snooping and smelling around.

The cook cabin was the biggest cabin in the quarters. It wasn't as big as the kitchen back at the Donner Plantation, nor was it made of bricks, but it was almost twice as big as the other little one-room cabins the slaves called home.

Joe was now bored. He had finally tired the goat out again, wouldn't even chase him anymore, just stood there and stared. Joe looked at Floy's cook cabin. What was inside there? This would be more of a challenge than any old goat. It was getting late in the afternoon. The slaves would be coming in from the fields soon, and smoke drifted from the chimney as it always did this time of day. The smell coming from the cabin made you want to take a bite out of one of the logs—not that Aunt Lillie's food wasn't first rate, but everybody knew that only colored women knew how to cook colored food. Joe loved colored food.

As he approached the door, five little Negro boys surrounded him. If a person didn't know about slaves as Joe did, the boys could easily have been mistaken for short-haired girls because of their long shirts, which resembled crude dresses. The boys wore the long shirts instead of pants—only older boys wore pants. Ten-year-old Washington led the pack. He went up to Joe. "You ain't fixing to go in Aunt Floy's cabin is ya, Massuh Joe?"

Joe didn't like Washington. He was a pest, and Joe had already socked him in the head a couple of times. "Go on, Wash, take your little niggers with you. Y'all ain't got no business bothering white folk."

"You fixing to get bothered by Aunt Floy if you go up to that cabin," Washington said. "She gonna pop you up side yo white head."

They all laughed and danced around like a pack of Indians.

"Wash, you little piccaninny, I wish you were old enough to go to the field. You ain't nothing but a little bother. If I were your master, things would be different, I tell you."

Washington laughed and danced. "You ain't none of my massuh. You juss young Massuh Joe."

The rest of the children started chanting, "Young Massuh Joe—Young Massuh Joe—"

Joe searched around and found a short stick. Before Washington could react, Joe hit him on the head with it; it made a hollow thud. Joe laughed, reminded him of someone thumping a watermelon.

Washington grabbed his head, checked for blood, found none.

He looked around and found the stick, then threw it back at Joe. Joe moved just in time.

Joe knew this little piccaninny would be no match in a chucking fight, but the others began hurling things at him: rocks, sticks, chicken shit, and anything else they could find. Joe ducked and weaved, but he was out-gunned. He ran for the cabin door, and just as he grabbed the latch, a hunk of mule shit hit the door. He snatched the door open, shot inside and slammed the door behind. Slowly he opened the door again and peeked out. He saw Wash rubbing his head. Joe laughed.

"You ain't got no bidness in my cook cabin!"

Uh oh, Aunt Floy. Joe eased the door shut and slowly turned to face her. Joe had not been this close to her before. She was big—not just fat, but big and very tall. She had the usual rag around her head, which they all wore, and flour on her arms and hands. But what concerned him the most was the big hickory stick in her left hand.

"Hello, Aunt Floy."

"Don't you 'Aunt Floy' me. This here is my cabin and Massuh Zeke and Mistus say so. Ain't no niggers or white folks pose to be in here."

Joe quickly pointed to the door. "They're chucking things at me and are bound to whoop up on me if I go out that door."

She jerked him from the door. He covered his head for the beating with the hickory stick he knew was coming. Instead, she yelled out the door. "You little monkeys get from this here cabin fo I smack you with this here stick!"

Joe looked around the big woman and watched the children scatter. She commanded respect, a person to be friends with.

She held the door open. "Now, Massuh Joe, I specks you is safe."

"Thank you Aunt Floy; obliged." Joe started for the door, stopped suddenly, sniffed. "Wait a minute. What is that smell? Why, I do declare; I believe it is catfish head soup." He left Floy holding the door and started for the pot.

Floy shut the door and followed him. "You ain't got no call to be a sniffing around my cabin."

"Is that catfish head soup?"

"What you know bout catfish head soup, anyhow?"

"I've had catfish head soup bunches of times. Back home in the Shenandoah Valley we ate it all the time." Joe knew it was a lie. He had only tried it at his friend Curtis's house in Helena, only then after laughing at the heads floating around in the pot.

Three large pots were over the fire, bubbling and fishy smelling, yet inviting. Floy retrieved a bowl, filled it with soup. When she placed it on the table, Joe pulled it to him and started right in.

"Lawd bless you, boy, that going to burn yo mouth."

It was good. Colored women could indeed cook. She placed a big hunk of ash-pone on a tin plate and slid it to him. Joe chomped a big bite and started talking with a full mouth. "Thank you, Aunt Floy."

She gave him a cup of water. He spilled it down his shirt as he chugged it.

"I ain't never seed a nigger eat bad as you is. Slow yourself down."

Joe kept eating. It was good, but he would have to save room for Aunt Lillie's supper; she was a fine cook, too. Joe sopped the bowl and declared the meal fit for a king. He knew this wouldn't be the last time he would come here for a meal.

He looked around the cabin. Floy ignored him as she busied herself with the cooking. The cabin was constructed of great big logs, with four windows, and air flowed perfectly through the cabin. It was early October, but Joe was surprised that it wasn't hotter than it was with the big fire going. Shelves lined the walls covered with an assortment of cans and bottles, and all sorts of cooking implements like the big kitchen at the Donner plantation. But no fancy bowls and plates here, mostly wood, tin, and iron. Joe spotted about fifteen gallon-sized pots in a row next to the big fireplace.

"What are those for?"

"You sho does ask a lot of foolish questions." She picked up one of the pots and set it on the table. "This here pot is what us folks get our supper in."

"I thought you got it from one of those big pots," Joe said, examining one of the little ones.

"Lawd, boy, you don't seem to know nothing bout nothing." She took the pot from Joe and placed it with the rest. "I fills these here pots up when the field hands comes in from the fields. They's one pot fo each cabin."

Joe understood it now. The workers would come in from the fields and not have to cook. Aunt Floy would have it already prepared. Joe knew this was not the case on all plantations. Some places they had to cook after they came in from working all day, even if it were late at night.

"Appears to me you've got the most important job on the place," Joe said, wiping crumbs from his shirt.

Aunt Floy almost smiled, but caught herself. "Well, I does got to feed a heap a hungry niggers fo sho."

"Sure you do, and if they don't eat, they don't work. Why, there ain't no studying on it; you have the highest position on the place. Why, you let one of the field hands get sick and can't pick, that ain't nothing, but you get sick and can't cook, the whole place would shut down tight."

Aunt Floy sat on the bench across the table from Joe. "Marse and Mistus do take a big store in my cooking."

"Sure they do, Aunt Floy. Uncle Zeke was just telling me when I got here how if it weren't for you, he wouldn't have a darky fit to work." Joe hoped this little white lie wouldn't be found out.

Aunt Floy finally smiled. "Did Marse say that on me fo sho?"

"Sure he did." Joe reached across the table and patted her big paw. "Uncle Zeke appreciates you very much."

"I ain't knowed it," she said. "Seth say I was important to the place, but I ain't believed it til white folk say so."

"Oh yeah, and Seth is important, too. Why, Uncle Zeke couldn't run the place without the two of you."

Floy suddenly got up from the table. "I got something special for young Massuh Joe. You juss wait right there." She went to one of the shelves and retrieved a wooden bowl. She placed another piece of ash-pone in it and poured sorghum molasses over it. She slid it to him.

Yes, Joe knew he had won her over.

"Now, Massuh Joe, you going to have to get. I's got to get this here supper ready. The field hands going to be a-coming in soon."

When Joe walked out of the cabin, he spotted the colored children climbing around in one of the trees. They were watching him eat the sticky treat—no doubt surprised that he had come out alive and eating on a pone, too. They seemed to be under a spell, didn't say anything, only stared.

Joe finished the treat, got a drink from the well, and washed the sticky syrup from his hands. From there he could see the slaves picking cotton. He spotted Zeke easily; not only was he white, but the biggest man in the field. He saw Peter, too. What was he doing out there? He was a free man. Joe reckoned he was like the rest on them. He didn't have any more brains than a field hand.

Joe caught something out of the corner of his eye, the billy goat. They stared at each other for a long minute. Joe kicked dirt at the goat. The goat charged.

"Whooie!" Joe yelled. "Come on you, stinking goat!" Joe struck out for the big house. The goat was quickly gaining.

Chapter 10

The cotton field spread like a white sea past the houses and barns down to the trees, which hid the Tallahatchie beyond. The Negroes harvested the bolls like machines, moving down the rows, always moving, moving. The cotton jerked and rippled like waves as black hands snatched and pulled at the plants, reaping the white bounty. Many of the women wore red calico bandanas, and the color reminded Peter of a flock of redbirds in the snow. Fill the baskets; dump the baskets into the wagon. Do it over again and again, all day—a very long day.

Peter had never picked cotton before, and his basket filled slower than the rest, even slower than the younger pickers. His fingers were cut and scraped from the rough backs of the cotton bolls, and his back felt like needles. He had volunteered to go to the field, never thought it was that much work, but he wanted to show his worth.

He had thanked God many times for saving him from slavery. Now he thanked him more. But even though he wasn't a slave, he felt a bond with these people. They were his people, his ancestry, all sons and daughters of Africa.

"Ben, get off your ass and start picking!" Zeke yelled across the field. Peter turned to see Ben rise in the cotton. Ben was a tall skinny fourteen-year-old. He was known for his shirking.

"You done heard Marse. You best fill that basket right smart,"

Seth backed Zeke. Peter knew it was no joke; Seth was respected and feared, too.

One or the other two barked orders often to the younger pickers, seldom to the adults—they knew their job and did it.

Seth stayed with the wagon and picked cotton close to it. When it was full, he drove it to the gin house, then came back with an empty one. He watched closely as the pickers dumped their cotton in the wagon, knew who was picking fast and who was not.

Zeke picked and was one of the fastest pickers in the field. He moved around the field, not going down just one row. Peter figured this way he could monitor everyone's work. Zeke said little, not much on small talk.

The fieldwork was not quiet—oh no. There was singing. When one song would end, someone else would start up another. Peter had heard Mam sing many of the songs. He felt close to her now. She had told him of the cotton fields, had told him of the never-ending rows. Now he understood.

When someone would pick close to Peter, they would laugh and tease. Stepto laughed, too, but showed Peter ways to make the picking go faster and easier. Before Stepto moved on, he dumped some of his basket into Peter's. Peter would look better at the wagon. Peter knew he had found a friend.

The cotton wagon was at the end of Peter's row. He dumped his basket and moved to the water bucket.

"Peter, you is doing good, right good," Seth said. He handed Peter the dipper gourd. "Dr. Taylor sho nuff be proud at you, boy. Sho would."

"Thank you, Seth. It is kind of you to say so."

The water was cool coming from the wooden bucket, and Peter gulped it.

Zeke came to the wagon. "Slow down Peter. If you drink too fast, it will make you ill."

"Sho will," Seth said. "Make ya head hurt, too."

"I'm sorry—I mean—I'll slow down."

Zeke took the dipper and drank long and slow, looking over the field as he drank.

"Marse, we is making good time, good time, sho is," Seth said.

Zeke lowered the dipper. "Indeed we are, Seth." He handed the dipper to Seth. "I just hope the Yankees don't come and take it."

"I don't reckon them Yankees going to be coming this here way."

"We have been fortunate this far, but for how long?" Zeke said.

Seth hurried a swallow. "Sho is—sho is. General Forrest get 'em if they comes back down in Mississippi."

Zeke stared absently across the field. "Maybe so." He turned back toward Seth with a hard look. "For the life of me I can't find out what happened to Charlie. He should have been back here two weeks ago."

Peter had heard Charlie's name mentioned often and knew he lived in the big house, but he didn't clearly remember who he was. He barely remembered him from the past visit.

"Now Marse, don't be fretting over Massuh Charlie. He bees back by and by. You know he always stay too long when he go to Memphis. You knows how he is. You member bout that old widder woman up there he go see."

"I reckon, but he has been gone for damn near a month; we need those supplies. I know the Yankees are still buying cotton. Good thing cotton don't spoil."

"Well now, Massuh Charlie bees particular. He gonna heft a right good deal when he sell that bale."

"Master Charlie is probably drunk and has lost the cotton," Zeke said.

"Marse, don't let Mistus hear you say such truck. Lawd knows she set a lot of store on her brother."

Zeke kicked softly at a spoke. "I suppose you're right, Seth. If he ran into trouble with the Yankees, we would have heard something."

"You can depend on that there, Marse. You see, Massuh Charlie be coming back soon in high feather, ready to take this here cotton to Memphis. Oh yessuh. He be done fetched Marse up coffee and salt and everything."

Zeke didn't reply. He surveyed the fields, then studied the sky.

"Yessuh," Seth said to no one, as he drank from the dipper again.

"Sure would be a fine day to go fishing," Zeke said.

"Sho would—sho would," Seth said. "Floy is fixing fish head soup for us niggers this evening now that ya mentions it."

"That sounds good."

"Marse should come and fetch him some of the soup."

"Mrs. Taylor would storm if I ate Floy's cooking. You know that."

"Oh, yessuh, that a fact." Seth grinned.

Zeke turned to Seth. "I want you to go on in."

"Marse, we done settled this here. You ain't gonna be running me in from the field."

"Damn it, Seth; don't sass me."

"I can pick juss as good as any hand on the place."

Peter fumbled for his basket. He knew he was at the wrong location.

"You can pick better." Zeke took the dipper from Seth and placed it in the bucket. "But you are not as young as you used to be. You go on in and see if the boys got the gin ready."

"Marse, I knows the—"

Zeke put his hand up. "Take Peter with you. He has done plenty today for a first-time picker." With that he gathered his sack and headed back to the field.

Peter knew Seth had more liberties than any other on the place, but he knew when not to push it. He had always seemed happy and content on the farm. But how content could a slave be? Peter could only guess at the answer.

"Come on, boy; let us see is them boys got the gin in order," Seth said. They started across the field toward the gin house. "Marse don't know his place no how, picking cotton like a field hand." He rubbed his gnarly hand across his white head. Frowning like a spoiled child, he looked back at Zeke. "Niggers all over these parts laughing at us Taylor niggers for such a foolish marster."

"I would think you would be pleased to have such a master," Peter said.

Trudging on, Seth turned to Peter. A smile grew on his weathered face. "Boy, I declare," Seth laughed. "I is pleased with Marse. I specs he is the bestest marster anywhere."

"But you said—"

"Peter, don't take everything fo sho nuff. I juss wish Marse would let niggers do the nigger work and him do the white folk work."

Peter could not understand this thinking. It seemed to him that they should be happy to have a master working with them, instead of holding it high and mighty over them. He was beginning to see there was more than black and white on many issues.

Seth showed Peter around the gin house. Seth was in charge of the ginning, and the men in the gin house scurried when he walked in. The gin was driven by mules to separate the seed from the cotton fiber. In another building was a large press for baling the ginned cotton.

Peter learned that last year there had been a white man running the gin, but Mr. Taylor had forced him to leave. In fact, the room where Peter now slept had been his. When Peter asked why he was made to leave, Seth told him not to speak on it. Peter later discovered the man left before Mr. Taylor could kill him. Peter suspected he knew what bad thing the man had done. He had noticed it the first day he and Joe had arrived.

***

Joe sat at the supper table beside Fanny. The more he looked at her, the prettier she looked. He believed his own sister, Sarah, would have looked like her some day. Fanny was sweet to him, and she was good to Peter, too.

Zeke took his usual place at the head of the table. He didn't talk much—he didn't have to. Lillie kept everything he needed for supper at his arms' length. Joe saw everything had an order at the table.

Lillie busied herself back and forth from the kitchen, even as everyone else ate. She finally sat when everyone else was half-finished. She dipped food onto her plate in small orderly piles.

"Joe, I didn't see you much today. What did you find to do?" Lillie asked.

"Nothing much." Joe shoveled beans into his mouth. "I visited Aunt Floy in her cabin."

Everything fell silent. Everyone looked at Joe. Joe realized he had done something wrong. What? The silence stretched as he slowly drank his milk.

Fanny broke the silence. "You really went into Aunt Floy's cabin?"

Joe wiped milk from his mouth, noticed all eyes still on him. Zuey appeared at the doorway. Joe tried to figure what he had done wrong. Suddenly he realized what it was. Aunt Floy had told. "I hope you are not mad, Aunt Lillie, but Aunt Floy gave me some soup."

"She gave you soup?" Zuey said.

Joe looked at her. What was going on? "Yeah," he said slowly, "and ash-pone, too."

"She gave you soup and ash-pone?" Fanny said, turning to face Joe.

"Nation, the soup had to have some bread with it. But the sorghum molasses was the best."

"Sorghum!" Fanny and Zuey declared at the same time.

"Well, Joseph, it seems you have done the impossible," Lillie said.

"I will say so," Zeke said. "Not many can come it around Floy."

"Aunt Floy is a fine cook," Lillie said. "All the servants say just that."

"Yes, Ma'am, first rate. That was the best soup I ever ate." Joe quickly realized his mistake. "But as good a cook as Aunt Floy is, she is a far stretch from you, Aunt Lillie."

"Why, thank you," Lillie said, and handed him another biscuit.

Zeke smiled, shook his head as he started back eating.

Suddenly, someone banged on the front door. Zeke went to the door. Joe followed. It was Stepto.

"Wagon a coming, Marse—wagon a coming!"

"Who is it?"

"It bees Massuh Charlie."

"About time."

Joe heard the chairs scooting away from the table.

The wagon lumbered up the drive. All the servants turned out to watch the wagon approach. Children ran along side, some climbed aboard, and some fell off. All were laughing and in high spirits. Many shouted, "What did ya fetch us, Massuh Charlie?"

Firmly, Lillie told Stepto to get the children away from the wagon lest they get hurt. Stepto quickly dispersed the jubilant, then disappointed children.

The wagon finally stopped in front of the house. It was covered with a big, white canvas. The man driving wore a large Panama hat and whitish clothes—they were now dirty from the ride. He was a short, plump man. When he took his hat off to bow to the ladies, Joe saw he was gray and balding. He had a smile on his round, red face from the first, and it was still there now.

"Hello, family," he said as he strained to get down from the wagon.

Still standing on the veranda, Zeke asked, "Where have you been?" His eyes bore down on the man.

Lillie grabbed Zeke's arm. "Now, Zeke, there will be none of that." She let go and walked down the steps to hug Charlie.

"Oh, Sis, it is good to see you. I fetched the needles you wanted." He took them from his vest pocket and handed them to her. He turned to the crowd of servants. It seemed to Joe all the Negroes had turned out and were standing around the wagon. "Stepto, Ben, fetch that cover from the wagon," Charlie said.

The two flipped the cover off revealing a wagon loaded with supplies: two big bags of salt, sugar, coffee, hoes, clothes, and all sorts of merchandise.

Charlie looked at Zeke. "I fetched some bargains, I tell you. They was only allowing one sack of salt, but I come away with two, to be sure."

"It took you long enough," Zeke said. "You should have all of Memphis in the wagon."

"Now, Zeke, don't you be a-talking to me so. The road is not safe, not safe indeed."

The children gathered around him, and he rubbed a girl on her head.

"Others have been coming and going with no problems," Zeke said.

"Well now, I spect so—I spect so. But Zeke, I had to get the news on the war. You know how those falsehoods are spread. Why, you remember we heard Lee had won at Gettysburg only to find out it wasn't true. I got a passel of news—good for sure news, too. I also had to wait on some of them boats to come down from the North, and those Yankees get their merchandise first, pray. And I had to hunt high and low for everything we needed. And Zeke, you can't just go through just any picket line. No, sir. You have to choose a particular lot. Them white Yankee boys, they search everything. Them darky soldiers, why you can come it over on them—yes, sir, indeed—and I did, too."

"You are here now. I reckon that is all that counts."

Fanny and Zuey descended the steps and both hugged Charlie at the same time.

The servants pushed in close. They asked question after question. Charlie answered most of them.

Lillie took Joe's hand and led him to the wagon. The Negroes parted as she walked to Charlie. "This is Joseph. He is Josh's boy."

"Well, I'll be hanged. Last time I saw you boy, you was just a baby." Charlie rubbed his head. "I reckon I'm your Uncle Charlie or close enough to it."

The servants grew loud again, asking what was brought for them.

Charlie turned to address them. "Now, my good people, y'all go on back to your cabins. I'll give you yours later. You know I won't let you down. I know what tonight is."

Joe thought he sounded like some kind of king addressing his subjects. They were clearly disappointed, but they slowly drifted away.

After Stepto finished bringing the supplies into the house, the white folks gathered in the parlor, while Zuey and Peter sat in the kitchen. Joe wished they could sit in the parlor, too, but he knew better than to say so. At least they were close enough to hear what was going on.

Fanny pulled a chair next to Charlie. "Do tell me about Memphis. It has been ever so long since I have been there."

"Oh, child, the town is busier than a mule's tail in July. Steamboats a-coming and a-going all the time. Plenty of everything you want there."

"How did the Yankees treat you?"

"Why they's just as friendly as home folk. They don't seem to get the bad humor until they get out of town. That ain't counting the pickets. They rummaged and dug all in my belongings. They're right confounding, I tell you. Now them darky pickets, they just let me go on by with just one little peek inside."

"Oh, Charlie, you always were good with the colored people," Lillie said, sitting the coffee down in front of the men. "I know it is so late for this, but it has been a stretch since we had coffee."

Joe remembered the coffee in his bag and felt guilty. He could have given it to Aunt Lillie, best not to mention it now.

Zeke pulled a knife from a desk drawer next to his chair, dug and cut at his fingernails. "What news did you hear up there that kept you so long?"

Joe inched closer. Maybe he had news from Virginia.

"Well now, I tell you I do have some news. It seems our General Chalmers made a raid up around Collierville. He was a-confounding the Yankees hither and thither, made off with wagons and prisoners, handsomely. Yes, sir. Ole Chalmers was in high feather. Why them Yankees didn't no more know what was about than a goose." He squeezed Joe's shoulder. "And y'all know what's more than that? Ole Sherman himself saw the whole thing."

"No!" Fanny said, putting her hand to her mouth.

"That's flat! Him and his whole escort was a passing through Collierville when Chalmers was a kicking up his shines."

"I suspect you are going to tell us that is why it took you so long to get back," Zeke said. He wiped the knife on his pants and placed it back in the drawer.

Lillie gave him a hard look.

"Indeed—indeed! That along with other unforeseen reasons."

Zeke got up from his chair. "I'm turning in." He lit another candle, shook his head, and went up the stairs.

It was eight o'clock when Charlie told his last tale of Memphis. He was tired now, so he went to his room, too. Fanny and Lillie wanted to catch up on their sewing; now they had new needles and it was Saturday night.

Joe looked for Peter, but he wasn't in the kitchen; neither was Zuey. He checked Peter's room, but he wasn't there either. Nation, where did that darky get off to?

***

Zuey took Peter's hand, and they eased out of the kitchen while the white folks were talking. They raced toward the quarters. Peter didn't know what to expect when Zuey asked him to come with her, but the melting feeling inside urged him to go.

The quarters were unusually quiet. Peter thought this strange. There was generally some commotion, especially on Saturday night. Mr. Taylor didn't make them work on Sunday if they were ahead on the work. The weather had been good; the picking was ahead of the ginning and storage. There should have been singing, laughing—something, but it was nothing of the sort. Most of the cabins were dark. Peter slowed as they ran by the cabins; something was wrong.

Zuey tugged at his hand. "Come on, goose."

He smiled, followed.

They ran past the last cabin and came to a trail leading through the woods. Peter felt the hairs on the back of his neck stand up as they entered the darkness. Zuey giggled, pulled, ran down the dark path. It was evident she had been down the trail many times. Soon they came to a road, and Zuey hauled him down it. They went about a half mile, and she took him down another trail.

"Why, Peter, I do believe you is scared."

"Not at all. Why would you even think that?"

She said nothing, only giggled and pulled harder at his hand.

The stars danced in and out of the treetops, and the moon was big as it rose in the east. It was orange—harvest moon, Peter had heard it called. It chased them from tree to tree, as they ran. It slowly turned yellow as it climbed.

Zuey knew the trails well, dodging and weaving through the woods. Peter was getting tired, and he was lost, totally depending on Zuey. He felt as if they had been running for hours, though it was only around fifteen minutes.

Up ahead, Peter saw a glow in the woods, brighter than the moon, much brighter. He thought the woods were on fire. As they got closer, he heard people—he heard singing, smelled smoke—pleasant, inviting, like a campfire.

Suddenly, they burst out of the woods into a large opening. There were people, a hundred, maybe more, a large fire in the middle of the clearing and people gathered around it, also several smaller fires scattered around with small groups of people around them. Negroes, all Negroes, laughing and singing. There was music, banjos and tambourines. Peter had never seen anything like it.

Zuey tugged at his hand, and he looked down at her. The orange firelight danced on her face. She was smiling, so beautiful. She put a tender hand behind his head, slowly pulled his face to hers, her lips to his. His legs suddenly grew weak, chest fluttered. His heart hurt for her. It was a feeling he had never known.

A familiar voice trespassed on the special moment. "I see you fetched him here," Stepto said. He gave Peter a mocking punch on the shoulder.

Peter looked around, took it all in. It was a festival of some kind. Zuey hugged him around his body. Whatever it was, it was where he wanted to be.

Joe was at the well, half way between the house and the quarters. It was quiet, too quiet. The only sounds were an owl down by the river and the squeaking windlass as he reeled up the bucket. Where was everybody? He dipped the dipper into the bucket. A frog leaped from the dipper at Joe's face. He dropped the dipper and started. He looked around. He saw no one. The big orange moon had everything lit up like morning, and he could see the goat standing on a wagon. Stupid goat.

Where did Peter go? Where were all the darkies? It was strange, no talking or anything coming from the quarters. Only a few cabins even had light showing. Tomorrow was Sunday, no work.

He saw a shadow or something move at one of the cabins. He squatted behind the well. Someone climbed out the window. When the person slid to the ground, the moonlight revealed his face. It was Washington, that fuzzy head. What was he doing dropping from a window like a tomcat?

Washington crept along the side of the cabin and peeked around the front. He looked back behind him, then darted toward a path leading into the woods and away from the quarters.

Where was he going? Joe looked back toward the big house. The only light was coming from the parlor. Zeke was in the bed. Joe couldn't stand not knowing what was afoot with Washington. He struck out after him. Joe was fast, and he could have caught the younger boy, but that was no good, so he stayed back a ways. Washington never looked back.

Joe had no problem following the boy; the moon was bright. He followed him forever, and finally Joe saw a giant glow in the woods up ahead. He didn't know what it was, but it was where Washington was going. Joe remembered being surprised at Mrs. Donner's and again by Uncle Zeke. He wasn't going to be surprised again. He left the trail and circled around the glow. He crawled on his belly to a big oak. It sounded like a large party or something in the clearing.

He saw more Negroes there than he had ever seen at one time, except at the camp at Helena. Maybe they were planning a revolt like at Haiti. They might kill all of the white folks in their sleep. He should run back and tell Uncle Zeke.

To his left he heard something, moaning. It was close. He felt his pulse rushing in his ears. He snaked over to the sound, had to see what it was, might be captured white people. He saw a black man on top of a black woman. Joe was embarrassed—he knew what they were doing. He crawled far away to another tree.

What were all of these Negroes doing out here? Didn't they know they would get in trouble if found out?

He had to get closer. He crawled to a handcart and slid under it, had to be careful. He saw people sitting on stumps just a few feet away.

A light-colored boy jumped upon a tall stump and started sawing away with a fiddle. Most turned to him. They started clapping their hands and stomping the ground with some queer dance.

Joe spotted three hogs cooking over one of the fires. There would be trouble for sure if it was ever found out they had stolen hogs from their masters. What are these ignorant darkies thinking? Joe had always heard Negroes weren't as smart as whites—this settled the hash.

Two people danced right over to the cart. Joe buried down like a tick. They were jumping and stomping and laughing. They stopped when the music did. Joe heard them talking—it was Peter and Zuey.

So Peter was in with them! You couldn't trust any of them. Fanny was back home tending to Zuey's baby, and Zuey here at this revolt.

Joe thought he heard something behind him. He strained to listen. If only the darkies would hush a minute, he could hear. It was horse's hooves. A horse was coming up the trail. Now these darkies would get it.

What about Peter and Zuey? Well, they had it coming, didn't they? They didn't have any business coming out here. They should have stayed back on the place where they belonged.

The horse came closer.

Peter may not be such a free nigger after this. If they catch him out here with this revolt, he will be a slave sure enough.

Joe could hear the horse plainly, clop—clop—clop.

Damn it, Joe thought. "Peter," he whispered.

Clop—clop—clop.

"Peter!"

Clop—clop—clop.

Peter and Zuey were standing closer to the cart. Joe reached out to grab Peter's leg. Peter moved. Pshaw—he had heard the horse.

Slowly, like wild ducks, they all turned toward the sound of the horse. The place fell silent, except for the crackling fires. Joe saw one stupid nigger was still turning a pig on the fire. Why didn't they run?

Clop—clop—clop.

It was no use. Joe couldn't reach Peter's leg. If he yelled, he would be discovered, and no telling what the darkies would do to him.

The horse finally emerged from the woods. The rider was a white man for sure, but the darkies weren't afraid. They ran to the horse and helped the man down. They greeted him as an old friend. The fiddler started back up, as well as a banjo player on the other side of the pigs. Ben set a chair by the pig-roasting fire. The white man patted the cook on the back, then sat in the chair. The cook tore a piece of meat from a ham and gave it to the man. The man raised the meat up and everyone cheered. The white man turned to face everyone, then ate the meat. It was Uncle Charlie.

He was in with them, Joe thought. But this made no sense, none at all.

Washington crawled into Charlie's lap. Charlie pulled something from his coat pocket and gave it to the boy. It must have been a sweet because Washington gobbled it down.

The cook gave Uncle Charlie another piece of meat. He took a bite and nodded his approval. Charlie gave the rest to Washington.

Joe didn't know the cook. He recognized many of the people from the farm, but most he didn't know. Where did they all come from? The people made their way to the pigs. Joe also saw people going to carts near the fire. They had food on them. Joe realized the cart he was under might have food, too. He had seen enough, so he backed out from under the cart and struck out for the path. The smell of the cooking pigs drifted to him. It smelled good. He hesitated. But he quickly decided against the temptation and left for the farm.

The moon was high now as he left the path and hit the road. He saw horsemen coming. He slid behind a tree. There were five men. Joe felt a shot of fear for Peter. The men were paddy rollers. Joe saw at least two shotguns. This was not good, not good at all.

He ran down his options. He could do nothing and let Peter get his own self out of this fix. Joe knew he couldn't do that. He would have to try to beat the men back to the gathering, but that was almost impossible.

The men stopped at the path. Joe hugged the tree like a lizard. They all looked toward the glow of the big fires. Joe could see the bright glow plainly.

"King Charlie and his African subjects," one said. The others laughed, and they moved past the path and continued down the road.

Why didn't they go check out the fire? After all, that is what paddy rollers did—keep the slaves in line. And what did that man mean by "King Charlie?"

Joe footed it back to the farm. The goat was still standing in the wagon, and his head followed Joe's movement. His big eyes shined like white lights under the full moon. Joe wasn't afraid of the goat during the day, but he looked scary in the dark. All of the lights were out in the quarters, and there were no lights coming from the big house either. Joe walked under a tree and stopped to watch the goat.

Suddenly, rustling and loud squawking came from the tree limbs overhead. Joe dashed for the house. The goat leaped from the wagon and went for Joe. Joe tripped and landed face first in a pile of cow shit. He turned. Chickens were flying down from the tree. The goat was closing in. Joe jumped up and pulled the tomahawk from his belt. The goat skidded to a stop. He stared with his moon-white eyes, bobbed his head a couple of times and went back to the wagon.

Joe wiped the shit from his face and shirt, glad no one saw him running from a bunch of chickens. At least the goat knew who was boss. Joe spit straw. "Damn cow shit." Joe put the tomahawk back and turned for the house. Instantly, he felt as if he had walked into a wall.

"What are you doing out here?" It was Uncle Zeke.

No wonder the goat ran.

"Answer me, boy."

Joe had to come up with a story, and the story had to keep him out of trouble.

"You've been down to the fires, haven't you?"

How did he know? "I've been...a...over at the—"

"Boy, I'll smoke you if you lie to—"

"Yes, sir. I've been to the fires."

Zeke smiled. Joe was relieved.

Zeke looked up at the moon. "Pretty night."

Pretty night for what? Joe wondered. A pretty night for rounding up runaway slaves, a revolt, what?

"Let us go to bed," Zeke said. "We will go to church tomorrow." Zeke turned to go to the house.

"But what about the darkies?" Joe didn't know why he blurted that. He didn't want Peter and Zuey to get into trouble. But damn it, what were all of those niggers doing down there in the woods?

Zeke turned back toward Joe, stood there for a minute looking down at him. "Did you go down there with someone or did you spy on them?"

"Well...I...kind of..."

Zeke looked serious. He looked toward the house, then toward the quarters suspiciously. "I reckon you can come along now that you know. I heard a few blacks were going to gather there, but I didn't want to believe it. We need to get the guns from the house. We shall put a stop to this matter before they rise up and kill us in our beds."

"But it's over a hundred of them!"

"Yes—yes, we shall get help. We shall get Mr. Johnson up the road and his four boys."

That wouldn't be enough white men. They needed an army.

Joe thought of Peter again. "But what about Peter and Zuey?"

"They should have weighed the consequences before going way down there. And Charlie should have known better, too."

Wait a minute. Joe knew he had not mentioned Charlie's name, and why didn't the paddy rollers do something? Joe smiled.

Zeke saw the smile and laughed aloud. "I had you going, didn't I, boy?"

"Yes sir, you got me and good."

"The whites around here let the Negroes have their fun, just as long as it doesn't get out of hand. They have a big Juba a couple times a year."

"But ain't you scared your slaves will run off?"

Zeke frowned. "My slaves? Joseph, I don't own a slave, not one."

Of course, he owned slaves. They called him "Marse," and they worked on his farm. "You are saying the darkies on this farm are not slaves?" Joe asked.

"Yes, they are slaves, but they are not my slaves. They are Charlie's slaves."

"But you—"

"Charlie and Lillie's father was a well-to-do man. He was a speculator. He owned most of the land around here at one time. When he died, he left everything to Charlie, including the slaves."

"But you run the plantation."

"I do. Charlie could never manage anything. In fact, Lillie and I own the farm now."

"Why do you not have slaves?"

Zeke looked up at the moon again, studied it a time, then back at Joe. "No man should own another man."

Joe could not believe he heard it. "But you work the slaves."

"I work them because they are here. I work them because we have to eat, black and white. We have to live, and as long as Charlie keeps his slaves here, they shall have to work."

"If you are so set against slavery, why don't you have Uncle Charlie sell them?"

"Charlie sell his people?" Zeke laughed. "That's like telling a king to sell his loyal subjects." He laughed again. "No one has that kind of money."

Joe followed Zeke into the house. The house seemed different now. Everything was different. Uncle Zeke was more like Uncle Wilbur than Joe had realized.

Chapter 11

Blue jays scolded Joe and Peter as the mules pulled the wagon under the frosty oak tree. Joe wanted to knock them from the tree with a rock, but Peter would have none of that.

The air was fresh and crisp. Joe loved November, his favorite month. Some people liked the flowery smell of spring, but Joe enjoyed fall smells: cotton and fallen leaves.

"Here you go," Peter said, handing Joe the reins. "I reckon we are far enough that Mr. Taylor won't see."

Joe was glad to drive the mules again. He had gotten in trouble a few days back for driving the mules too fast. The wagon rode rough. The hard wheels found every rut and rock on the road to New Albany. Joe wondered how people kept their teeth while riding in such vehicles. He'd rather ride a horse or walk, but a man couldn't haul much that way.

Four Confederate soldiers rode past, gave the boys a hard stare. The rider in the back stopped, didn't like something.

Peter squeezed Joe's hand. He thought Peter was going to break it.

The man turned and saw his companions still going, so he kicked the horse and followed them.

After the soldiers rounded a bend, Peter turned on Joe. "It's the Yankee kepi. You are going to bring peril on us yet."

"Pshaw."

"Why do you insist on wearing it?"

Joe reached up and pulled it down so tight his ears stuck out. "It is mine, so I reckon I can wear it."

"Well, as long as we are in land held by the Confederacy, why don't you not wear it?"

"You won't have to worry about it much longer," Joe said. He snapped the reins. "Get up, mules."

"What are you talking about?"

"Nothing. I said get up there, mules." The wagon lurched forward, and Peter grabbed hold of the seat.

"What did you mean, Joseph?"

Joe looked at Peter, then back at the road. "We've stayed in Mississippi too long."

Peter said nothing.

"We were only going to stay long enough to get fitted and move on. It is time to move on."

Peter stared down the road and said nothing.

"I know you're fond of Zuey, so I aim to go on alone."

Peter continued to look past the mules's ears. A rabbit sprinted across the road.

Joe turned to Peter. "Nation, ain't you going to say nothing."

Peter slowly turned in the seat. "Joe, Mr. Taylor sent a letter to your pa."

Joe wheeled around on the bench. "When? Did he get a reply?"

"Seth said he sent it by Mr. Johnson when he took a load of cotton to Memphis. It was about a week after we got here. No, he hasn't received a reply."

"Don't mean nothing. Mail is just sometimey around here anyhow. You know that. He didn't get any of the mail from Uncle Wilbur at Helena, or he would have known we were there."

"All that doesn't matter. Mr. Taylor has said we aren't leaving until he hears from your pa."

Joe saw it was no use talking to Peter; he wanted to stay with Zuey, so let him stay, but Joe was leaving and soon.

Joe had turned thirteen last month, and he could fend for himself. He had handled himself just fine since Helena. After all, what could they do if he struck out at night? By the time he was missed, he would be in the wind.

"I know what you are thinking. Listen, Joe; winter is coming on.

Wait until spring, and I will go with you."

Joe nodded to satisfy Peter. It seemed to work. There was no need talking about it. Some people's mind was like a steel trap, and Peter's trap was snapped shut.

They neared New Albany and saw the evidence of the Yankees. They had been through during the summer, burned houses and downed fences. Joe now saw how lucky the Taylor place was because it was off the main road, nestled back against the river. They rode on not saying much. What was there to say? The Yankees had said enough with the flame. Joe had been friends with some of the Yankees in Helena, but those Yankees didn't burn Helena. Damn these Yankees. Joe wished they would carry their stealing and murdering asses back up north where they belonged.

They arrived at their destination, the tanyard outside of town. The owner wasn't there, so they had to wait. Joe couldn't stand the smell of the place.

"Peter, let me walk on into town," Joe said.

"You stay right here with me."

"Nation Peter, what could happen just going into New Albany?"

Peter thought for a minute, then reluctantly let Joe go.

***

Many of the buildings had been burned. A lot had been cleaned, but no one could deny the stinking Yankees had been there.

Joe saw the people staring at him as he walked down the street. It was the kepi, but he didn't care. It was his kepi—damn them. He wasn't a Yankee—anyone could plainly see that. He hadn't seen a man yet that scared him enough to make him remove it.

Joe found the store Washington had told him about. Well, it really wasn't a store building—they had been burned along with the churches. It was more like a barn with merchandise in it, but it had sweets. He had to use money from the bag, but he wasn't bothered; he was sure he still had enough money to get him to Virginia. Joe found more items in the barn than he had expected, but the stuff was ridiculously expensive. The storekeeper evidently had made a few cotton trades in Memphis. You couldn't get stuff anywhere else, and the Yankees wanted the fluffy white gold.

Joe realized what the war was all about: cotton. The Yankees wanted it, and they wanted it something bad. He knew they would trade escaped slaves for it; they had done just that in Helena. Now the people in Northern Mississippi were getting whatever they wanted from Memphis. Take a load of cotton—get a load of supplies.

Joe prowled around in the store a bit, then stepped outside to suck on the hard candy he had bought. He sprawled out on a bench and watched the lazy town. It was a different town than he had been used to in Helena—no Yankees.

No sooner had that thought left, when he heard the rumble of horses coming from the south. Everyone in town turned out to see. The riders were a ragged sort; no uniform matched—they were Rebels. They came like a long snake, horses kicking up dirt, men shouting, and waving caps. Joe counted over a hundred before he gave up counting. Some piled from their horses here and there, while others rode on through town. It reminded Joe of a swarm of locusts or the like. After a time the dust settled, and the solders were everywhere and in high spirits.

The town folks descended on them with presents from bread to wine, everyone in high feather. These were their heroes—Joe could plainly see that. These were the warriors with the job of keeping the blue demons out of Mississippi. The Rebels were a tough-looking lot. If that counted for everything, they could keep out the Yankees and the Roman Legions, too.

As Joe was beating dust from his clothes, the storekeeper came out of the barn. "I see they's back again."

"Yeah, and they brought all the dirt in Mississippi."

The storekeeper nodded his head to something across the street. "You see that tall 'un over yonder?"

Joe saw an officer with his staff surrounding him. He was still on his horse surveying the town, had a leather face with a small black beard, and looked as if he wanted to bust somebody's head in.

"That there is General Forrest," the storekeeper said.

Joe stood.

"I knowed him before the war when he's a trading niggers. Saw a man cross him in Memphis once. Weren't no purty sight after Forrest finished up with him. Let them Yankees come on back down and burn us now. Ole Forrest will show 'em what's what."

Forrest continued surveying the town, then his eyes locked on Joe. Katie Bea's eyes were never more penetrating, not on her worst day.

"Son, if I's you, I'd be a taking that Yankee cap off," the storekeeper whispered. Joe slid it off like melting butter off hot corn.

Forrest smiled. He said something to one of his staff and sawed his horse around. He rode north out of town with his staff following like a long tail.

The storekeeper laughed and followed a couple of soldiers into the barn.

General Nathan Bedford Forrest, Joe thought. He will get the Yankees for sure. He is the best the South has. He can whip them coming and going.

Joe absently put the kepi back on and sat back down on the bench. Dust was thick, as was the stinking horse smell, so he put the rest of the candy in his pocket. The soldiers were also everywhere, moving about like flies on a dead possum.

Joe remembered Peter. So many Confederate soldiers would probably frighten him. Hell, he was afraid of everything. Joe couldn't wait to tell him he had seen Forrest. He would tell him Forrest was snatching up big, young darkies to help the army. That would scare the britches off him. He would tell him he had heard Forrest was heading to the tanyard. That would be a hoot.

Joe kicked at horse turds as he headed for the tanyard. Before Joe could leave town, he saw Peter coming in with the wagon. He just couldn't wait. A boy couldn't do anything without a woman or a darky getting in the way. If they would put all the darkies and all the women on a boat and send them—

Joe was knocked to the ground. His ears hummed like a million bees were in his head. He rolled over, saw a soldier on a horse holding a sword. He hit me with the broad side of that, Joe thought. He felt for blood at the back of his head, found none.

"If you ain't no Yankee, you must be a Yankee lover," the soldier said.

The kepi—hit me because of my kepi. Joe could kill the Rebel bastard if he had a way. Joe reached for his kepi lying on the ground beside him. The soldier reared his sword back. The man flew backwards from the horse, and the sword fell to the ground close to Joe. The horse reared, stomped, and fled down the street.

It was Peter. He had pulled the man from the horse, but now the soldier was up and had a revolver in Peter's face.

"You damn stinking nigger, I'll blow you brains out!"

Joe scurried over and raked the soldier's legs from under him. As he went down, the revolver fired.

Peter fell.

Joe and the soldier scrambled to their feet. The man stuck the barrel of the revolver in Joe's chest. The revolver popped. Joe thought he was dead. The gun had misfired, only the cap fired. Joe realized he had the sword in his own hand. He placed the point under the soldier's chin. A drop of blood stained the tip.

The man lowered the revolver. "Careful boy, that thing is sharp."

"You didn't let that concern you when you struck me with it!" Joe felt himself spinning. Things were going in and out of focus—he was looking through a tunnel. He had never felt such rage. He felt hot. Just an inch, he thought. If he pushed just one inch, the man would die. "You killed Peter, you bastard!" Joe believed he could do it—he could push it. Rotten, stinking Rebel.

"All right, son, let him go." Joe heard someone talking, but the voice seemed far away. Everything seemed far away except the end of the sword. "You are the better man," the voice said. It sounded as if the voice was in a hollow cave.

The soldier swallowed hard, and Joe felt it through the sword.

"Put it down, boy," Joe saw the man talking now as he walked behind the soldier. He was an officer.

"He killed Peter, so I aim to kill him."

"No," the officer said. "Peter is still with us."

Slowly the tunnel melted away. The humming in his ears faded. Joe saw behind the officer, Peter on his knees holding the side of his neck. Joe felt his heart rise with relief.

"See." The officer pointed to Peter. "Now put down the sword."

Joe slowly lowered the weapon.

The soldier jerked the revolver up to fire. The officer slapped his hand. "You've done enough, Swortz! Now get the hell out of here."

The soldier cussed and started for his horse, turned. Joe threw the sword at his feet. The soldier picked it up, kicked Peter. "I'll kill you another time, boy."

Peter grimaced as the soldier went to his horse.

Joe started for the soldier.

"Whoa!" The officer caught Joe's arm. "Let it go boy."

Joe pulled free and went to Peter. The bullet had only grazed him.

"Son, don't wear that Yankee cap anymore," the officer said. "The next time someone might be killed." He climbed on his horse. "When you get a little older, come ride with us," he laughed. "We can use you." He whipped the horse and galloped back into town.

Joe helped Peter into the wagon, then ran back and retrieved his kepi. He climbed up beside Peter. Peter said nothing, only stared ahead. Joe pulled his kepi on tight. "Get up mules."

***

The ride back was quiet, just the rattling of the wagon and the clopping of the mules' hooves. It went on that way for a couple of miles; Joe couldn't stand it. "Nation, Peter, it wasn't my fault. That man hit me with that sword."

Peter said nothing.

"Well, I'm leaving in the morning, and you won't have to worry about me no more."

Peter turned on Joe. "You are not going any place! I promised Dr. Taylor I would look after you, and I'm going to do just that, so you get that notion about Virginia out of your fool head."

Peter had never talked to Joe in that tone—he had talked to no one in that fashion. Joe believed he had lost his mind.

Now Peter was sobbing. "You could have been killed back there."

"So! You could have been killed, too."

"That is right, Joseph. We both could be dead right this very minute, and for what?" Peter pulled the cap from Joe's head. "Because of this."

Joe pulled at the cap, but Peter wouldn't let it go. "Give it back."

"No, Joseph. You need to wise up. There is a war going on—a war!"

"I'm not scared."

"I am." Peter wiped his eyes. "I'm very afraid."

Big baby. He's big as a bull and scared of the war. Joe should have left him back at Helena.

Peter touched Joe's arm. "Look, Joe, will you just stay here through the winter? I promise we shall leave in the spring."

Joe studied him. He felt his heart sink. Peter couldn't really handle things well. If he left, who would look out for Peter? After all, spring wasn't that far away.

"The war may be over soon. Vicksburg has fallen, and the Yankees seem to be winning everywhere. You saw what they did at Helena."

Joe shot back. "Uncle Charlie said the Confederates won at Chickamauga!"

"At any rate, maybe it will be over no matter who wins. Even if it is not, we will leave for Virginia in the spring."

Joe studied on it. It was, indeed, getting cold in Virginia by now. It wouldn't be good to be caught on the road when it turned cold. Besides, he had better keep an eye on Peter. He couldn't make it on his own. "We'll wait until spring, but no later."

"That is capital, Joe, capital!" Peter wiped his eyes and sniffed. "Spring will be much better. You will see. We may even get a letter, yet, from your pa."

Joe reached for his kepi. Peter looked at it, then looked into Joe's eyes. Joe slowly pulled the cap from Peter's hand.

Peter turned suddenly. Joe looked around. Ten Rebel soldiers were coming up the road. Joe eased the kepi under his leg. Peter smiled. Joe felt better. He didn't want to fight with Peter. Peter was too soft for that. Peter needed Joe to look after him, so he may as well be good to Peter.

**

The hayloft was the warmest place Peter could find without being inside the house. It was a nice haven for reading the Bible. No one bothered him there, except for Joe—you couldn't hide from him anywhere.

The Bible was the most comfort in the world. Yes, Zuey was a comfort, but not the same comfort as the Lord's book. Zuey made him fluttery inside and melted his heart, but the Bible made him soar, made him free of the world. The words within it were magic, a guide to anything and everything in life. If every man would take the Lord's words to heart, there would be no war. There would be peace in the land and in the heart. *In God is my salvation and my glory: the rock of my strength, and my refuge, is in God. Trust in him at all times; ye people, pour out your heart before him: God is a refuge for us.*

Peter held the Bible close as he thought of Joe. Joe was true to his word. It was now February, and Joe was still on the farm. Thank the Lord for that. Peter knew if Joe struck out for Virginia, he would certainly have to follow. The boy would be protected. Peter had promised. He had promised Dr. Taylor. He had promised himself.

Peter had been awakened by nightmares since the incident in town. In the nightmares, the sword didn't hit Joe flat across the back—it was a deadly cut instead. Peter tried to run as the soldier raised the sword. Peter tried, but he couldn't close the distance. The sword came down like the devil's sickle. Peter couldn't get there in time. He screamed, but no sound came forth. His feet became lead. Joe turned, saw the sword. He looked pleadingly at Peter. Peter didn't have time. He could not move fast enough. The blade carved a crimson swath across Joe's middle. Joe screamed, "Why, Peter?" Peter always woke screaming. Peter stopped. It did no good to remember the dreams, no good at all. He squeezed the Bible tight and prayed for relief from the nightmares. They were God's will, but he prayed God's will would change.

He ran his hands over his worn Bible. Just the feel of the leather moved him, so much power, so much love and wisdom. He could not read all of the pages in it, not because of wear, but the cavity carved in the center. He had cut a neat hole in the center, not too big, just big enough for its purpose. Only Proverbs through Daniel was sacrificed, and he could still read most of that.

Peter looked out the loft door, no one around. He untied the blue ribbon, which bound the book, and carefully opened it to the cavity. He slowly drew out the golden necklace. It was one of the prettiest things he had ever seen. It wasn't only the piece of jewelry, but also the memories that accompanied it.

He remembered Dr. Taylor giving it to him the very day he was killed. He remembered Mrs. Taylor wearing it long before that. She was as much a lady as Dr. Taylor was a gentleman. She always wore it on special occasions. She even wore it when Peter was baptized. He remembered how it stood out so much in Mrs. Taylor's picture over the fireplace.

Peter ran his finger across it, two golden wild pigeons—passenger pigeons. They were feeding each other as doves do while courting. An eye of each bird shown with the profiles: red eyes made of rubies. The birds were enclosed in a circle of gold, studded with small diamonds. Dr. Taylor had said the passenger pigeons represented an abundance of love. Peter knew why. There were billions upon billions of wild pigeons. They were beautiful birds, sleek, swift, and majestic.

Peter kissed the birds, knew he held in his hands an object worth a large sum of money. It was the most prized possession the Taylor family had owned, and now it was his, given to him with love—love that was more valuable than the precious jewelry itself. It was given to him because he was loved.

Now Doctor and Mrs. Taylor were gone, waiting for him in heaven. Mam was there too with his father, and it was a great comfort to know that. However, it was so lonely on earth without them. Peter wiped the tears with his coat sleeve. Thank the Lord for Zuey, and he reckoned for Joe, too.

"Peter!" Joe called from the ground.

Peter dabbed at his eyes and laughed. Never was much time alone before Joe showed up. He placed the necklace back into the Bible and bound the book tight with the ribbon.

"Peter!"

Peter leaned from the loft. "I'm up here."

Joe looked up. "Nation, Peter, you are all the time up there in that old loft."

But you always find me, Peter thought.

"Come on down. They're fixing to kill hogs. Uncle Zeke said everybody's got to help."

Peter took the Bible back to his room and placed it at the bottom of his carpetbag. He climbed on the bed, pulled a loose board aside on the ceiling, and slid the bag in.

***

When Peter rounded the barn, Zeke and Stepto were dragging a dead hog to the pots. Peter counted three big black pots full of boiling water, and twenty people were gathered for the killing. Knives were sticking in chop blocks, ready for the work, and children were sharpening sticks to roast pieces of guts in the fire for a treat. Joe punched the dead hog.

"Massuh Joe, stop that," Seth said. "You is gonna spoil the meat." Joe gave it one last punch.

"Peter, grab hold," Zeke said.

Peter grabbed a leg. The men doused the hog headfirst into the scalding water. They quickly swapped ends without the hog touching the ground and stuck the hog in rear-first. The women went to work on the hog from there and began scraping the hair from the animal. They removed most of the hair, but another dousing was needed, so the men scalded the hog again. Then four men hefted the hog to the poles, hanging it from its hind legs. Joe punched the hog again.

"Boy!" Zeke said.

Peter knew Joe couldn't help himself. Trouble always pecked Joe on his shoulder.

Stepto and Peter grabbed the second hog. It was bleeding from its head where Stepto had hit it with a big hammer. Suddenly the hog started squirming and squealing. They would have stuck that live hog in boiling water. The thought turned Peter's heart.

"Where's the hammer?" Zeke yelled. "Get the hammer!"

They scrambled for the hammer, but it was lost.

The hog squealed—almost screamed.

Peter covered his ears. It was unbearable. It was horrible.

The hammer could not be found, so Zeke pulled a knife from the block.

Peter turned from the terrible scene. He prayed to the Lord for mercy.

Peter heard a thud, then the hog was silent. There was another thud, then another, and another. He turned. Joe was over the hog swinging his tomahawk. Over and over it landed on the hog's head. The hog had stopped moving, and everything was quiet, except the whacking of the tomahawk.

"That's enough," Zeke said.

Joe continued swinging.

Zeke grabbed his arm. "That's enough, Joseph."

Joe looked at Zeke. Joe appeared far away, like someone who has awakened from a deep sleep and doesn't know where he is. Blood was splattered over his face like mud. He wiped the tomahawk on his pants and stuck it back into his belt. He stepped away from the hog. Everyone watched him. His chest rose and fell with heavy breaths. "He won't squeal now," Joe whispered. "Never again."

Joe's face was red and flushed. Peter had never seen him like that. His eyes were wild—animal eyes. He had taken no joy in putting the hog out of its misery. No, it needed to be done, so he did it. But he did it too coolly. He didn't kill the suffering animal as a farmer would. He killed it as a soldier would kill his enemy.

The men dragged the hog to the pot, and the chore continued, many hogs to kill, and time was wasting.

Joe slipped away to the house. Peter watched him go and wondered what was going through his mind. What gave him such control when it was needed? But Peter knew Joe was not made of iron. Joe stealing away to the house proved that.

"Fetch on over here and catch a leg," Seth said.

Peter felt his stomach roll. Things faded to a gray, then slowly to almost white. Peter ran. He had to get away. He found himself behind the barn leaning against the wall turning his stomach out. He heaved until it hurt and nothing left.

I'm not much of a man. How could anyone stand that? How could anyone stand the screaming? How could Joe whack away at the hog in such a manner?

"Peter?"

It was Zuey. Not now, he thought. Please don't see me this way.

She placed a light hand on his shoulder. "Peter?"

Peter wiped his mouth, then his eyes.

"Is you... Is you all right?"

Peter could have crawled in a hole and died right there. He wished she would just go away.

"Please answer me, Peter."

He turned to her. "I'll be fine."

"Let us go to the well and fetch you some water."

Peter wished he could hide in the well.

Charlie was standing at the well. "Peter, do you feel ill?"

"I believe he will be fine, Massuh Charlie," Zuey said. "He juss done et something that don't agree with his belly."

"Do tell, do tell," Charlie said, cranking the bucket from the well. "Here, my boy; let me fetch you some cool water. It's bound to make your belly feel a mite better." Peter knew Charlie had seen the whole thing.

Zuey dipped the dipper into the bucket and gave it to Peter. "Thank you, Massuh Charlie."

The cool water did help. It was soothing going down, but it did nothing for the embarrassment now that the incident was over.

Washington ran to the well. He started squealing like a pig and laughing. He danced around Peter and was soon joined by other children, dancing and squealing.

"Stop that!" Zuey said. "Y'all stop that right now."

Peter wished he could melt into the ground.

Charlie grabbed Washington and held him over the well. The other children stopped and fell silent.

"Well now, Wash, I do declare you don't seem to be in such good humor now," Charlie said. "And I reckon you other little people want to come around to the fun Mr. Washington is a having right here and now?" He smiled, and his face glowed like a red ball.

"Mass—Mass—Massuh Charlie—I's be good—I's be good. I swear!" Washington said.

"I don't know on it, Wash. Your shines is powerful hurtful to folks." Charlie winked at Peter and Zuey. "What do you reckon on it, Peter? Do you think young Washington here has done learned a lesson?"

Peter felt better. Charlie had taken the attention away from him and placed it on that little bother, Washington.

"Mr. Charlie, I declare I do believe he has," Peter said.

"I is—I is!"

"Madam Zuey, what is your opinion on this particular matter?" Charlie said.

"Massuh Charlie, I's of the opinion we should be asking Washington," she said.

"I had not studied on that, Madam, but you are surely correct. He is, after all, the one in a predicament."

"Please, Massuh Charlie!" Washington said. His eyes were wide, looking down the well.

"Boy, if I fetch you down, are you going to be a good little fellow?"

"I bees a angel!"

Zuey and Peter laughed.

Charlie put Washington down and rubbed his head. Charlie moved to his chair under the big shade tree. The children followed him, and when he sat, they all tried to climb into his lap. He laughed. "I declare my, little people, there ain't enough dog for the fleas."

Zuey took Peter's hand. "Massuh Charlie is a good man."

Peter agreed with that for sure. Charlie was one of those rare men that oozed goodness. Obviously, he wasn't a responsible man, because if he were, he would be helping with the hog slaughtering. But he was still a good man.

"Is you feeling better?" Zuey asked. She smiled. Peter thought it the prettiest smile in the world.

"Better."

She smiled bigger.

He wished he hadn't promised Joe he would leave with him in the spring. He believed he could stay on the farm with Zuey forever.

"Come, Peter, walk to the house with me. I's got to tend the babies."

"No, you go. I've something I must do."

"I'll see you at dinner then." She left for the house.

Peter took several deep breaths, watched the children climbing around on Charlie, clinched his fists and relaxed them several times. There were more hogs to be killed and butchered, then salted. He would do his part—somehow. Another deep breath, then he went toward the butchering.

***

After washing off the hog blood, Joe went to his room and closed the door, sank on the bed and stared at the blue striped paper on the wall. Helena crept into his mind like a bad dream. It was the hog butchering that carried him back there. He could see the house where Uncle Wilbur and the surgeons were tending to the wounded—the blood and the smell like hog guts.

He wished he had not thought of Helena. Now he couldn't get dying out of his head: Ma, Sarah, Uncle Wilbur, Katie Bea. He could see all of them dying all over again. He could see the explosions on the hill behind the house, and men flying into bits. But the worst was the dead captain in the gully. He got up from the bed before he started crying. Crying was no good. It never helped anything. Besides, what would he be crying over, hog butchering?

He went to the window and looked down at Charlie and the little Negro children. They were having fun climbing about Charlie as if it were the best game in the world. They were so ignorant. Didn't they know what waited for them when they were old enough? They would be in the field. They would be doing whatever the master wanted them to do. Joe would rather be dead. Joe reckoned it was all they knew. It was home to them, and life.

Joe looked up toward the eastern horizon and thought of Virginia. Somewhere to the north and east was home, the Shenandoah Valley, mountains and clear streams and cornfields like a yellow sea. Joe prayed his pa was there, too—he had to be there. Joe was tired of Arkansas and Mississippi and its baggage. He wanted to go home and see people he knew. He wanted to see familiar sights, like the mills, and Mr. Cain's big red barn. He wanted to see home.

He heard someone coming up the stairs, then a knock at the door. Fanny walked in. As usual, she looked as sweet as honey.

"Hello, Joe." She moved to the window. "Uncle Charlie sure has a way with the children."

"I don't know why they are so happy," Joe said. "They ain't nothing but slaves."

She put her tender hand on his shoulder. "Why, Joe, you know they are treated well here."

"But don't you reckon they would rather be free?"

She smiled. "Pa says they will be freed soon."

"You think the Yankees are going to win the war?"

"Oh, I hope not. Pa says slavery is doomed even if the Confederacy prevails."

"Pshaw! You ain't never been on one of those big plantations that has a couple of hundred niggers, have you?"

"Joe, don't call them that. They are Negroes." She smiled warmly, and Joe felt embarrassed. "Yes, I have seen those big plantations."

"Well, you know those rich planters ain't never going to set their nig—Negroes free."

"Pa believes we will see the time."

"I wish the Negroes were still in Africa," Joe said. "If they weren't here, there would be no war."

"But they are here, Joe, and we must take care of them."

Joe studied on that a minute. Take care of them? "What do you mean?"

She pulled his kepi off and rubbed his hair down, then placed it back on. "We are a more educated people and know more things. They are a loving, but ignorant people, so we should guide them and show them the ways of the world."

"Why not just set them free and let them fend for themselves?"

Fanny laughed. "Joe, you are a silly boy. You sound like Pa, but I believe you are so wrong. We must take care of them. We must guide them in the right direction in life, since they are not as intelligent as we."

Joe saw no point in this discussion. Darkies were a lot of trouble, but Peter was as smart as any white person that Joe knew and smarter than most.

"Joe, the reason I came up here was to tell you Mother wants you to take some coffee to Pa. It is ever so cold outside."

"Tell her I will be down in a few minutes."

After Fanny left the room, Joe watched Charlie with the children. Past them, he saw two servants hauling firewood up to the house.

Take care of them? Joe thought. It is cold outside, but are they offered coffee?

Chapter 12

Joe liked his job in the barn that afternoon. All he had to do was whack the salt with an ax handle. Peter had to smear it on the hog meat.

"This salt burns," Peter said. He waved his hands like a squirrel's tail.

Joe laughed. "I told you it would find that little cut on your hand. Here let me help with the meat."

Joe worked the salt over the hams and shoulders while Peter found a bucket and rinsed the salt from the cut.

Joe didn't mind work as long as he wasn't working in the cotton fields. That was field hand work, and if they didn't grow it in the Shenandoah Valley, it wasn't worth messing with.

Joe watched Peter attack the meat again. Peter didn't miss a spot, always took pride in his work. Joe knew Peter had always done his best at everything. He was the most dependable Negro Joe had ever seen. The more Joe thought on it, Peter was the most dependable person—black or white—he had ever known. He now worked fast and whistled some Negro song Joe had heard before, but didn't know the name. Katie Bea had whistled it, too.

Joe missed Katie Bea. He and Peter had something in common: they had both lost their mother. Joe could see both of them in his mind. It only—

"Where is your mind again, Joseph?" Peter asked, dabbing the salt from the cut on his hand.

Joe knew better than to tell him he was thinking of Katie Bea—no need to upset him, so he stretched the truth. "I'm thinking about home in the Valley."

"I should have reckoned on that," Peter said. He smiled.

"The Shenandoah Valley must be a special place."

Joe perked up. "It is the prettiest place on earth."

"Oh, yes; you've told me." Peter laughed. "Helena was pretty to me."

"That swamp hole?" Joe grabbed another handful of salt. "The Valley beats it decidedly."

"Well, I can't argue on it because I don't remember Virginia, but I think you are cutting Helena short."

"Pshaw!" Joe whacked the salt as if he were mad at it.

"Helena has its swampy places to be sure," Peter said, "but mainly because there were too many Union soldiers crowded into a small area." Peter turned over a pork shoulder and layered it with salt. "In the spring, you will be hard pressed to find something as pretty as the hills and ravines when the dogwoods and redbuds are in full bloom."

Joe thought about it, and Peter had a good point. The hills around Helena were beautiful with the red and white blossoms.

"And where did you ever see and hear prettier birds than up and down Crowley's Ridge in the spring?" Peter blew at the cut. "I think we see good where we want and bad where we want."

Peter may be right. Joe remembered the sun peeking over the Mississippi River, and he often thought it was as if God himself was peeking out of Mississippi and into Arkansas. The mighty river was a marvel, too. It seemed a mile wide at Helena. You would have to go to the ocean to see more water at one time.

"I know what Helena is like," Peter said. "Tell me more about the Shenandoah Valley again. I like hearing it."

Joe rubbed his hands together, knocking off the salt and leaned on the wooden table. "The Valley is about a hundred miles long."

"That big?" Peter said. "I figured it to be smaller."

"In places it is over twenty miles wide. There are mountains to the east and west. The whole valley is gentle rolling hills, and there are streams and small rivers throughout, including the Shenandoah River."

"Sounds nice."

"Oh, it is Peter. The farms are well kept, and there are mills everywhere, and beautiful barns." Joe fell silent. He longed for home even more now that he talked about it. He wanted to splash in the millstreams. He wanted to see the sun climb over the mountains in the mornings.

"What do they grow there?"

"Mostly corn and wheat, but they grow a little of everything. It's some of the prettiest farmland you will see anywhere."

"I reckon they have many slaves there with all of that farmland," Peter said, salting the last ham.

"Some." Joe wiped his hands on his pants, getting the last of the salt off. "Our neighbor, Mr. Karl Stein and his boys were against slavery. They said they would never fight for the Confederacy."

"They were abolitionists?"

"I don't know about that, but they were Mennonites."

"What are Mennonites?" Peter asked.

"They are church people." Joe tried to remember more about them, but now it seemed so long ago. "I believe they were Germans."

Joe and Peter placed the last of the meat in wooden boxes and covered it with a big blanket.

"Did your pa have slaves?"

"Naw. Pa said there wasn't any work that a Negro could do that he couldn't." But Joe remembered his father did hire a slave one time named Jack from his owner, Mr. Culler. Jack helped with planting sometimes. But that wasn't like owning a slave. Mr. Culler owned him. It was more like a hired hand.

A rider came pounding down the lane. Joe and Peter ran outside. It was a Confederate soldier. He dismounted and Washington took his horse—that was one thing Washington could do. The soldier slid his cap off and went to the front door. Lillie invited him in.

Joe looked toward the house. "What do you reckon?"

Peter rinsed his hands in a bucket and looked past Joe to see the man's horse. "I'm sure I don't know, but he has ridden that horse hard."

"I'm going to slip through the backdoor and see what's about," Joe said.

When he opened the door, he heard crying. He looked around

the doorway into the parlor. Fanny was on the sofa with her face in her hands, sobbing. Zuey and Lillie were sitting on both sides of her, and Charlie was in the rocker.

"How did it happen, Tom?" Lillie asked.

"We was up around Nonconnah, gonna skirt below Memphis when they jumped us. We thought we had got away clean, but one of them made a long rifle shot. Robert never felt no pain. But Fanny, I'm afraid we couldn't get him. I'm sure them Yankees saw to his burying."

Fanny dropped her head on Lillie's shoulder.

"I shall fetch him home, Fanny," Charlie said. "Me and the boys will fetch him right home—I declare it."

Joe was so involved in the story, he hadn't noticed that Zeke had come up behind him, until he walked by into the parlor.

"Hello Tom," Zeke said.

Tom stood and shook Zeke's hand. "Hello, Mr. Taylor. I was telling—"

"I heard."

Tom turned his cap absently in his hands. "I sure am sorry."

Tears welled in Zeke's eyes; he nodded, went to Fanny and stroked her hair as she sobbed on Lillie's shoulder.

"Mr. Taylor, there is more bad news. The Yankees are on their way back down from Memphis. They are coming from Holly Springs way. The captain believes they will come through New Albany. Sir, you better get ready for them."

"How many?"

"We reckon six or seven thousand."

"Oh, my God!" Lillie said, moving her hand to her mouth. "What shall we do?"

"Will Forrest stop them?" Zeke asked.

"We will make a stand I'm sure, but it will probably be south of here. I'm sorry, sir."

Zeke nodded.

"I must catch my outfit," Tom said, as he turned for the door. He turned back. "Mr. Taylor, the Yankees will be here within hours I believe." He crammed his cap back on and bolted through the door.

"Lillie, we must be ready," Zeke said. He touched her cheek, then went out the door.

Joe wanted to say something comforting to Fanny, but he didn't know what to say, so he said nothing.

"Zuey, get someone to help you dig a hole behind the springhouse," Lillie said. "We must hide our valuables. When you cover it up, it must not be recognizable. Do you understand?"

"Yessum." Zuey stood, waiting for further orders.

"Go now, Zuey!" Lillie said.

Zuey fled though the backdoor.

Charlie kissed Fanny and exited through the front door.

Lillie held Fanny's face in her hands. "Honey, we must prepare for the Yankees."

Fanny wiped her eyes and put on the strongest face that she could. "I will be ready, Ma."

Lillie hugged Fanny one last time before they went to work.

When Joe went to the backyard, it was all activity. Mules and cows were being led toward the woods down by the river. The salted meat was being placed in a wagon. It was almost like Mrs. Donner's Plantation back in Mississippi.

"Now my people, we must be orderly," Charlie said. "We must have the Yankees believing this here is a poor farm." He strolled back and forth like a real overseer seeing to every detail. Joe had never seen Charlie do anything with such a purpose.

Peter ran to Joe. "The Yankees are coming!" Peter looked around. "We must help hide the stock."

Joe grabbed Peter's arm. "Fanny's husband, Robert, was killed by the Yankees."

Peter looked toward the house. "Poor Mrs. Fanny. And now the Yankees are bearing down on us. Never got to meet him."

Charlie called to Joe. "Fetch as many chickens as you can, boy. Get the children to help you."

Joe saw Zeke pulling the white mare from behind the barn. He said something to Stepto, and Stepto mounted the mare and galloped up the lane toward the main road.

Joe and the children chased the chickens, but it was no use. The birds squawked and darted about, then flew up on the buildings or up in the trees. They only caught a few and had to give up on the rest.

The slave women helped hide the valuables from the big house. They labored along side Lillie and Fanny. Men had dug a hole behind the springhouse and what would fit was deposited there. They piled hay over the hole.

Negroes were coming back from the woods after another round of livestock when they started pointing toward the northwest. It looked like smoke just above the trees. Zeke studied it as he pulled on one of the milk cows.

"What is it, Uncle Zeke?" Joe asked.

"Dust."

"Dust? From what—"

"Hush!" Zeke cupped his hand to his ear.

Joe listened. He heard it—the rumbling from horses' hooves from the main road over a mile away. Now he remembered the Iowa Cavalry back at LaGrange. How could he have forgotten that.

Stepto came tearing back down the lane. He reined the mare just short of Zeke and Joe. "Marse—Marse!" Stepto was almost out of breath as if he had done the running instead of the horse. "Marse Johnson's nigger, Lue, fetched me up at the end of the lane. He say the Yankees done went and killed Marse Johnson and his boy Phillip. He say they was tearing up the house, and Marse Johnson tried to stop 'em, and they shot him dead. He say Young Massuh Phillip pulled a gun and they shot him, too. He say it a million of them blue bellies. Lue say they ain't ten minutes behind me."

Joe looked around and the women were on the back porch; they had heard it all. Lillie ran down to Zeke and threw her arms around him. "Zeke, you go to the woods with the livestock and hide there," she said.

"I'll stay right here."

The dust cloud was at the end of the lane now.

"Take the mare and go now," Charlie said.

"If they are going to kill someone, they will kill you just as well as me," Zeke said.

"I'm an old man. I'm harmless for heaven's sake." Charlie took the reins from Stepto and handed it to Zeke. "They see me, they may take pity, but your temper will get us all killed."

"Please Ezekiel," Lillie said.

He looked down at Lillie, then looked up and saw the dust getting close; he jumped on the mare. "Do what the Yankees say and maybe it will come out right." He sawed the horse around. "Heah!" He galloped through the field toward the river.

"Everyone, try to appear as normal as possible," Lillie said. "Please don't let on that our stock is down by the river. Please, I pray you." She lifted her dress slightly and ran to the house, ushered Fanny and Zuey inside.

"All right my people, it will be fine, just fine," Charlie said. "The Yankees ain't here to bother us. They are after Forrest—not us. We will not give them cause to cross with us."

Soon about twenty-five horses galloped down the lane. Charlie moved to the front of the house. Dust rolled through the yard as the soldiers dismounted.

A fat sergeant, looking the place over, walked up to Charlie. "This your place?"

"I reckon it is. Is there something I can do for you, Sergeant?"

"I see you have a lot of slaves on the place." The man moved past Charlie and looked at one of the young women. "Lots of slaves means lots of wealth."

"The well is around here, if you men need water." Charlie pointed in the direction of the well.

The man grinned. Joe thought he looked like a smiling fat egg. The sergeant gestured to the other soldiers, and they scattered like a covey of quails. They had the routine well rehearsed. Some went into the house, others went to the barn, and outbuildings, while others raided the slave quarters.

"Sergeant, I have nothing to hide," Charlie said, stepping between the man and the Negro woman.

"Well now, that's fine, just fine." The man shoved past Charlie and went to the house.

Joe ran around to the backdoor. The soldiers were rummaging through the kitchen. They hardly noticed Joe when he came in. The women were sitting in the parlor, comforting each other. The soldiers stomped the floor and poked at the ceiling with their rifles, looking for loose boards and hiding places. Joe could see they had plenty of experience at this type of soldiering. He heard some of them knocking around upstairs; then one man came down with a armload of Fanny's dresses.

"Oh, Ma!" Fanny said and buried her face on Lillie's shoulder.

"You ain't going to take those are you?" Joe said. He grabbed at the dresses, and the soldier pushed him down.

"Don't hurt him!" Lillie said and helped Joe to his feet.

"What you got that kepi on for, boy?" the soldier said. "You want to be a Union man?" He laughed and snorted like a pig.

Another man came down the stairs with some of Zeke's clothes. Another followed with shirts and Joe's carpetbag.

"Rotten, stinking thieves," Joe said, pulling at Lillie's grip.

Zuey stood. "You is not soldiers. You is cowards and robbers."

"Shut up, nigger," the sergeant said as he came from the kitchen. "We came here to free your black ass." He squeezed Zuey's cheek. "You is a handsome gal, I tell you." He turned toward the soldiers at the foot of the stairs. "What say, boys? I think I'll take this wench for mine."

They laughed.

Fanny leaped from the couch and swung a lamp at the sergeant. He moved to the side and grabbed her arm. "You stinking murderers! Y'all killed my Robert."

The man shoved her back down on the couch. "I'll burn this house down if you try a shine like that again."

Zuey and Lillie went to Fanny. The babies began to cry, so Zuey went to them.

A gunshot cracked outside. The men dropped the loot, grabbed their guns, and ran out the doors. Joe followed one out the backdoor. Two of the slave cabins were on fire, and soldiers were coming out of others like rats. They are even robbing the Negroes, Joe thought. The goat was dead—they had speared a sword through his neck.

Joe saw Seth kneeling beside Floy at the front of their cabin. Charlie was sitting flat on his butt holding one of her big hands in his. Her eyes were closed.

"This damn big fat-ass nigger hit me with that big stick," a little skinny soldier told the sergeant. He turned toward Floy. "You won't hit nobody else with it, will you, Aunt?" He laughed.

Seth placed Floy's head in his lap and wept. Lillie ran past Joe and moved Charlie out of the way so she could tend Floy.

"What sort of men are y'all?" Charlie asked. Crying, he staggered to his feet and started toward the skinny man. The man raised his revolver and Charlie stopped as if he had been struck.

"I'll give you what that fat-ass woman got."

Joe saw Zeke coming across the field on the mare. A shot rang out. Zeke and horse tumbled. The Negroes shrieked as they ran toward him. Lillie screamed and put her face in her hands.

Joe ran to the house. This was a nightmare. He stormed into the kitchen.

Zuey was holding both babies. "What's happening Joe?"

He ignored her. Where was Fanny he wondered, but he didn't have time for that. Joe pulled his revolver from the bag the soldier had dropped. He ran around to the back of the house and stopped at the corner. All of the soldiers were either looking in the direction of Floy or Zeke. Joe ran to the barn and climbed to the hayloft. He scurried to the opened door and slid under the hay. Now he would pick off the one that needed shot the most.

Before Joe could draw a bead, he heard a loud whop. Fanny had popped one of the soldiers over the head with a shovel. She went after another, but the egg-shaped sergeant came up behind her and punched her in the head with his fist. She fell instantly. The sergeant kicked her for good measure.

Peter ran screaming and hit the sergeant like a train. Before they were on the ground good, he straddled the man and pounded him in the face with his fist. Joe had never seen Peter in such a state. Joe wished he was down there helping Peter. Joe felt surprise and pride.

A corporal hit Peter in the face with the butt of his rifle. Peter fell over slowly like a falling tree. The man turned the rifle around and pointed the muzzle at Peter.

Lillie screamed at the man as she ran toward Fanny and Peter. They were lying side by side like corpses.

Joe couldn't get a clear shot. He was afraid he would miss and hit one of his friends on the ground.

The corporal turned and yelled at Lillie. Joe saw his chance as the man moved. He fired. The revolver sounded like a cannon inside the loft. The man dropped the gun and grabbed his shoulder as he twisted to the ground and fell over the sergeant, who was trying to get to his feet. All the soldiers were looking for the shooter, but Joe was buried in the hay like a flea.

The sergeant wallowed on the ground like a hog trying to get up. "I think it came from the barn."

The men started for the barn with their rifles at ready.

"Just burn the damn thing!" the sergeant yelled.

The corporal scrambled to his feet and ran into Floy's cabin. He came back with a stick of firewood.

Soon Joe saw the smoke rising in the barn, but he stayed buried in the hay. He would take another as soon as he got a clear shot.

More Yankees galloped up. A lieutenant jumped from his horse. "What is going on here?" He didn't wait for an answer. "Sergeant, get this bunch of sorry excuses for soldiers on their damn animals and get back in the column."

"Sir, they attacked one of my men, and—"

"They should have killed him. Get his ass across a saddle and let's move out."

Charlie ran to the lieutenant. "These here men have shot two people, and my barns afire."

The lieutenant looked around, then spat on Charlie's shoes. "I've seen a good many of my men killed by you damn Southerners. So I don't give a damn." He watched the flames climbing in the barn. "You've got all of these slaves. Get them to put it out." He yelled out to the Negroes, "If any of you darkies want your freedom, follow us. If not, keep your black asses here." He climbed on his horse. When he saw none of the Negroes were coming, he muttered, "What the hell are we doing down here?" He spurred his horse, and the troops left up the lane like a long snake.

The Negroes were throwing water on the fire when Joe lowered himself down with the hoist rope, but it was no use. The barn was full of hay, and the flames were overwhelming.

Chickens that had taken refuge in barn were squawking in the barn, but nothing could be done.

Zeke came into the yard, stopped and stared at the burning barn. He made no effort to put it out. Joe knew as Zeke did: it was too late. At least Zeke was alive—thank God for that.

Lillie ran to Zeke. "Oh, Zeke, I thought you were dead."

Zuey helped Peter and Fanny to the house. Good, Joe thought, they will be all right.

"Marse, why them Yankees kill my Floy?" Seth put his fists to his eyes. "Why they do that?"

"Seth, you hush now," Lillie said. "The lead is just below the skin. I shall get it out."

"Why she ain't talking to me?" Seth said, pouting.

"Shut up, you foolish old man," Floy whispered, and slowly opened her eyes."

Lillie called to Stepto, "Get Ben to help you, and you carry Aunt

Floy to her bed. Come on now, and do be gentle."

The two young men gently picked her off the ground. They groaned under the weight. Seth followed them into the cabin like a worried bitch dog.

Zeke picked Floy's hickory stick from the ground. There was a bullet hole blasted in the side of it. "I reckon this slowed the ball just enough."

Lillie wrapped her arms around Zeke. "I thought they had killed you."

"No, but they killed the mare, shot in the head.

Washington ran to Zeke. "Marse, they done got the stuff!"

They all went to the springhouse. The hole had been discovered. Hay was scattered everywhere, and a few pieces of silverware were left scattered, along with a few other precious items where the Yankees had dropped them.

"Damn this war!" Zeke said. "Damn it all." He kicked at the hay and hit the springhouse with his fist.

Fanny approached. She appeared lost as she picked up a small picture frame and wiped the dirt from it. She said nothing as she turned and went to the house.

Joe felt a rage growing. It grew like fire being rushed with a bellows. He went back around the springhouse. The barn was almost down. The Negro women were crying. Their cabins had been robbed of the few possessions, and two cabins were set afire, but at least they had been saved. Joe stood as close to the barn as the heat would allow. The rage inside him grew hotter as the last wall caved in. Yankees had done this and for what? Was Fanny a Rebel? Was Uncle Zeke a Confederate? Was Aunt Floy a Secessionist? Joe pulled the kepi from his head and chucked it into the fire. He pulled his shirttail over the revolver. He didn't want the family to see it and take it—may need it again.

Chapter 13

Pink and red-painted clouds covered the setting sun when Peter led the last milk cow to the barn. The new barn wasn't much, just rough lumber and scraps, but it would do until a better one could be built; little hay was left to put in it anyway. Peter was proud of it even if it was shoddy—he had helped build it.

He closed the door to the barn, thought about the day the Yankees came. He would always remember it, had to keep from hating them. He bowed his head and turned to the Lord once again. *Be ye angry, and sin not: let not the sun go down upon your wrath: Neither give place to the devil.*

Peter still could not understand the Yankees. They were supposed to be fighting against slavery. Yet, they were no different from the Rebels. What difference did it make the color of the uniforms if they burned the citizens's barns and even shot them? At least, Forrest had run them back to Memphis.

Fanny sat on the porch swing with her baby, looked blankly across the fields; her black dress dusted the floor as she swung. She didn't talk much anymore, and she smiled less. Poor girl, Peter thought. This war commanded a high price from many people—too many. He knew too well how Fanny felt. Time would ease the pain—time is magic that way, but the war goes on, and new pains can come, and they do come, over and over and over. Peter prayed God would ease Fanny's suffering through this difficult time.

The door to Floy's cabin opened, and Joe stepped outside gnawing on a biscuit. Floy patted Joe on the top of his head and smiled. Then she saw Peter looking and quickly scowled at Joe. "Now you get outta here, Massuh Joe," she said as she shoved him. "I ain't got no time to be a fooling with the likes of you." She reached inside, grabbed the hickory stick, and waved it in the air. Peter saw the bullet hole in it. She looked around to show she was still boss of the cabin, then went back in and slammed the door.

"Want a bite?" Joe asked, molasses running down his chin.

"No thank you. Floy would hit me with that stick if I ate part of your biscuit."

Joe turned back toward the closed door and smiled.

"I'm sure happy that bullet didn't do much harm," Peter said.

Joe stuffed the rest of the biscuit in his mouth. With his cheeks swelled like a chipmunk, he sputtered, "Me, too."

Charlie called to Peter. Charlie was sitting in his favorite spot under the big shade tree. Peter reckoned it didn't matter to him if it cast a shade or not, certainly no shade in March.

Peter sat in the chair across from him. "Yes, sir, can I do something for you?"

"I was just sitting here thinking before I went into the house." Charlie lit a cigar. "This here warm weather done got me to thinking about springtime, and that done got me to thinking about catfish." Charlie rubbed his round belly. "Wouldn't some catfish be first rate?"

"Yes sir, that would be fine, indeed."

"Reckon you and the boy can go fetch us some from the river in the morning?"

"I'm not that good at fishing, Uncle Charlie."

Charlie waved that off with his fat hand. Blowing smoke, he said, "Hog wash, boy. Anybody can catch a catfish, I'll be bound. Just put something rotten on a hook and they'll bite it. Joseph will show you how it's done."

"Mr. Taylor says we have to get things done around here before plowing—"

"Plowing can wait, mind you. There ain't nothing more important that I know on than catching us a mess of catfish tomorrow. My people can tend to the work."

Peter didn't want to upset Charlie, but Zeke would be angry if he didn't work tomorrow. Peter sat there quietly for a time. He was between a rock and a hard place.

Charlie saw his dilemma. "Oh bother, boy, I'll talk to Zeke tonight. Now that settles the hash. You two shall get after them fish tomorrow."

***

Peter ate supper at the kitchen table with Zuey, watched as she chewed food and gave it to her baby. He felt so relaxed and comfortable.

Zuey looked at him. "You best eat your food before it get cold."

"Who's his father?" Peter was more surprised than Zuey at the question, but since it was out, he let it stand.

Zuey looked at him as if he had pulled a gun.

He would not take it back. He didn't want to pry, but for some reason he didn't understand, he wanted to know. But didn't he already know?

She looked down at the table. "It was a white man," she whispered.

Peter wanted to comfort her. He wanted to say he was sorry for even asking. After all, was it any of his business? He said nothing.

"He was a hired man on the place," she continued. "Marse thought a heap on 'em." She smashed a pea and put it in the little boy's birdlike mouth. "He was like part of the family. He stay in the room you is now staying in. He all the time doing little things for me. A kind man—bout twenty-five I reckon. I believed he was purty. He say I was, too." She pushed the food aside and rocked the baby. She wiped her eyes with her sleeve.

Peter felt a hurt growing. It pulled at his heart and his soul. "Did you love him?" After he asked it, he realized he didn't know if he could handle the answer.

Her eyes met his. "I believed I did at the time."

"What happened to him?"

"Things went too far." She looked down at the baby, then back to Peter. "When I got with child, Marse and Mistus was so upset. Oh my, it hurt now so much to remember. They got us together in the parlor and asked him what his intentions was. He say he fond of me, but that was all. Marse pitched all hell. He put the man in the road right then and there. Then Marse say he ought to sell me off and be rid of me. But Massuh Charlie say he would not sell none of his peoples for no reason. I knowed Marse was just upset and did not mean it." She looked down at the baby again. "I reckon you can see for yourself the rest."

"I reckon I can."

She kissed her baby. "Lawd knows I wish it ain't happen, but I loves my baby."

Peter caressed her arm. "And you are a very good mother." Then he surprised himself. "I love you, Zuey." It felt good to say it, like a dam had been breached and a flood finally released.

Tears came so fast Zuey didn't bother to wipe them. She sniffed. "You is good Peter. You is the best man I know."

She called him a man. He was only seventeen, but she called him a man. He was proud, and coming from her, it was capital. But slowly the pride faded like snow on warm ground. He realized she had not said she loved him, too.

***

Fog floated on the lazy river like a blanket of smoke. "Why did we have to be here so early," Peter asked. "It's not even good daylight, yet."

Joe leaned his pole against a tree. "Is too."

Two wood ducks zipped above the foggy water and flared when they saw the two boys on the riverbank. They squealed their eerie call as they disappeared through the trees.

"See that?" Joe said.

Before Peter could answer, a wild turkey gobbled down the river, echoing through the woods like a yodeler.

Peter turned to Joe and smiled. This is a perfect morning, Joe thought. The air is cool and crisp, and the animals are active—maybe the fish, too.

A big swirl broke the surface of the river, leaving wave rings that grew like a bull's eye.

The river wasn't wide—Joe could easily chuck a rock across it and wade it most places, but there were fish in it sure enough.

He didn't know why Peter wanted to go fishing—just wasn't like Peter. Peter didn't even know what to use for bait, but Joe took care of that. Aunt Floy had given him scrap meat and chicken guts. Peter knew nothing about catfish, but Joe knew plenty. Peter had said Uncle Zeke gave them permission to stay as long as they wanted, said he didn't care what they did. He had been acting strange lately.

Joe crammed a piece of meat on his hook and found a stump by the river's edge, a ready-made seat. He plopped his line into the water, knew any minute a big ole catfish would be tugging. He looked around and saw Peter trying to put chicken guts on his hook. He had his nose curled, holding the hook and guts at arm's length.

"Nation, Peter, just joog the hook in it."

Peter finally attached the guts. "Nothing to it." He went to the riverbank and flung the line toward the water. The guts fell off before the line hit the water.

Joe laughed. "You're wasting all the guts."

Joe felt a tug on his line. He snatched the pole. The fish was strong, wouldn't come up. "I got a big one—I got a big one!"

Peter dropped his own pole and ran to Joe. "Pull it out!"

"It's too big. It must weigh a hundred pounds."

Peter grabbed the pole with Joe, and they tugged together. Finally, a head grew out of the water.

"Pshaw, it's just a big ole loggerhead turtle."

"We can have turtle soup," Peter said.

"Nation, I didn't think of that."

Peter could always make chicken soup outta chicken shit.

They pulled and fought with the turtle for what seemed like hours to Joe—though it was only minutes—before they finally got it close to the bank. The big snapper dug its claws into the mud and would come no closer. It roared a loud hiss; startled both boys. Joe laughed.

"Hold the pole, Peter." Joe let go and jerked the tomahawk from his belt. He attacked the turtle's head, and in short order and a few whacks, the struggle was over.

"That is one huge turtle," Peter said, laying the pole down. "He pulled like so many mules."

"I'd say so," Joe said as he washed the tomahawk in the river. "He's big as a tub."

They dragged the big turtle up the bank, then went back to the fishing poles. Soon Peter got the hang of baiting the hook, and both boys managed to catch a few catfish. They tied them on a long line and agreed they would head home with their catch when the line was full.

"Hey, Joe, come here." Pointing, Peter asked, "What is that large fish floating just under the water?"

Joe set his pole down and went to investigate. "That's a big ole gar." More floated just under the surface like submerged logs. "I'm going to make me a spear and stick me a couple of 'em."

Joe found a bitter pecan sapling and went to work on it with his tomahawk. He honed a barbed, pointed end to it. On the other end, he made a notch to tie a line so he could retrieve it. He went to the edge of the water with the stick. "See one?"

Peter pointed. "Right there."

"I see it." Joe launched the spear toward the fish. Missed. "Pshaw!"

"There's another one, Joe; he's even bigger!"

Joe threw the spear again, and once again, missed.

Peter laughed. "I see now why you and Curtis never came back with fish when you went spear fishing."

"It ain't as easy as it looks." Joe pulled the spear back in with the line and threw it to the ground.

"Let me have a go at it," Peter said, picking up the stick.

"Pray, do try your hand at it," Joe said, as he swept his hand and bowed.

"There's one right there." Peter flung the spear.

The water exploded with a swirl and a splash.

"You got it, Peter—you got it!" Joe jumped up and down. "Grab the line—grab the line!"

Peter was so surprised that he just stood looking, but Joe's yelling made him realize to grab the fast disappearing line at his feet. The line burned at first as it cut threw his hands, but he soon planted his feet and held fast. When Peter stopped the escaping line, the huge fish came plumb out of the water.

Joe ran up and down the bank. "Nation, it's a whale. That's it, Peter; wrap the line around your hand. Don't let him get away. It's a whale Peter—a whale!"

Peter wrapped the line around his fist, turned, and pulled like a mule. The gar gave way as Peter marched up the bank.

When the fish drew up at the water's edge, Joe pounced on it. It was a scary thing with its rows of teeth, but Joe wasn't about to let it get away now that Peter had pulled it this far. He bear hugged the fish with all he had, wrapping his arms and legs around the wiggling, bucking creature. Uncle Charlie would be proud of this one.

Peter slid down the muddy bank and pulled Joe and the fish up on dry ground.

Joe let go of the flopping fish. "You did good, Peter—real good."

"That is the biggest fish I've ever caught," Peter said, smiling. Peter hefting the dying fish. "What do you reckon he weighs, Joe?"

"Twenty pounds, depend on it," Joe said.

"Twenty pounds," Peter whispered.

***

Joe smacked on the chicken Lillie had packed and watched Peter. Peter ate, too, but couldn't take his eyes off the line that held the many fish, smiling like a little child.

"Mr. Taylor will sure be happy with the catch, won't he, Joe?"

"I suspect so." Joe had never seen Peter so excited, and it was important to him that Zeke be happy. If Uncle Zeke is happy—fine, Joe thought; if not—tough. He hadn't been happy since the Yankee's had come to the place.

Joe watched Peter; he was big and strong, but he was soft. What would become of him if Joe weren't there to look after him? If someone tried to make a slave of him, it would do him in. Well, it was no need thinking on it. Joe knew he would have to take care of him; that was the tall and short of it.

"We should try gigging more gars after we finish eating," Peter said.

"You think you can get lucky again?" Joe asked, sucking on the chicken leg.

"Perhaps."

"I reckon I ain't no good with that spear." Joe threw the chicken bone toward the water. "I'm handy at throwing my tomahawk, though."

"You can't throw that at fish; you will lose it."

He doesn't think I'm that stupid, does he, Joe thought.

Joe stood and brushed the crumbs from his slimy pants. "Let me show you how I can fling this thing." He pulled the tomahawk from his belt. "See that hollow tree over there?" He pointed to a big sycamore with a large opening at the base.

"I see it. That's about twenty yards from here."

"Yeah. You see that knot on the side of it?"

"I see—"

Before Peter could finish his sentence, the ax was on its way. It hit about an inch from the knot with a loud whack that echoed from the hollow tree.

"That's very good, but can you do it again?"

Joe knew he bragged about many things he couldn't pull off, but this wasn't one of them. He yanked the tomahawk from the tree, stepped it off, and hurled it again. This time it hit dead center.

"How did you learn to throw like that?"

"Me and Curtis got to chucking it back at Helena, and it just came natural like."

"Let me try." Peter pulled the tomahawk from the tree, went to the same spot from where Joe had thrown. He heaved the tomahawk; it landed inside the hollow.

Joe laughed and ran after it. When he reached inside the tree, he saw the hollow was huge—like a small cave. He could lie down inside if he had a mind to.

"Let me try it again," Peter said.

Joe started back toward Peter. Peter was good with the spear or maybe just lucky, but he was no good with the tomahawk.

Joe stopped, heard a roaring in the distance. He looked toward the sound, but saw nothing.

"What is that?" Peter asked.

It sounded like a train or something, but the nearest train was many miles away. Joe looked the sky over. It was perfectly sunny—wasn't thunder.

Peter pointed toward the south. "Whatever it is, it has frightened those wild pigeons."

Joe looked to where Peter was pointing and saw a small flock of passenger pigeons coming over the trees.

The noise grew like a big storm approaching.

Joe had never heard such a roar, and it was building. He looked at Peter. Joe saw he wasn't the only one concerned.

"Look!" Peter pointed over the trees again.

Joe turned, saw a giant black cloud approaching.

"It's more wild pigeons!" Peter yelled.

As the pigeons closed the distance, Joe guessed it to be millions.

He had seen large flocks before that had stretched for miles, but he had never been in their path when they were so low. It was a sight, indeed, as they came over just above the treetops. The trees began to sway as if blown by a gale. It grew darker and darker as the birds covered the entire sky. The sound was overwhelming, like a locomotive in a tunnel.

Joe felt something tugging at his shirt. It was Peter. He was saying something, but the noise was so loud, Joe had to move close to hear.

"I've never been right under a big flock like this!" Peter yelled.

Suddenly it began to hail. No—it was pigeon shit. Joe covered his head with his arms, but it was no use. The ground was turning nasty white, like shitty snow.

He remembered the hollow tree and dashed for it. He dove in. Peter flew in behind him. Joe looked out from the cover of the tree. The leaves and sticks swirled above the ground as if moved by a cyclone.

Pigeons began landing everywhere: on the ground, on stumps, in the trees. Soon there was little room for another bird, but they kept coming, reminded Joe of ants. Large limbs moaned, cracked, then fell under their weight. A big one from the sycamore crashed to the ground killing scores of pigeons, yet they kept coming.

They pecked at the ground, walking around and over each other, fed as if they had never eaten before. They pecked at bugs and seeds and nuts and anything else they saw, turning over leaves and sticks. Joe and Peter shooed them away as they tried to come inside the hollow. It was a nightmare outside the hollow tree, but at the same time, it was a wonder of nature.

The pigeons were long and sleek with long tails, built for speed, not like Mrs. Donner's tame pigeons. These blue, chestnut and gray birds were beautiful.

Joe heard a faint popping noise. He barely heard it over the pigeons. "What's that?"

Peter listened. The popping sounds came again. "Sounds like gun shots."

Joe believed Peter was probably right. He looked at Peter and laughed.

"What is the matter with you?" Peter asked.

"You're covered in pigeon poop."

Peter looked at his arms, then back at Joe. He laughed, too. "Look at yourself."

Joe examined his own arms, laughed harder.

Joe shooed another pigeon from the opening. "Peter, why do they do like this?"

"I'm not sure, but I think they flock together to fly north. I've seen them way up in Pennsylvania."

Joe remembered his pa telling him how they used to kill them at the roost by the thousands. Joe now understood how that would not be a problem.

"How you reckon they know how to find their way north?" Joe asked.

"God gave them the wisdom," Peter said. "All of God's creatures have their special ways."

Joe believed that was probably true. He also believed there were more wild pigeons than any other creature on earth, and most of them were right there in front of him.

Peter said something Joe could not understand.

"What did you say?"

"I just said, 'Going north.'"

"What are you talking about?"

"All of these birds, at least the live ones, are headed north. They will take to the wing and be there in no time. So I reckon all we have to do is follow these wild pigeons and they will show us the way like the Star of Bethlehem." Everything was related to the Bible where Peter was concerned.

"The problem with that is they ain't going to wait on us like the star waited on the Wise Men," Joe said.

Suddenly all the pigeons rose from the ground with a deafening roar. The action was like a giant leapfrog or great wheel, as they rolled over the woods. Then more birds down the river rolled out, too. As the birds cleaned the food from the ground, they moved on. They left nothing but destruction. As suddenly as they appeared, they were gone.

Joe and Peter crawled from the tree. The pigeons were gone, except for the scores of dead and dying birds scattered across the ground, enough barely alive and twitching to give the ground a singular crawling appearance.

"A cyclone couldn't have done worse," Peter said.

That is exactly what it looked like to Joe. Limbs lay on the ground everywhere, even a few large trees were broken over. No one could have convinced him that birds were capable of doing such destruction. Just minutes before, the area was pretty and alive like any other woods in the area. Now it looked as if a war had been fought there—a war of bombs and pigeon shit.

They washed as much of the pigeon mess from them as they could, but the river ran nasty. They grabbed up the fish and made a drag for the turtle.

***

They walked down the road to home, saw a wagon coming.

"It's Mr. Taylor," Peter said.

Immediately, Joe thought they were in trouble for something.

Ten of the youngest field hands were in the wagon. Zeke stopped the wagon along side Joe and Peter. "You two have a good mess of fish, and that's a nice turtle," Zeke said.

"Yes, sir," Joe said. "We have more than enough for supper."

"You got caught under the pigeons, didn't you?" Zeke said.

The darkies in the wagon laughed.

Peter was embarrassed, but Joe wanted to whop them in the head with a catfish.

"It was like a storm," Peter said.

"Yes, we saw it. We killed as many as we could as they flew over the south field. We're headed to gather them now."

"I knew we heard shots," Peter said.

"There are hundreds of dead pigeons along the river, Uncle Zeke," Joe said, pointing back the way they had come.

"We're going to gather as many as we can draw and hang today," Zeke said. "Seth and some boys are bringing the hogs up to turn loose on the rest."

The thought of the hogs eating the dead pigeons made Joe's belly turn.

"There won't be much work in the fields today, but we can't let this opportunity for all this meat slip away," Zeke said. "We'll work the fields tomorrow."

Now that Joe had thought about it, he wanted to see the hogs eat some of those pigeons. "We'll help gather some of them birds." Joe started for the wagon.

"No Joe, you need to clean those fish. Take that big turtle to

Aunt Floy. She knows how to get it out of the shell and makes the best turtle soup." Zeke thought for a moment. "Don't tell your Aunt Lillie I said that."

***

When Joe and Peter approached Floy's cabin, Joe yelled, "Aunt Floy, come see what we got." The door sprung open and she waddled out.

Washington and the rest of the troops soon appeared from nowhere, like worrisome gnats.

"Lawd, that a big snapper," Floy said.

"Uncle Zeke said for me to fetch it to you."

"He all time dumping stuff off on me. What if I ain't got no notion to fool with it?"

Washington hit the turtle's tail with an ax handle.

"Get away from that turtle, you monkey!" Floy yelled.

The children backed away.

"Uncle Zeke said you were the best when it comes to cooking turtle."

Floy wiped here hands on her apron. "Well, I spect I can hull that turtle out right fast enough. We ain't had no turtle soup in a spell, and these niggers likes turtle soup, that fo sho."

Joe liked it, too. "Reckon I can get some of that soup when you get it made?"

"Marse say I ain't got to feed no white folk." She looked past Joe. "What you gonna do with that big old gar?"

Joe nudged it with his shoe. "You have to ask Peter—he caught it."

She turned on Peter. "Well, boy, what is you gonna do with it?"

Peter stepped back when she barked at him. Joe laughed.

"I was going to clean if for supper," Peter said after he composed himself.

"You is got a long rope full of catfish, ain't ya?"

Joe whispered, "Give it to her, Peter."

Peter looked down at the fish and back to the big woman. "Would you like this gar, Aunt Floy?"

"Ain't I got enough to do hulling out this turtle? You bad as white folk thinking you can just throw any critter at me." She kicked the gar over to the turtle. "Leave him there. I clean 'em both by and by." She turned to the children. "You chilluns touch nary one of 'em, and I'll brain you with my stick."

She labored back up the steps and into her cabin while the children stood over the turtle, trying to get the courage to mess with it.

"Come on, Peter. Let us go show off our fish to Aunt Lillie."

"Maybe she won't be so nice like Aunt Floy," Peter said as he picked up his end of the line.

Chapter 14

The smell of the freshly broken ground was pleasant to Peter, reminded him of Mam's garden back home. He had always turned the ground for her in the spring.

April was a magic month. The dogwoods were in bloom and the birds had come back up from the South; their sweet songs filled the air. Things were either green or turning green, and the smell in the air was fresh—new. Even the hum of the many bees was pleasant. And the temperature was nice, too. Katie Bea had said April was the month of beginnings. It really was.

Peter led one of the block-headed mules from the makeshift barn.

Beginnings were a good thing for sure. Peter was hoping for a new beginning some day in Pennsylvania, but when that beginning would happen, he didn't know. And would that beginning be a lonely one? He didn't know the answer to that, yet. Joe wanted to head north now, as Peter had promised him they would, and it was all but impossible to convince the boy to wait for the war to be over. Joe just didn't realize how dangerous it would be to go to Virginia now. Well, maybe he did. It was obvious the boy wasn't worried about a war or anything else. However, Peter knew the dangers, and he would stay where it was safe as long as possible.

"Peter, you ain't hitched those mules to the wagon, yet?" Charlie said. He rubbed one of the mules between the ears as Peter backed the other to the wagon.

"I'll be ready in just a minute, Mr. Charlie."

"I'm just spouting. There ain't no rush. We shall get to town by and by, I'll be bound."

Peter was happy Charlie had picked him to go along to New Albany. Peter didn't know why, but Charlie had taken a shine to him—Zuey had said so. He liked Charlie, too. How could someone not like the old man? He was gentle and always treated every soul kindly. That was a rare thing in these hard times.

***

The road to town was rougher than the last time Peter had taken it. No matter; it was still an enjoyable ride. The evidence of spring was everywhere. The smell of blossoms floated on the air.

"It is a lovely time of the year, I tell you," Charlie said. He sniffed and took in the scenery.

"Yes, sir."

"Just smell that air," Charlie said, taking a deep breath. Then he suddenly stopped sniffing and curled his nose. "Whoo."

Peter smelled it, too. He laughed.

"Peter, my boy, don't my people grow the feed for these beasts? Don't my people take care of them? Ain't they treated good, suh?

"I would say so Mr. Charlie."

"Then why pray would they put a heap of stink on me in that fashion?" Charlie fanned his hat.

Peter continued laughing. The mules' heads bobbed as they walked, and it appeared to Peter they were laughing. They sure didn't deliver delightful spring smells.

***

Things were quiet when they rolled into town. Peter saw where the Yankees had done more damage when they came back through in February, but life went on.

How did these people keep going after such devastation? They would build back, and the Yankees destroyed it again.

"Pull up in front that there shed," Charlie said, pointing to a shed used for a store. Roberts took a load of cotton to Memphis for me, and he's got the goods inside there."

Peter browsed while Charlie visited with two other men in the store. The owner eyed him, but didn't say anything. He knew he was one of Charlie's people.

Peter discovered a blue bonnet. It had white ruffles and dainty blue ribbons dangling from it. They would make a pretty bow under Zuey's chin. It would be perfect for her, but he had no money with him. He smiled. He could see her with it on when she went to the white folk's church with the Taylors. Oh, she would be a prize, yes indeed.

"What you studying on there, Peter?" Charlie had come up behind him.

"Nothing, Mr. Charlie." Peter felt as if he had been caught doing something wrong.

"Well now, you like that fashion, do you?" Charlie said, admiring the bonnet.

Peter admired it again. "It is a very pretty bonnet for sure."

"Indeed it is." Charlie rubbed his chin, smiled. "I fancy it would look handsome atop a pretty little duck back on the place, I'll be bound."

Peter felt his face grow hot. "I reckon it would look pretty on most girls."

"Fiddlesticks, boy, that there bonnet has Zuey's name all over it." He squeezed Peter's shoulder.

"Charlie, you ready to load now?" Roberts asked.

"I am, suh, and charge me for that bonnet."

Peter quickly looked at Charlie. He didn't know what to say.

"Ain't nobody got to know how you come about that parcel."

Peter smiled. "Yes, sir, Mr. Charlie."

***

Joe hurled a stick at the purple martins fluttering around the box. The swallows dived and shrieked at the bothersome boy. He had no intention of hitting one of the birds, but it tickled him when they dove at him and pulled up at the last second. But, even that grew old.

He wanted to go to town with Peter and Uncle Charlie, but he was being punished for tying the rooster's legs together. It wasn't that big a deal, but Aunt Lillie thought it was. She had said it was cruel. Nation, nobody got hurt—just a blamed old rooster. He shouldn't have flogged Joe anyhow.

He grabbed a spear he had whittled and headed to the river. Maybe he could stick one of those big gars floating around. As he walked toward the woods, he threw the spear ahead and ran after it.

He would try to throw it farther each time. He wasn't as good with it as Peter had turned out to be.

The people were planting cotton. It seemed a big deal to everyone that it be planted before the next rain. Seth had disagreed with Zeke on planting so early. "It much too early to plant now. Marse, know that there," Seth had said.

Zeke had been sharpening a plow. "It's not too early for me." He never looked up.

"But Marse, you can still see through the pecan trees. Ever nigger on the place know you has to wait til the leaves done gone and filled out. The ground too cold."

Zeke ignored him and scraped the file down the plow.

Joe, sharpening his spear, stood behind Seth. He saw Zeke's mind seemed a thousand miles away. He sensed Seth noticed it, too. Zeke was strange since the Yankees had been to the farm. In fact, no one on the place was the same. Everybody was quieter. Laughing seemed out of place. When someone did manage a chuckle, it was like a sour note on a piano. And someone was always looking down the lane, as if they expected the Yankees back any moment.

Poor Fanny was in the worst shape. She seemed to Joe to be lost. All she ever did was talk to her baby. She never looked down the road, though. She expected nothing to come and seemed not to care if anything ever did. She would answer Joe if he spoke to her, but she never began a conversation, and her pretty smile had been put out as sure as you would pinch the flame from a candle.

Peter and Zuey, that was another matter. They were always giggling and smiling, but only when they weren't in the company of the white folks—they were sneaky that way. They took long walks in the evening after all of the work was finished. Joe would follow sometimes at first, but he quickly got bored. All that kissy stuff made him feel sick.

Now that the planting had started, things were somewhat back to normal. Maybe it was because everyone was so busy. Maybe that's why Zeke wanted to get to planting so early. It would get idle minds back to a task.

Well, Joe's task now was to stick a gar with his spear. He was in luck. As soon as he reached the river, he saw one of the biggest fish he had ever seen. Maybe it wasn't luck, always gars at that spot. This gar was even bigger than the one Peter had killed. It floated under the surface; the fin on its back barely above the water. Joe took careful aim, launched the spear. It was a perfect shot. He hit the fish dead center. The gar shot out across the water with the spear dancing through the water like the mast of a ship. The pole danced from side to side, as the current rolled against it. Joe ran to the edge of the river. The pole suddenly disappeared under the water.

Ten minutes later the spear had not surfaced. Joe fell to his knees in disgust. It had all happened so fast. His luck was good. The fish was there as soon as he had arrived at the river. He had hit the fish. The spear stayed in the fish, but now the fish was gone, and with his spear, too. He had forgotten to tie a string to it.

Joe leaped to his feet. "Nation!" he yelled, and pulled the tomahawk from his belt. He quickly looked around and spotted the hollow sycamore they had hid in when the pigeons were there earlier. He threw the ax at the tree—hit it. That let off some of his steam. In fact, it was kind of funny how the gar stole his spear. The joke was on Joe. He was laughing by the time he pulled the tomahawk from the tree.

Placing the tomahawk back into his belt, he peered into the hollow tree. It was inviting, seemed like a good place to hide. After all, it had been a safe place when all of those pigeons were here. He climbed inside. From inside, the opening looked like a door—no a window, and as he looked out he felt comfortable inside the big tree, like a warm house on a rainy day. He laughed again at the disappearing spear. Maybe he would go back in a while and see if he could spot it, but not now. Now the hollow tree felt comfortable—safe, better than being in the cotton fields.

He lay flat on his belly with his chin on the back of his hands, looking out the opening. He could just see the river from there. The sunlight hit the surface of the river just right from that vantage point making the river shimmer like a thousand pieces of glass. It reminded him of the streams back home in the Valley. He felt if he stared long enough he might be able to see Garner's Mill, which was just a few miles from his home in the Valley. If he just concentrated hard, maybe it would appear. He narrowed his eyes. They were getting heavy anyway. If he just looked through his fluttering eyelashes. If he just thought real hard. If he just remem...

***

Bonnie Taylor called to her son, "Joseph, you and Sarah come and eat."

Joe looked toward his ma. She and his pa were sitting on a blanket under a shade tree with a dinner spread out before them. It was one of many blankets, as other families were there by the stream to celebrate the Fourth of July, too.

"I'm fixing to come in a few minutes, Ma," Joe shouted.

"Come now, Son," his pa, Josh, said. "The flies are going to eat more than we do."

"Hang on, Sarah," Joe said. His sister was riding piggyback while he walked in the stream.

"I'm hanging on, Joe."

He felt her little fingers lock under his chin as he ran through the water.

"Yee—ha!" she said, as Joe jumped from the water and onto the sand.

Joe ran with the small girl on his back, her long blonde hair flying in the wind. Sometimes she was such a bother, but it was a comfort now with her on his back. Joe gently lowered her to the blanket.

"You are so much fun, brother," she said.

"You have a wonderful brother," Bonnie said, brushing Sarah's hair from her eyes.

Josh knuckled Joe's head and said, "But not when he is pulling his many shines." The knuckling never hurt.

Bonnie pulled Joe to her and kissed him on the top of the head. "He's wet, but he's a good boy." That always made Joe's heart melt. He had the best ma in the world. He had the best family.

Joe heard a pinging sound coming from back toward the stream.

"Hey, the Reeds are driving spikes for horseshoes," Josh said. Let's hurry and we'll join them."

"Don't eat too fast," Bonnie said. "It will make you sick."

She always said that, but Joe never got sick from eating too fast. He rushed. He was good at pitching horseshoes, and he wanted to get in on it.

Mr.   Reed   drove   the   second   stake:
Ping—ping—ping—knock—knock—knock—

A woodpecker woke Joe, pecking on the hollow tree. Joe looked out over the river. It was not home—it was Mississippi. No place was home, but home—the Shenandoah Valley. He buried his face into his folded hands and wept. He couldn't help it, nor did he care. He wanted his ma—he wanted Sarah, but they were gone. They were all gone; maybe even his pa.

He sat up after a while and wiped his eyes. I'm going home, he thought. I'm going home! Peter can stay, but I'm going home.

He climbed out of the tree and stood by the river, wiping his eyes. Suddenly the spear bobbed to the surface and lazily drifted down the river. It slowed with the eddies and swirled with the current, but it never stopped. It moved as if on a preset course. It floated on until it disappeared like a ship on the horizon. He watched it until it was lost to the distance, then he turned for home.

***

Everyone was busy with the farm work, so it was easier than he had hoped sneaking his stuff out of the house without being noticed. He eased past the last outbuildings and onto the lane. He had made it without being caught—well, almost. Washington came running from quarters—that knot-head.

"Where is you going?" he said, as he caught up to Joe.

"Go on back, boy, for I give you a pounding."

"Is you running away, Joe? Is you?" The boy grinned big.

"Confound it, Wash, white folks don't run away. We can leave on our own free notion. Now get back up to the house."

Washington skipped along behind Joe. "You is running—you is!"

Joe wanted to pop the boy. He wanted to pop him real bad, but it would do no good. The boy would still go tell.

"I'm just going into town, and if you are good, I will bring you back a sweet."

"You ain't done it. You is leaving here." He laughed and pointed his finger at Joe.

Joe couldn't stand it. He threw his bag down and jumped the boy. They rolled around in the dirt, each trying to get a punch in. Joe climbed on top and began working Washington's head over, but soon he was jumped by Washington's troops. Little pickaninnies came from everywhere. Joe didn't know where they came from and how they got there so fast, but before he knew it, he had five more to battle. They knocked him off Washington and commenced to kicking and stomping. Joe, on his hands and knees, hit one of the two girls on the toes with his fist. She squealed and was out of the fight. One of the little boys bit Joe on the arm. Joe yelled and popped the boy in the nose—he cried and was out. But Washington was almost as big as Joe, and he was kneeing Joe in the ribs. Joe grabbed his leg and bit down. Washington screamed. Another one grabbed a stick and hit Joe across the butt. Joe kicked backwards and knocked him down. Two were on his back and pounding him on the head and butt. Joe was flailing like a wild horse, swinging, kicking, and gouging.

"Get off there!" Joe heard someone say.

He looked up and saw the wagon with Charlie in it. Peter was pulling the little bothers off him.

"You children get on back up to the place before I put this crop on you, I'll be bound," Charlie said.

The children ran toward the farm, some sobbing, and some mumbling.

"Don't let me hear any lip, or you will be sorry for a season," Charlie said.

Joe was mad at himself. Not only had he let those pickaninnies get the best of him, he had been found out.

Peter picked up Joe's carpetbag, said nothing, only looked at Joe with disappointed eyes.

Joe snatched it from him. They should have left a long time ago. What right did he have to look disappointed? Joe would try it another time. And there would be another time. You bet there would.

***

Joe's free reign on the farm had come to an end. He was made to work like the rest. He didn't mind the work, but he was surprised at the trouble he had gotten from Zeke. Why should he be blamed for wanting to go home? He had come on his on free will. Why couldn't he leave the same way? Zeke had said Joe wasn't going anywhere until the war was over and not to try that again. But by the time June had rolled around the "escape" was almost forgotten.

Days in the field chopping cotton weren't too bad. At least he could chuck dirt clods at Washington. Zeke had said if he were big enough to fight with Joe, he was big enough to work, too. But sometimes when Joe was daydreaming of home, he would catch a dirt clod to the back of the head. Wash could give as well as receive.

Joe stayed angry at Peter. If Peter had wanted, they could have, and should have, been gone long ago. But Peter was so taken with Zuey that he thought of little else. They were together almost every moment possible. It made Joe sick. Yeah, he would leave Peter. He didn't need him anyway.

Joe had learned a lesson from getting caught. He wouldn't make that mistake again. He began stashing his stuff at the hollow tree. He would take a piece from his carpetbag every chance he got and sneak it to the tree. When Lillie came into his room, the carpetbag would be there. And if he had to, he could leave without it. He would simply go to the tree first, and then move on. It was a good plan.

***

Peter felt sorry for Joe, but it was good for the boy to work, and it was good that Zeke had finally laid the law down on Joe about going to Virginia. The war couldn't last forever, and when it was over, he would carry the boy to Virginia if the boy's father was still alive. He prayed the boy's father was still alive.

Peter was deeply in love with Zuey now, but he wasn't sure she felt the same for him. Oh, he knew she was fond of him, but he didn't know how deep that ran.

He enjoyed playing with the baby. He could easily see himself being a father some day. He even thought of the notion of purchasing Zuey and the baby. In Pennsylvania, they would be happy, and they would be free to do as they pleased.

Free? Was he really a free man here in the South? Not really. He always had to have his papers with him. He had to bow to the white folks' will. There were some good white people in the South, for sure. The Taylors were all good people, and there were many others. But he was not equal to them—not in the South, no doubt in that. When he got to the North, it would be different he prayed. Go to Pennsylvania is what he had promised Katie Bea, and that is what he intended to do once this horrible war was over. He hoped Zuey and the baby would be going, too.

***

The rain had fallen on and off for the last two days. Chopping in the fields was muddy work. Zeke finally let the people rest for a day. Lillie was afraid working in the rain was going to make the people sick. Zeke allowed them to work around the cabins until the rain let up, then it would be back to the fields.

Charlie sat on the back piazza watching the sheets of rain wave across the fields. Many of the children were sitting around him, and he laughed and picked at them as he always did. Joe sat close by sharpening his tomahawk with a big file.

"Boy, I declare, you are going to open yourself up with that thing one of these days," Charlie said.

When the nosy children turned to look at Joe, Charlie thumped Washington on the head. He yowled and everyone laughed. Charlie rubbed the back of the boy's head, grinning.

Joe laughed. "That sounded like a hollow pumpkin."

"Why, fancy that. Are you a pumpkin head, Wash?" Charlie said.

Washington grinned and the other children laughed.

Charlie laughed, too. "I have high hopes for you, boy. Someday you are going to be the best man on the place."

Washington drew himself up with pride. "Does you think so, Massuh Charlie?"

"Pshaw," Joe said. "They'll have to sell you down the river."

Washington screwed his face into a frown and started toward Joe.

Charlie laughed and grabbed Washington's arm. "He's only funning you, boy."

Zeke walked out onto the piazza, and the atmosphere changed as surely as you would put out a lamp. He lit his pipe and stared out over the soggy fields. The smoke drifted up to the ceiling and floated. No one talked for a time, and the only sound was the pattering rain and Joe drawing the file across the tomahawk.

Charlie broke the silence. "Well, Zeke, I do believe this rain will help the crops, to be sure."

Zeke took a big pull on the pipe and slowly let it out. "I hope it don't rain too much. It's been coming down like forty."

"That's right—that's right," Charlie said. "A coming down full chisel is as bad as too little." He picked one of the little girls up, placed her on his lap, and touched her nose. She giggled.

Joe laid the file down and crammed the tomahawk into his belt. He didn't care for Zeke's company too much anymore. Zeke was always sour and focused on something just out of sight like a hound looking toward the woods.

"I told Uncle Seth I would help him build some pegs for Aunt

Floy's pans." With that, Joe jumped from the porch and ran toward the cabin before anyone could say anything.

Seth was sitting at the table with his feet soaking in a pan, and Floy was pouring fresh hot water in when Joe popped through the door.

"Them feet bothering you again, Uncle?" Joe dropped down on the bench beside him.

"Massuh Joe, you just don't knows what it bees to get old, now I tells you."

The cabin smelled like supper. It was always a comfort in there. Joe could hear the rain picking up. It was pinging on a tub outside.

"Boy, does you want a ash-pone?" Floy set the bread in front of Joe before he had a chance to answer.

"Uncle Seth," Joe spoke with a mouthful, "do you still want to mount those pegs?"

Seth pointed to a board on the wall. "I's made the holes, just need some pegs."

"I've got that fashion," Joe said. I've got me some sticks left from when I was making my spear. They're behind the corncrib. I'll get them."

He heard Floy say something about the rain as he shot out the door.

He found the sticks where he had left them. He stepped under the eaves of the corncrib and shaved the stick down with his tomahawk. He was busy at it when someone stood in front of him. He looked up. It was Zeke.

"Boy, what are you doing out in this rain?" He was angry again. "The purpose of not being in the fields is so no one would get sick in this weather. Now look at you. You're dripping."

"But Uncle Zeke, I was just going to shave these pegs for Seth, and then I—"

Zeke yanked the stick from Joe's hands. "Go to the veranda."

Joe saw a look in Zeke's eyes he had never seen before. Something had come over him. Something was wrong with him. As Joe marched to the porch, he realized this wasn't new at all. It had been slowly growing. The signs began about a week after the Yankees had raided the farm.

As they stepped onto the porch, Zeke told the Negro children to go to their cabins. They scattered.

Charlie stood. "What's the matter, Zeke? You look madder than a March hare."

"This boy is going to get what for." He bent Joe over a chair. "He will be made to learn to mind."

"You don't mean to whip the boy with that stick, do you, Zeke?"

Zeke turned on Charlie. "You look here, Charlie." He pointed a finger at him. "You have never been a help with discipline with the Negroes or anybody else, so you hold your tongue."

The whipping Joe could stand, but he couldn't bear to see Zeke take it out on Charlie.

Zeke whirled around with the stick and caught Joe across the butt. There was pain, but it wasn't as severe as the humiliation.

"Zeke!" Charlie said. "There is no need for that. You are not yourself, pray." He reached for the stick.

"You grab that stick and I'll put it to you!"

Charlie stepped back as if he were struck.

Zeke whacked Joe across the butt a few more times before Joe heard Seth coming across the yard.

"Marse—Marse! You don't need to be a doing that to the boy."

Joe saw Seth standing at the bottom of the steps dripping wet and barefooted. Floy was standing behind him with an apron over her head.

"I don't believe my ears," Zeke said. "Are you really talking to me in that tone, Seth?"

"Oh, Marse, you knows the boy is high-strung. He bees like a young stud horse. He can't help his self he got so much go."

"I run this farm, Seth—"

"I knows you does, Marse, and you is a good man, but—"

"What are you wanting to say, Seth." Zeke patted the stick in his palm.

"Yessuh, Marse. The boy was just getting me some pegs for my wall. Only he left out the cabin before I could tell him not to be in this here bad weather."

"Maybe you are the one that I should be whipping, allowing the boy to run wild."

Seth lowered his gray head, and rain ran from his nose. Joe thought it could have been tears.

"I will not have Negroes telling me what to do!" Zeke pointed the stick toward Seth. "Do I have to beat you with this to have you understand, you old fool?"

"Father!"

Joe looked around to see Fanny and Lillie standing at the door. Zuey and Peter were behind them.

Zeke turned around. It was as if someone had slapped him. It was as if he had been awakened. Zeke looked down at the stick, then at Seth. He dropped the stick and it rattled when it hit the floor. Joe stood. Fanny went to Zeke and put her arms around him. Fanny and Lillie led them into the house. Zeke suddenly looked like a lost child.

Floy and Seth shuffled back to their cabin. Seth never raised his head. Floy put an arm around him. That was something Joe had never seen her do before.

Charlie followed the family inside, and Peter came outside.

Joe had never felt the pain. The whole affair was like a bad dream.

Peter studied Joe with soft eyes.

Joe sat on one of the chairs and looked at Seth and Floy's cabin. "Did you see the hurt in Uncle Seth's eyes?"

Peter sat in the swing. "Yes."

"Why would Uncle Zeke be so mean?"

"I think he is sick," Peter said. "I think the war has taken a toll on him."

Joe wheeled around. "Damn the war!"

"Joseph!"

Joe stood. "Damn this place!"

"Watch you mouth."

Joe softened. Peter was only concerned for him. "Peter, I'm leaving."

"Now Joe, we talked about—"

"No! I'm leaving! We started out for Virginia, and we have stayed here too long!" Joe sighed. "I want to go home, Peter. I want to go home, and I'm going."

Peter looked at Joe, but said nothing.

"You have been like family since I first met you. We left together, but I won't hold it against you if you stay," Joe said.

Peter shook his head, but said nothing.

"I know you love Zuey. So maybe it is fitting that you stay. I'm leaving tonight."

"Tonight!"

"Tonight." Joe nodded. "That's right, and if you tell them, I will leave tomorrow; if not then, then the next day."

Peter stood. "Joe, let's just wait until the war is over. You know it can't last much longer."

"'The War!' That is all we hear. Look what the war is doing to everyone. I'm not going to let it sockdologer me any more. It could last years. I'm leaving."

Peter lowered his head.

"Do you remember the hollow sycamore we hid in when the pigeons came?"

Peter nodded.

"I've hid my things there. I'm fixing to get my bag and stay the night there. Everyone is so concerned about Uncle Zeke they won't miss me until tomorrow. If you are not there by first light, I'm leaving without you, and I wish you well."

Joe opened the door, then looked back at Peter. He had his head in his hands. Poor Peter. But it couldn't be helped. Joe was going home.

***

The hollow tree was dry, considering how wet it was out, and the candle lit it nicely. Joe stretched out and laid his head on the carpetbag. The big revolver rested close by. Now and then, an owl would scream out, and crickets and peepers sang down by the river.

Joe thought about his pa. Was he still alive? Where was he? Why didn't he come? He had to be alive. He just had to.

The rain was steady, and Joe was thankful for the dryness of the tree. He would have built a fire, but everything was wet. The candle would have to do.

It sure was lonely. He had to admit it was going to be a long trip without Peter. Peter was a good companion. He had never tried to hold it over on Joe that he was older, never tried to be boss. That thought struck Joe funny: a darky being boss. But Peter wasn't just any ole darky. He was free. A free Negro. Joe thought about that, wondered what that would be like. It wasn't the same as a free white man, was it?

What were those people up north called—abol something. They wanted to free the slaves. What would a slave do if he were free anyway? Joe guessed they would all go back to Africa.

He wondered what they lived like in Africa. Maybe they hunted lions and elephants. There are no lions here—only panthers.

Suddenly Joe sat up. Something was wrong. The crickets and peepers had stopped singing. Maybe it is a panther outside of the tree right this very minute. Joe grabbed the revolver.

He heard a stick pop. He cocked the gun. He felt his pulse pounding. He aimed the gun at the outside. Suddenly Peter's face appeared.

Joe lowered the gun and breathed a deep breath.

Peter threw his bag in and scooted in beside him.

Joe was relieved that he had decided to come. Joe didn't want to bring up Zuey or the family, so he thought of something else. "Remember when we hid from the pigeons in here?"

Peter showed a half smile that was surely forced. "Yes, Joseph, and I reckon we shall now chase the wild pigeons to the Shenandoah Valley."

Chapter 15

The rain stopped during the night, and by sunup, Joe and Peter were near New Albany. Joe had learned a train track ran north and south through the town of Baldwyn, east of there. The plan was to catch the cars and ride them north to Tennessee. Once they made it to Tennessee, they would make a new plan. It was Joe's plan and Peter had to see how it played out since he had nothing better.

A slave hauling wood outside of New Albany showed them the road to Baldwyn. It was a poor one with many low places in it, and the rain of the past few days had filled all the puddles. Mud was the rule, and both boys were muddy to their knees.

"I'm not sure, Joe, but now that I think about it, doesn't that track go north to Corinth?" Peter asked.

"Nation, I'm sure I don't know." Joe kicked his foot, slinging red mud high in the air. "It don't matter if it goes through New York. It's the way home, and we're going to hop the cars."

"I believe I heard the Yankees hold Corinth, Mississippi."

"I reckon they might. I heard they have most of Tennessee, but that don't matter none." Joe looked at Peter. "Fire, Peter, they were in Helena and that didn't hinder you none."

"They seem different now, somehow." Peter slipped in the muck, but caught his balance.

"Pshaw, Yankees is Yankees."

Peter reckoned he would never understand Joe. How could he

forget what they had done to his uncle's farm? How could he not see how they had turned his uncle from a strong and assertive man to—well—confused? Peter could not forget—never.

Joe saw Peter staring at him. "What are you gawking at? You are always gawking."

Peter said nothing, just slipped again and stared straight ahead.

"Look, Peter, if you are scared of the bad ole Yankees, when we come across 'em, I'll find the biggest toad in the pond and give him a sockdologer, and the rest will fall in line." Joe laughed aloud.

Peter tried not to laugh, but it came anyway. He knew Joe was funning, but he wouldn't put it past him to hit the biggest one to stir the pot.

The day heated up as they trudged on. They didn't talk much. Both boys were dealing with their own thoughts. Peter's mind was on Zuey. He tried not to think on it, but it was no use. He was in love with her, and he missed her already. It was going to be a long trip to Virginia, indeed. What was he doing? All he had to do was turn around and go back. It would be the sensible thing to do; it would be the sane thing to do. How could he be letting a thirteen-year-old boy lead him into God only knew what? It was foolish trekking across the country with a war flaring. It was insane.

However, there really wasn't any choice when it came down to it, and he knew it. He loved Zuey deeply, and he hoped she felt the same, but all that was second. He had promised to take care of the boy, and he would. Joe was going to Virginia, with or without him, so he had no choice but to go along. He had promised Katie Bea he would go to Pennsylvania, and now he was headed that direction.

They both saw the rider coming at the same time. It was too late to hide because the rider had seen them, too. It turned out to be an old man on a ragged black mare.

"Whoa." He pulled along side the boys. "Where y'all going?"

Joe answered, "We're headed to Baldwyn to catch the cars."

The rider put a finger to one nostril and blew snot out of the other. He eyed Peter; asked Joe. "This here your boy?"

Peter didn't like the looks of this. It was usually trouble when they asked that type question right off.

"He's a free man," Joe said. "He don't belong to nobody."

"Um, that a fact." It wasn't really a question.

"That sure is a sorry horse," Joe said. He rubbed the horse's neck.

Oh no, Peter thought. Why can't he just hold his tongue for once?

The man smiled, and tobacco dripped from his lip. "It's all Forrest's men left me a while back."

"They didn't think much of you, did they, mister?" Joe said.

"Mister, how far to Baldwyn?" Peter said, trying to change the subject.

The man looked at Peter for a short time, then spit. "I reckon 'bout seven or eight miles. But if I's you boys, I'd not be a going there; heard Yankees are a coming down that way. You won't be a fetching up on the cars there no how—not a going north no ways."

"Why can't we get on the cars at Baldwyn?" Joe said.

"I done told you boy. The Yankees are up the tracks. They is at Ripley, too."

"I ain't worried about no Yankees," Joe said.

"I am," the man said. "Where y'all from anyhow?"

Joe avoided the question. "We're headed to the Shenandoah Valley."

"Virginia?" The man hit his leg and laughed. The horse started. The man pulled the horse's head forward. "Well, I'm fetching up west away from the Yankees. You tell 'em I said hi, won't you?" The man laughed again and moved on down the road.

Peter didn't like the looks of things, not at all. The Yankees coming down meant fighting, but Joe would not be detoured. He was set on Baldwyn. That meant Peter was bound there.

***

Close to sundown, they neared a crossroads and came upon a man leading some mules. Peter knew what that meant: he had been hiding them, and now it was getting late, so he was taking them back home.

"Hidy," the man said.

He was a young red-haired man, maybe twenty or so. He had a friendly round face. Peter saw right off he was a good person; sometimes it's easy to tell.

"Hi," Joe said. "Why you toting them mules?"

"Rumor is the Yankees are coming down from Ripley. Don't much believe it, though. Always rumors and not half pan out." He offered Joe his hand. "My name is Jason Wells."

Joe shook it. "I'm Joe, and this is Peter."

Jason reached for Peter's hand. Peter was surprised, not too many white men shook his hand. Peter took it. "Glad to know you, Mr. Wells."

"Where you fellas headed?"

"Baldwyn," Joe said.

"Y'all come from New Albany way?"

"Yes, sir," Peter said.

Jason smiled at Peter. "You're not a slave, are you?"

Before Peter could answer, Joe said, "He's as free as we are."

Peter didn't totally agree with Joe, but he left it at that.

Jason invited them to his home, convinced them it would be better to stay there for the night and strike out for Baldwyn bright and early. Peter liked the idea, and he helped persuade Joe.

Jason lived with his parents on a nice farm. The farm wasn't the size of the Taylor farm, but they had a nice crop of cotton in the field, plenty of hogs and chickens about the place, too.

The boys were invited to sleep in the barn, and that was fine with both. Jason brought them beans and potatoes. They were cold, but they were still good.

Jason didn't invite them into the big house. Peter knew why he wasn't, but he didn't know why Joe wasn't. It didn't seem to bother the boy, so it didn't matter.

Jason sat with them in the barn until well after dark. He was friendly and talkative. He had told them that he had heard the Yankees were north of there in Ripley Mississippi. He didn't know if it were true or not—a new rumor everyday—but he did say he had seen Rebel patrols coming and going.

"I don't believe the Yankees will come down this back road," Jason said. "They'll follow the rails." He stuffed some hay behind his back as he leaned against the barn wall. "Maybe go through New Albany again. You hear all sorts."

A very dark, middle-aged black man entered the barn. "Marster Jason, I's brought you some cider to share with these here fine gentmens."

Jason took the jug. "Thank you, Black Bill."

Bill started for the door.

"Wait a minute, Bill," Jason said. "Won't you join us?"

Bill grinned big. "I sho was hoping you'd say such."

"Black Bill?" Joe asked.

"Oh, yessuh, Marster. I's Black Bill. The other Bill on the place is Yellar Bill."

Jason winked; Joe and Peter laughed.

They passed the jug around quickly the first time, each one declaring it a fine cider, then they drew themselves into a circle and passed it more slowly as they talked.

Peter enjoyed the friendly chat. They talked of better times, before the war. Peter told of his family and of Dr. Taylor. Joe spoke fondly of his own family and told how he had to get home. Jason told his story and Bill told his.

Bill belonged to Jason's father, but to hear him talk, he owned the farm. He had always been there on the place, so he was part of it and it was part of him.

Peter found why he liked Jason right off. He was a preacher, rode the local circuit. Peter had wondered why he wasn't in the army; now he knew.

Jason told about his family, then he told Bible stories. Peter liked the way he told them, made it sound like the Bible stories happened yesterday, and left no doubt the stories were true.

Peter got the most laughs talking about Joe and his cutups. Bill hawed so hard he choked, then they laughed at him.

Peter had not felt so relaxed in a long time, and with total strangers, too. Good times were in short supply with the war raging.

"Mr. Wells, what exactly have you heard on the Yankees?" Joe asked.

So much for good times, Peter thought.

"George Fannon sent word down that the Yankees were up the Ripley road. Don't know if it is true, but I hid our mules this afternoon. I heard that General Forrest was at Rienzi, a piece south, and there have been patrols up this road coming and a going."

"Oh, them Yankees is about, sho nuff," Bill said. He pulled on the cider jug.

"Well now, Bill, do tell us what you know, pray," Jason said. He smiled at Joe and Peter.

Bill wiped his thick lips. "I tells ya, Marster Jason. And I tells you two fellars, too." He looked from side to side to make sure no one else heard this secret information. He tried to speak softly, but his booming voice was like a bull. "We niggers knows what's about.

Marster Jason know that true on that there head."

Jason winked and nodded.

"Wayne-Wayne come down from Ripley yesterday. That bees Marster Ryan's nigger cross the ways. He say he seed a bunch a them Yankees up 'bout Ripley. He say they's 'bout a million of 'em done come down from Memphis."

"But Bill, you know Wayne-Wayne has been known to stretch the truth," Jason said. "You remember last year when that Rebel patrol came through? He said he saw General Lee, himself, and we know that was a falsehood."

"That be true—that be true." Bill nodded. "But I believes Wayne-Wayne be on the level this here time, Marster Jason. He described them there Yankees to me cause he know I wouldn't believe on it no sorta ways, and he know I bees a authority on them blue bellies."

"Authority?" Peter asked.

"Well, yes, Peter," Jason said. He winked again. "Black Bill is our resident infinite store of knowledge."

Bill drew himself up. "That there a fact. That not to confuse me with Yellar Bill, what knowledge come some harder."

"Now Bill, don't be talking down on Yellow Bill," Jason said. "It ain't Christian."

"Oh, Lawd bless you, Marster Jason. Yellar Bill got his good side and that is a go." Bill patted Jason's knee and turned to Peter. "You see, Peter, I knows about them Yankees cause I done been to Memphis and seed 'em."

Joe laughed. "What did they look like, Black Bill?"

"Well, they's all got them blue suits on, juss like a bluebird. And didn't they all talk queer, too. That sorta talk can't answer to no kinda smart, I will fancy to add."

Joe nudged Peter in the side, said, "Bill, I heard they looked sort of like that. I heard they are all pretty big—bigger than our soldiers."

"Marster Joe, that there hits the thing 'bout in the middle. They's big like Goliath in the Bible."

Joe laughed.

"But if them Yankees come it down this here road, they gonna catch it a-coming and a-going. That there a fact." Bill smacked his fist in the palm of his hand.

"Black Bill," a soft voice came from the barn door."

Peter turned to see a lady, maybe in her fifties, standing inside the door, a very tidy woman, her hair in a bun.

Bill jumped to his feet, handing Jason the jug. "Lawd sakes, Missus, I done plumb forgot I spose to come straight back."

The other three rose, dusting hay from their butts.

"These are the two I was telling you about, Mother," Jason said. He pointed to them. "This is Joe and that is Peter."

"Hello, boys. I hope you find the barn comfortable. It is the only room that we have for you."

"It's fine, Ma'am," Joe and Peter replied at the same time.

"Well, good." She turned to Bill. "You were supposed to take the cider, then return to help Mr. Wells and the girls with the lamp oil."

"Lawd bless you, Missus, I just done forgot. I'm headed there now, sho is." Bill slipped from the barn like a child.

Mrs. Wells smiled as Bill left, turned to Joe and Peter. "I hope you boys rest well." She left when the two boys assured her the barn was comfortable enough.

Jason left shortly after, leaving the two nestled in the hay and the dark.

Joe was soon asleep. This left Peter alone with his thoughts and the night. Now and then a mule would bray or a horse would whinny. A mockingbird on the barn roof believed it was a good time to sing. Therefore, the night wasn't totally quiet, but they were good night sounds to Peter.

The smells of the farm were strong after the rainy days. Peter was used to these smells: hay, manure, leather, and even wildflowers. The smells reminded him of the farm he had just left.

The Taylors would be looking for the two boys. Lillie would be worried sick over Joe. However, they would not search far from the farm. If Joe was not close, they knew he was bound for Virginia. If the rumors of the Yankees were in the air there, too, they would stay tight at the farm and try to hide what they could from the Yankees.

Peter wished he was there to protect Zuey and the baby, to protect them all from the Yankees. But what could he do? He could hide, as the rest should. What could any man do against an army with weapons? A man could comply or die, that was all.

He couldn't let Joe lead them right to the Yankees, though. They had to avoid the armies—North and South. If they were going to Virginia, they had to slip by them all. But how? How were they going to walk all the way to Virginia? And they would have to walk if they were going to avoid the armies.

How were they going to eat? They had a little money left from the bag, but was it enough? Where would they stay at night? What would happen if one of them got hurt on the way? What would they do if they were robbed?

Peter reached for his bag in the dark. He fumbled around in it, pulled the Bible from it, and hugged it close. He didn't have to read the passage, knew it by heart: *In God is my salvation and my glory: the rock of my strength, and my refuge, is in God. Trust in him at all times; ye people, pour out your heart before him: God is a refuge for us.* Soon sleep found him with his arm around his Bible.

***

When Joe awoke the next morning, it was still dark. Peter was asleep, clutching his Bible. He did that a lot. Joe looked out the window and saw lights on at the house and at the little slave huts. He had heard horsemen on the road during the night and was curious. "Wake up, Peter; it's morning." Joe nudged him, and he sat up, rubbed his eyes.

Soon Jason arrived at the door with some flapjacks. "Y'all have this. I'm going to take the mules to the woodlot. There have been riders during the night, and I'm afraid the Yankees may come down this road, yet."

"Do you believe that, Mr. Wells?" Peter asked, getting to his feet.

"Pa doesn't want to take chance with the mules. We've just received word that the Yankees are at Stubb's farm just a few miles up the road." He smiled. "It seems Wayne-Wayne was telling the truth for once. I need to take a little more stock in the 'Negro network.'"

Joe dug into the breakfast. It was good, too. Peter didn't appear to want any, so Joe stuffed the rest in his bag.

The boys helped Jason gather the mules and horses.

"Jason, if you will show us the way to Baldwyn, we will head out," Joe said.

"No, we won't!" Peter said. "We are going to wait until

daylight."

What was the matter with him Joe wondered

Jason suggested they go to the woodlot with him until daylight. He would give them directions to Baldwyn and point the road out after the threat of Yankees was over.

***

They had just settled the animals in the woods when they heard horsemen on the road. They heard a few shots, then horses galloping south.

"What does it mean, you reckon?" Joe asked.

"I'm not sure," Jason said. "Sounds like they are headed toward Brice's Crossroads. You boys stay here. I'm going to cut through the woods to my cousin's to see if there is news." He mounted one of the horses and dodged his way through the dense woods and out of sight.

***

The boys were still in the woods at late morning. They could hear the armies moving on the road—cavalry they believed. Joe could tell Peter was scared. He held his Bible tight and prayed a lot. Joe wanted to leave, was restless as a mink in a cage, but Peter would not leave the spot until he believed it was safe. Hours had passed and Jason had not returned.

The musketry started, and the popping sounded like a crackling fire. The battle was growing like a storm.

"Reckon something done happened to Jason?" Joe asked.

"He'll be back soon," Peter said.

"I'm sick and tired of waiting in these woods like a squirrel. Let's just head east and take our chances."

Suddenly a loud boom exploded to the south. It shook the ground.

"Cannon!" Joe said. He jumped to his feet. "Did you hear it?"

Peter looked at Joe as if he had lost his mind. "I heard it. Lord, my God, not again."

Joe didn't know what was happening, and it was eating at him like a hunger. He wanted to see, wanted to know. He had waited in the blasted woods all day. If he couldn't leave, at least he wanted to know what was going on, but Peter wouldn't allow it.

***

In the afternoon, Jason appeared in the woods leading his horse.

Joe ran to him. "What did you find out? What's going on?"

Jason tied the horse to a sapling, took his hat off and wiped his brow. "Yankees were at my cousin's house. They took his horse and shot at him as he ran away. They seem to be everywhere. We hid out behind his place, too scared to move. I believe Forrest has made a stand near Brice's. That's the house at the crossroads where I met y'all."

They heard something coming and they all wheeled around. It was Black Bill. "Marster Jason, them Yankees is at the farm!" Bill was dripping with sweat, and his eyes were wild.

"Is the family all right?"

"I believe they is. Them Yankees is tearing up everything and eating everything on the place. They killing the chickens and the pigs. And they's a lot of colored Yankees, too. They tried to get me to go along with them, but I ain't joining no Yankee niggers, but that worthless Yellar Bill done gone and throwed in with 'em."

"Tell me it ain't so."

"He say it ain't nothing on the folks, but he want his freedom."

"That foolish simpleton—he's gonna get killed."

"I knowed it weren't no sorta good," Bill said.

"What about father?"

"He done skint out after you did, but I don't know where he go. The womans is still at the house."

Joe saw his opportunity. He sneaked away while Jason and Peter were getting the news from Bill. When he was out of their sight, he ran. Peter would be mad, but he would get over it. Joe had to see what was going on.

The woods were thick, and briars tore at him as he jumped rabbits and quails. After a good run, he saw a clearing and crept to the edge. It was the road, and Yankees were everywhere. He saw wagons stretched up and down the road and in the fields.

He saw many Negro soldiers. They were fanning out across the fields and woods. Joe guessed they were getting ready to defend that position. Smoke hung over the fields like a cloud, and the soldiers appeared and disappeared in it like demons.

An explosion shook everything and orange hell appeared past the smoke. The small trees behind him disappeared in splinters. Debris rained down on him. He dove to the ground and flattened out like an adder snake. Cannons thundered again, and he saw a wad of soldiers blow apart. Pieces of bodies rained down. The Yankees returned fire, their muskets making a loud ripping sound. Men were screaming and cussing and yelling, but nothing could be understood.

He wanted to run back to Peter. This was the mistake of all mistakes coming here. He was too scared to move. He had never been scared like this—never. His whole body trembled like a wet dog.

He now saw the Confederates coming out of the smoke like devils. This was surely hell. They were slowly advancing, and he saw the cannons at the front. Instantly all he saw was fire and smoke as the cannoneers fired.

What the hell was he doing here? Had he gone insane? He scurried behind a tree and buried into the dirt like a groundhog.

Cannons roared again. The ground in front of him ripped away as if an invisible plow had been flung through it. Little circles of smoke rose from the ground.

Shortly two Yankees ran across the field, coming toward him and the cover of the trees. The cannons came alive again, and they disappeared. Guts strung down the field, and blood flew like red paint.

Smoke rolled across the field and into the woods. It burned Joe's throat, but he tried not to cough—could not let anyone know where he was. Then he thought: how are they going to hear me above all of this?

A soldier ran out of the smoke and slid behind a tree not ten feet from him. He was a Negro Yankee. Joe stared at him and he stared back at Joe. The soldier was shaking all over. His teeth were chattering so loud, Joe could hear them above the battle. He said nothing to Joe, and Joe said nothing to him. They both simply turned back to watch the battle.

When the smoke drifted away for a spell, Joe saw wagons stacked up on the road. Some were turned over and wedged, and the Yankees were abandoning them and running for their lives.

Joe saw the Rebel cavalry swooping around the ends of the Yankees with their revolvers blazing. He felt sorry for the Negro soldiers—some were running and some seemed to be melting to the ground.

Confederate soldiers pushed the cannons down the road by

hand. They would stop, shoot, then push them farther. The gray army would not be stopped. Joe had no doubt of that. This was not Helena.

Out of the corner of Joe's eye, he saw the Negro soldier move. Joe turned. The Negro was raising his hands. Confederate soldiers materialized in the woods from behind like spirits. They were ragged and ghostly. Joe wondered what they would do with their Negro prisoner. He prayed they realized he wasn't a Yankee like the Negro.

A nasty black-bearded man walked up to the Negro, raised his revolver, and shot his left eye out.

The Negro fell over slowly like a felled tree. Joe looked at the Rebel. Joe saw the man's mouth move, but he couldn't hear him. Strange. The man pointed back the way he had come. He bent down to Joe's face and yelled something, but Joe only saw his mouth move. The man rose and shook his head, then charged on with the other ghosts.

Joe looked at the Negro. Green flies were already on the hole in his face. Joe slowly looked around, couldn't believe it was all real. The Rebels drove past him.

Joe looked at his hands. They were shaking, and he couldn't stop them. He was numb all over, and it was hard for him to breathe. He placed his trembling hands under his armpits to steady them.

Slowly he recognized sound again, then he shot back to reality like a slap on the face. The sound of war was suddenly too loud to bear. The sight of the dead soldier was too much to stand. He slowly lifted himself from the ground and slipped back to the camp.

***

Jason and Bill were sitting on a log when Joe returned.

"Where have you been?" Jason said.

Joe looked around. "Where is Peter?"

"Them Rebels done took him," Bill said.

"What are you talking about?" Joe said. "Took him where?" Joe fell to his butt.

"We don't know," Jason said. "We tried to tell them that he was with us, but they would not believe it. They said he talked too good. They said he had a Yankee talk."

"No," Joe said. "Didn't you tell them he was free?"

"We tried," Jason said.

223

"They's gonna kill him at first," Bill said. "But one a them sesesh mens said being he didn't have on no uniform they would have to see the captain. So they fetched him off with a gun in his back."

"I got to find him," Joe said. He jumped to his feet and started for the road.

Jason grabbed his arm. "He told me to look out for you until this matter is resolved."

Joe jerked free. "Where did they take him?"

"We will find out tomorrow. Nothing can be done now while they are still fighting. We could all be killed."

Joe settled down; Jason was right. When the fighting was over, it would be easier to find him. But how easy would it be? There were hundreds of Negroes in that one field alone. But Peter wasn't a soldier. Why did they grab him? They didn't get Bill. Damn Peter for talking so good. Damn himself—he should have stayed to protect Peter.

The fighting moved north. Joe could hear it like a storm moving across the land. This left no doubt that the Confederates were winning since they had come up from the south, and from the sound of things and what Joe had seen in the field, they were going to have a total victory. What would it mean in the morning?

They settled in for the night. Jason had made a little shelter from an Indian rubber coat and some saplings. It was just big enough for the three of them to lay huddled together. It was a good thing they had the shelter because it began to rain again at dark. It was a nasty rain—an unwelcome one, but it did settle the sulfur smell a bit.

**

At daylight, Jason and Joe left the mules with Bill and sneaked to the farm. What they found when they left the woods was a nightmare. Bodies lay everywhere and in all sorts of distorted positions. Joe began to count the bodies, but it made him sick to his stomach. The dead Negro soldiers stood out. They made him think of the poor soldier rotting in the woods.

The road was littered with debris: guns, knapsacks, shoes, clothes, canteens, and many other articles that Joe couldn't identify.

He saw Yankee wagons, too, and the local people were going through them until some Confederate soldiers came up and ran them off.

There were many Rebel troops at Jason's home—what was left

of his home. The cannons had taken a toll on it. Hunks of the house were gone. It was full of holes like a woodpecker tree.

They found Jason's mother and his sisters in the house. They were safe, but told how they had hid in the parlor as the war enveloped them. They said the Yankees had stolen most of their possessions.

The Yankees had stolen from the slaves, too. The war had turned into a war to free the darkies, so why would the very army that was coming to free them steal from them? It was like back at Uncle Zeke's farm. War gave men a free pass to do bad things, and they did bad things wholesale.

The women were especially shocked when the black soldiers had raided their home. The colored soldiers had said they were going to make Forrest pay for Fort Pillow. Joe remembered something about Yankees accusing Forrest's men of murdering surrendering soldiers there. Hours later when the battle was lost for the Yankees, some of the Negro troops were horrified and begged the civilians for protection. Joe saw why: the black troops lay scattered.

A portion of the Confederate army came back down the road with hundreds of prisoners—very few were black. The prisoners were a sad looking lot. Joe felt sorry for them. But he still saw no sign of Peter.

He stayed in Jason's barn again that night. It was a long night. Confederate outfits were camped all about the farm, so there was a different feeling than the night before, and no cider.

Joe found it hard to sleep for once. Where was Peter? How long would he look for him? The answer to the last question was simple: until he found him. He was going nowhere without Peter.

As Joe lay in the hay, he listened to the men in the camps laughing and talking. The longer he lay there, the more he missed Peter. Finally, he came up with a plan. Tomorrow he would go from camp to camp searching. He knew he had to start first thing. He had no idea when the Rebels would pull out, but when they did, it would be too late—who knew where they would go. With the plan set, he finally found sleep.

***

Joe awoke the next day to a dreary rain. He would just have to get wet because he was determined to find Peter.

When Joe left the barn, he saw someone had been burying the

dead. They weren't burying them six feet either. In fact, Joe saw a black hand sticking out of one the graves like a marker stick in a garden. Dead horses had been set afire, but the rain had put the fire out, leaving something Joe had to turn away from. As horrible as it was, the cooked animals smelled like a smokehouse. At that instant, Joe felt he could never eat smoked ham again.

The rain poured. Everything was miserable and wet. Joe wondered if the rain would ever end. The rain had even run the gravediggers in. The bodies along the road were hard to witness. They were beginning to swell, and buttons were begging on the clothes. The smell was starting. It wouldn't be long before it would be unbearable. He hoped to be gone by then.

That was enough. It was foolish to think he could find Peter in all of this rain. Everyone had taken shelter. He was alone with the death, with the leftovers of war. Joe ran all the way back to Jason's barn. He threw himself on the hay. He was wet and cold, had seen things that a thirteen-year-old should never see. And he was alone. He was alone somewhere in Mississippi far from the Shenandoah Valley. The closest thing to family that he had now was Peter. And where was he? Where was everyone that he cared for? Dead! His mother and sister were dead. Uncle Wilbur and Katie Bea were dead. Who knew where his pa was? And now Peter is gone.

Joe tried to hold it in, but it was no use, and he cried. He couldn't stop. It was totally out of his control. Everyone was dead—everyone.

Joe felt a hand on his back. He rose from the hay. It was Black Bill. "What the matter with the young marster?"

Joe rubbed at his eyes and tried to pull himself together, but the sobbing wouldn't let go. Joe couldn't find the words to answer.

"Bill know. It Peter." Bill softly patted Joe's shoulder.

Joe simply nodded.

"I tells you what." Bill perked and stood. "I can't helps you today, cause Bill's gotta help fix up things around here, but tomorrow we take a couple of horses and we go find Peter. I'll talks it over with the marster and we'll be off."

Joe felt hope.

***

Peter rode with the soldiers as they left Ripley headed back south. He had nowhere to run. If he tried to escape, he would be shot; he had no doubt of that. The best plan would be to just go right along. They were going back south and down the road that went by the farm.

He counted himself fortunate. The Rebels treated him well compared to the way they treated the Negro prisoners. In fact, they had killed many of the black soldiers, and the others were marching back to certain bondage.

The pitiful look on the Negro soldiers was surprise and horror. They had believed they could win the fight. They had not expected Forrest's army to be so strong. Now they were bound back into slavery. One had told Peter he now believed the North could never defeat the South, not even if Joshua led the army and they had a million men.

Peter didn't have to march on foot. He had a mule to ride. A Corporal Green had appointed Peter as his body servant. Green had taken Peter's free papers and crammed them in his knapsack. He had told Peter if he was a good nigger, he would set him free when the outfit was on the move again. Peter didn't take much stock in that, but he didn't have too many options at the present.

The most urgent thing on Peter's mind was Joe. Was he all right? Where did he slip off to during the battle? He had to find him. But how?

Green rode beside Peter. "See them niggers going there?" Green said, pointing to some prisoners trudging in the mud.

Peter nodded. He wondered where Green was going with this.

"Ain't you lucky you ain't them?" Green smiled. "You are a good boy, Peter. I believe I will keep you for mine."

"Mr. Gree—"

"Master Green." Green said.

Peter hated it, but he had no choice. "Massuh Green."

"That's much better. I think we'll get along good together."

"You said you would let me go, and what about young Joe I was telling you about?"

"I'm sure Joe will be fine. I'll think on the matter."

Green put spurs to the horse and moved on ahead.

Peter knew Green was not going to let him go. He would have to make a move when he neared Jason's farm, or he may never see Joe again.

Peter didn't have to wait long. He spotted Joe's blonde hair. He was riding one of Jason's horses and Bill on another. They were riding against the flowing tide, and the soldiers cursed them.

Peter saw the instant Joe spotted him. Joe stood in the stirrups and yelled. It was a deep comfort, hearing Joe call his name. Finally, he would be free, and more: the boy was safe.

Joe and Bill pulled along side Peter.

"What are you doing on that mule?" Joe said.

What a foolish thing to say. He knew well what he was doing there.

Before Peter could say a word, Green galloped up. "Boy, you need to leave my nigger alone."

Joe wheeled in the saddle. "Peter is a free man, and if you are holding him against his will, you are a thief and a scoundrel."

Bill's eyes got big, and Peter saw he was looking for a quick get-away, but with so many black prisoners passing, it would be best to stay right there atop that horse.

Green spurred his horse toward Joe. Just as he got to Joe, Joe jumped from the horse, and like a shot, he was under Green's horse. Green's horse reared, and he tumbled off.

Joe turned to Peter. "Come on, Peter; jump on my horse!"

Peter leaped from the mule and was on the horse in an instant. He reached for Joe, but Green grabbed Joe from behind and pulled him to the ground. Peter started down from the horse. Green pulled his revolver with a free hand and pointed it at him. He could do nothing, but stay on the animal.

"Massuh Green, don't harm the boy," Peter said.

Green started to say something to Peter.

Joe drew back and popped Green in the face with his fist. He groaned and let go of Joe for an instant. That was all Joe needed. He ran, jumped for the horse.

Green fired the revolver at Joe. The horse began bucking and stomping.

Peter couldn't believe it. It happened so fast. He couldn't see Joe under the horse, but heard him yelling.

Peter leaped from his horse and pulled the bucking beast away from Joe.

Joe was rolling around, moaning.

"Joe! Where are you hit? Where are you hit?" Peter rolled him over. He was holding his left leg.

A soldier pulled Peter aside and looked at Joe's leg.

Peter saw it was an officer.

"Son, where are you injured?"

Joe tried to answer, but he could only moan and hold his leg.

"General, he was trying to steal my servant," Green said.

At that instant, Peter knew it was General Forrest.

Joe moaned, and through gritted teeth, he said, "That man is a liar and a thief. Peter is not his servant. He is not even a slave. He is a free man, and he is with me. That man stole him, and I aim to get him back."

Forrest looked at Green. Green's nose was bleeding where Joe had hit him. "Corporal, I believe this boy is telling the truth."

Green opened his mouth, but thought better of it.

"Son, are you shot?" Forrest asked.

"No, sir, the horse stepped on my leg."

Forrest took Joe's arm; Peter quickly grabbed the other arm.

Joe moaned. He couldn't stand on the leg, so he leaned on Peter.

Forrest had the surgeon look at it. It was just badly bruised.

"Do you live around here?" Forrest asked.

"We are headed to the Shenandoah Valley. We just got caught here in this battle," Joe said.

Forrest looked at Peter. Forrest was a tall man and intimidating. Peter was frightened just being in his presence. "You going with this boy to Virginia?"

"Yes, sir," Peter said. "He has family there. His uncle died in Arkansas, so now we are going to Virginia. His father is fighting in General Lee's army"

Peter had a pain in his gut. Even though this was true, it was misleading because Joe also had family in Mississippi. He hoped that General Forrest would not see through it.

Forrest stared into Peter's eyes. Peter felt his knees get weak. Then Forrest looked at Joe gritting his teeth and leaning on Peter. He slowly nodded. Peter didn't know what it meant.

"Corporal," Forrest called out.

Green ran to Forrest. "Sir?"

Forrest looked at Green for a long minute. "I would hit you myself, but it looks as if the boy has fetched enough blood from you."

Green said nothing and Peter saw he was frightened and

embarrassed with the blood still running from his nose.

Forrest looked past Green to a train of mules. "Someone bring me one of those mules."

An officer with Forrest started one that way.

"No—we must have the poorest beast," Forrest said. "We need the strong ones for the army."

Eventually one of the soldiers led a swayback to the general. It was a funny looking animal with a big "US" branded on its rump.

Forrest bent down to Joe. "Son, my man brought you harm. He stole your Negro, and I want to make it right. I don't know how long that leg will bother you so I'm going to give you a mule, such as it is."

Joe smiled through the pain.

Forrest got Joe and Peter's names. He walked to one of his aids, retrieved some paper, and wrote something. He came back and handed it to Peter.

"Peter, I see you are watching out for the boy. I also see that he is watching out for you, but I believe you are the best one to hold on to this. It is a pass that will let you get through our lines. I can't speak for the Yankees."

Peter remembered his free papers. "General, Sir, that man has my free papers."

Green quickly dug them from his bag and handed them to Peter.

Forrest mounted his horse and turned to one of his officers. "Now let us see if we can put a stop to the citizens stealing from my wagons." He turned back to Joe. "Oh, boy, I'm happy to see you no longer have that Yankee cap you had on in New Albany."

Joe looked surprised. Peter remembered Joe telling him he saw General Forrest at New Albany.

When Forrest galloped away, the army kept moving south.

Peter felt they were fortunate. General Forrest was upset about things being stolen from the captured wagons, yet gave them a mule. They could have all been killed instead. He put Joe on the mule, then mounted the horse Bill was holding.

"Bill, can you show us a road that will carry us east?" Peter asked.

Through gritted teeth, Joe said, "Good idea, Peter."

"I knows the way," Bill said. "Get up, hoss. Lay some hoofs."

Chapter 16

The ragged shelter wasn't much protection against the swarm of mosquitoes, so Lucius sat by the small fire drinking coffee made from stolen Yankee coffee beans, hoping the smoke would keep the bugs away.

The eastern sky glowed pink above the Mississippi River as wood ducks whistled overhead. Oh, if he could get his hands on one of those ducks it would be a satisfying meal, indeed.

Right on time, he heard the Yankees beating the morning drums in town. The damn Yankees were no different from any other white people. They were comfortable in town and had plenty to eat, didn't give a damn about the Negroes. One white was like the next.

Lucius looked at his small rickety shelter, about like the rest in the freedom camp, made of scrapped boards, sticks, cloth, and anything else he could find to throw together. White people's dogs had it better. It was no way for anyone to live.

He stood up and looked over the camp. It was a nasty sight, simply a garbage dump. He heard more ducks overhead, was a wonder he heard them at all because of the coughing. He couldn't really tell one cough from another. There were so many—they made one song and it echoed every morning, a song he was tired of hearing. Other people were coming out of their holes, mostly women. They would start their morning ritual cooking breakfast. They would stew up whatever the good white folks had allowed them, or whatever rat or critter they had found.

Some had gone north and some had gone to work on the government farms. But to Lucius that was no better than being a slave all over again. He would die first. He would never—never serve another master. He was his own master now. He owned his body and his soul. His direction was of his choosing.

Now he was beginning to think he had chosen poorly. He should have let the doctor live. If he had, he would be comfortable now and well fed. He must learn from this mistake, must be willing to bow down, but only for what is necessary and as long as necessary.

He placed a chunk of wood on the fire, then sat on the piece of chair he had found and stared into the small blaze. The fire popped and crackled. He remembered the store fire from almost a year ago. That was not in his plans. The store was not supposed to burn. He had figured someone would acquire the store after the good doctor was found dead. That someone would surely keep him on because he was a good worker. That was his backup plan, anyhow. That damn white-headed boy was to blame. If he ever got his hands on that boy, he would pay for all of the suffering Lucius had endured—before and after the store burned. And if that nigger, Peter, stood in the way, he would pay the price. All niggers that cuddled up to white folks had it coming anyhow.

He bent forward and held his hands close to the fire, studied his hands; they were big and strong. He made two fists; they were like cannonballs. They were strong weapons and nothing could stand up under a pounding from them. Men had died from blows of the weapons, black and white. The most prized trophy— or victim—was his old master.

As he thought about his master, his hands went to his shoulders. He felt the scars even through his shirt. They crossed his back like a spider web. He didn't get them all at one time—oh, no. They grew slowly—a few whelps today, a few more tomorrow, and still a few more next week until it looked like the web of a garden spider. As he touched them, he remembered the pain—not from the whippings, but from the salt that was rubbed in.

He remembered the shame from hanging from his tied wrists without any clothes on, still remembered the dogs licking him as he hung there, and him too weak to run them away. They licked him all over, even down below. Everyone could see, but nothing could be done. But his master paid. Lucius smiled.

Now one of the Negro women approached Lucius. "Let me have just a small stick of wood."

Lucius shot to his feet so fast the chair flipped out behind him.

"No! I told y'all to never come near my camp."

"I's got to cook for my children. They is—"

"No!"

She retreated, looking back over her shoulder like a scared dog.

Lucius set the chair close to the fire and stared into it again. The coals glowed bright, then dim, then bright again. It reminded him of something flying—bright, dim, bright, dim—like wings—up, down, up, down.

His mind went where it always went when there was idle time to think—his mother's story of the African birds.

***

"Your father was a black African; he was a chief," she had said as she plucked the feathers from a chicken. "He didn't talk no American at first. He only talked that African talk."

Lucius wished he could have known him, wished he could have seen him.

"What did he look like?" he asked as he put the feathers in a sack.

"Lawd sakes, he was black. He was blacker'n any darky on the place, but he was a purty man and a brave man. When they first brung him here, he had bracelets on his wrists made up of lion claws."

"Did he kill them lions?"

"Sho he did." She flipped the chicken over and went to work on the other side. "He had a tiger skin wrapped around him, and he killed that, too."

Lucius smiled, and his mother smiled back.

"But the thing I remembers the most is the hoodoo charm he had around his neck. The chain was made a real gold, and birds hung from it—African birds."

"Tell me more 'bout them birds." Lucius's young eyes were wide, now.

She had plucked the chicken clean and had cut a hole in it to get to the guts. She smiled. "Now let me see. Well now, them birds was in a yellow ring like the sun and they had red eyes of fire. They was gold birds. I reckon I remember that 'bout right."

"What happened to the charm?"

"Well, when Massuh sold your pa, the charm was still around his neck."

"Why didn't they take the charm from him like they take everything else?"

"Heaven sake, boy, that was a hoodoo charm—African magic. They couldn't take it from him lessen he was dead, no ways. It had powers, and them white folk knowed it." She smiled bigger and cut her eyes. "Oh, they knowed your pa was wild, so Massuh sold him to a trader a going to the frontier. I specs he done crossed the Mississippi into Arkansas or there 'bouts."

"How far is it to Arkansas?"

"Child, I don't know." She pulled a long gut from the chicken. "Let me see. We is in Georgia. The next state bees Alabama, then Mississippi, then you is got the Mississippi River. Lawd be, child, I don't know. It that way some place."

"Reckon that charm make me a king?"

She stopped pulling guts and sadly looked at him. She studied so long, Lucius wondered if she was going to answer. "I spec you find that charm, you be a king," she said softly.

Lucius grinned. "I's going to find them African birds some day. I's going to be a king. I's going to kill tigers and lions."

His mother started to speak, but the words didn't come. She looked down at the chicken, but looked through it. Then she slowly started pulling the guts again.

Lucius sensed something wrong. "You all right, Mammy?"

"Son, you knows peoples tells stories sometimes. Now bout them African birds—"

Lucius slapped his leg and spun around. "I's going to find them African birds. I is—I is! I is going to be king."

***

The wind changed direction now and blew the smoke on Lucius. He fanned it away and stood up. He had found Arkansas. He had also found the charm. What else could it be? As he had gotten older, he had begun to believe it was just a story his mammy had made up, and maybe some of it was, but now it was different. He had found the birds. The Taylor necklace was the charm. It had to be. Now what was he going to do about it? How long was he going to stay at this camp like a hog?

He kicked dirt into the fire and went into his shelter. He swept dirt from some hidden floorboards, raised them up, and pulled two bottles labeled laudanum from a hole. He next pulled a smaller bottle that contained a white powder. He placed them in a ragged haversack, then he pulled a long knife from the hole and stuck it in his boot. He went outside, thought about telling the woman she could have all of the firewood, but instead he turned and started for Helena.

***

Helena made Lucius sick. He hated to see the Negroes begging for work. Hell, if they had to beg, why didn't they just go back to their masters? The Yankees were the masters now. What was the difference? At least the Southern masters took care that their property stayed healthy like they did their animals. He despised the Negro soldiers, too. They fooled they selves if they thought they were like the white Yankees.

Lucius walked past the place where the Taylor store had stood. Someone had cleaned the lot. He looked in the storage shed. It was empty.

"What you looking for, darky?"

Lucius turned to see a Yankee standing there.

"Lawd sakes, Massuh, I's looking for Massuh Theo. Is you done seen 'em?"

The Yankee studied his feet. Lucius saw he was trying to remember the name. The Yankee looked up suddenly and snapped his fingers. "That fat man that worked in the store."

"Yessuh." Lucius grinned a big toothy grin. "He bees round."

"I don't know what you want with that piece." The Yankee shook his head. "But you will find him down by the wharf."

"He working there?"

"Working? Drinking and begging is his lot now."

***

The wharf was busy as an anthill. Steamboats were always coming and going. Cotton was stacked everywhere, and the Negroes were doing most of the work. Lucius could plainly see these Yankees were not interested in a Negro's freedom. They were only interested in the cotton. They traded for it or stole it.

"Hey, boy, you want work," a sailor called from a ramp.

"No, suh, I's got a heap a work," Lucius said. "I's looking for my massuh."

The sailor shook his head and started up the gangway.

Lucius found Theo huddled next to a bale of cotton. He was asleep and had pulled loose cotton over him for a blanket. His clothes were rags and he had lost weight, but he was still fat. He reminded Lucius of a dog. "Why, Massuh Theo, you is a right sad sight," Lucius said.

Theo jumped and his bloodshot eyes flashed open.

"Good, good, I was feared you had done gone up," Lucius said.

"Damn you, Lucius. You gave me a start. Now go way and stop meddling me."

Lucius could think of nothing better than placing his boot across Theo's neck. Instead, he pulled a tin cup from his bag and poured some laudanum into it.

"What you got there, boy?"

"Boy" cut like a knife, but Lucius knew he had to let it go for now.

"This here make you feel a heap better, Massuh Theo. Yessuh, a heap better."

"What is it?"

"It a good tonic."

"I don't want none of your nigger potions."

"Just sniff it Massuh. You change your mind, by and by."

Theo took the cup, ran it under his nose, and gulped it. He wobbled to his feet. "Give me the rest of that."

"I will give you more later," Lucius said.

Theo reached for it, and Lucius easily pushed him away. Theo started yelling something about a nigger, but Lucius hit him with one of his cannonballs, and Theo crumpled like a shot hog. Lucius slung him over his shoulder and headed for a hiding spot by the river he had found earlier. He walked by a white man and two Negroes heading toward the wharf. "Massuh done had way too much licker."

The white man looked at Theo's face, recognized him. "You need to keep your master away from down here before somebody cuts his begging throat."

"Yessuh, Massuh, sho will—sho will."

Lucius made his way to the cottonwood and willow tangle he had found earlier, dumped Theo on the ground. He hit the ground hard, jarred him awake.

Theo blinked his eyes a few times, then focused on Lucius. "You sorry nig—"

Lucius grabbed him around the throat with his huge hands. Theo's face grew red as blood.

"Don't you ever call me 'nigger' again. Don't call me 'boy.' You call me 'Lucius.' Does you understand me?" Theo tried to nod, so Lucius relaxed his grip.

Theo rubbed his throat. "What do you want with me?"

A smile bloomed on Lucius. "Why, Massuh Theo, I wants to do business with you."

"What sort of business?"

"It seem like I needs a massuh where I is going to."

"What you talking about, Lucius?" Theo sat up and rubbed his jaw where Lucius had hit him earlier.

"I's going over to Mississippi, and I needs you to come along as my massuh."

"Mississippi?" Theo stumbled to his feet. "I ain't going, I'll be bound. Ole Forrest will have me in his cavalry."

"You is going, and you is going right off tonight." Lucius pulled a bottle of laudanum from his bag. "I got a passel of this here, and you can have it. All you got to do is be my massuh til I find what I's looking for."

Theo reached for the bottle, but Lucius pulled it back. Lucius poured him a small shot in a cup. "I's got plenty and I's got opium, too."

Theo gulped the liquid from the cup. "What are you after in Mississippi?" He handed the cup back to Lucius.

"I's after the Taylor boy. I's after the Taylor money, and I will split it with Massuh Theo."

Theo grinned. That was exactly what Lucius believed he would do, the greedy ape.

Lucius pulled some clothes from a bag. "Put these here clothes on. You don't looks like no massuh in them tore up rags."

"Where did you get those?"

"One thing Massuh Theo gots to know—I is a sourceful nigger."

The muddy river appeared lazy as Lucius moved away from the bank, and the torches at the wharf made soft reflections on the water.

The night was black as tar, and the stars looked so close Lucius might could pluck them like grapes if he had a mind to. However, at that minute he just wanted to get across the river before the two were discovered. He pulled at the oars hard, but the current showed him that though Old Man River may appear tame, it was always wild and strong. Theo was of no use; he lay in the boat drunk, or whatever the laudanum did to him. Lucius would give a smaller dose next time.

As Lucius fought with the churning current, he remembered how two years ago he had swum the river hanging onto a log, fighting for his life to get to Helena and freedom. Now here he was trying to get back across the Mississippi in a stolen skiff with a stupid, drunk white man. Was it worth it? Were the African birds worth all of this?

Was the story true about the African birds? It could have been a wild story his mammy had told for fun. That seemed more likely than not. No—it had to be true. There had to be more to life than just the freedom camp. Maybe there wasn't magic in it, but still it belonged to his father. Or did it? He shook his head, reached into the cool water, and splashed some on his face. He would think no more of it. It was useless. The story had to be true. There had to be a reason to life. He had not escaped slavery just to wind up in a Yankee hellhole. There had to be something else. That something was his father's charm—the key to Africa.

The Taylor boy would pay for taking it. Lucius could feel the boy's scrawny little neck in his hands even now as he squeezed the oars. The boy didn't know what he had. It meant nothing to him, just another piece of jewelry. White people had everything and the blacks had nothing, but that would change soon, and it would start changing when Lucius found that white-headed boy.

The little black boy paddled across the lake and loaded Lucius and Theo into the leaking boat. Lucius saw the bridge was gone. It was there when he came through two years ago, but many things can change in two years.

The boy stayed at the lake while the two men went on. Lucius figured out the boy was a lookout. It must have seemed to the boy these two posed no threat. That was good. Lucius had schooled Theo on what he wanted him to do and say, and Lucius was surprised at how well Theo played the part. Maybe this plan would work after all. It had to—it was the only plan Lucius had.

The Negroes in the fields chopping cotton looked up briefly, but went back to work. Lucius assumed that one Negro and a white man was nothing to be worried about.

When they arrived at the big house, there was a pretty white woman standing on the porch. On the steps below her was a gray-headed Negro. Lucius could see right off by the arrogant look he was boss nigger.

As they approached the gate, Theo played his part, swept his cap off and bowed. "Good morning, my dear lady."

The woman bowed her head slightly.

"Ma'am, could we bother you for a drink from your well?" Theo asked.

"Cluck, show this gentleman and his servant to the well."

Niggers will answer to anything, Lucius thought. He'd be damned if he would answer to such a ridiculous name.

"Right this here way, Marster," Cluck said.

A little black boy was drawing the water when they went to the well.

"Efficient lot of darkies, I tell you," Theo said to Lucius. "You take notice, Lucius, and you will do well."

Lucius bowed. "Yessuh, Massuh. I's do good like these here niggers does."

"If Marster don't mind me asking, why is y'all coming from Helena way?" Cluck asked.

"Not at all—not at all, my good boy. I've just been to Helena to fetch my boy, Lucius, back. He reckoned he wanted his freedom, but now he realizes that he belongs back home on the place. Ain't that right Lucius?"

Lucius nodded his head vigorously. "Oh, yessuh, Massuh, yessuh, I's so glad to be headed back to home. I sho is."

"If the marster don't mind, we didn't see you come this here way a-going to Helena," Cluck said.

"You sure didn't—you sure didn't—that's a fact. I came

Memphis way."

A little Negro girl ran from the front of the house. "Marster, Missus would like to see you on the veranda."

This would be the test, Lucius thought. If Theo didn't give up the goods now, they might just make the plan work.

When Theo went to the house, Cluck stared at Lucius for a long time without saying anything. Lucius was beginning to think something was going wrong until Cluck finally spoke.

"What it like at Helena? What so bad there that you give up your freedom to come back to Mississippi?"

Now it was time for Lucius to play his part. "Freedom? Niggers is dying over there in Helena. Them Yankees is worser than any massuh. They make you work just the same, but they don't take care of you like most massuhs does."

Cluck drank a dipper of water, then handed it to Lucius.

"We don't get many a-coming and a-going from Helena. I spec most of them niggers in Helena is from Arkansas," Cluck said.

"Most is, but not all."

"We had a white boy and a nigger come from that way last year," Cluck said, taking the dipper from Lucius.

Lucius's heart leaped.

"They said what you said 'bout that camp at Helena. I sho wouldn't want to be there."

"Where was that white boy and nigger headed to?"

Cluck eyed Lucius. "Why does you want to know?"

"I just making talk—that all."

Cluck studied on it for a spell, then said, "They's headed toward New Albany I believes they say."

"I reckon I never heard of this place called New Albany. Must be a far piece."

"I specs it bees far enough, if you have to walk it. I's never been there, but I knows about it."

"I reckon you knows a lot. You's the head man on the place, ain't you?" Lucius showed a toothy grin.

"I is that. We ain't got no need for no overseer with me on the place. The Missus got total trust in old Cluck, and I aim to do right by her, too." Cluck clucked his tongue.

"You look after this whole plantation?" Lucius asked.

"In fact I do."

Lucius looked all around and made sure the wonder showed on his face. "Massuh would never trust a nigger like me to a small job, let alone nothing like this here," Lucius said.

"Well, I specs not." Cluck clucked his tongue, again. "You's done gone and runned off to Helena, and he had to fetch you back." Cluck narrowed his eyes. "Now that I thinks on it, how come he knowed you was in Helena and was wanting to come back home?"

Damn, Lucius thought. This was a smart nigger here. Now he's got to go and ask these wise-ass questions. "Well, you see now. It like this here. There was this preacher man that come to the camp, and this preacher man, well, he was from the parts that I runned off from. I knowed him right off, and he knowed me, so I asked him if he would ask my massuh to come fetch me, cause I was ready to come home. Then one day I look up and there my massuh; he done come to fetch me juss like I ask."

Cluck frowned and was starting to say something when a shot rang out from the front of the house. Cluck and Lucius raced toward the front.

This couldn't be good in any way, Lucius thought. What the hell could Theo be up to?

"You," Mrs. Donner said to Lucius when he rounded the house. "I have a mind to shoot your master. You are welcome to stay on with us if I do."

What the hell happened? Lucius couldn't believe his eyes. The woman had a big revolver leveled at Theo's head. She didn't look bashful about using it, either. He had to think fast.

"Oh, please don't shoot Massuh. He got a family back home."

She took aim at Theo.

Theo squeezed his eyes shut.

"Does your master have a wife back home?" she asked.

"Yessum, and some chilluns, too."

"Then you best get him off my veranda and my property, or they will be widow and orphans."

Lucius ran up the porch and seized Theo by the arm. "Come on, Massuh. We best being going on down the road."

Theo said nothing. No one else said anything. Everyone just stared as the two went through the white gate. After they had gone down the road a piece, Lucius looked back and they were still staring. Strange place.

***

Just after dark they passed though some small town, didn't bother to find out the name. Lucius figured the farther they were from people the better. He was still steamed at Theo. The man was as ignorant as a cow. He had grabbed the woman after she invited him in for coffee. What a fool. She had stuck the gun in Theo's lard belly before he had a clue. He could have ruined everything if she had pulled the trigger then. Instead, she waited until she marched him outside, and then she shot between his legs.

They set up camp close to a stream. The frogs sang their strange songs and night birds whistled in the woods. It felt good to be there. It felt free compared to Helena.

Lucius placed a few more sticks on the fire. Theo lay beside it with his fat head propped on his hand.

"That was a fine woman, I tell you," Theo said. "What I could do if only I had just a little time."

"Shut up, you fool. You almost ruined my plan."

"That ain't no way to be a talking to your master."

Quick as a rattler, Lucius kicked Theo's arm from under his head and his face crashed to the dirt.

"What the hell did you do that for?" Theo sat up and brushed dirt from his face.

Lucius quickly wrapped his big arm around Theo's head and clamped down. Theo grabbed at his arm, but could not budge it.

"What the hell are you doing?"

"The next time you pulls a foolish shine like that, I'll squash your head like a punkin. Does you understand me, white man?"

Theo said nothing.

Lucius clamped down harder. "Does you?"

Theo shrieked, "I do—I do!"

Lucius moved to the opposite side of the fire, sat, and smiled at Theo. Theo rubbed his big head.

Lucius pulled a piece of bread from his bag, pulled a chunk off for himself and handed the rest to Theo. Lucius took a big bite. With a mouth full he said, "We can have all the Taylor money, but you got to does like I say."

Theo said nothing, just nibbled at the bread. He was puffed up like a toad-frog.

Lucius laughed aloud. He stopped when he heard a horse coming down the road. He started to put out the fire, but thought it best to look normal.

"All right, Theo, you bees a good massuh. Remember, we could have the Taylor money."

"Yo at the fire," called the rider.

Theo looked angrily at Lucius, then smiled and called back. "Approach the camp, and welcome."

It was a young Rebel lieutenant. He looked barely twenty. His clothes were ragged and dirty. He tied his horse to a sapling.

"Sit down by the fire here, soldier," Theo said.

"Yessum, Massuh, sit by the fire and let it chase them skeeters away," Lucius said.

The young soldier sat by Lucius. "Thank y'all kindly. It would do me some good to be off of that beast for a spell."

"Wish we could offer you some coffee, but times is hard and appears we are fresh out," Theo said.

"Indeed, times are hard all over," the soldier said. He reached across Lucius and offered his hand to Theo. "I'm Ralph Reed."

Theo shook his hand. "Well, I'm pleased to meet you, Lieutenant Reed." Theo pointed to Lucius. "This here is my nigger, Lucius."

Reed nodded at Lucius. It was a friendly enough nod.

"Where you bound, Lieutenant?" Theo asked.

"To tell you the truth, I'm lost. I took a wrong road some place. I'm not from around here, but I'm supposed to meet my wife and little girl in a town call Sardis. Have you heard of it?"

"I have, I have," Theo said.

"Capital," Reed said. "I haven't seen my wife in two years. And my little girl was newborn when I left for the army. Look here." He reached in his inside pocket and pulled out a little doll. "I bought this thing about five months ago when I was at Atlanta. I've been carrying it ever since. I can't wait to give it to Ann. That's my little girl's name, Ann." He stuck it back into his pocket.

"That is fine," Theo said, "Mighty fine, ain't it, Lucius?"

"Sho is Massuh, real fine."

Theo threw a bottle at Lucius. "Go down there to the creek and find a clear spot and bring me and the lieutenant some clean water."

"Yessuh, Massuh," Lucius grabbed the bottle and scrambled to the creek. Lucius knew they had done well. The soldier was fooled real good. It was a shame how things were going to turn out.

It was good and dark now, and the white men couldn't see Lucius at the creek. Lucius left the bottle at the water and crept in a circle around the fire. It was just as he suspected. The soldier had his revolver drawn and was waiting. The two white men were still looking toward the creek. That worthless Theo had betrayed him. Lucius came up behind the soldier and jerked the gun from his hand. He grabbed the soldier's neck before the man had time to react. He slowly tightened his hold like a chicken snake on a rat. The soldier clawed at the air. Lucius stared into Theo's eyes. They were wide in horror. Lucius slowly—very slowly—tightened his grip. Reed's eyes rolled back in his head. Theo's lips began to tremble, but he said nothing—he did nothing. Reed's face was purple, and he slowly went limp. Lucius relaxed his grip and smiled. Reed gulped a coughing breath.

"Thank God," Theo said. "There weren't no need in you killing that boy."

Lucius jerked his arm up with a quick snatch. Reed's neck made a loud pop and lay over on his shoulder. Only skin was holding it from falling off. Lucius flung the body over the fire, and it landed across Theo's legs. The doll popped out and landed by the fire.

Theo crawfished from the body. His eyes were big as balls.

"Next time you go against me, I'll pull your big ass head plumb off, juss like this po boy here. Does you understand me?"

Theo said nothing, but Lucius could see in his eyes that he understood perfectly. The wet spot growing between Theo's legs was a good enough answer.

Lucius kicked the soldier's body. "I reckon his sweet family won't be a-meeting him after all." He reached down and picked up the doll, looked at it for a long minute, then tossed it into the fire.

Chapter 17

General Forrest had been right about the pass; one look and the Confederates let the boys through. The Yankees laughed at the swayback mule. Peter realized they must look a sight with the pathetic-looking animal. The Yankee's were probably glad to be shed of it. It had been days since the boys had left Mississippi. Peter had lost count. He just wanted the ordeal to be over.

The farms were beginning to look alike. One Yankee was as blue as the next. One Confederate as ragged as the others. The citizens suffering the insufferable, but yet, not turning the two wayfarers away.

As they headed north, Peter found the eastern part of Tennessee to be a beautiful country, plenty of trees, hills, and valleys. Of course, Joe said it was lacking compared to Virginia.

As Peter led the mule, Joe lay on the animal facing the blue sky whistling *Shenandoah*. Peter was waiting for him to fall off so he could laugh.

Peter stopped, thought he heard something. Joe continued his whistling, lost somewhere daydreaming.

"Joe, hush a minute."

Joe continued.

Peter slapped him on the shoulder.

Joe rose up on the mule. "Why did you go and do that for?"

"Listen."

There was a moaning coming from the woods on the right of the road.

"Do you hear it?" Peter asked.

Joe nodded.

"You stay put and I'll go see what it is," Peter said.

Joe ignored him and leaped from the mule. "Sounds like a person." He ran to the sound.

"Joe wait!" Why even bother? He was uncontrollable, just as well talked to the mule.

Joe disappeared into the woods before Peter could follow, yelled, "It's a man."

It was an old man. He had been shot several times, once in the arm, once in the side, and once in the back.

"Reckon he's going to die, Peter?"

Peter didn't answer, looked the man over. It appeared the bleeding had stopped and the wounds were beginning to clot.

"Mister, can you hear me?" Peter said.

The man slowly opened his eyes.

"He's alive," Joe said.

Very softly, the man whispered, "Help me home."

"Where do you live?" Peter asked.

"Follow the..." the man said, but then had to rest.

"Take your time," Peter said. He turned to Joe. "Bring the water from the mule."

Joe ran for the water.

The man whispered, "Follow the road to the left, and go to the end of it." The man passed out.

The boys loaded the man on the mule. As they started down the road, he fell off and hit the ground like a sack of corn.

The boys rushed to help him.

The man moaned, "Are you'uns trying to help me or kill me?"

They loaded him back on, then tied him on like a parcel.

The road wasn't much of a road, more like a pig trail. It cut between two big hills. They traveled for about a mile down the narrow trail before it opened up to a small farm. Everything was made of logs or stone: barn, corncrib, sheds, and the cabin. Everything was old and had fallen into disrepair. Weeds grew high among the split-rail fences. A graying black man came from the cabin.

"Oh, my Lawd, Massuh Albert," the black man said. He hobbled to the mule. "Has he done gone up?"

"No, but he's hurt pretty bad," Peter said.

"If he ain't dead, why is y'all got him tied to that mule like a dead deer?"

"We didn't want—" Peter said.

"Shush up that jabbering and help me get him down from there and into the cabin."

Peter looked at Joe; Joe shrugged.

The inside was well kept, Peter noticed, but he could tell there wasn't a woman in the house. It didn't have a woman's touch. It was clean, but not cozy.

The man examined the wounds and declared all of the bullets had passed clean through. He put bandages on them and made the boys stand clear. Peter saw the work was hard for the black man; his hands were gnarled and twisted with arthritis.

"Where did y'all find him?"

Joe answered before Peter could speak. "He's beside the road a few miles back."

"I reckon y'all ain't seed no horse."

"There was no horse," Peter said.

"Fetch me some water, Gus," Albert whispered.

"Just you hold right there, Massuh Albert. I fetch it right off." Gus scrambled for the pitcher. He raised Albert's head with his crippled hand, but he was shaking too much to hold the cup with the other.

"Here, let me help," Peter said, taking the cup from Gus.

After he finished with the water, the old man opened his eyes and looked around as if to get his bearing. Peter could see it slowly coming back to the man. His thick gray eyebrows looked like gray caterpillars, and they slowly rose and fell as he became more conscious and looked about the room. It looked to Peter as if they would crawl from his face.

Gus moved Peter from the side of the bed and moved close. "Massuh, is you gonna be all right?"

The thick eyebrows drew down into one long caterpillar. "Hell, Gus, how the hell do I know?" He tried to sit up, but quickly thought better of it as the pain hit. "Dumb darky, always asking fool questions. Can't you see with those damn bloodshot eyes of yourn that I done been shot?"

Gus folded his arms. "Yessum, I does see that. Yessum, I sho does. And you can't specks nobody to take the blame but yourself. You is too thick-headed."

"Go on, you damn ignorant darky, before I get up and flog you."

"Oh, I's a going." Gus headed for a back room. "I was going to leave this here farm, but now I's got to wait til you is healed up some. I reckon you done gone and got shot so I would be bound to stay." Gus went to the back room.

Joe turned to Peter. "Strange."

Peter nodded.

"I reckon we better get going," Joe said.

Gus came from the room. "No, you ain't! You two is going to let me fix you something to eat." Before they could answer, he went back into the room.

"Boys, I want to thank you'uns for fetching me home," Albert said.

"What happened to you?" Joe asked. Did the Yankees shoot you?

Albert stared at the ceiling for a long minute taking deep breaths before he answered. "Damn Lincolnites shot me, bunch of damn cowards."

"What are Lincolnites?" Joe asked. He sat on the edge of the bed.

"Tories, Yankee lovers," Albert said. "This here country is crawling with them. Hell, they'd shoot their own momma if they thought she was sesech."

"Where did they come from?" Joe asked.

"Hell, boy!" Albert coughed and spit into the water cup. "You don't know nothing do you? They's born here. They's my neighbors. Until this war, they's my friends—some of 'em."

Peter saw Albert was getting upset. He squeezed Joe's shoulder. "I think we will go out and check on the mule."

"Y'all ain't a leaving til y'all done et!" Gus called from the back."

"We'll be right outside," Peter said as they went out the door.

Joe led the mule to a patch of weeds by the fence to graze.

Peter looked over the place. The little farm was nestled in a cove. A small stream ran close to the cabin, only a trickle flowing through it now, but it formed a pretty pool before it moved on down the cove. Small fields of wheat and corn were overgrown head-high with weeds. A garden was the only thing that seemed to have been tended lately, and it was very small.

Joe disappeared into the barn for a few minutes, then popped out. Next, he went into one of the outbuildings. Peter shook his head at the boy; he just could not be still. After Joe was satisfied with the shed, he went back to Peter.

"How do you reckon they live?" Joe said. "Everything is falling down around here."

"I was just thinking the same thing."

They heard a crash from inside the cabin. They found Albert trying to get out of the bed.

"No, you stay there," Peter said.

"Well, check on that damn darky," Albert said, pointing to the fireplace.

Gus was holding his hand and staring at a kettle he had spilt on the hearth. Big tears were trailing down his dark cheeks.

"Are you hurt?" Peter asked.

Joe picked up the kettle and raked the food into it.

Gus went back to the little room. Peter followed him in. It was a bedroom and pantry combined. There were pans, kettles, pots, and utensils hanging from the wall. There was a small bed, and Peter saw cornhusks protruding from the mattress. Gus sat on the mattress and placed his crippled hands between his legs.

"What are you doing, you old fool?" Albert called from the main room.

Joe appeared at the door.

"That was the last of the beans, and I just wasted it," Gus said slowly, looking at Peter. "We is going to starve for long. I's too cripple, and he too old."

Peter knew Gus was too old, too.

Joe sat on the bed beside Gus. "Does your master not have family?"

"His boy was killed in the army. He had two more servants and they ran away with the Yankees."

Peter looked around the room, found it hard to believe Albert could afford to buy slaves. Gus looked at Peter, grew a faint smile.

"He won us in a card game down in Chattanooga 'bout twenty-five years ago."

"Are there no friends?" Peter asked.

"Some; they moved over into North Carolina when the Yankees come. Some is Lincolnites now, and the rest is looking out for they own skin. Times is hard. Massuh don't make friends none too good."

"What the hell you'uns a-doing in there, holding a town meeting?" Albert said, then coughed.

"What about the little garden?" Joe asked.

"Not much left to it, now. We had a pair of oxen, but they done wondered into the hills, and so is our hogs. We both too old to do nothing 'bout it. Now Massuh done gone and lost our horse. It too bad. He had went to Knoxville to sell some old jewelry that the late missus had, but I spects that gone with the horse."

"Gus, you go on ahead and get that pot ready, and I'll get something from the garden to cook," Joe said. He jumped from the bed and left the room.

"Are you a Christian, Gus?" Peter asked, placing a hand on Gus's crippled hand.

Gus looked into Peter's eyes. "I is for sho."

"Well, pray hard and God will provide. The Bible says, *Ask, and it shall be given you; seek, and ye shall find; knock, and it shall be opened unto you; for every one that asketh receiveth; and he that seeketh findeth; and to him that knocketh it shall be opened.*"

"You and your young massuh sho is good people."

Peter walked to the door. "Thank you for the compliment, but Joe is not my master. I'm a free man." Gus's eyes widened. Peter smiled and left the room.

Peter found Joe scrapping what few beans were left in the ragged garden. Peter searched for the right words to convince Joe that they needed to stay a few days to help these old men get settled. Joe saw Peter, pointed to the garden, and shook his head. "Ain't much of a garden, is it?" Joe said.

"Not much of a farm."

Joe handed the basket of beans to Peter. "I think we should kick around here for a few days, see if we can help these old men, maybe get them settled a little so they can make it on their own."

There was always a new facet to the boy to be discovered.

Joe wandered about the farm while Peter worked around the cabin. Joe looked for things that could be used by the old men, things they could eat, or things to make life a little easier.

He followed the spring to the springhouse at the edge of a big hill. It was a stone building covered with moss and vines, shaded all the time by two big chestnut trees. Inside, it was cool as a cave. The spring sprouted from the side of the hill and ran down the far edge of the floor. Little minnows darted about in the stream, and bats clung upside-down from the rotting, wood ceiling. Joe found dusty shelves along the walls with jars that once held food, but now the contents were just a greenish-brown mush.

Joe spotted a rope behind the jars, could be handy if he found one of the hogs or one of the steers later. He pulled the rope from the rotten shelf. It wrapped around his arm. Joe flung his arm—the rope grew tighter. He ran out of the dark springhouse yelling and flapping his arm like a crippled bird. In the sunlight, he saw it was a long, black, chicken snake. He grabbed it behind the head and pulled, but it only squeezed tighter. He plunged his arm with the snake under the water. The stream was so shallow the snake raised his head from under the water. He grabbed for the head again. It bit him. Joe yelled. He yanked the tomahawk from his belt. Joe caught himself just before he started whacking; the snake was only protecting himself. The snake was a benefit, because it ate rats and mice, a good snake to have around the farm if it was kept out of the chicken house. He laid the tomahawk down, grabbed the snake behind the head, and held it under the water. Slowly the creature uncoiled. Joe raised his arm out of the water and tossed the snake to the ground. The snake seemed dazed, but slowly slithered back to the springhouse. Joe examined his arm: red, but fine. He picked up his tomahawk and breathed relief, better be a little more careful—that could have been a copperhead, and things would have been a lot different.

The small wheat field behind the fence, which had grown wild, seemed to have enough wheat to salvage, and blackberries grew along the fence. He found a little volunteer corn, too, enough to harvest. There was more to eat on the farm then first appeared, and he found where hogs had been eating some of the corn.

Behind the overgrown corn patch, he found another little stream. He followed it toward one of the big hills. Maybe he would find a hog.

There were different tracks in the mud: deer, coon, possum, hog, and even the steer's tracks. It was a highway from the big hills to the farm.

As Joe climbed the hill, the mud played out and the stream had a rock bottom, so there were no tracks to follow. That didn't matter; he knew he would find something. He followed the rocky stream higher. He had seen a bald knob at the top, and if he could get there, he could survey the entire farm. He picked up a stick to knock the spider webs from his path. It was hot going, and the cool stream was refreshing. It ended at a spring well before he reached the top of the small mountain, but he went on to the knob. He could see even farther than he had expected.

The farm below resembled a toy farm. The farm was in a cove, surrounded by small mountains, and he could see its layout: the springhouse nestled into the side of the hill, corncrib, log cabin, barn, the road they had come in on—it snaked though the valley. It all looked like a map. He could even see the mule, no bigger than an ant.

The mule wasn't all that he saw, saw both steers standing by the overgrown corn. He must have walked right by them. He even saw two pigs walking the road. He would get Peter and they would catch them. The sooner they caught the animals, the sooner they could help the two old men and the sooner they could be on their way.

A buzzard circled slowly overhead, drifting along like a lazy kite. Warblers held a chorus in the dark woods, and some little birds came close into the opening to scold Joe. Every now and then a squirrel would bark somewhere deep in the forest. He could smell the woodsy smell, too. It was a comfortable feeling up there. It reminded him of Massanutten Mountain back home above the Shenandoah Valley.

He moved to the shade of a large rock, would rest there a few minutes, then make his way back down to the farm. He leaned his back to the rock and his eyes quickly became heavy. He was soon dreaming of the Shenandoah Valley, playing in the millstream with Sarah.

He awoke with a start as a hawk screamed overhead. At first, he didn't remember where he was. He felt something crawling on his neck. He grabbed it. It was cold and scaly. He chucked it, just a lizard—harmless. He rubbed his eyes and yawned. Looking down at the valley, he quickly remembered the day's events, saw the mule. But wait! There was more than one. No, there were horses, too—ten or twelve of them.

There were men prowling around the dooryard. They could have been Yankees, but it was too far to be sure. Joe sensed they were up to no good. He just knew it. Why would they be crawling all about the place like rats if they were friends?

Joe placed his hand on the tomahawk. But what good would that be? He needed the revolver, and it was on the mule. Everything they owned was on the mule. Damn!

Joe ran down the mountain, sliding and skidding. He followed the stream back by the corn, snuck through the corn until he came to the overgrown fence, crawled beside it, closer and closer to the cabin.

He peeked through the split-rail fence. They were not Yankees, but worse—bushwhackers. They had enough blue on that Joe assumed they were from the North, but he needed to get closer to see what was going on. He slithered through the weeds next to the fence, saw a couple coming out of the barn. Suddenly there was an explosion in front of his face. He felt his heart stop. A covey of quail! He relaxed, remembered the men. They were pointing to the quail, then they started his way. He backed out fast, keeping low. He crawled for the corn as fast as a racer snake.

The men got closer. "Something scared them quails," one of them said. One climbed on the fence, had a rifle in his hand. Joe lay flat as a fawn, felt his back rise every time he took a breath. He prayed they wouldn't see it.

"There it is!" the man on the fence yelled.

Joe squeezed his eyes shut.

The rifle rang out. Joe jerked, then breathed relief. He wasn't shot.

A man yelled from the cabin, "What is it?"

The man leaped from the fence, and they headed back to the cabin. "Weren't nothing."

"Well, damn it, don't be a wasting leads!"

Joe took several deep breaths, then crawled back to the fence. The man had shot a possum. It lay there dead and grinning. Joe looked through the fence again and saw smoke coming from the barn and sheds. The men were on their horses, and one was pulling the mule.

"You ain't gonna take that sorry beast, are you, Brown?" the leader said.

Brown took another look at the mule and threw the rope to the ground.

"Heah!" the leader spurred his horse and they thundered toward the pass and out of the small cove.

Peter was fighting at the flames of the barn when Joe ran to the yard. But it was no use. Peter stopped and looked at Joe, then back at the burning barn.

"Who were they, Peter?"

Peter wiped the back of his hand across his nose. "They were partisans."

They were the Lincolnites that Albert was talking about. Joe suddenly thought of Albert. He pointed toward the cabin. "Are they all right?"

Peter slowly turned to Joe. He was not crying, looked too sad to cry. "They beat him to death," Peter said so softly that Joe almost didn't understand him.

Joe followed Peter into the cabin. Gus was wiping Albert's face.

Peter looked astonished. "Is he still alive?"

Gus said nothing, just nodded.

Peter turned to Joe. "Fetch some more water from the stream." Peter took the wet rag from Gus's crippled hand and dabbed at Albert's shattered face.

Joe took the bucket to the stream and scooped water. He picked a small crawfish from the bucket. His mother had taught him not to hate, but he hated those men. They weren't even real soldiers—they were murderers and thieves. How could a god let this happen? How could a god let wars happen? If this thing was happening here in Tennessee, what was happening in Virginia? Peter could pray, but Joe was done with it. He took the water to the cabin.

***

The next day Peter sat beside Albert's bed with Gus watching Albert take shallow breaths, thinking each would be the last. Peter had never felt more helpless in his life. Could he have done more? He had asked himself that question repeatedly for the last few days, but the answer was the same: no. The men had held him at gunpoint while they beat Albert with the butt of a rifle. Why Albert was still alive, only God knew.

Peter had gathered from the cursing and yelling that the men knew Albert. They were local men. This made less sense than the war. North against South was one thing, and it was horrible enough, but neighbor against neighbor was—well—worse than horrible.

Peter began to think of the war as a kind of hell. There was always fire. From Arkansas to East Tennessee—fire. Biblical stories of war were not worse. It was cruel and hard to bear. Peter prayed more and more, and he hated to think it, but when would God intervene? How much longer would this war go on—forever?

Was it not bad enough for Albert to be shot three times? Was it not bad enough that he and Gus, a cripple, to be alone with no help from neighbors? Why did they have to come and bludgeon him with a rifle? War brought out the devil in people. Why did Joe have to see all of this? Would he ever get over it?

Peter heard a ruckus outside and looked enquiring at Gus. Gus shrugged. Peter went to the door, and for the first time in days, he laughed. Joe had roped one of the pigs. Joe was muddy and dirty from head to toe. The pig was cleaner.

Joe laughed aloud. "I got one of 'em." He yanked the rope, but the pig didn't budge. He yanked harder and the pig took to running. He ran past Joe and pulled him to the ground, but Joe held fast. "No, you don't!" The pig skidded to a stop and had the rope stretched to the limit.

Peter laughed. "Who has whom?"

Joe looked at the pig at the end of the rope, then he looked at his dirty self. He grinned—his teeth seemed brilliant white in contrast with his nasty face. It touched Peter's heart.

***

The boys patched up the pigsty. They decided to catch one more. Peter saw no need penning up more than they could feed—more than Gus could feed when they left in a few days.

When Joe was done with the pen, he peeled his clothes off and barreled off in the small pool in the stream. Peter laughed as he picked up Joe's clothes.

"I'll wash these nasty things out for you," Peter said.

Joe splashed water on Peter. Peter dropped the clothes and reached down to throw water on Joe. Joe grabbed his arm and pulled him into the pool. Before Peter realized it, Joe was on his back.

"Get up, mule!" Joe laughed as he hung on.

Peter ran forward quickly, then stopped suddenly and bent forward. Joe flew over Peter's back, his feet high in the air and his white butt flashing. Joe came up coughing and laughing at the same time. Joe dove under the water and pulled Peter's legs from under him. Peter fanned with his arms, trying to keep his balance, but it was no use; he landed flat on his butt. Joe jumped him and they rolled in the water like alligators, tumbling, spinning, and splashing. Peter finally got his footing and grabbed Joe up over his head.

"I'm the king of the pool. Do you doubt it, Joseph Taylor?"

"Let me down and I'll show the king!" Joe flailed, but it was no use; Peter had him tight. He held Joe up naked as a newborn, and Joe could do nothing about it.

"Say 'Hail to the king' and I will let you down, my disloyal subject," Peter said, laughing like a little kid. He didn't get the best of Joe often, so he was going to milk it for all he could.

Joe yelled back, "You're not the king. I'm the k—"

Peter was facing the cabin, smiling. He noticed Joe shut up quickly. He slowly turned, still holding Joe over his head. There was a wagon on the road with a lady and a girl of about twelve. The lady had covered her face and was trying to hide the girl's face, but she was giggling and trying to see.

"How do you do, Ma'am?" Peter said.

"Peter, do you want to let me down?" Joe said. "I think they have about seen all that I have to show."

Peter eased Joe to the water. Joe slid around behind him.

The lady composed herself after Joe hid his body from view. "My name is Mrs. Sawyer, and I have come to call on Mr. Stokes."

Peter realized he didn't know Albert's last name—surely it had to be Stokes.

"Ma'am, he is in the cabin, but he is hurt pretty bad."

"Hurt?"

Joe spoke, but didn't even lean around Peter. "Yes, Ma'am. Some Lincolnites shot him, then came back and beat him darn near to death."

"Lincolnites?"

"Partisans, Ma'am," Peter said.

"Boy, I know what Lincolnites are!" She gave Peter a hard stare that cut, and he wished he had not opened his mouth.

She picked up the reins and gave the boys a contemptuous glare. She shook the reins. "Get up, Jack." The horse started forward. The girl looked back over the seat as they rode toward the cabin. The lady scolded her and made her turn in her seat.

Joe grabbed his clothes when the two females went into the cabin. "Well, I have no secrets from those two ladies."

Peter looked at Joe. He saw Joe wasn't embarrassed at all. In fact, he was grinning. Peter thought it was funny, too, now that the females were gone.

"Joe, you know something about East Tennessee; there are some pretty views here."

"Funny, Peter—you are so very funny."

"Not only are there big, green mountains, there are small white mounds, too."

Joe picked up a crawfish hill at the edge of the water and flung it at Peter. Peter ducked as the hill went by, but a crawfish ejected from it and landed squarely in his hair. Peter hopped in the water, frantically raking at his hair. The crawfish flopped to the water. This frightened Peter more than he cared for Joe to know. He looked around, and Joe was on is knees at the edge of the water holding his side, laughing. Dang it, Joe had the last laugh again. Peter realized how funny he must have looked raking at the crawfish and dancing in the water. He laughed, too.

Chapter 18

Joe eased open the cabin door, but didn't go in—Mrs. Sawyer might bite. She was tending to Albert and muttering something about worthless people. The girl was getting things from a black bag—a doctor's bag it appeared—and handing them to her mother. Gus stood at the foot of the bed wringing his hands; he looked like a big toad.

Peter pushed past Joe. "Ma'am, can we help in any way?"

She turned on Peter. "Help?" She threw a cloth on the bed she had been using to tend Albert's wounds. "If you cared to help, you would have been in here and not in that pond playing like a pair of otters."

"But Ma'am—"

"You listen here, darky, don't you talk back to me. I'll have you shot!" She moved toward Peter—he stepped back. "We are fighting this war to free you people and you frolic around like an animal while a white man is fighting for his life. You didn't even care enough to go for a doctor. Now get out of this house and take that piece of white trash with you."

Peter lowered his head and slunk out of the cabin like a whipped dog.

Joe watched Peter go. He would have rather the woman scolded him than Peter—Peter couldn't handle such things. He was soft, way too soft. Joe stepped inside and slammed the door.

The woman immediately jumped him. "I told you to—"

"No, Ma'am!" Joe planted his feet squarely. "Didn't we find this man shot and a laying on the roadside? Didn't we fetch him here to this cabin? Didn't we catch a couple of his hogs for him to have something to eat? Didn't we risk our lives when the bushwhackers come a calling?" Joe took a step forward. The woman stepped back. "Yes, Ma'am, we did. We are a couple of wayfarers. We don't know nothing about this country. I reckon we got our own broke wagon, and here you are a blaming us for his. Ma'am, you're bound to get my Irish up talking to Peter in that fashion. You had no call, and I reckon I won't stand for it."

The girl went to her mother and put her arms around her as if she believed Joe meant them harm. Though Joe was furious, he still noticed she was a pretty girl.

Albert moaned; Mrs. Sawyer turned to examine him.

Joe still felt the fire, but let it go and stormed from the cabin. He found Peter loading the mule. That was good. The sooner they got on the road the better. Try to help strangers and what happens? You get blamed for everything under the sun. The quicker they got shed of Tennessee the better.

"That lady is right," Peter said, as he checked the mule's shoe.

Why did Peter always have to think that everyone else was right and they were wrong?

"We didn't even go for a doctor," Peter said. He turned to Joe. "Now why didn't we go for a doctor?"

Joe saw Peter had an overpowering weight on him. However, the question hung there because Joe didn't know the answer.

"I'll tell you why," Peter said. "Because we are children. We have set out on a march across this war-torn country and we are still children. We can't even take care of ourselves. How are we supposed to take care of someone else? How am I supposed to take care of..." Peter turned back toward the mule without finishing the sentence. Joe knew how it ended, though. But Joe was thirteen now and that was not exactly a child's age, and Peter was seventeen, almost a man.

The door of the cabin squeaked open. The girl flowed out onto the porch. The sunlight hit her right, and Joe forgot all about Peter and being angry. She had soft blue eyes—they were dreamy eyes—and her hair was gold as wheat.

"Hello," she said.

Her voice surprised him. It was a high-pitched voice, but not high and squeaky, but high and bird-like, like a sweet songbird. "My name is Mary."

Joe said nothing. She was much shorter than she appeared in the buggy, but it suited her.

"Mary Sawyer."

Like a china doll, she seemed fragile—like she might break if she was to fall.

"Do you have a name?" she asked. She smiled.

"Joe." It came automatically, without any help from him.

Her hair was long and it flowed all the way to her butt.

"Joe what?"

She was barefoot; she had small feet. He wouldn't have been able to see them for the long dress if she had not been rocking, making the dress come and go across her toes.

She noticed Joe looking. "Joe with no last name, I have shoes, but they are back at home."

Joe suddenly remembered himself and said, "Taylor."

Mary laughed. Peter laughed, too. Joe felt his face glow.

Joe glared at Peter, but he only laughed more. At least he wasn't still upset.

"You were pretty angry at Mother, weren't you?"

Joe stuck his hands in his pockets, not knowing what to do with them. "I reckon I was. She had no call to jump me and Peter in that fashion."

Mary sat on the edge of the porch. Joe leaned against the post.

"She's not really angry with you," Mary said. She's angry with herself."

Peter leaned against the other side of the post. "Why is she mad at herself?"

Mary looked toward the door, then lowering her voice. "We are Union people. She feels responsible for what happened here."

"She didn't do this," Peter said.

"I know, but we knew that something like this might happen."

Joe could hear Albert moan loudly. They all turned toward the window.

"Mary!" Mrs. Sawyer called, and Mary brushed herself off and ran inside.

"I reckon we should probably wait until morning before we strike out," Peter said.

Joe nodded. His mind was on something else.

"I'm going to see if I can find something to fix for supper," Peter said. "There are a few more things in the garden." He took the pack back off the mule and led him around the cabin.

Joe went back into the cabin; no one noticed. Albert was jerking violently on the bed. Mary and Mrs. Sawyer were putting cool rags over his body. Gus poured water from the bucket into a pan, but spilled as much as went into the pan. Albert called out names, but Joe could barely make them out—maybe family members or something. Joe grabbed the empty bucket to refill at the stream. Mrs. Sawyer's eyes met his. There was a faint smile. He believed the smile also said, "I'm sorry."

***

Joe lowered the bucket into the stream and his mind wandered. Was the world going upside down? These people were neighbors and they were killing each other. Neighbors were supposed to help each other. That's what they did in the Shenandoah Valley. Well, Mrs. Sawyer was helping Albert, but she said she was Union.

Joe heard the cabin door shut and saw Mary coming. He hoped she didn't slip on something; she would surely break. "Nice of you to fetch the water, Joe." Here voice was like a song. She smiled and Joe felt a tingle in his chest. She took one side of the rope handle. "I will help you carry it."

"I reckon I can manage."

"To be sure, but I just like to help."

Joe felt his face warming. He had never felt like this—never. He wanted to say something, but he felt he would make a fool of himself.

They carried the bucket to the porch and set it down.

"Mother thinks Mr. Stokes will pull out of the fever." Mary sat down on the porch.

"Is your ma a doctor?" It came out sounding arrogant and Joe wished he hadn't said it.

"My father was." She smiled up at Joe.

He sat beside her and studied his shoes.

"Mother assisted him all the time."

"Your father off fighting?"

"He was killed by bushwhackers because he didn't support the South."

Joe felt awful. He was so busy thinking about the Tories and Lincolnites being killers, he had forgotten that killing had no bounds. "I'm sorry."

"Where you from, Joe?" she asked, smiling with a face too pretty to be real.

Joe watched her eyes. They danced and seemed to be unable to stay still.

"I'm from Virginia, the Shenandoah Valley, near a town called Dayton."

"What are you doing in Tennessee?"

She placed her soft hand on his arm.

He had to take a deep breath. There was no place on earth he would rather be than right there on that porch, but at the same time, he felt like a tied coon. He couldn't breathe.

"Hey, Joe, come here," Peter called from around the cabin.

Joe jumped from the porch. "I need to see what Peter wants."

She smiled and slowly picked herself from the porch. When Joe was cornering the cabin, he saw her struggling through the door with the bucket.

Why did he want to get away from her so fast when he wanted to be close to her?

Peter was standing by the corncrib. "Look what's inside."

Joe looked in. A big possum was grinning and staring back.

"Supper," Peter said, smiling.

Joe smiled back. Mary left his thoughts. He stepped inside and with one quick blow from the tomahawk, the possum knotted up. Joe grabbed him by the tail and brought him out. "Reckon you can find enough in that garden to make possum stew?" Joe said, holding the dead animal in front of him.

"I believe I saw some carrots over among those weeds," Peter said.

The mule was munching in the weeds, and Peter pushed him out of the way. The boys raked around in the weeds with their feet.

"There are some!" Joe said pointing with the dead possum.

Suddenly, the possum came back to life. He hissed and tried to reach around at Joe. Joe yelled and flung the possum in the air. He went head over end and landed at the base of the mule's tail. The mule went crazy, braying and kicking. The possum fell off and started for the weeds. While on the run, Joe pulled the tomahawk from his belt. He jumped the possum again, and with five blows from the ax, took the head clean off.

He looked up, saw Peter chasing the mule. Joe struck out behind him. He had never seen an animal so unstrung. For heaven's sake, it was just an ole possum. The mule hit the stream and fell, but quickly jumped back up. Peter grabbed for the lead, but the mule jerked his head and Peter fell into the water. Joe ran for the mule and grabbed the rope. The mule smelled the possum blood on Joe's hand and started kicking and braying again. Joe danced around trying to hold the animal. Joe fell over Peter and back into the water. The mule took off up the valley road.

The boys dragged themselves from the water. Joe looked at Peter and laughed. Peter laughed, too. They started back toward the cabin, saw Mrs. Sawyer and Mary standing on the porch laughing. Gus was standing in the door laughing, too. They must have heard the ruckus and came out to watch the show.

"You boys really like that stream, don't you?" Mrs. Sawyer said.

She seemed a different person. He now knew where Mary got her handsome face.

Gus went around the cabin and fetched the possum. They had seen more than Joe had thought.

"I will cook that animal if you boys will skin it," Mrs. Sawyer said.

They would catch that stupid mule later. No one would steal the old swayback anyhow. Possum stew, now that sounded fine.

After supper, Mrs. Sawyer said she would be back in a couple of days to check on Albert. Joe hated to see them go.

Mrs. Sawyer wasn't so bad, just a little testy, but Joe could handle that. It was a small price to see Mary again.

***

Joe and Peter pulled weeds in the garden after Mary and Mrs. Sawyer left. Joe figured they should stay a few more days. They needed to be sure that Albert was going to be all right. He reckoned they could help Gus get lined up to take care of things. Peter had found some seeds, so they may as well plant that late garden, maybe something would make it, and Mrs. Sawyer said she had collards and things to plant in the late garden, too. She said Mary liked

263

working in the garden. Joe believed working in the garden wouldn't be too bad when she returned.

The sun sank behind the west mountain and crickets began their serenade. Two owls called back and forth in the distance. "You know, I've always liked this time of day," Peter said, leaning on the hoe and looking toward the mountains. "Not really day, but not night yet, either."

Joe looked around. It was a nice time of day he reckoned. He looked back at Peter; Peter was staring at the mountains, but he was miles away.

"Listen at those ole hoot owls calling to each other," Peter said. "Zuey and I used to walk down the path to the river about this time of day and those owls would call just like that—whippoorwills, too."

"More skeeters back there in Mississippi than here," Joe said.

Peter looked at Joe, but more looked past him. "Reckon what Zuey is doing now."

Joe had a sudden sinking feeling. Now he had a small idea what Zuey really meant to Peter. If he felt so silly about Mary, what did Peter feel for Zuey? Joe had been selfish. He had not really appreciated what Peter had left behind to go with him, not really. He would bet his last coin that Peter had a heavy weighing in his chest at this very moment in this very garden. Joe felt he could sink right in the ground. He knew what Peter had sacrificed, and he knew why he had done it.

"Peter," Joe said softly. Peter looked at him and Joe felt even worse. "I know...a...how..."

"What are you talking about?" Peter said.

Joe turned, reached down, and grabbed a mean-looking weed. "Nothing."

Peter took Joe's cue and started hoeing weeds again.

***

Joe and Peter had made their bed on the floor of the cabin. Peter had found it to be all right—at least it was not a barn. When he awoke, Joe was already gone. Peter knew he was in the garden. He had been working it as if his life depended on it. No doubt, he wanted to impress Mary when she returned—if she returned. It had now been five days and Mrs. Sawyer had said they would be back in a couple.

Joe was already soaked with sweat when Peter found him working. The boys had some of the garden planted, and now were waiting for Mrs. Sawyer to bring the seeds for the collards and what ever else she had. Joe was leaning on a hoe and staring toward the overgrown fields. He did not see Peter. Peter watched him. He had seen that look on Joe's face many times. Something was about to happen. Joe threw the hoe down, kicked dirt, squatted, picked up a clod, rolled it around in his hand, and crushed it, all the while staring at the overgrown field.

Peter could not stand it any longer. He went to the garden. "What goes?"

Joe didn't take his eyes from the overgrown fields. "I aim to catch them steers."

Peter looked to where Joe was looking, but didn't see anything but overgrown fields and thick saplings over head high.

"I've seen them," Joe said. The day the bushwhackers came I saw both of them, and I believe I saw one go into that old corn field."

"Joe, that's a jungle now, not a field, and what do we need with them? We aren't going to be here long enough to plow fields, and Gus or Albert will not be able to use the beasts."

Joe looked at Peter as if he had said the most ridiculous thing in the world. "We can sell them, Peter."

Peter smiled, of course, they could. Why didn't he think of that? If they sold the oxen, they could buy things for the two elderly men and be on their way.

Joe grabbed a length of rope from around a fence post. "Come on, Peter, let's get skinning."

***

Peter saw Joe's white hair above the tall weeds, but that was all he could see of him. Peter didn't like it. There could be creatures and only the Good Lord knew what else lurking in the overgrown field. There could be snakes. He hated snakes.

Joe had a plan: they would align themselves about fifty yards apart and walk up and down the field until they spotted a steer. It seemed like a good enough plan to Peter. An ox was big; there should be no problem finding one if it was in the field. Peter quickly realized the flaw in the plan. True enough an ox was big, but this overgrown field was more like a forest, old corn over head-high and weeds even higher.

There were trails in the field that seemed like pikes, tracks of all sort—Peter had no idea what animal left them. There could be bears or even elephants as far as he knew. However, there were ox and hog tracks. He knew what they were, and he saw them wholesale. Maybe Joe knew what he was doing after all.

Peter bent down to examine a track further. Was it a cat track? Oh, lord, Peter thought—a panther. He looked it over. It sure looked like a big cat. He rose, suddenly realized he had lost his bearing. He scanned the weeds, looking for that white head, but saw it nowhere. He turned. He jumped to get above the weeds, but couldn't see Joe.

"Joe!"

He didn't answer.

"Joe, where are you? I seemed to be turned around."

Still no answer.

Peter eased through the weeds. The wind started to blow; a dark cloud had covered the sun. The dried leaves on the corn rattled. He didn't want to yell too loudly. He didn't want Joe to think he was afraid. Cockleburs clung all over his clothes, and he was beginning to sweat—more from discomfort than the heat, though it was the middle of August.

He hated to admit it, even to himself, but he was scared. Scared of what? There was nothing to harm him in the field. He bet Joe wasn't afraid, and he was just a thirteen-year-old boy.

Thirteen. Joe had turned thirteen and he hadn't even noticed. It was hard to believe the boy was that old. He was so short—much too short for a thirteen-year-old. He would have to acknowledge the boy's birthday just as soon as—

Suddenly, Peter heard a rattle and something slapped against his leg. He wanted to yell, but it caught in his throat. He leaped aside, but couldn't make his legs move to run. He felt his whole body quake with fear. It was a snake—he knew it. He wanted to look down, but he couldn't make himself do it. He began to tremble. He was shaking all over and couldn't stop. Everything went snowy, then a pink, then red. He shook his head to clear his senses. It would do no good to pass out. Slowly he realized he wasn't bitten—there was no pain. He looked down at his pants and found no holes. He looked to see the snake. It was a blown-over corn stalk. He had stepped on the root, and it kicked up and slapped his leg. He didn't feel foolish. He felt relieved.

However, he was still lost, and that dark cloud was just the lead for more. It was going to storm. He needed to find Joe and they needed to get back to the cabin.

"Peter!" Joe yelled. "Coming your way."

Peter spotted Joe ahead of him. He saw his arms waving. What was coming his way? It didn't matter now. He had found Joe and he was going to him.

"Coming your way!" Joe shouted again.

Peter saw the weeds and corn parting and something moving toward him. It was coming quickly—too quickly. Peter yelled at whatever it was. It stopped about twenty feet from him. The wind blew from that direction, and Peter smelled cow manure, but he could still see nothing.

Now what? Peter saw the weeds moving behind the ox—that was Joe coming. The ox must have seen it, too. It eased forward, and suddenly Peter and the white-faced ox were eye to eye. Peter slowly lifted his hand to the animal. The ox didn't move. Peter rubbed his floppy ear; the animal seemed to relax.

"Where are you, Peter?" Joe called.

Peter raised his hand and waved.

Joe barreled up beside Peter, almost knocking him over. He looked at the big ox, then at Peter. "Well, there is an ox."

Peter grinned, then laughed. "Yeah, there he is." He laughed not just at Joe's ridiculous statement, but also at the snake that wasn't there. He laughed at being in an overgrown cornfield in Tennessee hundreds of miles from anything or anybody he knew, except this strange white-headed boy that did the craziest things. He pointed to the ox, which had a stalk hanging from its mouth that looked like a fat cigar, and laughed harder still.

Joe moved the looped rope over the ox and looked at Peter. "Peter, are you all right?"

Peter stopped laughing suddenly. With a straight face he said, "I got lost looking for this animal, but he found me instead of me finding him." He laughed again. He didn't know why he was laughing, but he couldn't stop.

Joe looked at Peter as if he had lost his mind. "Lost? All you had to do was look above the weeds at the mountains and get yourself straight with them."

Peter stopped laughing and rubbed his nose. Of course, Joe was right. He should have thought of that, but he hadn't. Joe always thought clearly—always. Joe may have done some foolish things, but he was clear-headed.

Now Peter knew what he had always known, but had not wanted to admit it. He knew it back in the little house when Joe shot the man with the revolver. He knew it when he lost control when the hog revived at the Taylor farm. He had promised Dr. Taylor he would watch out for Joe. But Joe was the one looking out for him. A heavy weight hung inside his chest. Dr. Taylor must have known. He knew the two boys' different personalities—yes, he knew.

"Peter, are you feeling all right?"

Peter forced a smile. He wished he had Joe's self-confidence.

Lightening flashed and thunder rumbled in the distance.

"We better get back to the cabin," Peter said. "You lead the way."

Peter followed Joe and the ox through the weeds and corn. Joe whistled and hummed *Shenandoah* as he led the beast. Peter lowered his head and just followed.

***

Two weeks had passed and Joe was beginning to think Mrs. Sawyer and Mary were not coming back. It was like most people; they mean things when they say it, but they never get around to doing it. He wasn't that way—if he said it, he did it.

Peter and Gus fussed over Albert; he was coming around nicely. Joe found the man to be a mean old coot, gave orders like a sergeant, but not to Joe. He stayed away and explored the farm. That was the way to stay clear of that noise.

He had caught four hogs now, and he had both steers. As he fed the hogs what little feed he could find, he knew he had to make a move. Food was running short. There was only one thing to do: go to town and find someone to buy the steers. They could use the money for food for Albert and Gus and feed for the hogs.

Peter came around the cabin to dump the slop jar. Joe went to him, steering clear of the discarded contents.

"I'm fixing to go to town and sell them steers," Joe said.

Peter shook the last of the piss from the slop jar. "You don't know anything about driving a team of oxen."

This was true, Joe thought. "Do you have a better plan?"

"Take the mule to town and see if you can find someone interested in purchasing the oxen, then bring them out here."

Peter was right. In less than five minutes, Joe was on the mule. He rode out of the valley, and it felt like coming out of a well. They had been there over three weeks. They should have been in Virginia a month ago. That settled the hash; when he got back to the farm, they would hit the road for the Valley.

***

Joe was about five miles from the farm when he saw cavalry coming. He wasn't going to hide. Damn the Yankees, but for that matter, they could be Rebels; damn them, too.

They were Yankees all right. They rode by him, laughing and pointing. He put his hand over his face, but the dust got through, and he gagged and coughed long after the troopers had ridden on by. The last troopers were leading mules and cows. They had stolen them, no doubt. Cavalry on both sides were nothing but thieves.

Joe waddled on down the road on the swayback mule. He knew he would have to give the buyer a very good deal for the team. Times were hard here, but someone would need them, especially with the Yankees stealing from the farmers.

Joe stopped the mule. Those Yankees were stealing for sure, and now they were riding straight for the farm. They would turn down the little road—of course they would. They would probably raid every farm. Joe sawed the mule around, but he was much slower than the horses. He prodded the mule as fast as it would go.

What would he do when he arrived there? Hadn't every farmer argued to keep his livestock? Hadn't the Yankees taken it anyway? What could he do different? This was the sorry truth of war.

The blue troopers were pouring from the little valley road like a blue serpent when he finally got there. He saw the pigs laying in a wagon. He climbed down from the mule, saw both oxen being pulled individually behind troopers. How could this be fair? Where was God? Peter said God helped the ones that couldn't help themselves. Where was that help now? Slowly the thieves disappeared up the road in a dusty cloud.

Peter sat on the porch staring into space when Joe stepped down from the mule. He seemed strange to Joe, just sat there. "Did they hurt anybody?" Joe asked. He tied the mule to the post. Peter didn't answer—he hadn't even acknowledged Joe's arrival. Joe shook Peter's shoulder.

Peter slowly found Joe's eyes. "They took all the animals, every last one."

Joe looked at the cabin door.

Peter saw him looking. "They didn't hurt anyone—not physically, anyway."

What did he mean by that? Did they hurt anybody or not?

Joe stepped up to open the door, but hesitated. He could hear Gus talking. He was talking in a soothing voice to Albert. "Things be fine by and by, Massuh Albert. The boys done got us a garden started. I know that fine lady, Mrs. Sawyer, be back soon. We be fine, you'll see."

Albert said nothing.

Joe stepped away from the door. Peter was still just sitting staring blankly up the road. They had lost. They tried to do good by these old men, but they had failed. There was nothing else to be done; it was time to move on. It was now September and past time to leave.

Joe sat beside Peter. "It's time."

"Yes, I know," Peter said, looking at Joe.

"There is nothing more we can do here, but live day to day and that is no good," Joe said.

"Right."

"We have a little money left we can give them," Joe said.

"Yes."

They looked at each other for a minute, not knowing what else to say.

Joe stood and looked at the door, squared his shoulders, and advanced on it. He felt Peter behind him. They went in.

***

They turned onto the main road to Knoxville, had gone a few hundred yards when Joe turned and saw Mrs. Sawyer and Mary coming from the other direction. Peter had the reins and seemed not to notice. Mrs. Sawyer turned the wagon onto the road leading down to the farm from where Joe and Peter had just come. She seemed to not notice the boys on the mule. Joe wondered if Peter and Mrs. Sawyer were that blind.

Mary slowly raised her hand and waved. She was so very pretty.

Joe raised his hand. He watched the wagon disappear down the lane as the swayback mule walked on. Joe turned to tell Peter to go back. He changed his mind when he saw a tear streaming down Peter's cheek. When Joe turned back to the wagon, it was hidden behind the trees, hidden to be seen no more. Joe turned, slowly pulled his harmonica from his pocket, and soon *Shenandoah* echoed from the trees with the mules bobbing head keeping time.

Chapter 19

Lucius grimaced when he saw the slave quarters at the Taylor farm, looked too much like the ones at the plantation where he had escaped, like dog houses lined up in a neat row. After all, to white men, slaves were dogs.

He looked back down the road; there was Theo dragging behind. If Theo weren't a necessity, he would have killed him long ago. The fat toad was not much of a man. Lucius hated all white men, but worthless, lazy, cowards were the worst.

"Fetch on up here," Lucius said. "Look like a massuh; look respectful and honorable."

Theo puffed on up to Lucius, sweating like a pig and red-faced. Lucius looked the man over and simply shook his head in disgust.

"Just let me have one little swig of that laudanum," Theo said.

"No suh." Lucius patted his bag containing all his stuff. "Only after you plays your part here will you get a snort. You ain't gonna get us killed here like you about did back in Oxford."

"We got out of that fix just fine, didn't we?"

"You's done got us into too many tight fixes. Now shut your trap and do like I says, and things will be right."

If Theo fudged up this time, he was a dead man, "play massuh" or no "play massuh." They had left Helena in June. Now here it was August, and they still hadn't caught up to the boy, too many obstacles, and that damn Theo caused most of them. They spent a week in jail at Oxford—he should have killed the fat man then. However, Lucius reckoned it was his own fault, gave Theo too much laudanum; he would have to ration it better. No matter now, they had finally found New Albany and with good luck, found the farm of Dr. Taylor's brother. He could thank Theo for that. He was finally acting like a master.

When had they passed a farmer a ways back, he actually struck up a sensible conversation with the man and had discovered this handy information. Just when Lucius doubted Theo and his own plan, things seemed to be turning for the better.

This farm was a nice one. The cotton was swelling in the bowls. In just a couple of weeks, the land would look snow-covered. The corn had been harvested, and he saw many Negroes cutting the stalks and stacking them. A large white man worked along side them. A few of the Negroes watched as Lucius and Theo approached, but the white man only gave them a glance and went back to cutting the stalks.

Lucius moved behind Theo. "You leads the way, and remember how we studied on what to say."

Theo spoke over his shoulder. "Just follow your master and things will be well."

They crossed the field to the white man. He finally looked up when they were only a few feet from him. Some of the Negroes looked on, but most kept cutting and stacking stalks.

"How do?" Theo said, extending his fat hand. "My name is Theo Caldwell."

Lucius grimaced inside. Theo's acting still needed a lot of work.

The man looked at Theo's hand for a long moment, then looked up and slowly took the chubby hand in his. Lucius noticed the contrast: Theo's hand was pudgy and pink, but the other man's hand was hard, and his arms were muscular, no stranger to work.

"Zeke Taylor."

"Mr. Taylor," Theo said, nodding. He placed his hands on his hips and smiled. "I'm so glad to finally meet you."

Confusion grew on Zeke's face.

Theo pulled a handkerchief from his pocket and wiped his brow. "I can tell by the bewildered look on your face you are wondering just who this fellow is."

Zeke handed the scythe to one of the Negroes. "Stepto, y'all finish this field and we'll call it a day." Stepto nodded, and the Negroes went back to work.

Zeke started toward the farmhouse without saying a word. Theo looked at Lucius—he was at a loss for what to do. Lucius motioned with his eyes to follow Zeke. Theo tailed Zeke, Lucius behind him. "Mr. Taylor, if you would just speak with me for a moment, I am sure you will find it worth your while."

Zeke stopped suddenly and turned. "Mr. Caldwell, nothing about you would be worth my while."

"But Mr. Taylor, you haven't given me a chance to—"

"Mister, you come walking up to my farm; you have no horse, no wagon, nothing. You ain't from around here, so you had to come from afar. If you were an important man, you would be riding, not walking. You are too fat and soft to be accustomed to walking. You got this big Negro following you and that don't look good. Either you stole him or you are trying to sell him. Either way I don't like the looks of it." Zeke turned and started walking, again.

Lucius quickly realized this man was a hard man and would not be easily fooled. He tried to form a new plan, but before he could think of the first idea, Theo surprised him: "I was good friends with Doctor Taylor." That wasn't in the plan—not at all, but it would work if Theo played it right.

Zeke turned, but said nothing, waiting for Theo to continue. For once Theo didn't disappoint Lucius.

"I worked in the store for him." Theo looked sheepishly at his shoes. "I reckon you could say I was his right-hand man."

Zeke still said nothing.

"To tell you the truth, Mr. Taylor, life was hard in Helena with the Yankees and all, and Dr. Taylor fetched me from hard scrabble—I tell you that for a fact."

Lucius couldn't believe his luck. Theo was an actor of first rate. He had totally underestimated this fat ass.

"Wilbur always did have a big heart," Zeke said. He had loosened a little. "Yes, he did. What did you say your name was again?"

"Theo, Theo Caldwell." Theo bowed slightly.

"Mr. Caldwell, I don't have a big heart, and I am a busy man. If you want something, why don't you come on out with it?"

Theo seemed to have come to the end of his acting talent. He just stood there. Lucius begged his brain for an idea. He blurted out, "Massuh Caldwell, let us don't bother Massuh Taylor no more. I specks we can scrounge enough food to go up to Pennsylvania."

Zeke shot a look toward Lucius, then back to Theo. "You aim on going to Pennsylvania?" He shook his head. "Mister, I don't know if you give a good caring damn, but there is a war going on. I don't reckon you would get far with that run-away. I'm damn sure you won't make it to Pennsylvania with Rebel troopers on the roads between here and there."

Theo said, "He is not a run—"

"Oh, Massuh Theo, let us not be lying to Massuh Taylor. He can see right through that there," Lucius said.

Lucius saw that Theo was at a loss to where he was going with this. He didn't know himself, but he just let his mouth take him. "Massuh Taylor, please forgive Massuh Caldwell. We is just desperate. We wants to get to Pennsylvania. That where Dr. Taylor say we should go." Lucius lowered his head. "That is before he die." Lucius shook his head slowly. "He sho was a good man, a very good man. He sho was that."

Zeke said nothing for a long minute. Lucius knew he had said all he could; he hoped it would work. Zeke looked across the land, surveyed it as if he was seeing where he could put the Negroes to work next, then his eyes settled on Theo, studied him for a time. Theo said nothing. "You come with me," Zeke said, then he looked at Lucius. "Boy, what is your name?"

Lucius reckoned it was no harm in using his real name now—Theo had. "My name is Lucius, suh."

"You come along, too. I don't want no strange Negro gabbing it up with mine while they are working."

***

It had been thirty minutes since Zeke had taken Theo into the house and left him on the porch. Lucius hoped Theo didn't mess things up. He had convinced Theo the boy had plenty of money. Maybe that was a good enough reason to not screw the whole thing up. All they needed to do was find the boy. For that, they had to fool Zeke into believing they were good folks.

Lucius heard a commotion from around the house. A little Negro boy came around the house shooing a sow and a litter of half-grown pigs. Those little pigs would be some good eating. They probably weighed about forty to fifty pounds each; he could easily carry one of them away, would make some fine eating down the road.

Mr. Taylor came out of a side door and went toward the slave cabins. Lucius wondered about Theo. Mr. Taylor went to the door of the largest cabin. He stood in the door for a long spell talking to the Negroes inside. He left and went back in the side door of the big house. Shortly an old Negro man came out of the cabin and headed for Lucius. Not another boss nigger, Lucius thought.

"Lucius, I is Seth."

Lucius nodded. It was probably best to say little, but listen a lot.

"Marse want me to find you a place to bed down for the night. It won't be much seeing how the Yankees burned down the good barn, but least you won't be under the stars."

Lucius nodded again.

Seth eyed him suspiciously. "Can you talk?"

"I can talk."

Seth nodded his head one slow nod. "Well, then, come on along, gabby."

Lucius followed the old man to a shed, which was being used for a make-shift barn. It wasn't much, but as Seth had said, it would keep him from under the stars. However, what was even better, he could see everything from there. It was located right in the middle of the farm. If the boy was around, he would surely see him from there.

"Marse say to see is you hungry."

Lucius said nothing.

After waiting a couple of minutes and getting impatient, Seth said, "Well, is you?"

"I reckon I could stand something."

"Boy, lets me tell you something right here and now," Seth said, pointing his finger at Lucius. "I ain't in the habit of chewing my cabbage twice. When you is asked something here on this here place, you best answer."

Lucius thought about hitting the old fool, but simply nodded.

Seth took him to his cabin. Lucius found that Seth was mild compared to his woman, Floy. She was a big fat woman with a big fat mouth. No sooner had he entered the cabin, she started with the mouth. Lucius reckoned it was best to just do what she said and say nothing himself. She shoved a bowl of grits in front of him. He didn't realize how hungry he was. He ate like a starving animal, and the two stared at him.

"You needs to slow down," Floy said. "If you puke on my floor, you is going to clean it up. I won't stands for no nigger to puke on my floor."

He wanted to slap her hound dog jaws. She was just a damn slave, yet here she was giving orders to him as if she were a master. He was stewing inside, but he just told her he would be careful, and he ate slower.

When he finished eating, Seth took him back to the shed and told him to wait on his master. He wanted to tell the old man he served no master, but kept his mouth shut.

He saw Zeke back in the field working, must have gone back out while he was in the cabin eating. He heard Theo's loud mouth in the house. He was having a high time, laughing and carrying on. Lucius hated him for it, but at the same time, he was pleased that things were going well.

Lucius backed up in a pile of hay and waited for Theo to come out. He hoped Theo was finding out about the boy, also hoped he would get food for the road; he was tired of scrounging for food.

A kitten came meowing up to him. He lay his big hand down and the kitten crawled in it. He raised it to his face, looked at the slit eyes. Cats had eyes that you couldn't trust, never knew what a cat would do—they weren't like dogs. A dog stood by you and helped you. He had a dog when he was a boy. It was the only good friend he ever had. Cats only wanted from you. They were like white folks—the only time they were nice to you was when they wanted something from you. The minute they got it, they turned on you. The cat nuzzled at Lucius's nose. Lucius squeezed his hands slightly, and the cat's eyes grew large. Lucius smiled.

Oh, yes, surprise. Lucius had seen the same look on white folks when he had turned on them. They hadn't suspected it—oh no, they had not thought the good Negro would do such a thing. He had seen the horror in their eyes—first surprise, then sheer terror. He smiled. At least ten white folks had known that surprise. He felt his iron fist tighten on the kitten.

"I see you found my kitten."

Lucius was startled. It was the Negro that had been out in the field with Mr. Taylor. He remembered Mr. Taylor had called him Stepto.

"He's a purty little kitty, ain't he?" Lucius said, as he set the kitten down.

The kitten scrambled away from Lucius and up Stepto's pants leg. Stepto pried him from his leg. "Why, Puss, he ain't gonna hurt you. You is just a little kitty." Stepto stroked the kitten, then turned to Lucius. "We is finished for the day and seeing how it is Saturday, Marse say we can play and sing round the fire if we keep it low. You is welcome to come around if you wants."

Lucius simply nodded.

Stepto looked at him for a spell. "Well, you is been invited. Come if you want." He rubbed the kitten as he left the shed.

In just a few minutes, Lucius heard Theo on the porch laughing and carrying on. He was standing beside a white woman, Mr. Taylor's wife no doubt. He took his hat off and bowed, then strolled toward the shed. The woman looked toward the shed and half smiled at Lucius, and then disappeared back inside the house.

"Well, my good boy, this has been a delight, I tell you," Theo said, rubbing his plump belly as he went into the shed.

Lucius grabbed him by the shirt and shoved him against the wall. "Don't call me 'boy!'" Lucius hated the fat man even more. Theo smelled of meat. No doubt, he had filled his fat ass with good food while Lucius ate grits.

"What goes, Lucius? The good lady was just—"

Lucius punched Theo in the gut. Theo shot out a loud fart and doubled over. Lucius snatched him back up straight, realizing he, himself, was about to blow the game.

Theo gasped, "You have got to stop handling me in such a fashion." He straightened his hat and took several deep breaths.

Lucius steadied Theo on his feet, while looking around to see if anyone had seen the punch. He saw no one. "You is right, Theo. That was foolish on me." Lucius smiled. "You just smelled good with that smoked meat on your clothes; it just make me mad."

Theo raised a faint smile. It looked peculiar with him holding his belly in obvious pain. He reached into his vest pocket, pulled out a napkin, and handed it to Lucius.

Lucius snatched it from him and pulled the folds open, revealing a large lean piece of pork. In two bites, Lucius had devoured all but a small piece, which he deposited into his pocket for later.

"Ain't that worth a swig?" Theo said with a growing smile

Lucius grinned. "Yessuh, Massuh, I reckon it is."

Lucius pulled the bottle from the bag and handed it to Theo. Theo gulped and Lucius had to wrestle it from him. "Easy, easy, you keep up the good job and you will get more." Lucius looked around and then placed the bottle back into the bag.

Theo rubbed his mouth. "Well, they've asked me to come back to the house and tell them all about Helena."

"Did you find out about the Taylor boy?"

"I will find out tonight, I'm sure."

"Plays it real good, Theo. Don't let on what we's up to."

Theo nodded. "They have a spare room around back. That's where I'll sleep. They say you are to stay here in this shed."

"That bees fine. You just find out about the boy."

It was growing late when Theo went back into the house. Lucius lay in the hay to try to sleep, wanted to get his sleep now before it was very dark, wanted to be awake when the night came. He placed his bag at his feet and covered it with straw.

He was about to drift off when the sounds of Negroes singing and wagons rolling into the farm aroused him. The sound was too familiar, and sleep was gone now.

The end of the day was a good time for most slaves—if there was a good time, Lucius thought. The hard day's work for the master was over and the rest of what was left of the day was for the slave. They could work their small garden if they had one, or do work around the quarters to make life a little more bearable. But the best time was the ride in the wagon back from the fields or the walk. Lucius remembered it well. There was one time he remembered most of all.

***

His mother had sat beside him in the rocking and swaying wagon. They had both been tired from the cotton fields. However, the ride from the fields had been pleasant because she had told him of his father again. He never tired of the story.

"No, Lucius, your father was not a slave in Africa," she had said. "He was a great king. He had peoples that tended him. He had his own slaves."

Lucius had studied on that. His father owned slaves. It would be better to own slaves than to be a slave. He was now twelve. He would be a boy prince and have his own slaves some day.

"How did father come to America?"

"Bad mens come there to Africa and catched him and some more of his peoples."

"If he was a great king, how did he get catched?"

His mother pulled the rag down tight on her head and smiled at Lucius. "You see, Lucius, he had killed a great lion, and they had a big juba cause he had killed the lion. The lion's spirit floated on over to the elephant."

"What is a elephant?" Lucius asked.

"That bees a big animal—bigger than a bull, and he got a long nose and two long tushes that stick out in front. The Missus show me one in a picture book."

Lucius was wide-eyed. "Is that elephant bigger than Massuh's red bull?"

"Lawd sakes, boy, that elephant make four or five of Massuh's red bull."

Lucius stared around in amazement. He never thought there was any animal bigger than the red bull.

"Now that elephant done gone and told the monkey, and that monkey done gone and told some bad white mens, what was on a ship. Now the king and all his peoples done gone and drinked too much magic potion cause they was celebrating. The bad white mens just went right up and catched them."

"Didn't they put up no fight?"

"Oh—a—well, yeah, but they's too weak from the magic potion."

The wagon stopped in front of the big house. The master marched to the wagon.

Lucius was scared. The master was a bad man—a mean man.

The master addressed Lucius's mother, "Martha, you and the boy have been talking too much in the field, not enough work is getting done."

"Oh, Massuh, we is—"

"Quiet, wench! I pay my overseer top dollar, and he is a good man. He would not lie. He said he has warned you, but he is too damn soft."

"Please Massuh, don't whip me again."

The master slapped the woman across the face. Blood sprayed on Lucius. His own blood ran cold.

"I won't whip you." He turned to the overseer. "Hang the boy up."

"Oh no, Massuh!" She held Lucius's arm.

The overseer cracked her across her back with his whip. She screamed, and it tore at Lucius's heart. He pulled Lucius from the wagon. It was like a dream. Everything went slowly, but at the same time, it happened so fast. One minute he was in the wagon talking about an animal bigger than the red bull; the next, he was naked, hung by the arms to a gum tree, his feet barely touching the ground.

The master stepped up to him. Lucius wanted to scream, but something inside would not dare let him.

"Boy, you will give me a good day's work from your black ass."

Lucius saw his mother on her knees behind the wagon sobbing. All of the other slaves that were in the wagon were gone. Lucius didn't remember seeing them go. It was like magic. Maybe they disappeared.

"Are you listening, Lucius?" The master grabbed Lucius's face and squeezed it hard. "You will be a good nigger, and this evening we will give you some reminders, so you don't ever forget."

Lucius looked into the mean man's gray eyes. "White man, I am a prince and one day I—"

The man screamed with rage. He rammed his fist into Lucius's belly. Lucius felt searing pain.

His mother ran screaming. "Massuh, please don't hurt my boy."

He grabbed her around the throat and began strangling her.

Lucius wanted to yell, but he couldn't even breathe.

After long minutes the overseer couldn't stand it and tried to pry the master's hands away, but when the master screamed curses at him, he backed away.

Lucius croaked with a weak breath, "Mammy, Mammy." He knew the master would let her go before she died. But he did not. He held on even after she melted to the ground. Lucius did not cry. He felt something leave his body. He felt numb.

The master stood over the body and stared for a few minutes. Suddenly he started screaming and began kicking the body. He was a mad man. The overseer stood back, wide-eyed. When the master finally tired of kicking her, he pulled his manhood from his trousers and pissed on her face.

Lucius felt a fire kindle somewhere down deep. He was numb now, but he felt a small ember flame up.

The master turned on the overseer. "Whip the damn boy before I whip you."

The overseer stumbled back, regained himself, and pulled up the whip.

***

Lucius was wrestled from the horrible memory and back to the present when he saw movement near his feet. He held still. He saw an arm reach for the bag. He sprang around and came up with a small, black boy. Lucius had his large hand over the boys whole face and had the boy held so tight that the boy could only move his feet.

Lucius looked into the boy's eyes and saw horror. There it was again, the shock of being in his vice and not knowing what had happened. Lucius backed into the shadows, like an animal might do with its freshly caught prey. The boy's eyes couldn't have been opened wider without popping from his head.

"What is you doing, boy? I's going to let you speak, but if you squeak too loud, I will snap your neck."

He lowered his hand.

"I—I—just wanted to see what was in the bottle the fat white man was drinking."

If the boy had seen that, then he had overheard them talking.

"It ain't good for little boys to be snooping around when a massuh is talking to his nigger," Lucius said.

The boy said nothing. His wide eyes said it all. Lucius could feel him tremble in his grasp. He felt pity. He seldom felt that for anyone, but he felt it now. For once, he was bothered.

He clamped his hand back over the boy's mouth and slowly began to twist his head. The boy squirmed, but it was of as much use as a mouse squirming in a cat's paw.

"Washington!" called a voice from the porch of the big house. Lucius knew it was a white man calling. He felt the boy flinch when the boy heard the voice. The boy was Washington. He studied on it a minute. If the boy came up missing, the white folks may not wait until tomorrow to look for him. Maybe there was another way to handle this.

"Washington. You is Washington, ain't you?"

Washington tried to nod, but Lucius held him too tightly. Lucius relaxed his grip a bit.

"Boy, if I lets you go, you don't tell nobody what happened here. Does you understand me?"

Washington nodded swiftly.

"Is you scared of me?"

Washington nodded again.

"Good." Lucius looked around, then stood up, holding the boy. He looked out of the shed and saw an older fat white man. He was looking about for Washington. Lucius backed to the back of the shed. "I tells you what, I ain't the only big nigger that Massuh has—oh, no. He gots more in the woods just a waiting on us now as we talks. If anything happen to us, they comes in and kill everybody." He waited to let the boy study on it. "Boy, I'm going to let you go cause you's just in the wrong place at the wrong time. Now if I lets you go, is you going to say anything about me and my massuh?"

Washington shook his head.

Lucius took his hand away from the boy's face and set him down. Washington just stood there.

Lucius got down on his knees and grabbed both of the boy's shoulders. He eyed the boy for a long time then said, "Do you know the white boy, Joseph Taylor?"

The boy flinched, but said nothing.

Lucius smiled. "Tell me where the white boy is and I will let you go."

The white man called for Washington, again.

Washington looked in that direction. He turned back to Lucius. "Will you swear to let me go if I tells you?"

Lucius stood up and rubbed the boy's head. "Lucius is a man of his word."

***

Lucius put his hand over Theo's mouth, and Theo awoke with a start. "Quiet, it just me. We needs to get away from here while it is dark."

Theo sat up in the bed and rubbed his face. "Why not wait until morning."

"Don't be asking foolish questions. Now get your stuff and let's go."

Lucius waited outside for Theo. Theo was slower than a woman. When Theo came out the door, Lucius motioned him to follow, and he put his forefinger to his lip signaling Theo to be quiet. They went into the shed and Lucius grabbed his bag and a bundle wrapped with a horse blanket.

"What do you have in the bundle?" Theo asked.

"I've killed us a little pig. They have a few, and they ain't going to miss one. Least ways, they won't think we carried it away." He saw Theo smile.

***

Lucius waited until they were on the main road before he spoke. "That Taylor boy is gone to Virginia."

"Virginia? Have you gone crazy?" Theo stopped walking. "They are fighting hard up there. We can't go there."

Lucius studied Theo. Did he still need him? He knew where the boy was headed. He could leave this bag of shit right here on the side of the road and go on. Not yet—not just yet.

"It is where the boy is, and it is where we is going," Lucius said, then turned and continued down the road. He heard Theo huffing to keep up. If he said another word, he would regret it.

They walked for about two miles without saying a word, then finally Theo spoke. "Where is the boy at in Virginia?"

Lucius smiled. He knew that greedy bastard would come along, not just because he was scared, but because he wanted the money and, of course, the laudanum.

***

Close to dawn, Lucius felt they needed to get a little nap before daylight. They would walk all day and rest was necessary. He found a spot off the road a ways where they couldn't be seen by travelers. He set the bundle down and stepped into the bushes looking for the right spot. He had just found the spot he was looking for when he heard Theo scream. He drew his knife from his boot and crept around to Theo. He was standing over the bundle with his hand over his mouth.

Theo stepped back when Lucius walked up. "I-I-just wanted to see the pig."

Lucius reached down and hefted the dead boy.

"Why, Lucius? He was just a little boy."

Lucius felt like taking his knife and cutting Theo's tongue out.

"Don't you talk on it—don't ever talk on it again!"

Lucius carried the body to the spot he had found in the bushes. There was a big log. He heaved at it, but it would not roll. He heaved again and the log slowly rolled over. With the knife and his hands, he dug out a shallow depression, then placed the body into it. He stood and stared at the boy. It would be a while before they found the body. They should be long gone by then—yes, long gone. He rolled the heavy log back over the body, then went around the log sweeping the area with a leafy branch. When he was satisfied that all evidence was covered, he sat down on the log—something snapped under the log. He let out a deep breath, then whispered, "Little Washington, I will make that white boy pay for what he done to you." He reached into his pocket and pulled out the filthy piece of meat Theo had given him back at the Taylor farm. He blew on it, but it didn't clean away anything; then he crammed it into his mouth. "Yep," he said and chewed. "Joseph Taylor will die for what he done to you."

Chapter 20

Peter's belly rumbled as they stopped at the grove of trees. They had eaten little since they had left Gus and Albert, and they had given the two old men most of their money. The small trees had big leaves, bigger than any others around. Peter knew they would be turning yellow before long. Soon the leaves from all of the trees would be turning their fall colors: reds, yellows, browns.

Joe shook one of the trees, but nothing fell. "Ah, maybe ain't any," Joe said. "It ain't ever too many on them anyhow."

Peter tied the mule to a tree and went down the hill to Joe. He found the biggest tree in the grove, squared his legs for support, and shook the tree.

"Ain't nothing in them, I done told you," Joe said.

The treetop whipped like it was caught in a gale. The big leaves sailed down like kites. Suddenly four missiles dropped from the tree; one smacked Joe on top of the head.

"Yowl!" Joe grabbed his head with both hands.

Peter picked up one of the pawpaws, then split it in half. "You going to eat or are you going to hold your head?"

Joe grabbed up a couple and sat at the base of the tree, laughing and rubbing his head. He pulled the tomahawk from his belt and dug into the fruit. Soon he had yellow pulp all over his face.

Peter laughed at him, digging with the tomahawk. "Me like um pawpaw."

Joe giggled harder and spit a seed at Peter.

Peter sat on a log. The pawpaw was good; at least it would curb the growling in his belly.

He watched Joe eat. The boy acted as if he didn't have a care in the world. Just yesterday, they were both blue for having to leave the old men in such a situation. Peter wished he could be more like Joe in that regard. But, someone had to worry. Someone had to be concerned for the war. At least they were not alone in this. God was with them, and that's what kept Peter going when things were at their lowest.

Peter went back up the hill away from Joe, removed his bag from his shoulder, reached in, and retrieved the Bible. He needed that comfort now. They were getting closer to Virginia and what they found there may not be—well—God only knew what they would find. He sat by a tree with his back toward Joe and opened the Bible. He had forgotten the necklace, and it fell into his lap. He looked up—good, Joe had not seen it. He held the necklace in his hand, admired the two passenger pigeons. Doves were in the Bible; Noah released the dove from the ark to find land. A pigeon was really a dove, after all. Here he held a family heirloom, but not his family.

He thought about that—his family. He had no family. He looked at Joe, busy shaking another tree. Joe felt like family. Peter turned the pigeons in his hand. Dr. Taylor had given him his most valued possession. He was like a father to him. He was white, but it hadn't mattered. It surely didn't matter to God. It didn't seem to matter to Dr. Taylor. Does Joe feel as if I'm family, he wondered. He looked at Joe.

Something was wrong. Joe was staring past him like a deer. His eyes met Peter's, then looked past him again. He had his hand on the tomahawk. Peter slid the necklace back into the Bible and slowly closed it, then dropped it back into the bag. He was afraid to turn around, but he had to.

Two men were coming from the trees, black men. Peter saw another to his right, and as he turned to him, he saw one coming from the road.

"What do y'all want?" Joe said.

The one from the road marched to Joe and pushed him down. Peter ran to Joe. The man grabbed Peter's shoulder as Peter reached to help Joe.

"Leave him be," the man said.

Peter pulled loose from his grip and hauled Joe to his feet. Then he held Joe tight, so he wouldn't do something stupid.

"Let me go!" Joe said, squirming.

Peter ignored him. He looked the men over. They had all come up close, surrounding them. They were runaways—Peter could tell that plainly now. "You touch him again and it will be at your peril," Peter said. He felt Joe look up at him.

"At my what?" The man laughed. The man was bald, and his head shined like a new cannonball.

Peter was bigger than any of them, but he knew he couldn't take them all. "You men be on your way and let us alone."

"We's come to help you, boy," the bald man said. "They's Yankees in all directions. You can fetch up with us and be free."

Peter let his guard down and Joe jerked free. Before he could react, Joe had his tomahawk in his hand and advancing on baldy.

"He's already free," Joe said, "and if you put your hands on me again, you'll have stumps."

The man slowly backed off. The others started forward.

"Tell them to back off, or I will spill your guts like the nasty hog you are!"

They stopped. The bald man looked to Peter with fright.

"He is pretty good with that ax," Peter said. "I do appreciate your concern for me, but as my friend said, I'm already a free man. I've always been a free man."

"Come on, John; that nigger don't need no help," another man said to the bald man.

Peter heard horses coming down the road from the north. The men heard them, too, and darted for the trees like rabbits. Peter followed Joe to the mule. Just as they got to the animal, eight men pulled up to them. They were a ragged lot. They wore all manner of clothes, but Peter saw enough gray and butternut through the dust and grime to figure who they were.

The lead man climbed down from his pitiful horse and looked the mule over. "What you boys doing here?" he said, running his hand over the animal.

"What are you doing here?" Joe said.

No, Joe! Peter thought. Why dive right into trouble when you may can avoid it?

Without moving a muscle, the man shot a stare at Joe. Peter saw they all had revolvers. He and Joe were at their mercy and Joe was too foolish to know it.

The man slowly turned, climbed back on his horse. "Well, boy, I'll tell you what I'm a-doing here." He pointed north. "Back up that way is Virginia, and in Virginia is the Shenandoah Valley. In the Shenandoah Valley is a General Early." The man looked at the other men. They smiled. "I used to belong to General Early; well, I don't belong to his ass no more."

Joe stepped forward. "I'm from the Shenandoah Valley and there is where I'm headed. I'm not scared like you deserters."

Peter grabbed Joe.

The man stopped smiling. "Boy, there is another general up there, too, and his name is Sheridan, and he aims to have the Valley. I've already lost two brothers up there fighting his ass." He nodded toward the south. "I'm going home. I have a little girl about your age, and I'm going to see her." The man said nothing for a long minute; then he simply spurred the horse and never looked back. The other soldiers fell in behind him—they didn't speak.

As the soldiers rode out of sight, the Negroes came out of hiding like roaches. Peter found John to be their leader. "We is obliged to you not telling them soldiers we was a hid in them woods," John said. He peeped down the road in both directions to make sure the soldiers were gone.

Joe mounted the mule.

Peter turned to John. "Well, we best be on our way, too."

"Wait juss a minute," John said. "We seed y'all eating them pawpaws, so y'all must be hungry. Follow us; we is got food." The men turned back to the woods.

"Thank you, but we best be on our way," Peter said.

Joe jumped from the mule. "Come on, Peter, let's eat."

Peter led the mule and followed Joe. Just a few minutes ago, Joe wanted to cut this man's guts open; now he was following him as if he were an old friend.

The men led them farther into the woods. Peter worried. There could be more men; they could easily jump them and that would be the end.

Peter was right—there were more men, and women and

children, too. It was a camp with about 20 people. There were four mules, a wagon, and a cart, and there was a big pot over a fire. Peter looked closer—no, the fire was out. The people watched Joe and Peter as if they were a couple of rabid dogs.

John raised his hand. "It fine—it fine. These peoples bees good peoples." Slowly Peter could feel the camp relax.

"Where's the food?" Joe said.

***

They ate on a makeshift table fashioned from a plank. They had ash-pone and cold grits. The grits had small pieces of meat in it. Peter believed it was rabbit.

The camp was hidden back in the woods. They had posted lookouts, and as a whole, the camp was kept quiet.

"I hopes y'all don't mind the cold food, but we can't afford to build too many fires," John said.

Joe nodded and said with a mouth full of food, "Smoke."

"That right," John said, as a woman shoved more food into the boys' plates. "We does our cooking at night; then we does our traveling after."

"Where are you going," Peter said, then took a bite of the bread.

John stood up and rubbed his shiny head with charcoal-colored hands. "We's juss heading north. Don't know where else to go."

"You're runaways, ain't you?" Joe said.

"No, not really—well, most of us ain't. We done picked up a couple that might be, don't know for sho."

"I don't understand," Peter said.

"Yankees done killed our massuh and the missus left us. Yankees burned down the place, even the quarters. We had a good massuh, but we don't want nobody else to get us, so we is headed north."

"Where you from?" Joe said

"Georgia—most of us. Don't know where some from. They just took a notion to fall in with us. Even got a white man." John pointed to the cart. "He asleep over yonder behind that cart." He looked at Peter, then Joe. "Did I hear you tell that soldier you is from Virginia?"

Joe finished his meal and stood up. "That's right and headed there now."

He started for the mule, then turned. "Oh, thank you for the grub."

"Wait til dark and we'll fall in with y'all," John said.

"I have to look out for the boy's welfare, and that wouldn't be a good thing," Peter said.

John whispered, "Don't you think it time we looked out for our own?"

Peter shook John's hand. "He is my own." Peter mounted the mule with Joe. He felt pity for the Negroes. Then he thought of himself and his own troubles as they maneuvered the mule through the woods and toward the road. It was enough trouble to worry about.

***

Like a hungry lion, Lucius peered from under the cart at the boys on the mule and watched them disappear back toward the road. Good! Very, very good!

He looked over at Theo sleeping. He could kill him now, didn't need him any longer. He slid the knife from his boot. He looked around and thought differently. Hell, one of these damn ignorant niggers might get mixed up in it and try to help Theo. As Theo snored, Lucius came up with an idea. Why kill this white man? Don't need to. He took the last bottle of laudanum from his bag, poured the opium into it, and leaned it onto Theo's belly. Lucius smiled and headed for the road.

***

Joe felt lighter, as if he were floating. They had passed a man on the road that said they were in Virginia. Finally, after all the time wasted, he was in Virginia. Now he just had to make it to the Shenandoah Valley. He pulled his harmonica from his pocket, played better than he ever had—no mistakes.

It was September. The Valley would be golden with corn; he could earn money with the harvest, could work in one of the mills. The opportunities were endless. He would have the farm up and going in no time. Wait until Peter sees the Valley. He won't believe how beautiful land can be.

Joe put the harmonica in his pocket and turned to Peter, leading the mule. "We got anything left to eat? This excitement makes me hungry."

"No. The bread we purchased at Bristol is gone."

"Well, we'll just buy something at the next town."

Peter shook his head. "Money's gone, too."

"Reckon we gave too much to Albert and Gus," Joe said, digging in his pockets.

Peter smiled and said, "The Lord will provide. The Bible says, *For I was a hungred, and ye gave me meat: I was thirsty, and ye gave me drink: I was a stranger, and ye—*"

"Shut that up!" Joe turned on Peter and the mule reared. "I'm sick and tired of you and the Bible. Where the hell was your Lord when they beat the hell out of Albert? Where was God when your own mother was killed? What about my mother and sister? What about Uncle Wilbur?"

"Now Joseph, you—"

"No, Peter, you just don't say anything else about the Bible." Joe turned and ran up the road ahead of Peter. His chest was rising and falling with anger, but slowly he wished he hadn't said it, not because he didn't feel it, but he wished he hadn't hurt Peter. Peter believed in God with all his might, but Joe had more doubts than a wagonload. Finally, he was feeling good, and Peter had to bring up the Bible and a god that had been absent too long. He looked back and saw Peter wiping tears. It tore at Joe's heart.

They were in front of a well-kept farm. The house was white and bordered with a whitewashed fence. The yard was neat and clean as was common before the war. There were even late flowers around the place like spilt paint. Joe saw no animals, but that wasn't unusual being this close to a busy road. Soldiers and partisans had probably long ago swiped them.

A dog barked. Joe spotted it by a smokehouse. It was a little dog—no danger from it.

Someone was shoveling something in the doorway of the smokehouse. Joe walked over, and the dog ran to him and sniffed his legs. Joe rubbed him behind his ears, and they were immediately friends.

"That's it Itchy, protect Momma from the bad boy," said an old woman leaning on the shovel. Her hair was in a tight bun, and her face was wrinkled as if it had been in bathwater much too long. She was stooped and had a large hump on her back like someone riding piggyback under her dress. She held the shovel with hands gnarled like an elbow bush. Joe stared at her distorted hands.

"Hello, Ma'am," Peter said. "We are sorry to intrude."

Joe caught himself staring. "Oh—a yes, Ma'am. We are hungry."

"Joseph!" Peter pushed Joe's shoulder.

"Well, Hun, you cut right to it, don't ye?" The woman smiled and leaned the shovel against the smokehouse wall.

"Sorry, Ma'am. I'm Joe, and this here is Peter."

She extended her crippled hand. "I'm Belle."

Joe looked at her hand as if what she had were contagious.

"Take it, Hun. It won't bite ye. It's just rheumatism."

Joe took her hand. It was hard and calloused, felt like a twisted tree limb.

"Don't ye squeeze too hard." She chuckled.

She dropped Joe's hand and looked at Peter. "Ain't ye a fine looking darky, so well kept and all."

Peter extended his hand. She looked at it in surprise.

"Never shook a stranger darky's hand before. Things are changing so." She took it.

Peter pointed to the shovel. "Ma'am, maybe we could do some work in exchange for something to eat."

"Ye don't talk in the fashion of a regular Negro." She leaned the shovel toward Peter, and he took it. "You'uns ain't from around here, are ye?"

"Yes, Ma'am," Joe said. "I'm from the Shenandoah Valley, and that's where we're headed."

"The Valley?" She wiped her knotty hand across her lips. "You'uns is a long ways from home."

Joe saw no point in keeping any secrets now. What could this old woman do? "We've come from Arkansas."

"Well, that is a fir piece to travel." She nodded toward Peter. "This here your boy?"

Joe looked at Peter. "He is a free man."

"There's a good many of them now," she said.

Joe turned back to the woman. "No, Ma'am, he's always been free." Joe looked into the smokehouse. "What about Peter's offer on the work?"

"Ye boys is welcome to eat without working." She looked at her cramped hands, then to Joe. "But I ain't a gonna turn down no free labor."

"What were you doing here?" Peter asked.

"Why I was scooping up salt offin the dirt; then I's gonna bile it down for the salt."

"Getting salt off the dirt?" Joe said. "You mean you can't get salt? Don't your neighbors have salt?"

"Boy, where have ye been? Times ain't hard south of here?"

Joe said nothing. Sure things were hard everywhere.

"Why, ye can't get salt around here, nor coffee, nor flour, nor such. Ye mean to tell me ye can get them things betwixt here and Arkansas?"

Joe and Peter were on the move so much, he didn't think much about it. The Yankees were at Helena, so there was plenty, and the Taylors had swapped cotton in Memphis with the Yankees for supplies. Now he was feeling guilty just for wanting to swap food for labor here in this depressed place. Why did Peter even ask?

"Ma'am, we'll scoop the salt for you for nothing and shove on," Joe said.

"Hun, I don't think so. I said times is hard, but I still get by. I got some beans simmering now, and I got a mater or two. Ye two young men come around the back of the house when ye get me a bucket or two of dirt shoveled up. Just scoop the very top."

When she left for the house, Peter started scooping while Joe looked around the smokehouse.

"Smells good in here, but ain't even middlings left," Joe said.

"I reckon the soldiers took everything," Peter said. "She's just too close to the road."

"Things must be hard for her here," Joe said.

"Did you see her dress?" Peter asked as he dumped a shovelful into the bucket.

"What about it?"

"Homespun."

Joe didn't understand.

"Homespun," Peter said as he leaned on the shovel. "Spinning wheel."

Joe looked toward the door. People hadn't spun their own thread for years, except for the poorest of people maybe. This lady had a nice farm. At one time, she must have had a little money. Times really are hard now.

***

Belle had set the food on a wooden table behind the house and had gone into the house for more. Between the house and table, a fire was tickling the bottom of a pot hanging from a trivet. An old oak shaded the table, and Peter could see from the arrangement of the table and the footpaths around it, many meals had been taken there. He imagined many days were spent around the table not only eating, but shelling beans or husking corn or just sitting and talking, as Mr. Charlie had done back in Mississippi.

A rope hung by the trunk of the tree, and Joe grabbed it and scaled the oak like a squirrel. He threw his legs across a big limb. "Hey, Peter, you can see for miles from up here."

Peter arranged things on the table and waited for Belle to bring the rest. He thought about asking her if she needed help, but he knew some white people didn't want Negroes in their house.

He sat on a bench and looked around. He could still smell the chickens, though they were gone now. There was a small duck pond at the back of the yard, but the ducks were missing. He was sure the hen house was empty of eggs, and the pigpen was vacant, too.

He spotted the garden and went to investigate. It was trampled and raped. It was a shame. He imagined a large family could sustain itself on such a garden.

There were three small houses on the opposite side of the yard away from the animal pens. They were whitewashed and well kept—slave quarters, no doubt. Each one had a small garden beside the porch, but they were empty, too. The small houses were fine slave houses as far as slave houses went.

Down from them was the burnt ruins of a large building—the barn more than likely.

"Peter, ye can come on out of that garden," Belle called as she dipped beans from the pot. "The new garden is hidden."

She placed the beans on the table, and without looking up she said, "Joe, ye best come on down before you fall."

Joe slid down the rope. "How did you know I was up there?"

"I had four boys," she said as they all sat.

She blessed the food and Peter admired the conviction in her voice. She didn't just say it; she meant it.

"Are you the only one here?" Joe asked with a mouthful of beans. "These beans are good."

"The only one."

"May I ask where are your servants?" Peter asked. "I see the quarters."

"Ye sure don't talk like no darky I ever done seen." She nibbled on a tomato slice, and Peter could see she was thinking. "Well, Peter, I tell ye; I want to say they ran off, but my heart won't let me. About a year ago, I looked up and all four was gone. Uncle Bill and Aunt Mary had been with my husband forever, Fred and Jack, about ten years."

"Yeah, niggers have been known to run off like that," Joe said, as he gave Itchy a couple of beans.

Belle looked at Joe and raised her brow, but Joe didn't notice. He was busy with his beans.

She turned back to Peter. "I believed they's happy to be here with us. I believed they loved us as we loved them."

"I'm sure, Mrs. Belle, they did," Peter said.

She picked up another tomato slice and looked at it. "Reckon we was wrong about slavery." She looked at Peter. "Uncle Bill and Aunt Mary wanted their freedom so much they left the safety and care of the farm."

Peter wondered how she could have ever thought anyone wouldn't want their freedom. How could someone be so detached from the truth? But he saw she was sincere and her heart appeared broken.

"A coin has two sides, and from one side you can't see the other even if you bend the coin," Joe said, and then looked up from his beans to see the two staring at him. "A Mennonite preacher told me that—it seemed fitting."

Peter believed it was fitting, and a shame.

Belle set the slice back in her plate. "Joe, you are wandering around with a Negro, so tell me; what do ye think about slavery?"

Joe didn't hesitate. "The long and short of it is: if there was no slavery, the Yankees wouldn't have invaded the South, and a lot of Southerners wouldn't be fighting for something they ain't got no stake in. I wouldn't own a slave if you gave him to me with a dollar in his pocket. They are more trouble than any gain. You can't trust someone if they are bound to do something they don't want to do."

"So, ye think slavery is wrong."

"I hold nothing against anybody, but, Ma'am, I wouldn't want to be no slave. I reckon that sums up what I think about it."

Joe cut to the heart of it. Peter wouldn't want to be a slave either, but the question of slavery was deeper, much deeper.

Peter looked around the dimly lit parlor. The pine knots didn't give off as much light as a good lamp, but the house didn't smell like oil.

The day had grown late, and she had asked the boys to stay the night after they helped her render the salt.

"Peter, this is new to me, having a Negro stay in the house," Belle said as she lit another pine knot.

"Don't worry, Mrs. Belle," Joe said, watching the smoke corkscrew from the pine knot. "I house trained him personally."

Peter looked at Joe and shook his head. Belle laughed.

Itchy curled up in front of the fireplace. Peter reckoned he loved the spot when there was a fire built in it, and that time wouldn't be too far away as the nights grew cooler.

Peter noticed a couple of shelves with daguerreotypes on them. "Your family?"

"Yes, indeed." She picked up one of the pictures, four Confederate soldiers. "These is my boys."

"Where are they?" Joe asked as he moved closer to see.

"They's killed, every one of them. Three killed at Manassas, and one killed at the Wilderness."

"I'm sorry," Peter said. He knew how she felt.

She picked up another picture. "This here was my Pat."

"He dead, too?" Joe asked.

"Killed right here in front of the house about four months ago when they burned our barn."

"Yankees?" Peter asked.

"I don't know what they was—bushwhackers, I reckon. They's gonna take our last milk cow, and Pat tried to stop them. They shot him down, and shot Itchy, too, but he ran under the house and later I patched him up. They throwed fire on the barn and the house. I put the fire out in the house, but lost the barn. I don't understand why they throwed the fire."

"You have other family close?" Peter asked.

"No. Pat came over from Ireland, and I came from below Knoxville. My family there moved to Mississippi or Alabama somewhere. We ain't in touch no more."

Peter hurt for her. At least he had Joe. She had no one, nothing but a dog.

"This war has been costly, ain't it?" she said.

"Nothing like it since biblical times," Peter said.

Joe piled up next to the dog and played his Hohner. Belle moved into her rocking chair behind the spinning wheel. She began humming, but soon was singing along with Joe's playing.

Peter sat on the sofa and enjoyed the music, and when Joe started with "Amazing Grace," he joined in.

The house was cozy to Peter. The little burning pine knots were just enough light for a warm glow with their little curly smokes. The place smelled of pine and cedar and smoked ham from the many years of living.

Peter could close his eyes and see the family sitting around the room. He could see the fire burning in the fireplace and lamps lighting the parlor. He could see the family quietly reading or even enjoying a song together as they were doing now.

A sinking came in his chest. Peter opened his eyes. As Belle sang, he realized she would never sing with her family again—not on earth, anyway. She was like Peter and Joe, victims of madness. It was a war, but it was madness. Who was not affected by it? Everyone in the South, and for all Peter knew, everyone in the North was touched, too.

Peter's eyes met Joe's. Joe was looking into Peter's mind as surely as he was looking through glass. Joe was playing as good as he ever had, but his eyes revealed he was thinking the same thing Peter was and not enjoying his music. Joe shook his head slowly. Peter understood.

Belle's eyes were closed, as she was lost in her singing. She was enjoying it—the company—the music—being close with friends, if not family.

No, Peter would not say anything to arrest the moment. There will be time enough tomorrow to remember the war and goodbyes.

Peter closed his eyes and remembered the Lord's words: *Take therefore no thought for the morrow: for the morrow shall take thought for the things of itself. Sufficient unto the day is the evil thereof.* Yes, Peter thought. Tomorrow will take care of itself. He opened his eyes and saw Joe and Belle looking at each other as they played and sang. He moved to the floor beside Joe and Itchy and joined in.

Chapter 21

Joe sprang up in bed with a start. He collected himself—Itchy was barking and growling. Joe stumbled to the bedroom door, saw Belle and the dog looking out the backdoor. The moonlight sprayed through the window, and Joe spotted the old musket in her hand.

Peter sat up in the other bed. "What is it?"

"Something's out there Itchy ain't liking," Joe pulled his pants on.

"Don't you go out there!"

Joe ignored him and slipped out the bedroom door.

"What do you reckon it is?" Joe asked as he moved beside Belle.

"Don't know. I ain't heard no horses, but that don't mean nothing."

Belle went to the window. "Could be—"

Joe cracked the door.

"Don't open the door!" Belle said.

Itchy nosed the door open and shot into the night, barking.

Belle jerked the door from Joe. "Itchy, fetch up here! Fetch up here now!"

Joe felt responsible. He grabbed his tomahawk from his belt and pushed past Belle.

"Joe, no!" Peter yelled from the bedroom door.

"Don't go out there!" Belle said.

Joe ran around the coals of the fire and around the table to the oak. He shimmied up the rope. The moon was bright. Maybe he could see something from there.

Itchy was barking at the henhouse, but Joe couldn't see him. He heard Belle calling to him, then to the dog.

Joe concentrated and soon had his night eyes. He made out the mule in the abandoned garden where Peter had tied him. He saw a possum on the table where they had eaten supper, but nothing else.

Joe could tell by the hollow sound of the barking Itchy had went into the henhouse. The barking stopped. Only a muffled sound came from the henhouse.

"Itchy!" Belle called from the door. "Itchy, ye come here!"

Joe strained to see the henhouse. What happened to that dog he wondered. Maybe it was just another possum, maybe a snake. Joe couldn't stand it. He had to know. It was no good sitting in the tree like a roosting chicken. He slid down the rope, and moved around to the side of the henhouse, holding the tomahawk at the ready.

"Itchy!" Belle called again.

Joe slipped to the henhouse door. He listened, heard muffled growling. That damn dog probably had a rat cornered. He rounded the door with his tomahawk ready to swing.

Someone grabbed his hand and the tomahawk fell to the ground. A hand went around his mouth before he could make a sound. Suddenly he was in a bearhug and unable to move, smelled sweat and musk. He got one arm free and reached for his attacker. He grabbed hair—Negro hair.

Joe couldn't get free. It was as if he were in the grip of a giant snake. He tried to yell, but the stinking hand covered his face—he believed he would smother if he didn't escape. He should have gone around to the back—damn it. If he could just wiggle loose, he could get to the tomahawk and this stinking darky would die. Where the hell is Peter when you need him?

"Don't hurt him," said a voice in the henhouse.

"I ain't gonna hurt him, John," said the attacker as he tried to pull his head back from Joe's grip.

Joe bit the hand—tasted like old leather. He stomped a bare toe. The man relaxed his grip and Joe squirmed free. The man grabbed for him, but Joe shot out the door.

Joe ran for the house. "Niggers in the henhouse! Shoot them!"

Belle ran past him and pointed the musket at the henhouse door.

"You'uns come outta there or I'll just shoot up in there."

Peter lit a stick from the coals by the table. He moved toward the henhouse door. He went past Belle, getting between her and the door, but still out of the line of fire. Joe knew what he was doing. He was not going to throw light on Belle as he lit the henhouse.

Joe stood beside Belle. "When they come out, blast them."

"Don't shoot—don't shoot. We is coming out."

Peter stood by the door, giving Belle enough light.

Two men came out the door. One was holding Itchy with his head wrapped in a gunnysack. He let him down, and Itchy ran for the house whimpering.

"John?" Peter said when the torch light fell on the men's faces.

"It's the niggers that fed us back a-ways," Joe said. He knew you couldn't trust any darkies.

"What you'uns doing in my henhouse?" Belle asked.

"Lawd, Missus, we's juss gonna take a few eggs," John said.

Belle laughed. "Take all you can find."

"So this is how you darkies been getting by," Joe said. "You ain't nothing but a bunch of thieves and scoundrels."

The two men said nothing, just stared at the gun.

"Trying to steal eggs isn't too bad, is it, Mrs. Belle?" Peter said, putting a hand on John's shoulder.

Joe cooled. Heck, Peter was right. A man will do most anything when he is hungry.

"I reckon I'll shoot 'em anyhow."

Joe looked at Belle. The moon reflected on her white nightgown. The hump on her back looked like a head under the cover. He wondered if the old woman was going to pull the trigger.

"Mrs. Belle, please don't shoot these men. They meant but just a little harm by taking a few eggs," Peter said.

"I ain't a gonna shoot 'em for stealing—I wanted some eggs, and they ain't found none." She lowered the gun and laughed.

Joe picked up his tomahawk from the doorway, saw John's legs shaking. Joe laughed, too. John had thought it was the end of earth for him. Joe had, too.

***

Joe put some sticks on the fire by the table as the dawn grew. Peter knew there would be no rooster here to greet it, just the chorus of birds.

John and his friend, Burt, sat on the bench at the table sipping a coffee substitute made of sweet potatoes that Belle had blended—they seemed to enjoy it. Peter found the stuff horrible.

Belle boiled oats in the pot for breakfast. Peter believed she was happy to do it. She seemed in good spirits when she was doing something for someone else. That particular spirit was becoming more rare across the land.

"Where are the other people that were with you?" Joe asked as he poked in the fire.

"We has a camp back down the road a piece," John said. "Spect they be getting worried bout us."

"They'd really be worried if you had gotten shot," Joe said.

"Now, Joe, that's enough of that," Belle said. "Weren't no harm done. They's just after some eggs."

"Yeah, like a thieving chicken snake, leaving nothing in return but snake shit."

"Joseph, your mouth is getting foul," Peter said.

"Pshaw," Joe said. He threw the stick into the fire and walked over to the mule.

Peter felt a knife in his heart seeing Joe becoming so cross. Peter knew he would have to do better with him—his responsibility until Mr. Taylor was found—if he were found.

"Mrs. Belle, I sho is mighty sorry bout yo dog," John said. Itchy was peeping from under the steps.

Belle laughed. She filled bowls from the pot. "Well, you'uns didn't find no eggs, but I reckon I found a chicken."

Belle set the bowls on the table. "Come on away from that animal Joe and let's eat."

Joe slipped in between John and Burt. "Pass that honey, Peter."

"We should thank the Lord first," Peter said.

"That right—that right," John said.

Joe glared at Peter, and it cut to his soul. Had Joe really turned from God? Had this war really damned his soul?

"Peter, will you please thank the All Mighty for our blessings?" Belle said.

Peter bowed his head. He searched his heart for the right words. It was never hard before, but he never felt someone he loved was lost. Seconds dragged on, and he felt the others staring.

"Heavenly Father—" He couldn't think, couldn't find the

appropriate words.

"I'm hungry, Peter," Joe said.

"Ye shush!" Belle said.

Peter didn't think about it. It was no good. He just let the words come of their own accord.

"Dear God, please bless this food. It is a gift from a kind lady, a lady that doesn't have much to offer because of this horrible war."

Peter felt his lips tremble and felt the tears well in his eyes. It suddenly all became too heavy. It was all too much. He had been a witness to too much. He thought of the picture of Belle's sons. He thought of Joe turning from God. He thought of Dr. Taylor, thought of Mam, the unknown in the Valley. But he had to finish.

"Father in Heaven, please help us." His voice broke. "It is all madness. We seem to have lost our way. I don't understand how all of this can be happening." He wiped his eyes.

No one said anything. Only the bird songs could be heard.

"I know you have a plan, but we don't understand it. Please help us to understand. Please help us to find our way out of this nightmare. Please help Joe. I pray for help from you to look out for him. I love him so, but I'm afraid for him. Please help all of us at this table, and forgive us our sins. Forgive us all and help us to find the way. Help us to understand your will. Show us a sign. Show us...help us to..." Peter wiped his eyes again. "Amen."

When Peter looked up, all were looking at him. He wiped his eyes.

"Peter, that was a lovely prayer," Belle said.

"Amen," the two men said.

Joe looked at Peter for a long minute. Peter saw no anger in his eyes, maybe a small smile, but it was gone in an instant.

"Now, can I have the honey?" Joe said.

***

John guided his small group into the dooryard. Including John, Joe counted four men, three women, and three children. There were two mules, four goats, and two ducks. They had a wagon, and a shoddy cart. This wasn't near the number of people Joe and Peter had eaten with back down the road.

"You'uns pull around to the back of the house," Belle said.

Joe grabbed John's arm. "Where's everybody else?"

"Here and there. Some reckoned they'd go back to they massuh.

The white man with us went crazy yesterday, talking foolish. He staggered off down the road, and I reckon I don't know what happened to his nigger. We's all that's left. We ain't got no massuh to go to and we a little scared of them Yankees, so we is wandering like a Moses."

Joe couldn't understand why Belle would have all of these Negroes on the place. She had said they could stay there a few days until they figured where they were going. What would they eat? Well, whatever, Joe knew where he was going, and he and Peter were striking out tomorrow.

"You'uns pick ye out a cabin. They's ever bit as comfortable as my own house," Belle said. "They's still some firewood stacked up around the back." She seemed happy to have the Negroes on the place, and Itchy took to the children right off.

"Joe, come here," Peter called from behind the quarters.

Joe found him under a grove of huge chestnut trees. The trees looked to be over hundred feet tall, and three men couldn't reach around either one with joined hands. "These are some of the biggest trees I've ever seen," Peter said, looking up at the trees. "Look, they are loaded with nuts and it won't be long before they start to fall."

"Yeah, like right now," Joe said, as he picked up a stick.

The first limb was over twenty feet high, and Joe missed it. Peter retrieved the stick and gave it a toss. Nuts rained down on the boys. The burrs were still a little tight on the nuts, but they were soon peeled away. The sweet taste was just what Joe remembered.

"I see you'uns found the five kings," Belle said as she approached the boys.

"Five kings?" Peter asked.

"These five chestnut trees are some of the biggest anywhere, and five of them right together is a gift. My husband called them the five kings. Soon the ground will be covered deep with the nuts. I will gather them after I have killed me a few turkeys that'll come down out of the hills after them."

"You plant them?" Joe asked.

"Heaven no, boy, I ain't that old. I reckon they's just here when my husband settled the place. He never would cut them down, would have been some fine lumber."

Joe believed if they were older than Belle, they, indeed, were old.

"See that clearing back yonder?" Belle said, pointing.

"Yes, Ma'am," Peter said.

"That there is my real garden. You'uns help me get some things from it for supper."

Joe didn't see how this old humpbacked woman could work a garden of such size. Most of the vegetables were gone now, but there was still squash, pole beans, a few tomatoes, and different greens. It was a huge garden. Joe reckoned her husband had helped her, but without his help and a mule, she would never maintain such a plot.

"Ye see, ye can't see it from the house. The five kings and these bushes hide it," she said. "The Yankees think that little garden at the house is all I've got, but ain't they fooled."

Joe picked a tomato and bit into it. He smiled and thought, yeah, ain't they fooled. He liked old humpback more and more. She had fooled him, too, and that wasn't easy.

Joe spotted a stack of split rails behind the garden with bark piled on it. "What's that?"

"That there is my corncrib. I couldn't leave it close to the house or it would all be stoled."

"You have plenty to eat, don't you, Mrs. Belle?" Peter said. "More than we thought."

"Iffen I keep it all hid, I got right smart of it. I ain't got no salt and chickens and other stuff, but I got my garden."

Joe raised some planks behind the corncrib. It was a pit lined with hay and grass filled with Irish potatoes and sweet potatoes. "Pshaw, you have enough to feed an army. Can me and Peter take some with us?"

"Joseph!" Peter said.

"His'n manners ain't none too good, but his'n sense is first rate," Belle said. "Hun, you'uns can take whatever ye need for ye journey home."

Joe smiled at the woman. She was gnarled, old, and humpbacked, but she was beautiful. When he could, he would come back to visit her; he knew he had to. Some day things would be better and he would return her favors.

***

It had been the best meal Peter had eaten in a long time—sweet potatoes, squash, beans, and rabbit. Belle was a good cook and so was John's wife, Diane. John was a smart trapper and had snared three rabbits for supper.

Peter sat at the table listening to the women sing as they prepared their cabins. They sang happy songs. You could tell a lot about a place and time by the Negro songs, and this was a good place and a good time by that gauge.

The evening was cool, but not too cool, just nippy enough to make you appreciate the fire. Peter rubbed his arms and watched the flames dance. He heard Joe's voice over the singing. He was helping the Negroes arrange their things in the cabins—had to be in the middle of it, never content to just leave things alone. Peter smiled.

The stars were being born and they speckled the sky like scattered jewels. Peter locked his fingers behind his head and stared at them. How many soldiers were looking up right this instant at the very same stars? How many runaways were following a certain star to the North and freedom? Moses had looked up and gazed at these stars and Jesus, too. Suddenly two shooting stars streaked across the sky with green and orange trailers. God's doing. However, isn't it all God's doing? Of course it is. God has a hand in everything. We don't know why things are what they are, but he does have a hand in it all. It's all part of a greater plan.

Peter heard Joe behind him at the animals. He turned to see Joe and John rubbing on the mules. It was just enough daylight left to make out a big man and a short boy—a boy with very light hair reflecting the firelight.

"Yessuh, Massuh Joe, you has to take care of the animals so they can take care of you," John said.

"I had a horse back at the Shenandoah Valley, but I had to leave it behind," Joe said. "Probably gone now."

"I don't know on that. It might be right there a-waiting for you to come home."

Peter could hear a brush stroking the animal, but heard no talking for a long time; Joe broke the silence.

"John, what's it like being black?"

Peter strained to listen, but there was a long silence.

"I don't know, Massuh Joe. I don't know no different."

"Do you ever wish you were white?"

"Well, Massuh Joe, I has studied on that there. I reckon I don't want to be white. I just wants what a white man has. I just wants to come and go when I gets a notion, and I ain't got to answer to nobody."

Peter moved to the big oak behind the table to hear better.

"I wouldn't want to be no darky, I tell you," Joe said. "I've seen how slaves have to work on those plantations, and I don't want no part of it." Joe took the brush and started stroking the mule's side.

"Massuh Joe, now let me ask you: what it like being white?"

Peter heard the brush stop.

"Uncle John, I ain't never thought much about that." Joe began brushing again. "Let me see. Well, you can come and go when you like, but don't seem like such a big deal. I don't know, but it's better than being a nigger on a plantation."

"Massuh Joe, being a dog is better than that. I reckon—"

"John, come catch this here coon!" Diane called from the cabin. Joe and John ran toward the cabin.

Peter sat back at the table. Joe had never asked him such a question. Why?

He looked toward Belle's house, and through the windows, he saw her moving around in there.

Suddenly Itchy started barking. He had found Diane's coon. There was laughter at the cabin.

Peter moved back to the fire and placed a crooked stick on it. He believed he knew why Joe had never asked him about him being black. Of course, it was obvious: Joe didn't think of him being a Negro. Oh, he knew he was a Negro, but not like other Negroes—he was Peter. Peter couldn't explain it to himself, but he knew Joe thought of him differently.

Belle stepped out the back door and stood with her arms crossed. Her white hair glowed like the moon. She spotted Peter and went to the table.

"Lovely evening," Peter said as he wiped the bench for her to sit.

"I always like it at candle-lighting," she said as she lowered herself to the bench. "Just dark enough for the stars, yet still a little light to see by, a purple-blue sky."

"Yes, Ma'am."

She turned to Peter. "You'uns look behind the henhouse tomorrow and fetch that old buggy. It ain't much, but I reckon it'll get ye two boys to the Valley. That old mule should be able to tote it iffen you'uns don't go the whole hog."

"Thank you, Mrs. Belle. You have been most kind to us."

She looked at Peter for a long minute. "Peter, ye are a special person."

Peter said nothing.

"Ye think ye are taking care of Joe all by your lonesome, but ye ain't."

Peter looked into the gray-blue eyes. He could see the fire reflection fluttering in them. Those eyes had seen many things in many years—wisdom. He waited for more.

She looked up toward the sky. A shooting star flared. "See that?"

"Yes, Ma'am. They are beautiful, a good many this evening."

She looked back toward Peter. "Ye are a tool, Peter."

"Ma'am?"

"I knowed it when I first talked to ye. I see how ye are with the boy. The All Mighty is using ye. Ye ain't no ordinary young man. Ye are a huckleberry above a persimmon."

Peter didn't understand. Of course, he was ordinary.

Joe ran up to them with the dead raccoon held by the tail. "Look here, Mrs. Belle. We've got dinner for tomorrow." Itchy sniffed at the animal and barked. Joe swung it toward the dog. Itchy yelped and ran under the house. They laughed.

"Clean that critter and we'll cook him for you'uns trip."

Joe ran back toward the cabins, laughing and yelling.

Belle turned to Peter. "Ye are his shepherd."

Peter looked into those gray-blue eyes again. Suddenly the weight he had been carrying since Arkansas grew heavier.

***

The mule was reluctant to be hitched at first, but soon resigned itself to the harness. Anything other than this small covered buggy would be too much, but Peter believed the mule could pull it fair enough.

Peter loaded their bags into the buggy, making sure his Bible was secure and hidden under the seat. Joe's bag was the heaviest. Peter remembered the revolver. He didn't like it, but it had saved lives in the past, and no one knew the future.

Belle brought a basket to the buggy. "Here is you'uns dinner. I cooked Joe's coon and some vegetables to go along with it." It smelled delicious.

"Thank you, Mrs. Belle. You have been very generous to Joe and me."

"It has been a delight having you'uns two here." Belle looked directly into Peter's eyes. "Peter, last night I said ye was Joe's shepherd, and it is true, but at some point ye have to also live ye own life."

Peter looked down at the short bundle of a lady. Peter knew she was a store of knowledge. He had learned to always listen to the elderly, as he listened now.

She looked at the basket and handed it to Peter. "It's like cooking a coon. Ye have to cook it enough so's to get it done, but not cook it so much til it falls plumb apart." She put her gnarled hand on Peter's arm. "Ye have to know when it is done, Peter."

Peter could stay right here with this beautiful woman and be content. He had only known her for a brief time, but he felt a warm love for her. Other than with his own mother, he had never had such a feeling, a feeling you could only have with a mother or grandmother.

Joe and John came to the buggy.

"Joe, I reckon ye are ready to see the Valley," Belle said.

"Yes, ma'am. Mrs. Belle, can we have a few of those sweet potatoes in your pit?"

"Why, of course ye can."

"I'll go with you to get them," Peter said.

"I bet you will want some for supper, won't you, Mrs. Belle?" Joe said.

"Why, I reckon that would be a grand idea," she said.

Joe grabbed John's arm. "Come on, Uncle John, help us fetch them back."

Peter picked up a handful of chestnuts when they went under the trees. He watched Joe march ahead of John, always in the head. The sun was just coming over the eastern hills. This was a beautiful place, Peter thought. If the Shenandoah Valley was prettier, he understood why Joe loved it so.

Joe stopped at a squash vine and bent down to study a big squash. "Uncle John, grab those sweet potatoes while I pick this here squash." John lifted the cover over the pit.

Peter stood by Joe. "That is a pretty squa—"

John yelled and fell back away from the pit. Peter saw a white blur flapping and squawking go by John's head. It was one of the white ducks.

John grabbed his chest. "Lawd sakes alive. That bout put me in my grave."

Peter looked at Joe. He was on his knees again, red-faced, and laughing.

Peter smiled. "You put that duck in there."

John went to Joe. "Joe, why you want to do me in that fashion?" He wiped his brow. "I almost messed myself."

Joe bellowed laughing.

Peter shook his head and giggled.

Joe finally stopped laughing and took a few deep breaths. "Uncle John, remember when you pushed me down when I first saw you?"

"I's sorry for that Joe; I done told you that."

"Now we're square," Joe said as he went to the pit for the potatoes.

***

Joe saw tears on Peter's face as Peter pulled the buggy onto the road.

"Get up there, mule," Peter said, as he snapped the reins.

Joe waved at Mrs. Belle and the darkies, then turned and pulled the harmonica from his pocket. He struck up *Shenandoah*. He could hardly wait to get there.

The mule gassed them, and they both laughed.

Soon they were settled into the trip. The mule pulled the little buggy easily.

Joe thought of his pa. Where was he? Was he safe? He had to be safe, had to.

The farm would be fine, neighbors would see to that. They would probably even have wheat and hay stored for them. They had good neighbors, and everyone looked out for each other.

A quail ran down the middle of the road, weaving and bobbing, before flying into the woods. There were woods on both sides of the road, not big timber as it was along the Mississippi when they left Helena, but still a thick forest. Joe imagined deer and squirrels a plenty in there. Belle had mentioned turkeys eating the chestnuts. A turkey sure would be tasty.

Joe looked back down the road. They had made enough turns, that he couldn't see Belle's place any longer. "Hey, Peter, I know we haven't gone but about a mile, but I'm hungry. Want some of that coon?"

"Hungry already. We just had something a little while ago."

"Don't matter. I'm hungry now."

They came to a ford in a stream. Peter stopped the mule at the edge of the water, so the mule could drink.

Peter handed Joe two tin cups. "Dip us some of that water."

Joe took the cups and leaped from the buggy. The stream was clear. No one had crossed it in a long while. The stream was full of rocks, and little fish swam about. Joe climbed upon a big rock and dipped the cups in the stream. It would be a good place for a swim.

He turned to Peter. "Let's eat on this rock."

"No, come on back to the buggy. I've got the food here in the seat."

Joe handed Peter the cups and climbed back into the buggy. The coon was good. Joe knew it would be. Old ladies like Belle knew how to cook. What could she do with a turkey?

A wasp flew into the buggy. Peter swatted at it.

"It ain't going to hurt you, Peter. Let it light and we will smash it."

Peter swung again, knocking the basket of food to the floorboard.

"Now look at what you did," Joe said, as he bent to gather the food.

Peter bent to help. "I'm sorry. Maybe it won't get too dirty."

"I don't care how dirty it gets. I'm going to eat it. I can always spit out the dirt. A little dirt never killed anyone, did it? Did it, Peter?"

Peter didn't answer, so Joe looked up. Peter was staring toward the stream. Joe rose. Lucius was holding the mule's nose with his big hand and holding a knife with the other. He looked like Goliath.

Chapter 22

A sudden memory formed in Peter's brain like a vivid picture, clear as polished glass: the knife. He remembered the glint of it when they shoved off from the riverbank at Helena. That was Lucius. "Jesus, be with us," Peter prayed.

"Well, if ain't Massuh Joe." Lucius grinned. "Never reckoned you'd see Ole Lucius, did you?"

Peter grabbed Joe's leg, no time for Joe to do something foolish, just wait, see what this crazy man was after.

"Y'all is come a long piece, ain't you?" Lucius thumbed the knife blade. "I reckon I has, too."

"What are you about?" Joe said. "What business do you have here in Virginia, you damn sorry thief?"

Peter squeezed Joe's leg.

Lucius's grin vanished. "You is still got that smart ass mouth, ain't you." He raised his knife as to throw it. "I'll take that outta you."

Peter saw his chance, snapped the reins. "Heah, mule!"

The mule lunged forward. Lucius dropped the knife and grabbed the mule. The beast stopped as if it had hit a wall. Lucius squeezed the mule's nose and pushed. The animal gave ground, backing slowly. "That was the last foolish thing you is ever going to do, purty nigger."

Joe rummaged through his bag for the revolver.

Lucius shot around the mule like a cat and grabbed Joe by the shirt.

Joe hauled the revolver from the bag, jerked the barrel toward Lucius. Lucius grabbed Joe's hand. The gun fired into the top of the buggy; stinking smoke engulfed the buggy. Lucius flung the revolver from Joe's hand; it disappeared into the weeds at the edge of the road.

"Where is that charm?" Lucius said, hauling Joe from the buggy.

Peter leaped across, catching Lucius around the neck. They all tumbled to the ground in a heap.

Lucius kicked Peter away, then grabbed Joe around the neck. He scrambled to his feet with Joe's feet flailing in air. "I'll kill this boy if you don't stand clear."

Peter rose slowly to his feet.

"Now, where is that charm?" Lucius said.

"What charm?" Peter said. It was happening too fast. Peter couldn't think.

"This boy know."

"I don't know what you're talking about, and if I did, I wouldn't give it to you."

Lucius squeezed, and Joe's face grew red.

"Don't harm him." Peter said.

"I'll snap his neck like a twig. Where is them damn African birds? Where's the damn Taylor woman's necklace?"

"I don't know what—" Peter said.

Lucius squeezed. Joe yelled.

"All right—all right! Don't harm him," Peter said.

"Don't tell him anything," Joe groaned.

"I have it, and I will give it to you. Just let the boy go."

Lucius smiled. "So you have." The smile disappeared. "Let me see it."

"All right. I have to get it."

Peter moved to the buggy. The memories of Helena flooded to his mind like water through a broken dam. It was clear now. Lucius had followed them to the river at Helena after the necklace. He had come all this way for a piece of jewelry. What was the matter with this man? He could have stolen some valuables somewhere else without coming all the way to Virginia. My God! Peter realized Lucius had killed Dr. Taylor for it. "Jesus, please! Please help me."

Peter pulled the Bible from under the seat, slowly opened it, a small price for the boy's life. But would Lucius leave them alone after he got it? Of course, he wouldn't. Peter knew he had to do something, or Joe would die.

"Hid in the Bible. You is a smart boy," Lucius said.

"Peter, you stole Uncle Wilbur's property," Joe said.

"Hush, Joe," Peter said.

"Give it to me," Lucius said.

"First, you let the boy go."

"You're a stinking thief, Peter, just like he is."

"I'm fixing to let him go. Now hand me the necklace."

Lucius relaxed his grip just enough. Joe pounded Lucius in the groin and slithered from his grasp.

Peter threw the necklace into the stream.

Lucius whirled around, and his fist slammed Joe's face. It sounded like a stick breaking. Joe collapsed to the ground.

"No!" Peter screamed. His mind narrowed into a single purpose: kill Lucius. He dove into him with all his strength; they crashed to the ground. Peter fought his way atop the Devil. He pounded Lucius's face over and over.

Lucius tossed him like a pillow.

Peter leaped to his feet.

"I'll kill you, just like I did the boy," Lucius screamed. He kicked at Peter.

Peter caught his leg and drove him to the ground. Peter kicked him in the side. Lucius growled with pain. Peter stomped Lucius in the face, and he lay still.

Peter looked at the evil man for a long minute, couldn't believe he felt so much hatred for him—no fear, just hatred.

Peter remembered Joe, went to him. "Joseph?" He kneeled beside him.

Joe slowly opened his eyes. They were just slits in his puffy face.

Peter felt relief as he had never felt before. His eyes burned with tears. "Thank God."

"I know you didn't steal the necklace," Joe whispered.

"Dr. Taylor gave it to me." Peter smiled. "He said I was family like you, Joe."

Joe tried to smile, but his swollen face would not allow it. "I said that because I was trying to distract Lucius."

Peter felt the love for Joe grow even more, but he was worried about Joe's face. Blood was still running from his nose and his face was still swelling.

"Just lie right there. I will get some cool water and wipe the blood from your face."

"It hurts Peter."

Peter wiped his own tears from his face. "I know it does. I'll make it better."

Peter saw Joe's eyes suddenly grow wide. He whirled to face Lucius.

***

Lucius swung. Peter ducked. He grabbed Lucius and they tumbled into the stream.

Joe struggled to get to his feet, but he felt as if a horse were standing on his head. He managed to get to his knees.

Lucius and Peter thrashed and rolled into the water like two mighty bears. Joe couldn't get a bearing on who was winning. Suddenly, the thrashing stopped. Lucius had his powerful hands around Peter's throat. Peter flailed, but it was no use. Lucius plunged Peter's face under the water.

"No!" Joe blurted and spit blood. He had to find strength. He scurried for the weeds, had to find the revolver. He spread the weeds, feeling and groping—no use.

"The African birds is mine!" Lucius yelled like a wild man as he held Peter under the water. "I'll be a king. Do you hear me? No one will string me up again. I'll do the whipping from now on."

Joe staggered to his feet. He fought the pain. Peter had been under the water too long.

Lucius let go of Peter and stood over him. Peter's face stayed under the water. Peter was dead. Joe saw it. Joe quivered with rage. The pain was gone. Everything was gone but the rage.

Lucius fished in the clear water for the necklace, and like a lucky fisherman, he came up with it. "I have it," Lucius yelled. "After all of these years, I have it. I am a king! I am a king!"

***

Lucius finally had his history. He had his father's necklace. He had Africa in his hands. No white man had that over him now. Now he was a king.

He raised the necklace to the sky. He yelled at the top of his lungs, "I have it. I've searched forever, and now I have it."

He remembered his mother. He wished she could see him now. No man would ever rule him again. He had his African birds. From this point forward, he would—

***

Joe saw the look on Lucius's face: jubilation for killing Peter. He hated him. He would pay. Suddenly the look changed to surprise. Joe saw the tomahawk in the center of Lucius's face. Lucius stood still in the water for a time, a statue. Slowly he folded into the water. He lay on his back with the ax handle sticking up like a horn.

Joe looked at his own hands. He didn't remember throwing it, but he had. Somehow, he had found the strength—it found him.

Peter! Joe remembered.

He hobbled into the water and grabbed Peter. He pulled with all he had, managed to get him to the bank.

"Peter?" Joe shook him. "Peter, you can't be dead." Joe shook him again. "Peter?" Joe wiped tears and snot and blood from his own face. "Wake up, Peter." Joe felt the world caving in on him. "Peter, damn you. You can't die. You haven't seen the Valley, yet. I want to show you." Joe shook him. Water drooled from Peter's mouth. "Peter...Peter..."

Joe fell beside him. Everyone he cared about died—everyone. He buried his face in his hands, didn't care if he ever left that spot, just lay right there beside Peter.

The wind rippled the water and swirled in Joe's hair. He heard something fluttering. He looked up. The wind was rustling the pages of Peter's Bible on the ground by the buggy.

God!

Joe dragged himself to his knees. There is nothing left, and it is what Peter would do.

"God, Peter swears you're up there." Joe blew out a breath. Blood drooled down his bottom lip. "I haven't been good, but Peter has always been right with you." Joe looked down at Peter. It was too much; he wept. "God, he once told me the story about Lazarus, and I said he was a liar. Is it true? Can you bring Peter back?" Joe put his hands to his eyes. "Please help me." Joe pushed at his eyes with his fist. He felt the pain grow numb and saw flashes of white light behind his eyes. "God, please help poor Peter. I've let him down so."

"Joe!"

Joe lowered his fist, blinked his eyes. He looked around. It was John and Burt.

"He killed Peter, Uncle John," Joe sobbed.

John slid down beside Joe. "You is hurt."

"He killed Peter."

Burt rolled Peter over on his belly, pushed on Peter's back and pressed on his sides.

"He dead?" John asked.

"Look like," Burt said as he pushed.

John helped Joe to his feet. "We was coming this here way to snare rabbits and heard the shot. We knowed it was no good."

Joe watched Burt pushing on Peter, but Peter was dead.

John knelt down in front of Peter, grabbed his arms, and tugged. Water spewed from Peter's mouth.

Joe watched, but said nothing.

They pushed and pulled—pushed and pulled.

Peter wheezed, then vomited water.

Joe felt his heart in his throat.

Burt and John kept working on Peter. Suddenly, Peter gasped for air, opened his eyes.

Joe fell to his knees. "Peter!"

Burt and John stood.

Peter fought for breath. "Joe." He coughed and spit water. "Joe, I thought you were dead."

"I thought you were, too." Joe threw his arms around Peter's neck. It was a miracle. He felt his chest knot up, then untangle in an instant. He closed his swollen eyes, prayed: Thank you, Lord. I will never forget.

"Where is Lucius?" Peter whispered.

"Dead," Joe said.

John and Burt pulled Lucius from the river. There was a grinding, sucking sound as John pulled the tomahawk from Lucius's face.

Joe and Peter helped each other to their feet.

"What's this?" John said as he pulled the necklace from Lucius's hand."

Peter staggered toward him and took the necklace. He looked at Lucius's body. "It's just a necklace, a family heirloom, nothing more."

"He called them African birds," Joe said as he took the necklace from Peter. Joe examined the piece of jewelry. He had never really studied it before. "These are two wild pigeons, passenger pigeons. Why would he call them African birds, Peter?"

Peter looked down at Lucius's body again. "He was a lost soul, misguided. He followed the wrong spirit."

Peter fell to his knees.

Joe grabbed for him.

"We best get you two back to Mrs. Belle's," John said.

John and Burt helped Peter to the buggy.

Joe looked at the wild pigeons in his hand, thought about the massive flock at the Tallahatchie River. Billions of real wild pigeons in the world, and Lucius was chasing after these two. Why? Why had he killed for the necklace? Why had he followed them to Virginia? Joe shook his head, stuffed the necklace into his pants pocket. He looked down at Lucius. Lucius still had a smile on his face. "I reckon you found what you were looking for—whatever it was."

"Fetch up here, Joe," John said. "We is got to get you two back to the place to get tended."

Joe headed for the buggy, stopped, remembered the Bible. He picked it up and saw the cavity in it, smiled, placed the necklace in it. He found the ribbon on the ground and secured the Bible closed. Peter was one smart person.

Burt helped Joe into the buggy beside Peter. John turned the mule, and he and Burt led the buggy south.

***

Peter felt better the next day, but Joe lay in the bed for a week with a fever. His face had swollen like a pumpkin before it finally started to heal. Peter worried over him like a mother.

He felt of Joe's face as Joe slept—it was cool, good. It was very good, indeed, since Peter had thought Joe was dead after Lucius had smashed him with that massive fist.

He left Joe's bedside and wandered outside past the quarters, stopping under the Five Kings. The nuts were starting to fall. He picked up a couple and cracked them against each other. The nuts were sweet, as good as a pecan.

The sun was just threatening to show itself over the east

mountain. He leaned against the trunk of one of the old trees. They would soon leave again for the Valley. What would they find? He prayed Mr. Taylor would be there—someone would be there for Joe.

He watched a squirrel cutting a nut on one of the massive limbs. The cuttings rained down like flower petals.

He could smell autumn in the air, nothing like it. Soon color would paint everything: reds, yellows, oranges, browns. Then winter would come. Peter knew he would have to be in place by then—wherever that was.

He heard ducks overhead, saw them in a ragged V. They were heading south.

South—he thought about that. He remembered all of the misery and destruction and death. But then, he remembered the love—Zuey. He had never forgotten her. He saw her face every time he closed his eyes. It was her face he saw when everything went black as Lucius held him under the water. He had thought he would never see her again. He smelled her sometimes, too—only for a fleeting second, not the wildflowers beside the road—her.

The squirrel came down the trunk beside Peter's head. It stopped, whipped its tail, then jumped to the ground. It picked up a nut and climbed on Peter's leg to eat it. Peter smiled, feeling the squirrel's body move as he chomped the nut. Peter thought how men were destroying the country with war, and everything would be changed after the war. Men would never be the same, but squirrels had probably been living and eating in these five chestnut trees for a hundred years, and that would probably never change.

The squirrel suddenly darted up Peter's shirt and up the tree. Peter looked to see what had frightened the squirrel. He saw Joe coming.

He got to his feet. "What are you doing out of the bed?"

Joe picked up a nut. "They're falling good. We'll get us some for the trip."

Peter gently took Joe's face in his hands and inspected it.

"Nation, Peter, I couldn't stay in that bed any longer. Besides I feel better, and the swelling is most gone."

Peter let go of Joe's face. He was right. He looked much better. Peter smiled.

"Besides," Joe said, "I couldn't stand another minute of Mrs.

Belle fussing over me."

"She means well by you."

"I know she does. She is capital, but I feel like a cooped chicken." Joe spotted the squirrel on the limb. He threw a nut at it, and the squirrel vanished up the tree. Joe turned to Peter. "Let's leave tomorrow morning."

"Tomorrow?" Peter said. He thought for a minute. Joe seemed better, and it was getting cooler, especially at night. "I think you are right. Tomorrow sounds good."

Joe nodded and smiled. He picked up a handful of nuts and went back toward the quarters. Peter heard John say, "That hurt." Joe had hit him with a nut, Peter reckoned.

At least there would be no Lucius on the way, at least not a live one. He was buried only a few feet from where he died.

Slowly misery came over Peter again. It had haunted him since that day at the creek. He had hated Lucius. It was a sin of the worse sort. He had prayed for forgiveness, and he knew The Lord had forgiven him, but he couldn't forgive himself. He had hated Lucius so much, he would have killed him if he could—in fact, had tried. Peter knew he was protecting Joe, but that didn't mean he had to hate.

Peter leaned his head against the big trunk. When will all this be over? What will we find in the Shenandoah Valley? What will I do? Peter felt the weight again.

"Oh God, help me. Show me a guiding light. Please help me, won't you?" Peter sobbed into his arm. "Please take this weight from me. I can't bear it alone—I can't."

Peter saw his mother's face in his mind. He heard her voice telling him to go north. He remembered the promise. He wiped his eyes and sniffed, had to get ready for tomorrow. It was still a long way to the end.

***

The swayback mule pulled the buggy at a pretty good clip. Joe leaned back and watched the countryside pass by as the sun grew low in the west. He wasn't feeling well, tingled all over. He covered his face with a rag when the soldiers rode past. They saw more Confederates the farther they rode. A sergeant had asked where they were headed. He had said they were fools because the Yankees were in the Valley, had told them Lexington was just a few mile up the road and told them they should stay there until the Yankees were driven out of the Valley.

Peter put the back of his hand on Joe's forehead. "You're burning up. We should have waited a few more days."

Joe said nothing. He felt too sick to argue with Peter. He felt cold, though he was sweating.

He wished they would soon be at the farm, but he knew it took a long day's ride to get from Lexington to Dayton, remembered that from past trips with his pa.

He buried himself in the seat like a quail in a tuft of grass and thought of home. Later, he wouldn't be able to say if he had been asleep and dreaming or awake and just daydreaming as the buggy rocked along.

When spring came, he and his pa would plant a good crop of corn and wheat. The mule should be able to pull a plow—it pulled the buggy just fine. He didn't worry about the winter. There were many good neighbors, and there was plenty in the Valley. Good neighbors are like family, and family always helps each other through hard times. They could kill squirrels and rabbits to eat if they had to. Yes, there was plenty to eat in the Valley. Joe knew he could find work at the mills. He could do most anything. He could feed hogs or herd sheep. He could even milk cows, but Peter was better at that.

But all that planning was probably for nothing. His pa probably had the farm in order. If he couldn't do it himself, being in the army, he probably hired the work out. Probably hired a servant from one of the slave men. Joe smiled. Sure, that's what they'll find when they get there—the farm in good order.

Joe felt himself being lifted from the buggy. He realized they had stopped, and Peter had him in his arms. It was night. "What is it, Peter?"

"We are going to stay at this inn for the night," Peter said as he carried Joe through the door.

An old bald man with a cane looked at Joe. "Yes—yes, put him in the bed. The cistern is around the back. You need to cool him down I tell you."

"Thank you, sir," Peter said.

"I reckon you can sleep on the floor in his room," the man said. "I normally don't let coloreds stay inside, but I'll make an exception for the boy. There is a little soup left." He pointed toward the fireplace. "I'll leave it there for you."

The inn smelled like whiskey and tobacco spit. Joe saw a cat asleep on a long bar. There was a spittoon on the floor with brown spit all over it and on the floor beside it.

Peter maneuvered through a narrow door and placed Joe on the bed. The bed felt like rutted ground where cows had tramped through. It smelled like rotten hay. There was no pillow.

"Where did you get the money, Peter?"

"The man said we could stay for free, unless a paying customer comes, then we have to go."

Joe figured they were there for the night. No one would pay to stay in that place.

Peter left for a few minutes, then returned with a pan and a wet rag. Joe felt the coolness on his forehead. He looked up and saw his mother's face as she smoothed his hair back. He was still shivering, but he felt warmer inside as his mother tended him. Soon he was asleep.

***

Peter awoke with a start. He heard yelling coming from the front where the bar was.

"Sergeant, get these men outta here," the innkeeper said.

"We want a damn room—all of us!"

Peter heard rummaging and people yelling from the other rooms.

"I will be sure General Early, himself, hears of this," the innkeeper said.

"General Early my, ass," the sergeant said.

A gunshot exploded in the other room. There was more yelling.

Joe sat up. "What's going on, Peter?"

Peter raised the window and looked out—saw no one. He looped their bags over his arm and scooped Joe from the bed. They went out the window, and Peter found the buggy. He placed Joe in it and quickly hitched the mule.

"What is it, Peter?"

"I don't know, but we are making tracks."

Through the darkness, Peter saw a soldier coming toward them. The man rubbed the mule between the ears. "Where will you go this time of morning?"

"Mind your own dooryard," Joe said.

The man jumped. He hadn't seen Joe in the buggy.

Why couldn't Joe just keep his mouth shut Peter wondered. He would get them killed, yet.

The man went to the buggy. "Boy, don't I know you?"

"I don't know any scoundrels that will come in the night and put people out of an inn."

"Sir, the boy doesn't mean any harm," Peter said. "He has a fever and is talking out of his head." Peter stood beside the man, a Confederate private. "Joe, you shouldn't talk that way to our own soldiers."

The man looked at Peter, then back toward Joe. "Joe? Joseph Taylor?"

"How did you know that?" Peter asked.

The man ignored Peter and climbed into the buggy beside Joe. "Joe, I'm John Ebert. Remember me? My pa has a mill close to Bridgewater. Y'all bought a colt from us."

"I remember," Joe said. "You led me around on the colt." Joe's head rolled and rested on the side of the buggy. "I remember."

John felt of Joe's face. "He's burning up."

"I know he is, but you people ran us out of the inn," Peter said.

John climbed down. "Who are you?"

"My name is Peter, a friend. I told Joe's uncle I would get him back home."

"Home!" John said. "Yankees are crawling over the Valley like ants. You can't take him there."

"There is nowhere else," Peter said.

Another shot rang out from within the inn. They looked toward the inn.

"That's a mean bunch I'm with. I'm guiding them to General Early. That sergeant hates darkies, so you best be on your way." He looked at Peter. "You go back south."

Peter saw the young man meant well, but was caught in a bad situation.

"Sir, we have come all the way from Arkansas, and we are going on to Joe's farm near Dayton. He won't have it any other way."

People began coming out of the inn in their nightclothes. John shook his head. "Well, if that's that, you should be past Staunton, by daybreak. Now get, before the sergeant sees you." John went toward the people coming from the inn. He turned back. "Take care of that boy. His pa was wounded awhile back, and I don't know his fate."

Peter climbed in beside Joe and turned the mule onto the road. As they passed by the door of the inn, Peter heard John tell the sergeant that he couldn't turn these people into the night. The sergeant started yelling.

***

The stars were brilliant in the sky. Peter admired them, letting the mule follow the road on his own. He watched them twinkle and disappear, then reappear as a small cloud passed between heaven and earth. These same stars were also looking over Helena and Mam's and Dr. Taylor's graves. Their reflections were dancing in the current of the Mississippi. They were also decorating the sky over the Taylor farm in Mississippi. Zuey was surely asleep right this very instant under these very stars. Peter could see her face as surely, as if she were right in front of him. He longed for her like a thirst for water. He missed her in the fashion he missed his mother and Dr. Taylor, except she was still alive. She could walk out of the Taylor house this instant and look up at these very stars. His heart pulled inside. He would rather be with her this second than with anyone else on earth.

Joe stirred restlessly. Peter felt his forehead. The fever was breaking—good.

Peter smiled. Joe was one of a kind. He was not bad—not really. He was just mischievous. One thing was for sure—Joe was never indecisive. He knew what he wanted, and he went for it barrels blazing. Peter knew he could never be like Joe, but that was fine. God probably only intended for there to be one Joseph Taylor with his special Shenandoah Valley.

The mule did his business, and the smell engulfed the buggy. Peter knew if Joe were awake, he would laugh for a time.

Peter smoothed Joe's hair from his face. Joe moved to a better position, but didn't wake. Peter bent over and kissed Joe's head. Joe would have never allowed such a thing if he were awake. Peter smiled. Joe was tough as a pine knot and rough as a cob.

Peter smelled smoke, turned and looked up the road. He saw several wagons beside the road, a camp. What were they doing there? As the buggy drew near, Peter saw the wagons filled with furniture and the trappings of a home, but these wagons were from more than one home. He saw more wagons up the road. This was not good. They were running from something.

Peter rode past. What else was there to do? He couldn't turn back, no matter what was up ahead. They had no more money and no more food. He and Joe were not beggars. Besides, Joe needed to rest for a few days, and Joe would not turn back anyway.

***

It was still dark when they rolled into Staunton. Peter went on through. There was a stir in the town. Something wasn't right. He didn't want them to get involved in the mess. The mule was tired, but he would just have to go on.

Outside of town, Peter smelled smoke again, but saw no fires. He was looking for the source when he saw three horsemen in the road. He prayed things would go well. When he came along side the men, one rode over to the buggy and looked in, a Confederate soldier.

"Where you headed?" the man said. He was a young man, a captain, with a long dark beard.

"We are going to Dayton."

The man looked at Joe, then looked back up at Peter. "He sick?"

"Yes, sir, took a bad fall. Now he has a fever, but I think it is about to break." Peter didn't think the Lord would mind such a small falsehood. Peter didn't want to get into details with the soldier. "Our farm is on the other side of Dayton."

"Y'all been away?"

"Yes, sir, been to Mississippi."

The man looked up the road. "Boy, Yankees are up ahead of you. People are leaving the Valley coming and going, mostly going north with the Yankees's blessings. If you go up there, it could get nasty."

"We have to go."

Another man came along side. "Captain, that swayback has a US brand."

The captain looked, then looked back in the buggy. "How did y'all come about that animal?"

Peter hesitated. "General Forrest gave it to us in Mississippi when one of his men snatched me for a slave. Joe here came after me. There was a ruckus, and Joe was hurt by the man. The General was upset and gave us the mule to set it right."

The captain looked at his men, then back at Peter. "You're not a slave?"

"No, sir. I've never been a slave."

The captain wiped his face with his hand. "That's a hell of a story."

Peter said nothing, wished he hadn't lost the note from Forrest.

The captain reached for Joe. Peter grabbed his arm. The captain smiled, and Peter slowly released him. The captain sat back on his horse. "I believe your story. It's a hell of story, but I believe you. I can see you are looking out for the boy, so I'm not worried you will let him come to harm up the road." The captain pulled at his beard. "Be careful. Them Yankees may not cotton to you getting one of their mules from Forrest. Don't tell them that story." The captain turned his horse and the rest of the men silently followed him. Peter was relieved Joe never woke.

***

From the directions Joe had given him, Peter believed Bridgewater had to be near, and Dayton would be on the other side of that. All Peter had to do was keep the mule heading down the pike, and he would make his destination. Peter felt the weight lifting every mile, but at the same time, he felt a queer discomfort.

For the last few miles, Peter had been watching an orange glow up ahead. It was a fire, no doubt, maybe a house fire or a grass fire. He prayed no one was hurt.

He looked over at Joe, still sleeping. It was a good thing. The boy needed it. His fever was gone. He would feel better when he awoke. Peter felt his own eyes grow heavy. He leaned back. The mule would keep to the road.

***

Peter jumped. A wren flew from his knee. He smiled. Who was the most afraid? He looked around—daylight. Joe wasn't in the buggy. The mule had stopped the buggy in the middle of the road. Peter panicked, but looked up to find Joe standing in front of the mule staring up the road.

Peter smiled, started to say something to Joe, but he was suddenly overwhelmed. They were atop a rise, and Peter could see for miles. He had discovered the source of the smoke he had been smelling.

"Dear God above, please help my Joseph."

Chapter 23

Peter dropped from the buggy, drew his praying hands to his face. "Dear God, no."

From the rise, he could see for miles. He felt his heart tear in two. Down the valley smoke floated up from the ground like black pillars, the many pillars supporting a ceiling of smoke like thunderclouds. Houses were there, but the barns, sheds, and farm buildings were smoldering. Fence rails were scattered and burned. Some fields were black, some not. He saw no farm animals. This was not the beautiful valley Joe had bragged about. There were no bountiful fields, no friendly neighbors to meet them. This was a wasteland, raped and pillaged, as if the Goths or Huns from history had stormed through.

Down the rise, Peter saw a smoking stone foundation beside a stream. Next to it, he saw a burned out waterwheel steaming in the water. He wiped at his eyes. It had been one of the beautiful mills Joe had bragged on—now only a smoldering char.

What sort of people could have committed such senseless atrocities? How could these Yankees consider their cause right and just? These farms were not rebels, not armies. How would the people—women and children—of this great valley live through the winter? Where did the responsibility lie?

Peter squeezed Joe's shoulder. Joe turned, his face pleading—lost. The expression was as foreign to Joe's face as happiness was now to this valley. Joe looked to Peter for answers—a reason. Peter had none. God, he wished he could say something to comfort the boy. He had never seen such a bewildered and hurt expression as was trespassing on Joe's face.

Joe buried his face in Peter's chest. Peter hurt so much for him. He would do anything to take this unbearable pain from this boy—anything.

Everything had a limit. Everyone had a limit. Was this Joe's limit? Peter feared it was.

Peter felt his shirt grow warm and wet from Joe's tears. He squeezed Joe. He felt him quiver in his arms like a frightened puppy.

"I'm sorry," Peter whispered.

Joe had told so many stories of the Shenandoah Valley that Peter had come to love it, too. Now it felt as if someone had died. Peter squeezed Joe tighter. "I'm so sorry."

A breeze rolled across the rise, and a solitary cinder floated down and settled on Joe's hair like a small feather. Peter brushed it away, as if it were a wasp, daring to attack this boy at this horrible time. He smoothed Joe's hair, and held him tightly, but ever so gently, ever so gently.

***

The tired mule labored in front of the buggy as they passed through Dayton. It was just a couple of miles now to the farm, and Joe didn't want to stop in town.

Rebel cavalry moved about Dayton. Where were you when the Yankee's were here, Joe thought. Why didn't you fight to save this valley?

Joe reflected on what he had seen in Helena and on the trek to here. What was the South thinking? The Yankees had the best of everything: good clothes, better guns, more food, and more men. The dash of good generals like Forrest was not enough to counter.

"I don't know if the mule can go much farther, Joe."

"It ain't far. Just—"

They rounded a grove of trees. Joe had thought he had seen the worst the Yankees could do. He was wrong. He looked past the exhausted mule's ears into hell.

"They burned all the houses here," Peter said. He turned to Joe. "They burned everything."

Joe knew the farms. He remembered the people, his neighbors. He remembered the pretty house that stood right there beside the road, the Krauss's place—now a pile of ashes. Up the road, the Williams's—one wall left of the house. The jake was the only thing left not burned.

As they rode on, Joe paid no attention to people on the road. He didn't look to see if he recognized them. His farm was the only thing on his mind now.

They went another mile, and Peter stopped the mule in front of another burned out farm. The house was still standing, but one wall was black.

"We have to let this animal rest," Peter said.

Joe stared at the house and said nothing.

"Joe, did you hear me?"

Joe slid from the buggy. He felt his heart twist into a knot.

"Joe, where are you going?"

"This is it, Peter," Joe whispered.

Peter said nothing.

Joe stopped at the front dooryard and slowly looked over the house. He felt faint. He had the sensation of falling into a hole, and the entrance was getting smaller and smaller. He remembered crossing the river at Helena, Peter's pants down to his ankles. It came back to him like a story in a book he hadn't read in a long, long time. He remembered the homing pigeons at the Donner Plantation. Why was he remembering this now? He recalled the fight with Washington and his bunch. He remembered the big gar and Peter's delight catching it. He could see in his mind's eye the passenger pigeons just outside of the hollow sycamore. He recalled falling asleep on that mountain in Tennessee—it was so peaceful there. He remembered the comfort of having Peter there with him on the long journey. He didn't know it was a comfort then, but he remembers it that way now.

He knew he was wrong about Helena now. He shouldn't have thought badly about Curtis's hometown. The Yankee's made it bad—too many there. It was surely a pretty place before they destroyed it. Joe closed his eyes. He felt as if he were sliding on ice. He shook his head, hoping to clear his mind.

He went to the door, grabbed the latch. He didn't open it.

He remembered his family at the table the day before they left for Helena. "I'm sure we will be fine," Pa had said. "The war will be over soon, and we will all be back here like nothing ever happened."

He swallowed, but the lump wouldn't go down. He was the "we." There would be no one else. If his pa were still alive, he would have gotten word to him. Joe knew that now. He had known it for a long time, but now he admitted it to himself.

Joe felt Peter behind him. Peter said nothing, but Joe knew he was there; of course, he was. Wasn't he always?

Joe took a deep breath, opened the door. The place was not wrecked. There was very little furniture left, but it was in order. In fact, the place was clean. Why had the Yankees not burned this house like the neighbors'? They hadn't even trashed it.

Suddenly Peter grabbed Joe and pulled him close. Joe turned and saw the reason. There was a revolver right by his head. The man had been beside the door waiting.

Joe looked past the big gun to a man with a bandaged head. Joe's head swam; his knees grew weak. "P...Pa?"

The revolver slowly descended.

"Pa!"

The man dropped the revolver to the floor. "Joseph!"

Joe flew into his pa's arms. "Is it really you? I believed you were dead."

Josh lifted Joe from the floor in a great bear hug. "Son, thank God, you are still alive. I've worried for you so."

"I've been trying to come home," Joe sobbed. "We've been trying so desperately to come home."

"I know you have—I know you have. We are together now by God's grace, and together we will always be. I'll never leave you again. The war be damned."

Josh lowered Joe to the floor.

Joe wiped his eyes. "Ma and Sarah are dead, Pa."

Josh nodded. "I know, Son."

"Uncle Wilbur and Aunt Katie Bea—"

Josh touched Joe's lips. "I know, Joe. I received a letter from Zeke a few weeks ago."

Joe stepped back. "Why didn't you write me? Why didn't you answer my letters?"

Josh took Joe's hands. "Son, I was wounded. I didn't come back to myself until a few months ago. I was in a family's home in Maryland for a long time, badly wounded. They didn't know who I was. Son, I didn't know who I was."

Joe looked at the bandage on his pa's head. "Are you all right now?"

"I have pains sometimes, but they pass." He looked down at his leg. "But this will never pass."

Joe looked down. "You lost a leg!"

"Only below the knee. Thank Providence, it wasn't worse. God knows I've seen worse."

Joe looked into his pa's eyes, remembered the battle at Helena, remembered the dead captain in the gully, remembered the black soldier at Brice's Crossroads. He hugged his pa again.

"Who do we have here?" Josh said, looking at Peter.

Joe removed his arms from around his pa and turned. He had forgotten Peter.

Peter moved to Josh and extended his hand. "I'm Peter."

Joe smiled and looked at Peter. He realized how proud he was of his friend.

Josh looked at Peter questionably. He took his hand slowly. Suddenly he smiled. "Katie Bea's little Peter!" He dropped Peter's hand, pulled Peter close, and hugged him. "Of course—of course. Zeke said you were with him. My God, you are a man now." He turned to Joe. "You both are."

Joe had never felt prouder. Joe took a slow, deep breath. He was home.

✳✳✳

The next morning as they looked at the mule, Peter could still smell the burning in the air, reminded him of the smell of the burned-out barn in Mississippi.

Josh smiled. "He ain't much of an animal, but he should be able to pull a plow. Be better than us pulling it, won't it, men?"

Joe looked about the burned sheds and barn. "There's not much left, is it?"

"No," Josh said, "Sheridan's men did a good job." He looked absently across a naked field. "This went beyond the boundaries of war. We will never forget."

Joe went back to the mule and rubbed it between the ears. "Pa, why is ours the only house around here still standing?"

Peter had wondered the same thing, but was waiting for a better time to ask. He should have known Joe would cut right to it.

Josh moved toward Joe, stopped, straightened at his wooden leg. "I didn't run."

"Sir?"

Josh gave up with the leg and stamped down a couple of times until he was satisfied with the fit. He looked at Joe. "Most men ran from the raiding Yankees. I didn't. They saw my wounds and asked me my outfit. When I told them, a sergeant said we had whipped them good a couple of times. Out of respect for a wounded soldier, they would spare the house. Said they would set it afire, but would look the other way if I put it out. Said they hated what they were doing, but we shouldn't have killed Lieutenant Meigs."

"Who was that?" Peter asked.

Josh turned to Peter. "Seems he was one of Sheridan's favorites. It was said he was killed by bushwhackers near Wenger's place. In fact, he was killed in a fair fight by Southern cavalry scouts, but didn't matter. Truth seldom matters in war."

Peter knew that was a fact. Truth seems to get twisted in war. Right and wrong seem to lose their way as well.

Josh pulled himself up into the buggy. "You two stay close to home. The Yankees are pulling down the Valley. God help the people down there. If the Yankees do return, head for Mole Hill."

"Yes, sir." Joe said.

"I'm going to survey the damage, thanks to your mule. I'm going to check the neighbors farther out. I'm going to see how we are to survive the winter."

"Want us to go with you?" Joe asked.

Josh reached down and smoothed Joe's hair. "It would be more help if you two would help get what we have left in order, still a lot left to do."

After Josh left, Peter found there wasn't much food on the place. No one had worked the farm for a year or more. The only things left were a few farm implements, no barn, no sheds, no springhouse.

Peter watched Joe work around the house. The sadness caused by the devastation was still present, but he worked about the place with a determination Peter had never seen from him. Peter knew why. This was home to Joe. This was his goal for the last couple of years. This was his Shenandoah Valley.

Peter went to the bedroom Mr. Taylor had said was his for as long as he wanted it. It wasn't much, just a cot and a ragged desk, but it was his, was as good as they had. Peter sat on the cot and placed his face in his hands.

He had promised Mam he would go to Pennsylvania. It was the last promise he had made to her. She had wanted it badly for him. Pennsylvania would be safe. It would be a better place for a Negro. He could start new, better opportunities.

Peter got up from the cot and moved to the window, saw Joe pulling vines from a plow. Peter smiled. He loved Joe. No one could love a brother more.

Joe always knew what he wanted and went for it. Now it was time for him to do the same.

Peter wiped tears from his cheeks, went to the cot, and pulled his bag from under it. He sniffed and composed himself. He had to stand tall before Joe. He had to show Joe he was a man, or Joe would try to stand in his way.

Joe stopped pulling vines when he saw the bag. He stood up straight. Said nothing.

"We made it to the Shenandoah Valley, didn't we Joe?"

Joe nodded, said slowly, "We sure did."

Peter looked across the Valley, saw a distant flock of pigeons to the north. The burning smell was strong, but he could whiff autumn. He knew he must keep his composure; for once he had to.

The journey from Helena passed through his mind like a story—a dream. He longed to milk the cow and bring in firewood for Mam, but that was gone like chaff in the wind. He remembered the servants waking at the Donner plantation, the stirring and dawning of a new day. He could still feel the softness of the cotton as he picked beside Stepto at the Taylor farm, and Stepto helping him. He recalled the goat chasing Joe—ah, Joe. He remembered him and Joe wrestling in the stream in Tennessee. Then he remembered Zuey, her beautiful face, and her precious baby. His heart was still in Mississippi with them.

"You heading on to Pennsylvania, Peter?"

Peter wrestled the memories from his mind and looked Joe in the eyes. Joe was his friend. Joe was his companion, but Joe was no longer his responsibility. He loved no man more, and never would.

They had seen and done things together that bind as no cables ever could. They were brothers.

God had intervened. God had delivered them. Peter knew God would always watch over Joe. Peter knew he, himself, was an instrument of God—it was his calling, and he was being called away from Joe now.

Peter pulled Joe to him. "I love you, Joseph Taylor. Remember, God loves you, too."

Joe threw his arms around Peter. "I'm sorry about saying bad things about God." Joe sobbed. "I didn't mean it."

"I know you didn't. The Almighty knows it, too. You have been through much, but now I believe it is over." He put Joe at arms' length. "You are home, Joe. You are with your father. You can make a new start."

Joe wiped his eyes with his sleeve. "You can stay with us. Pa don't care you are a darky."

Peter smiled. "I know he doesn't. I know I'm welcome."

"Then stay with us."

Peter looked up, saw the flock of pigeons growing larger and closer.

"Joe, remember how much you wanted to come home? Remember how you longed for the Shenandoah Valley and nothing shorter?"

Joe nodded.

"Well, Joe, I have that longing now."

"Pennsylvania."

"Eventually. But first I'm going back to Mississippi."

Joe smiled, wiped his eyes. "Zuey."

"That's right. I have a pulling in my heart."

"I do understand, Peter. I had that pulling."

Peter squeezed Joe's shoulder. "I knew you would understand."

Joe headed to the house. "Let me leave Pa a note. He may not understand, but you helped me come home, now I'm gonna help you."

"Joseph."

Joe turned.

Peter walked to him. "No, Joe. You have realized your destination—your goal. You must stay here with your pa—he needs you."

"But, Peter, you need me to help you. We help each other."

Peter smiled. "Joe, you have helped me. I'm not the same helpless boy you knew in Arkansas. You have helped me to become a man."

Joe said nothing as he looked into Peter's eyes.

Peter pulled his Bible from the bag. "You keep this."

Joe opened the bible and turned to the cavity. He pulled the necklace and presented it to Peter. "This is yours. Uncle Wilbur gave it to you."

"That's right. He said I was like his own son." Peter took it. He closed his eyes and kissed it. It had caused grief, but now it would do good. "Here, Joe. It is worth a good deal of money. You and your pa will need money to get back going."

"But Peter, it's yours."

"You're mine too, Joe—my family. When we come back through, we will need your help to get to Pennsylvania. How can you help me if you don't help yourself? Dr. Taylor would have approved."

Joe took it. "Aunt Katie Bea would have approved of you going after Zuey."

That touched Peter's heart. He had to turn away.

Joe said, "I'll be waiting to help you get to Pennsylvania." He pulled his tomahawk from his belt. "Here, you will need this."

Peter hesitated, but took it. He looked it over. All the memories flooded back. He knew what it meant to Joe, and he had given it freely. He kissed Joe on the forehead. "I love you, Joseph."

"Pshaw." Joe kicked at a weed.

The pigeons were over them now, thousands of wild birds heading south for the winter. It was like a cloud covering the land. Peter and Joe looked up in amazement for a time. Slowly they looked at each other and smiled. Peter turned and started down the road following the pigeons' path south.

"Be careful Peter," Joe called above the noisy wings.

Peter didn't bother to wipe his tears, nor did he look back.

"Practice with the tomahawk. You know you ain't that good, yet." Joe's voice was growing fainter as Peter walked. "If you change your mind, Peter, I will help you."

Peter tried to find the lead pigeon, but he was long over the southern horizon.

"You are my best friend, Peter."

The pigeons resembled a wide, black serpent snaking across the sky. God's birds of abundance, Peter thought.

Peter's eyes burned. He would not turn back. If he did, he would not want to let go of Joe—his best friend.

Joe's voice was almost too faint now. "I love you, Peter."

Peter wiped at his eyes and nose.

"Hey, Peter, remember what you said when we were in the hollow tree? You have to chase the wild pigeons. They are headed south, too. That's what you have to do, chase the wild pigeons. Chase the wild pi..."

Chapter 24

Fort Stoddard, Alabama May 4ᵗʰ 1865

Sergeant Davis's sleeves were rolled up to his elbows as he dug the shovel into the bluff overlooking the Mobile River. He was hot and ready for this war to be over. It had gone on way too long. Lee had surrendered and Johnson, too.

Frank Jacks, a skinny, pimple-faced private accidentally threw dirt on Davis's shoe.

"Damn it, Jacks, I'm gonna pound you, yet."

"Sorry, Sergeant Davis."

"Sorry, my ass."

Davis threw down the shovel and went over to where Corporal Bill Gains was sitting drinking from his canteen, watching the men work. "Bill, building this fort is ridiculous. Why don't the damn Rebs give over. Hell, don't they know when they are licked."

He snatched the canteen from Gains and guzzled.

Gains laughed. "You're welcome."

Davis tossed the canteen to Gains and piled down beside him. "But if the Rebels retreat down from the Tombigbee, we're gonna pound them from up here."

Davis looked down at the Mobile River. It reminded him of the Mississippi at Helena. He knew he would never see another fight like the battle there—thank God.

He heard a rider coming fast toward them. He was yelling something.

"That's General Benton," Gains said.

He and Davis shot to their feet.

The general rode up to the division, and all the men ran toward him. The men knew the news was good.

General Benton stood in the stirrups. "Boys, the war is over; throw down your spades and let the fort go to hell. We don't want it. Taylor has surrendered to General Canby."

The men exploded with cheer and excitement.

Gains pounded Davis on the back and yelled, "Huzzah—huzzah!"

Davis sat flat on his ass. He couldn't believe it. Soon he would be going home to Iowa. Home—what a sweet thought.

There was a loud explosion. Davis jumped. He smiled when he realized it was the Gunboat Octorara anchored just off shore letting loose with its 200 pounders in celebration.

Suddenly, he remembered something. He went over to his knapsack, rummaged through it, and brought out a bottle wrapped in blue paper. He yanked the paper from it and pulled the cork.

"Gains, I've been saving this bottle since Helena for this very day." Davis turned the bottle up.

Gains bent down and picked up the blue paper.

Davis starting spitting. "Damn it. This taste like ammonia—no, piss!"

Gains laughed. "There is something written on the back side of your wrapper. Let me read it: 'Sergeant Davis, I've added a little southern tonic to your spirits. Your friend, the Dixie Whistler.'"

Davis spit again, then it hit him—he remembered. He threw the bottle toward the river.

"Joseph Taylor," he yelled, "you'll answer for this, you little runt!"

The End

Now look for John Gschwend's second novel, *Spirit In The Red Amber, A novel of an American Indian.* See what others are saying about it:

John Gschwend Jr. is a storyteller. He captures your attention immediately - page one -- and he has your attention until the last word. I liked the way he incorporated some of the Quapaw language throughout the story, made the story seem more authentic. The reader knows this author is a nature lover who has spent a lifetime in the woods. His descriptions of flora and fauna are beautifully and accurately written by someone who cherishes God's creatures and their habitats. The author also has a heart for those who have been mistreated. In this book he has great compassion for the American Indian. John Gillette - a strong name and a strong multidimensional character- takes us on an exciting adventure during the Civil War in Southeast Arkansas along the White River and on the prairie. Edwynne

I enjoyed how John painted the picture so clearly that I could imagine the White River, St. Charles and the other towns mentioned. I read the book in one day, I couldn't put it down. I loved his imagination... Beth

What a wonderful and interesting book this was about American Indian life... read it within a few days of getting it as I just knew it would be something that I would and should know about this culture. The author definitely has a wonderful knowledge about what he writes. Would recommend this book to high school children as well as adults who want to learn more about our country and its history. Cynthia

http://civilwarnovel.com

CPSIA information can be obtained
at www.ICGtesting.com
Printed in the USA
BVHW030807080520
579417BV00001B/82